Perhaps the aliens saw Earth. . . .

. . . as a vast storehouse of resources that would aid them to rebuild their own war-torn world, and the only way to avail themselves of those resources was to remove the humans first. With so much at stake there seemed to be no other explanation for the growing ferocity and frequency of the Grays' military actions.

Would history regard this time as the beginnings of the next world war? For that Thompson had no answer. For such history to be recorded at all meant that humans would have to survive whatever obstacles still lay before them. One thing he did know, and feared, was that there could very well come a time for humans to realize that they could not save the entire planet. They could very well be forced to decide which parts of it needed to be sacrificed if they were to save anything at all.

Was this simply the next world war, or the last?

THE LAST WORLD WAR

Dayton Ward

POCKET **STAR** BOOKS
New York   London   Toronto   Sydney

This book is a work of fiction. Names, characters, places and incidents are
products of the author's imagination or are used fictitiously. Any resemblance to actual events or locales or persons, living or dead, is entirely
coincidental.

An *Original* Publication of POCKET BOOKS

A Pocket Star Book published by
POCKET BOOKS, a division of Simon & Schuster Inc.
1230 Avenue of the Americas, New York, NY 10020

Copyright © 2003 by Dayton Ward

ISBN -13: 978-0-7434-5789-7
ISBN -10:   0-7434-5789-7

First Pockett Books printing September 2003

10 9 8 7 6 5

POCKET STAR BOOKS and colophon are registered
trademarks of Simon & Schuster Inc.

Front cover illustration by Gerber Studio

For information regarding special discounts for bulk purchases,
please contact Simon & Schuster Special Sales at 1-800-456-6798
or business@simonandschuster.com

Manufactured in the United States of America

"... the soldier, above all other people prays for peace, for he must suffer and bear the deepest wounds and scars of war."

Douglas MacArthur,
General of the Army
May 12, 1962

Dedicated to the men and women of the United States Armed Forces, past, present, and future.

Prelude

prelude

1

Why the hell did I volunteer for this?

The unspoken question screamed in Lance Corporal Bradley Gardner's mind at the very same instant the mosquito whined in his ear for the third time inside of a minute. Automatically he swatted at the side of his head, once again trying to drive the incessant bug away.

"Gardner," a voice hissed from a few meters to his left. "Keep quiet. You'll give our position away." The voice belonged to Sergeant Ronald Thurman, his squad leader.

What, and talking won't? Gardner had never met Thurman before the beginning of this past week, but it had taken him less than five minutes to decide that the Marine sergeant was a complete asshole.

Shaking his head, he reached up to wipe perspiration from his face. The sweatband he wore underneath his Kevlar helmet was soaked through, thanks in no small part to the oppressive August humidity. Summer heat, working in tandem with heavy rainfall in recent weeks had also given full bloom to armadas of mosquitoes that were out in force tonight. Even though Gardner had doused himself with insect repellent before leaving their unit's base camp, sweating had diluted its effectiveness.

Nothing could be done about it now, though. His thirteen-man rifle squad had established an ambush position and silence at this point was crucial to the success of their mission. If the information Thurman had briefed them with was correct, they would be encountering an enemy patrol while it was conducting its own security sweep of the area.

Looking to his left, Gardner regarded his companions, nestled as he was among the underbrush that conspired with the darkness to render his squad nearly invisible in the forest. They had taken up positions along one of the numerous trails that crisscrossed this part of the forest, arranging themselves in a line that followed the bend of the trail perhaps ten meters inside the trees. Thurman had informed them during their briefing that this trail led to an enemy camp.

The squad had fast-marched to this point along the trail, which Thurman had chosen as the ideal site for an ambush. They had established sectors of fire that allowed each Marine to interlock with the men to either side, creating a kill zone from which no member of an enemy patrol would be able to escape.

Like him, his fellow Marines had taken care to conceal themselves behind fallen logs, thick bushes, anything that could break up their outline and hide them from even the most attentive pair of eyes. A nearly full moon hovered in the cloudless sky, bathing everything in its soft, ghostly illumination. No one moved, spoke, used their flashlight, or even smoked a cigarette, as the telltale glow from even a cigarette butt could be enough to reveal their location. So long as they did not make any stupid mistakes, their enemy would never know the squad was here until it was too late.

Movement!

His mind screamed the warning at him before his eyes even fully registered the nearly imperceptible motion up the trail. Perhaps fifty meters away, the movement was so slow, so methodical, that at first Gardner thought he had imagined it. Darkness could play tricks on the human eye, after all. At first his eyes registered nothing but a patch of forest, looking very much to Gardner like just another tree.

Then it moved again.

To Gardner's left, Thurman silently indicated that he had seen it as well, first pointing to his eyes and then down the trail in the same direction Gardner had been looking. The hand signal was unmistakable: *Enemy ahead.*

Now that he knew what he was looking at, Gardner could begin to make out the shadowy form of a figure walking slowly up the trail and hugging the outside curve of the dirt road where the shadows helped to conceal him. His steps were measured and precise, each one taken with care so as not to step on anything that might make a noise and reveal his presence. He carried his rifle with the barrel lowered and out in front of him as if searching for potential targets.

Behind the first figure, Gardner could begin to make out the form of a second and then a third, each man keeping an interval of five or so meters between himself and the man in front of him. As the front man continued to move slowly forward, Gardner counted until he saw that the enemy patrol numbered six in all. Was that all there was? Thurman had not given them any information on enemy size or strength. After all, it was their squad's mission to gather such intelligence.

And dispose of any enemy patrols they encountered, of course.

Gardner felt his right forefinger tighten on the trigger of his M-16 rifle. The barrel of the weapon was already facing straight ahead within the area defined as his field of fire, and he knew well enough not to move it to face the approaching patrol. He need not do anything but wait until the enemy soldiers entered the kill zone established for the ambush.

Come on, just a little bit closer.

Adrenaline rushed through his veins and his pulse pounded in his ears. Keeping his breathing under control was a physical effort as his body prepared itself for the coming firefight. He studied the movements of the enemy patrol, trying to determine his first target and anticipate where the soldier would be when the shooting started. The six figures were still moving in the same slow, deliberate manner, each man's weapon tracking in a slow arc from one side of the trail to the other in search of danger. The rearmost soldier was taking the added precaution of turning to look back the way they had come, looking for threats to their rear.

Gardner held his breath when, as the patrol came abreast of the hidden ambush positions, the point man looked in their direction. His brain knew that his squad was all but invisible, but that did nothing to stop the lump from forming in his throat when the front man looked directly at where he lay hidden among the trees.

A little bit more, he knew. Only a few more paces and the entire patrol would be in the kill zone.

Gardner thought he had imagined it as the first shot, Sergeant Thurman's signal to launch the attack, rang out.

Then the brass casing from the round, still hot after ejecting from the sergeant's weapon, landed on his own exposed neck.

"Ow! Shit!"

His words were lost as thunder roared from the forest in
the form of the sharp metallic reports from the squad's M-
16 rifles. Gardner felt his own weapon buck slightly with
every pull of the trigger, though most of the recoil was absorbed by the large metal spring inside the weapon's stock.

The effect of their attack was immediate.

"Ambush!" somebody yelled from the road as the six
soldiers at first ducked instinctively and then turned in the
direction of the incoming fire, leaping from their exposed
positions on the dirt road into the shallow ditch separating
it from the tree line. Gardner saw the muzzle flashes of
their weapons as they opened fire in retaliation.

Their opponents were in the woods now, closing on
their ambush positions. Gardner heard the crunch of
twigs and leaves beneath their boots as they plunged
toward where he and his squad remained situated between the trees. He saw movement to his right and swung
his rifle in that direction, pulling the trigger as he did so.
The dark figure heading in his direction ducked behind a
tree at the sound of the round going off.

Then the first casualty came.

A shrill high-pitched whistle pierced the air, easily
heard over even the sounds of their weapons fire. No
sooner did Gardner register the noise than a second shriek
followed, signaling another kill. Damn it, they were winning! This thing would be over in a minute or two.

Then another wailing screech filled the air and he realized it was coming from his own body.

The Multiple Integrated Laser Engagement System, or MILES gear, was a series of sensors attached to a harness he wore over his combat gear. Originally developed in the late 1970s and early 1980s, MILES systems had long since become standard equipment in military training exercises for simulating ground combat. The sensors, working in conjunction with a special laser transmitter attached to the barrel of their weapons, allowed trainees to employ their respective weapons as they would in a real battle situation. When triggered by the sound of a blank cartridge being fired from the weapon, the laser transmitter emitted a special coded laser beam that, when registered by one of the sensors worn by another mock combatant, recorded a hit or near miss as appropriate.

Bradley Gardner's sensors were registering a direct hit.

He had seen the figure emerge from behind the tree less than three meters in front of him, but he had been a sitting duck with no way to get his weapon turned fast enough before the intruder opened up on him. Then there was the telltale muzzle flash just before his MILES vest betrayed him.

"Bang," the intruder taunted him, barely audible over the racket his MILES vest was creating. "You're dead."

Gardner was about to offer a colorful reply when he was cut off by weapons fire from his left. Then the intruder's own MILES gear started to shriek, followed by a similar sound uttered by its stunned wearer.

"Dammit!"

"You're dead, too," Sergeant Thurman said, stepping forward and firing another blank round at the other man for emphasis. "You're supposed to attack through the ambush, and keep attacking until all the ambushers are dead."

Corporal Daniel Melendez nodded as he stepped forward to allow Thurman to deactivate his MILES vest, which was still shrieking its death wail into the forest night. The sergeant inserted the key into the special lock on one strap of the man's harness and turned it, silencing the irritating signal.

Melendez shrugged as he stepped back. "I know all that, but when I heard all the vests going off I figured it was over." He smiled at that, the white of his teeth contrasting against dark skin further concealed under layers of green and brown grease paint.

Thurman was unimpressed. "All of the vests belong to your group, all but one that is." The sergeant cast an annoyed glance in Gardner's direction as he waved him over and deactivated his vest as well.

Gardner did not bother with a response. He was just happy that this little exercise was over so they could hot foot it back for the beer and pizza Captain Douglas had promised. It would be their last night here before their unit returned to Kansas City and each of the Marines, most of them reservists performing their annual two weeks of active duty, returned to their mundane, everyday lives.

At least I'll get to sleep in a real bed and eat real food.

Still, he had to admit that this was more fun than his normal job. He could handle the lousy food, the long hours, and living in a tin building for the last two weeks. Even dealing with people like Thurman, who was an auto mechanic in his regular civilian job and who took certain aspects of Marine Corps life much too seriously for Gardner's taste, was not really that difficult. Working as a hospital payroll administrator back in Kansas City and dealing with irate employees who confronted him with discrepancies in their checks just did not have the same appeal as running around in the woods and playing "war."

"All right, huddle up," Thurman said, and Gardner and the rest of his squad moved in closer to the sergeant along with the six members of the "enemy patrol" that they had successfully ambushed. All of them members of the 24th Marine Regiment, a reserve unit based in Kansas City, Gardner even counted several of the Marines as friends of his in civilian life. Like he and Thurman, none of them possessed an infantry-related job classification. They ran the gamut from computer technician to radio operator to administrative clerk, though there were also several Marines in the unit who were armorers or mechanics, trained to repair and refurbish various types of military weapons and vehicles.

All of that was forgotten during the past two weeks, as the fifty-three Marines had marched, run, and crawled over nearly every square inch of godforsaken real estate that was Camp Growding, the National Guard reservation located three hours south of Kansas City near the small city of Neosho, Missouri. The reservation was one of the few areas within a reasonable distance that contained the necessary firing ranges and other facilities the Marines needed to complete their combat skills refresher exercises.

The training, which consisted of weapons firing, small unit tactics, chemical warfare defense, and other "battle skills," was an annual requirement for all Marines, male and female, be they active duty or reservist. Even those like Gardner, whose military occupational specialty was that of a disbursing clerk, were required to demonstrate proficiency in a variety of infantry skills. This was in keeping with the Corps' longtime philosophy that every Ma-

rine, regardless of specialty or job assignment, was a rifle-
man first and capable of deployment to front line combat
situations if needed.

"Okay," Thurman continued, indicating the leader of
the now dead patrol, Sergeant Anthony Bonniker, "since
you all are out of it, you might as well head back to base
camp." Hitching a thumb in Gardner's direction he
added, "Take Gardner with you. The rest of us can keep
on with the game." He smiled at Bonniker. "I don't suppose you'd want to tell me where your camp is, would
you?"

The war game was straightforward. Most of the
Marines were divided into two teams and tasked with establishing a headquarters at designated locations in the
forest. The two groups were then given orders to send
troops into the woods in attempts to find their "enemy's"
headquarters and capture it while at the same time defending their own base from being taken.

"Sorry, dude," Melendez said, speaking up in lieu of
Bonniker, "but you already killed me, and corpses make
for lousy interrogation. I'm sure that's in the handbook
somewhere." He and Bonniker exchanged grins, the
young Mexican's droll delivery eliciting laughs from the
rest of the group. That is, except for Thurman, of course,
who so far as Gardner knew possessed no sense of humor
whatsoever.

Bristling, Thurman said nothing, instead waving the
rest of his squad to follow him as he moved off deeper into
the woods. "Get moving," he called over his shoulder at
the others, and Gardner could see that he was none too
happy about being the target of the joke. Undoubtedly,

the sergeant would have more to say on the subject when he had the chance to talk to Melendez alone.

"Sergeant Bonniker," a voice said from behind them. They turned to see a young private who Gardner remembered was named Nickerson. He had been given the task of carrying his team's bulky PRC-77 radio. Each squad moving through the forest had been given a radio in order to keep in touch with the base camp, as well as add an additional layer of realism to the war games, with the opposing base camps able to coordinate the movements of their roving patrols. They would also be used to recall any teams that might still be out in the woods once the games were officially declared over.

Bonniker turned to face the private. "What's up?"

The younger Marine was holding out the radio's handset, a look of puzzlement on his face. "I can't get a clean signal on this thing. I've looked it over and everything's still set properly, and there's no sign of anything broken, but I can only hear about every other word. Everything else is garbled."

Shrugging, Bonniker said, "Well, it's not like we're lost or anything. We'll have the comm folks check it out when we get back. Considering how old the damned thing is, I wouldn't be surprised if it was finally going toes up."

A relic from the early days of the Vietnam War, the PRC-77 had long ago proven its reliability in even the harshest of environments. Though it had since been superceded by newer models with greater range and ability, Marine Corps budgeting realities meant that a unit of reservists from Kansas City were unlikely to receive the newer equipment anytime soon. Therefore, they made do with what was available and in this case, it meant using a radio that was nearly twice as old as the Marine carrying it.

Bonniker gave the order for the team to move out, leading Gardner and his men back onto the trail. Gardner walked alongside Melendez, and once they were on the road the corporal turned to him, a mischievous smile on his face.

"Something tells me that Thurman's not going to want to share a slow dance with me at the party tonight."

Chuckling, Gardner shook his head. "He definitely takes this stuff seriously, that's for sure. I have to wonder why he didn't just sign up for the infantry in the first place."

"Better him than me," Melendez replied. "This stuff is fun, but only in small doses. Otherwise, leave me with the computers." The corporal's normal specialty was repairing computers, desktop and laptop models that had evolved from items of luxury enjoyed by high-ranking officers to vital tools used by nearly every facet of the modern-day military. Every unit, whether stationed in an administrative office or deployed to a forward combat area, used computers to compile, store, and transmit information.

"Didn't you used to do this full time?" Gardner asked.

Melendez nodded. "Four years. Got stationed in KC and ended up staying there until my time was up." The Marine Corps maintained a small presence in Kansas City, the location of its main finance center, tucked away inside a gargantuan government building in the south part of the city. Pay and personnel information for all active duty and reserve Marines was stored there, overseen by a group of military and civilian programmers and analysts who maintained and safeguarded each Marine's personal and financial information.

"Then I got out and took a job downtown," the corporal continued. "The pay is better, that's for damn sure. Part of me missed the Corps, though, so I decided to stay in the reserves." Shaking his head, he added. "I didn't think they'd actually make us do this stuff, though. A reservist computer tech is about as low on the combat totem pole as somebody can get."

That made definite sense to Gardner. "Yeah, no kidding. If it ever comes down to us having to win a war, America is in deep shit."

Randy Guff was drunk.

Despite his near incapacitation, he was still able to stagger from his seat near the campfire to the cooler sitting on the tailgate of his truck. Opening it, he looked down to see nothing but water and some remaining cubes of mostly melted ice. He plunged his hand into the cold water and fished around, only confirming that his eyes, impeded as they were from the large quantities of beer he had consumed that evening, were not deceiving him.

"What the fuck happened to all the beer?" he managed to slur, wrapping the last couple of words around a belch that reeked of the hamburger he had eaten an hour or so ago.

From where he lay reclined in a lounge chair he had swiped from his back porch when his wife was not looking, Jim Jacobs raised his head, lifting the brim of his ball cap to look at him. "You mean we're out?"

"No," Randy said as he let the cooler's lid slam shut. "I'm taking a survey, asshole. Somebody's gonna have to make a run to the store."

Jim shook his head. "Not me. I quit feelin' my goddamn feet an hour ago." He attempted to stand, using his shotgun as a crutch to aid him, but it was not enough to keep him from dropping back into the lounge chair. The chair, not designed for such abuse, promptly groaned in protest as its cheap aluminum front legs collapsed under the man's weight and spilled him onto the ground, much to Randy's raucous delight.

His laughter echoing in the forest night, Randy looked hopefully in the direction of the third member of their group, Greg Collins, only to see that Greg had already passed out, using a log they had dragged into their campsite from the surrounding woods as a backrest. Greg was a cheap drunk, and Randy knew he would be unconscious until morning.

Shit. If you want something done, you've got to do it your own damned self.

He kicked at an empty beer can as he stumbled across the uneven ground, sending it clattering away only to ricochet off another of the several cans that littered their makeshift campsite. A fleeting thought drifted through Randy's muddled brain that they should really think about cleaning up this pigsty, but it was just as quickly forgotten. They could worry about that in the morning, before they set out for one more day of hunting.

Maybe.

The hunting had not gone well at all. When he had planned this outing, Randy was sure that there would be plenty of deer to be had in the forest dominating the otherwise unused areas of the National Guard base. Except for a few weeks, most of the reservation was uninhabited and undisturbed by humans, and even then most of their activities were limited to designated training areas. Wildlife wandered over most of the remaining areas unfettered, just begging for the attentions of a resolute hunter despite the fact that hunting season would not begin for four more months. Not that it mattered, as the reservation was not a legally designated hunting area anyway.

Sneaking onto the base was a relatively simple task, as no fence or other type of barrier cordoned off the property. So long as they took care not to attract the attention of anyone working on the base, the trio would be able to come and go at will. Randy had reasoned that all of these factors should have placed the odds of finding game squarely in their favor.

Despite careful prior planning and execution, however, they had not seen a real deer all day, and the defeated hunters soon ended their attempts in pursuit of something far easier to capture. Beer, for example.

It took Randy a moment to remember that the keys to his pickup truck were in the pitiful little two-person tent he had partially erected to house himself and his gear. He had borrowed it from his son, who often used the tent on camping trips with his Boy Scout troop, and had failed utterly to understand how to pitch the thing despite its being designed to open in seconds. Instead of an inviting dome, its nylon construction supported by flexible plastic rods that aided in providing the correct shape, it sagged in the middle, and water from an earlier light rain storm had collected in the depression created by the tent's improper deployment.

He was not sure what irritated him more: that he had failed to pitch the tent properly or that his son had made it look so easy when he had shown Randy how to put the damned thing together.

Retrieving his keys from the sorry excuse for a tent, Randy started to make his way back toward his truck when the call of nature that he had been aware of for the past several minutes but had kept forgetting to do anything about repeated itself. His bladder once again begging for his attention, Randy shuffled toward the tree line as he fumbled with his zipper. He sighed in relief as the proper muscles relaxed and allowed yet another simple biological process to proceed without further impediment.

"WHAT THE HELL . . . ?"

The cry came from behind him, loud enough in the forest night to make Randy jump and cause him to evacuate the remainder of his bladder's contents down his pants leg. Cursing, Randy turned back toward the camp while at the same time trying to finish what he had started without catching himself in his zipper.

Back at the campfire, Jim was staggering to his feet, his hands gripping his shotgun. He could only stand and watch as his friend brought the weapon to his shoulder and aimed it toward the woods to Randy's left.

"What the hell are you doing?"

His question was drowned out as fire erupted from the shotgun's barrel. The echo of that first shot rolled through the trees as Jim racked the weapon's slide and fired a second round, then repeated the process a third time.

Then Randy sensed motion among the trees and jerked his head in the direction Jim had fired in time to see a bright muzzle flash erupt from the forest. A high-pitched whine of energy poured from the trees as what Randy thought might be a torrential rush of displaced air surged across the space toward Jim.

And then Jim was gone, disappearing in a haze of

shredded clothing and skin and viciously liberated muscle tissue and bone, little more than shrapnel enveloped in a rapidly expanding red haze. The cloud of body matter that had been Jim Jacobs splashed across trees, bushes, the ground, everywhere. What had not been disintegrated, the man's lower legs and the right arm that still gripped the shotgun, fell to the ground with a sickly thud and Randy could see blood from the severed extremities reflecting the flickering light of the fire.

"Holy Jesus . . ."

It was then that he remembered Greg, nearly comatose by the fire until now, as the man began to stir. Randy could see that his friend was still partially unaware of his surroundings or the very real peril he was in as Greg pulled himself into a sitting position from where he had collapsed against the fallen log.

"Hey," Greg said, his voice thick and slurred from the alcohol he had consumed, "What's going on?"

"GREG!" It was all that Randy managed to get out before Greg was vaporized in the same sickening plume of crimson, his body torn apart by the horrific power of whatever it was that still hid among the trees.

Movement behind him made Randy turn again, and his mouth fell open in utter shock as he beheld the monster standing among the forest undergrowth and looking directly at him.

"Fuck me."

At first he thought it might be a bear, or perhaps maybe even a gorilla that had escaped from a nearby zoo. Were there any zoos near Neosho? For an insane instant, Randy thought he might even be looking at Bigfoot. Though no one, so far as he knew, had ever reported seeing anything like that in this part of the country, his brain told him that this thing was certainly big enough to qualify. Well over seven feet tall, its shoulders were nearly twice as wide as Randy's own.

It was there that resemblance ended. It was not covered in dark brown hair like he had seen in those goofy specials on the Discovery Channel. Instead, its arms and legs, two of each, were cords of bulging muscles covered by hairless skin that looked the color of ash in the pale moonlight. Its head was as large as the pumpkin Randy had helped his son carve into that jack o'lantern last year, but unlike the classic Halloween moniker this thing's eyes were two pools of utter, bottomless black. While its mouth was wide and full of irregular-shaped teeth, its nose was little more than a pair of holes set into the middle of its face. Randy could see no ears, but noted that the creature appeared to be totally devoid of hair.

The creature wore what appeared to be body armor, cast and formed to fit its wearer's chest. More alarming, he decided through the fading alcoholic fog enveloping his brain, was that the thing was also carrying what could only be a weapon. A big weapon.

And it was pointing directly at him.

Muted in horror, Randy scrambled backward and away from the startling sight before him. His shock and terror were only compounded as four more of the creatures, varying slightly in size but wearing similar body armor and carrying identical weapons, bounded from the concealment of the forest. They spread out to encircle Randy, their speed uncanny as they covered ground in huge bounding leaps. Each of the creatures carried a weapon like their companion, and all of them were aiming at him.

"Help!" Randy called out, though there was no one to hear him. There was nowhere for him to go, either, he realized, and then there was only time for a silent farewell to his wife and son before he heard the weapons' gruesome whine one final time.

Excessive force, Raegyra realized in horror as they fired on the first creature. Cradling the shoulder wounded by the primitive projectile weapon, he could only watch the creature literally disappear before his very eyes under his companions' assault.

Only after the chaos had faded did Raegyra finally inspect the wound inflicted on him. The skin had been broken in several places by what looked to be small pellets, though there was only a slight amount of blood, and even that was already clotting. At closer range or employed against a vital organ, the weapon might have done more damage. They would have to be careful if they encountered any more of these creatures, especially if they possessed other, more powerful armaments.

As for their own weapons, they had only recently been implemented into general use and, rather than the projectile rifles they had replaced, were designed to target a living being's central nervous system. The power of the energy pulses discharged by the rifles was adjustable, capable of inflicting levels of damage varying from mere unconsciousness to physical destruction of body tissue and vital organs.

None of the power settings should have been capable of dispensing the kind of total carnage Raegyra had just witnessed. Though he had suspected the creatures' bod-

ies were more fragile then his own, he had not been prepared for how easily the scout's weapons had ravaged
them. He wanted to call out, to order the others to de-
crease their power settings, but by then it was too late
and all three creatures were dead, their bodies all but
vaporized.

It was the latest in a series of shocks that had befallen
Raegyra since he and his companions had passed through
the odd portal and emerged into this forested area.
Though he had been told what to expect, the information
supplied by his leaders had not been enough to prepare
him for what lay on this side of the portal.

He had but to look into the sky to realize his situation.
There was only one moon. Where were the other two?
Raegyra also noted that the stars he had used as naviga-
tional aids since his first childhood camping excursions
were not arranged as they should have been. The Plysserian scientists they had captured and tortured had been
telling the truth all along.

This was not Raegyra's world.

Somehow, whether through science or sorcery, they
had traveled across untold distances to this place, a new
planet. As a youth, he had read and seen many fictional
representations of such things, and he had always believed that life must exist on planets other than his own.
How could there not be? It was the height of arrogance to
believe that *Jontashreena* was the only world in the entire
universe capable of sustaining life.

And here he was, on another planet, and he had traveled here as easily as one might cross a threshold between
two separate rooms.

At first he could not bring himself to believe it, but

there was no denying the lone moon in the sky was of a different size and color than any of the three orbiting *Jontashreena*. There was no debating the altered placement of the stars, which shone much more brightly here than they ever had through the heavily polluted atmosphere of his own planet.

Then there were the local inhabitants.

Briefed by their commander before entering the portal, Raegyra had been hoping to find some type of intelligent alien life here. The scouting party had come upon the odd sounds of life as they made their way through the environs of this strange place, unsure if what they were hearing was actual speech. Their language was unlike anything Raegyra had heard before. Tracing the voices through the forest, he detected the glow of the fire piercing the darkness. Soon they saw the small clearing among the trees, and the three creatures inhabiting it.

He was struck at how odd they looked. Their skin was an odd pale shade, and judging from their physiques, they were small and weak. They wore garments that seemed inadequate for combat or protection from the weather. Raegyra had seen no recognizable weapons or other military equipment of any consequence, with the possible exception of a pair of what looked to be some type of ground vehicles. They bore some resemblance to the transports he was familiar with, though these specimens appeared to be, like the creatures that commanded them, slow and weak. He therefore doubted that these three aliens belonged to any sort of warrior caste.

Careful, Raegyra reminded himself. *You are the alien here.*

The thought hammered home as he watched the last

of the three creatures disappear under the force of his companions' weapons.

Worse than watching the effects of the pulse rifles was the realization that his fellow soldiers seemed to enjoy subjecting the obviously weaker beings to their weapons' hellish force. There had been no mistaking the looks of near glee on the faces of the other scouts as they had opened fire on the two remaining victims.

Yes, victims, Raegyra decided. Though the first animal had been armed and even if that weapon had proven to be more of an irritant than a true threat, its two companions had been unarmed noncombatants that had never stood a chance. It was all he could do to keep himself from vomiting at the image of the violent deaths the creatures had suffered at the hands of his friends.

Not friends, he reminded himself, but simply four brother soldiers, selected at random for this mission by the Leadership. Newly assigned to this combat unit, Raegyra had not had the opportunity to get to know many of the other soldiers. As he watched his four companions laughing and celebrating the deaths they had caused, he was not sure he wanted to befriend any of them.

It was not the first time he had witnessed this type of savagery, of course. Such sights were unavoidable after spending all of his adult life in service to the Chodrecai military. It had always sickened him to see such jubilation on the faces of soldiers who undertook the business of killing with far too much enjoyment for his taste, but experience had taught Raegyra that such impulses were difficult to stave off, particularly during the heat of battle.

Still, he believed that the Chodrecai could not afford to lose sight of the principles that had guided them this far. Giving in to baser instincts such as killing for no purpose would only hurt their cause, which Raegyra believed was what separated his people from the Plysserians. He knew that his was a minority opinion, far outnumbered by those who believed that the Chodrecai were justified in taking any action necessary to defend their way of life.

Did those beliefs extend to this planet if the War migrated here? Did they include the subjugation of the race of beings that called this place home? How would those beings feel about that? What if they possessed the might to repel the Chodrecai, or worse, stand beside the Plysserians as allies?

If what the Leadership had said was true, and scattered numbers of the Plysserian armies had escaped to here from *Jontashreena*, then they may very well have found renewed hope by fleeing to this place. Here was a whole planet upon which to hide and rebuild while waiting for the day when they were ready to stand against their enemies one final time.

Raegyra sighed in resignation as he looked about the strange forest surrounding him before casting his eyes upward once more to behold the lone moon hanging in the unfamiliar sky. Already weary from a lifetime of conflict, he felt his heart grow heavier still at the thought that the War, which he thought to be nearing its end, might instead be receiving an unwanted breath of life.

3

"This crap is hosed."

Listening to the less than formal report from her subordinate, Sergeant Belinda Russell released a long, exasperated sigh. She rubbed a hand across her face, trying unsuccessfully to wipe away the frustration and weariness she was beginning to feel.

It was not a summation she was pleased to hear. After nearly three hours of setting up, disassembling, reassembling, checking and double-checking the twelve PRC-77 radios that she and her team were responsible for, she was confident that every single piece of the communications equipment was functional and operating just as the manual said they should.

Her communications team, which consisted of two corporals, Keith Eshelman and Rebecca Sloane, sat at the table where the radios had been set up. In addition to the communications gear, an assortment of tools littered the table along with various notepads, pens, and three metal canteen cups. The cups had at one time contained hot coffee, a special blend that Russell had brought with her from home as a defense against the gut-rotting brew they had been served throughout the training exercise. The enticing beverages were long forgotten, though, as the three Marines worked to diagnose the reason for the radios' strange malfunctions.

It isn't the radios, she reminded herself. She, along with Eshelman and Sloane, had gone over every inch of all twelve radios and their accessories. Russell had personally tested each unit, by taking them, one at a time, into the woods and attempting to transmit back to the base camp's comm shack. From the spot she had picked out, several dozen meters into the woods, she had been able to communicate with the other two Marines with no problems.

On a whim, she had decided to see if distance was an issue and sure enough, problems at somewhere over a hundred meters. The farther she walked, the weaker the quality of the units' transmissions became. Finally, at what she guessed to be in the neighborhood of two hundred meters, the signal had degenerated completely. As that was well below the PRC-77's operational range, the signals being exchanged between the radios should have been nearly clear of any static or other interference. Each of the units had also been connected to the large base antenna erected on the top of the compound's only two-story metal building, which Russell had also tested and verified. Tuned to the proper frequencies, which they were, the radios should be able to receive clear and sharp signals transmitted from anywhere within Camp Growding's boundaries.

"Any improvement?" a voice asked, and Russell turned to see First Lieutenant Martin Stakely standing in the doorway. He was dressed as they were, in camouflage utilities and combat boots along with the webbed belt and harness combination that carried his canteens, first-aid kit, and magazine pouches for his service pistol. He had also taken the extra step of obscuring his features with face paint, the muted greens and browns breaking up the lines of his face in the same manner that his clothing would help to conceal his body while moving through the woods.

Considering that the lieutenant had absolutely no intention of leaving the command post area, Russell thought he looked ridiculous.

Stakely's question was delivered in that no-nonsense manner Russell recognized as meaning he was taking the business of overseeing a mock war very seriously. Taking an additional few seconds to blink away some of the fatigue gathering behind her eyes, she replied, "No, sir. We've run checks on everything and tested each unit. They work fine for a few hundred meters and then the signals begin to break up. We can't explain it yet."

Even through his face paint, Russell could see that the lieutenant was displeased with the report. "Well it doesn't do us any good to have these things if our patrols can't communicate with us, Sergeant."

I'm certainly glad we've got that straightened out, she mused, but instead said, "I understand that, Lieutenant. We can still talk to our people, but it's slow going because of the heavy squawk. We're working on it."

"Work faster," Stakely shot back. "The exercise will be over in another couple of hours, and we'll need the radios to recall our teams."

Before Russell could say anything further, Corporal Sloane piped up. "We think we might be getting some interference from local power lines, sir. If they're running within a mile or so of here, they could be strong enough to mess with us. Corporal Eshelman and I were about to check that out."

Russell could only barely stifle the urge to laugh as Sloane's words drew the lieutenant's attention like a siren calling to Odysseus. A slight smile replaced the expression of irritation and his tone softened as he regarded the younger woman.

"That sounds like a fine plan, Corporal. Be sure to let me know what you find." After looking at her in silence for a few seconds longer than Russell considered appropriate, Stakely leveled a final disgruntled glare at the sergeant before turning and stomping out of the room in an authoritative huff.

Once he was gone, Russell turned to Sloane with an appreciative smile on her face. "Nice save, Becky. So you think power lines could be part of the problem?"

"Pfffft," Sloane replied, rolling her eyes and waving the idea away. "No way, we checked that first thing. We're nowhere near any local power or phone lines. I just said that so he'd go away."

Eshelman added, "According to every check we've run, we should be getting comm traffic out the ass." He shrugged. "Might as well be sunspots, for all I know."

"Or maybe it's just Stakely's ego," Sloane offered.

The joke's delivery was so perfectly deadpan that Russell could not help laughing at it, or at the expense of the force of nature that was the only way to describe the raw sexual magnetism of one Martin Edward Stakely, First Lieutenant, United States Marine Corps (Reserved).

That is, if you asked him.

Rebecca Sloane numbered among the lithe blond female subsection of Marines who comprised their reserve unit, and Lieutenant Stakely had made no secret of his affinity for this particular demographic. Russell, whose dark skin and hair apparently shielded her from the lieutenant's wandering eye, had watched his attempts to charm, cajole, and pester most of these aforementioned lithe blond females in vain attempts to secure a few precious "moments alone" with whoever took him up on the offer. Russell had witnessed a few of the other women in the outfit accept the invitations, but not Sloane.

"I'm allergic to idiots," the corporal told her one night. "The moron could have at least pretended not to be married. Didn't even take off his wedding ring."

Even as she laughed at Sloane's joke, Russell could see her own aggravation mirrored in the younger woman's eyes. As goofy as the offered reason for the radios' malfunction sounded, Russell had to admit that it was still better than anything the three Marines had been able to come up with on their own.

Maybe I should write this down, she thought, glancing over to her portable field desk and the notebook she had left there hours ago. Russell had originally expected the evening to pass without much excitement. The quiet time, had things gone according to plan, would have allowed her to catch up on the hobby that she hoped would one day provide her with a new career: writing.

Her normal job as an overnight production technician at a local television station in Kansas City tended to provide her with no small amount of downtime to write when things were going well. Russell used that and any other time she could find to spin tales of mystery, science fiction, even romance and erotica depending on whatever interested her on a given day.

She had received more rejection letters from editors than she cared to count, but Russell could feel that she was getting close to making that first sale. Fueled by that goal, she had been working on her latest story, a fantasy piece she planned to send to a fiction magazine. It had been her intention to write a good portion of the story tonight, while the rest of the unit was engaged in the mock war and her responsibilities entailed little more than overseeing the operation of the group's communications equipment.

Instead, all she could do now was sigh in resignation as she consigned herself to the fact that the quiet, uneventful evening she had been hoping for was not going to happen.

"Well," Sloane said as she reached for her cup of coffee, "I guess we'd better come up with something else to try. I don't think I'll be able to buy much more time from Stakely with just my charm." Taking a sip from the cup, the young woman's face screwed up in disgust as she tasted the cold remnants of what had once been an enticing beverage.

"I could always put the moves on him if he gets bored with you," Eshelman offered, his eyebrows wiggling mischievously.

Russell laughed again, but her amusement was short lived. After all, Sloane was right. Fake war or not, Lieutenant Stakely would be very unhappy with them if they could not figure out what was causing the problems with their radios. Not that she would lose any amount of sleep over that, of course. She simply had no real desire to put up with any more of the man's shit than was necessary. As high strung as he seemed to be, how would he react if this was a real war?

Lucky for us this is just one big game.

4

Though he remembered to hold his voice to a whisper, Ronald Thurman still could not resist the need to curse as he snapped off his flashlight.

Where the hell are we?

He rose from his low crouch, flinging aside the poncho that he had used to cover himself and shield the glare of his flashlight while he consulted his map and compass. Freed from the poncho, his sweat-soaked skin welcomed the cooling effects of the slight breeze wafting through the forest. Summers in southern Missouri were bad enough without wrapping one's self in a cocoon of rubberized nylon.

"Any luck?" asked Lance Corporal Allyson Parker as Thurman handed her the poncho that she had volunteered.

He only shook his head as he refolded the map and returned it to the large cargo pocket on the right leg of his camouflage pants. Then he waited while Parker finished folding her poncho, taking the opportunity to study her figure one more time and imagine what she might look like unencumbered by the uniform and the gear she was carrying. With any luck, he would get to find out in a couple of days, once all this was over. Parker had seemed receptive to the idea of getting together once they had completed their training and their unit had returned to Kansas City.

That is, if they could find their way out of this god-damned forest.

"If I'm reading the map right, we should be less than a klick from the western border of the base." *One thousand meters*, he thought, easy walking distance to what should be the service road that ran around the outer perimeter of the reservation. The trouble was, by the pace count they had been keeping, a crude but surprisingly effective method of tracking walking distance, they should have reached the road by now.

During the land navigation training the Marines had undergone earlier in the week, Thurman had determined that his normal walking stride allowed him to cover a hundred meters in sixty-two paces. Coordinating this with the proper plotting of coordinates on the map and then using the compass to guide them, it should have been possible for any one in Thurman's squad to direct them through the woods to within ten meters of any point on the reservation. With the clear night sky and the moon offering a generous supply of illumination, navigating over land even in the dark should have been child's play.

The service road was nowhere in sight.

"Just great," a low voice said from somewhere behind him and Thurman whirled, searching for the speaker. The other members of his squad were standing nearby, waiting for him to issue them instructions.

"Who said that?" he hissed testily. His anger only deepened when he saw the various expressions of boredom and irritation on the faces of the others.

They were mocking him.

"Keep your mouths shut," he ordered, not even trying to keep the tone of his voice civil. After two weeks, he had grown tired of dealing with this collection of misfits.

They'd probably respond better if you weren't playing the hardass routine.

Darkness concealed his scowl from the other Marines as Thurman considered the mental rebuke. It was true that he was taking this stint of duty with a higher degree of seriousness than he had past assignments. He would have liked nothing better than to come to Camp Growding for the two weeks of training and have as much fun as possible doing it. Never truly comfortable barking orders to subordinates, Thurman had instead preferred a more laid-back leadership style. At his previous unit on the east coast, this approach had served him well, at least for a time.

The longer he served with that unit, however, the easier it became to discern that the sergeants who applied more direct methods, such as those employed by Marines in every bad movie he had ever seen, were the ones receiving the promotions. It had irritated Thurman to come to that realization, one that he felt powerless to do anything about. There was no way that he could simply change his own style of dealing with those Marines in his charge. They were his friends, after all.

Things had gotten worse after his divorce. With no children to worry about, Thurman opted to return home to Kansas City, where he wasted no time finding mechanic work at one of the city's numerous automotive dealerships. Transferring to the local Marine reserve unit had been easy enough, as well. Once attached to the new group, and with plenty of aggression looking to be channeled, he decided that a fresh approach toward his reserve duties was necessary if he wanted to secure eventual promotion to staff sergeant. Rather than the relaxed style he was comfortable with, he chose instead to adopt the more aggressive approach used by his peers at his previous command.

And you're going overboard with it.

"Does that radio work or not?" he asked, making a conscious effort to lessen the severity in his tone.

The Marine carrying the squad's radio, Private First Class Timothy Manelli, shook his head even as he held the radio's handset to his ear. "I can barely hear anyone over the static. I thought I caught a few words here and there, but it's like the antenna's broken or something."

"I'm guessing you already checked it."

The younger man nodded. "Twice."

Thurman shook his head in disgust. The radio had been working before they had left the command post. He had used the damned thing to talk to that sergeant, Russell or whatever the hell her name was, during a test less than ten minutes after setting out on their patrol. There had been no need to use it after that, and he really had not wanted to take it along on patrol in the first place. A squawking radio would do nothing but give away his squad's position while they were moving through the forest, and he had wanted to maintain strict noise discipline. This, despite Lieutenant Stakely's insistence that each patrol carry a radio for safety, giving the patrols the ability to contact their command posts in the event a Marine was injured or a group became lost in the dark woods.

Fat lot of good it's doing us now, though.

Studying the hapless young radioman and the rest of his squad for an additional few seconds, Thurman finally turned his back on the group and instead allowed his eyes to scan the forest around him. The moon cast an eerie glow that filtered down through the thick overhead canopy of trees, elongating and stretching the shadows. Every tree, every bush looked identical to the one next to it. There were no distinguishing landmarks or anything else to offer him the slightest indication of what direction he should take. Essentially, they were lost.

We're not lost, he scolded himself. If nothing else, they would proceed due west until they ran into the reservation's perimeter road. Once there, they could march either north or south until they came across some landmark or intersection with another road that would match up to a point on his map. From there it should be simple enough to find their way back to the base camp.

"Psst," a voice said from behind him, and Thurman turned to see that some of the other squad members were reacting to something. One of the Marines, a corporal named Jenkins, was pointing at something through the trees. Thurman tried looking where the man was pointing into the darkness but could see nothing.

"What is it?" he finally asked, his own voice barely above a whisper.

"Don't you hear it?" the voice asked, and now Thurman recognized it as belonging to Corporal Alex McLanahan. Not saying anything, he instead listened and that's when he heard the faint sounds.

Music? He directed a questioning look in McLanahan's direction.

The corporal nodded. "Yeah, coming from somewhere over there." He indicated the trees in the distance again. "You think maybe we're near somebody's house?"

"According to the map, there aren't any houses near this part of the base."

"Maybe it's a park ranger or one of them National Guard guys," the younger man offered. "You know, found himself a nice place to hide for a while. Maybe he's got some beer or his honey or something." A wide smile suddenly brightened the corporal's face. "Let's go see."

Thurman frowned at the idea, at first hesitant to do anything that might distract them from the wargame. They were supposed to be trying to find their "enemy's" base camp, but at the rate they were going, the exercise would be over before he got the squad back on the proper track.

Since they were going to be late getting back to base anyway, was there really any harm in checking out the source of the music? Who knew what they might find there? Nodding for McLanahan to lead the way through the trees in search of the faint music, Thurman at the same time gave the "move out" signal to the rest of the squad.

As they proceeded through the forest, Thurman was pleased to note that McLanahan was still taking his responsibilities as point man seriously. Even though they had abandoned their "mission," at least for the moment, the man was proceeding slowly and deliberately, taking each step with care so as not to make undue noise while continuing to scan their surroundings in search of potential threats. After all, it was still possible that other squads could be in the area.

They continued their advance as festive sounds grew louder with each passing moment. Along with music Thurman could also hear voices, and he saw flickering light filtering through the trees. The gaps between trees were growing wider and he could see that they were approaching a clearing of some kind, with what had to be a huge campfire casting ominous shadows on the surrounding foliage.

Who the hell was this? Had they stumbled across some other unit that had set up camp for their own training exercise?

Ahead of him, McLanahan moved closer to the light, stopping behind a large oak tree before raising his fist, the signal to halt in place. Thurman passed the silent command back down the line to the rest of the squad before moving up to join the corporal at the tree.

"What's up?" he asked, his voice barely audible even to the other man. He did not need a real answer, though, as he got his first good look at what McLanahan had found.

The clearing could not have been more than twenty meters across at its widest point, and he did not see any indication of a road or trail that might lead out of the area. There were two small tents, the civilian nylon kind that probably slept two or three people at most. A fire pit was in the center of the clearing, and Thurman could see four people, two men and two women, seated or standing around it.

All four people were young, early twenties at the outside, each in varying stages of undress. The brunette woman's ensemble, he noted, consisted of denim cut offs and a bikini top. Her breasts were threatening to spill out of the top, and the shorts had been cut in such a manner that they revealed more of her backside than Levi Strauss had probably intended. The other woman, a blonde, was dressed in what looked to be spandex shorts and a tank top, its bottom tied in a knot that left her stomach bare.

"Hello," McLanahan whispered. "Those ain't no Guardsmen."

"No kidding." Thurman could see that both men were holding beer cans, each one no doubt intoxicated as they enjoyed watching the girls move about the small campsite. At first he thought he imagined the faint odor of marijuana in the air, but his suspicions were confirmed when he saw one of the men bring a small hand-rolled cigarette to his lips.

"Now that's what I'm talkin' about," Ruiz said suddenly from just behind Thurman. How had he managed to sneak up without being heard? The sergeant had to give the man credit for his surprising stealth.

Not that it mattered though.

Even before he issued a warning to keep quiet, Thurman saw one of the men near the campfire turn his head in their direction, his brow creased in concentration.

He had heard something.

"Mike?" the man's companion asked. "What's wrong?"

Rising from where he had been sitting with his back resting against a tree, the man who had apparently heard Ruiz pointed into the forest, directly at Thurman. "I think someone's out there."

"Maybe it's some of those soldiers," the brunette in the denim shorts offered. "They were shooting off their guns before."

The Marines watched as the first man, Mike, continued to look in their direction, ignoring his friends as he tried to find whatever it was that had attracted his attention. Thurman doubted that the man could even see them, as the fire would have impaired his ability to see in the dark, though it was obvious by his posture that Mike was convinced someone or something was hiding among the trees surrounding the campsite. If any of the Marines tried to move away, they would be spotted instantly. Their only choice was to wait until Mike grew tired of searching for something he could not see.

"Who's out there?" he finally shouted. Maybe it was the beer, or the grass, or just the simple fact that the man was scared of the dark, but Thurman could see that he was becoming more and more agitated. How much greater would that anxiety grow before Mike did something stupid?

As it turned out, the Marines did not have to wait long, as Mike turned and stumbled his way to one of the campsite's two tents. After burrowing around inside the tent for several seconds, the man emerged carrying something in his hand.

"Shit," Thurman breathed, already trying to mold himself into the bark of the tree he was hiding behind. There was no mistaking the pistol, the polished metal of its barrel reflecting the light from the campfire. It looked to be a nine-millimeter Beretta semiautomatic, very similar to the sidearms issued to military personnel. Thurman watched as Mike, with hands made more than a little unsteady by alcohol, pulled the pistol's slide back and released it, chambering a round.

This had the unforeseen effect of causing Mike to drop the weapon onto his foot, which like his other one was for some unknown reason lacking a shoe. The result was immediate, with the drunken man uttering a mostly unintelligible string of profanities as he hopped around and tried to cradle his assaulted foot in his hands. Mike's impaired balance and coordination suffered another setback when he fell backward onto his ass, crashing into his tent and collapsing the fragile nylon structure around him. His three friends found no small amount of amusement in this string of events as their laughter echoed through the forest.

"Okay, so maybe he is Guard," Ruiz said, eliciting a chuckle from McLanahan, though Thurman frowned at the joke. After all, now that he was angry and humiliated, the drunken Mike was almost certain to do something idiotic now, such as firing blindly into the woods.

"I don't know about you," Ruiz said, "but I'm not gonna stand here and wait for that shithead to shoot us."

Thurman did not realize what the other man meant until after Ruiz stepped forward, leaving the security of their hiding place and heading for the campsite. "Ruiz, wait!" he hissed, asking himself as he did so why he bothered to keep his voice low in the first place as Ruiz stomped forward through the foliage, making no effort to conceal his approach. "Dammit," he finally said, running to catch up to the other man.

The four campers were startled at the sudden new noise, but to Thurman's relief he saw that they relaxed somewhat as he and Ruiz stepped into the clearing. Both men had taken the precaution of slinging their M-16s across their backs, and Thurman made sure to keep his empty hands visible and away from his body as he walked.

"No cause for alarm, ladies," Ruiz offered, his voice oozing that particular flavor of charm that Thurman recognized from the countless bars and clubs he had caroused. "Just me and my friends out on a little stroll through the woods."

Mike, still lying amid the ruins of this tent, glared at the Marine. "I knew I heard something," he said, his voice slurred from the beer. "What the fuck are you doing out there?"

"War games, you moron," his companion said, his own voice only slightly less impeded. "They're training or something." Looking over at Ruiz he added, "Ain't that right? I'll bet that shit's fun, ain't it?"

"Yep," Ruiz replied. "Looks to me, though, that you're the ones having all the fun." Thurman noted how he made no attempt to downplay his candid appraisal of the two women as he talked, his eyes raking over each of their bodies. As far as he could tell, the girls did not object to Ruiz's wanton stares, appearing instead to warm to the newfound attention.

What is this, Penthouse Letters?

"You guys feel like hanging out for a while?" the blonde asked, batting eyes at Ruiz who in turn looked to Thurman with a wicked smile on his face that spoke volumes.

After several seconds of silent deliberation with himself, Thurman sighed in resignation. "Why not?"

The response was greeted with a host of disbelieving looks from the other Marines as he waved them forward from their hiding places in the forest. Stepping closer, McLanahan regarded the sergeant with incredulity, an expression that deepened as Thurman accepted a proffered beer from the brunette.

"What the hell is this about?" McLanahan asked, the skepticism evident on his face.

"We're going to be late getting back, anyway," Thurman replied. "Might as well have a little fun while we're at it."

As she stepped into the clearing, Parker regarded the sergeant with a teasing smile. "And here I thought you were King of the Pricks."

Thurman held up the beer. "I figure it's the least I could do after leading us around this shitty forest all night."

"Captain Douglas is going to be pissed if we're out here all night," McLanahan said, his eyes catching on the sight of Ruiz and the blonde sidling up to each other near the fire.

His attention focusing on Parker, Thurman shrugged. "What's the worst that can happen?" he asked as he stepped closer to her.

5

"Ambush!"

Bradley Gardner saw movement among the trees a heartbeat before he heard Daniel Melendez's shouted warning. For a brief instant he cursed the corporal's willingness to give their position away in the darkness, but then he realized that it really did not matter. Whoever they had stumbled upon already knew who he and his companions were and they were reacting accordingly. Fleeting figures scurried amid the forest undergrowth, scattering in numerous directions even as Melendez directed the rest of his squad to find cover. The squad moved quickly, abandoning the vulnerable open area of the service road to take up defensive positions just inside the tree line.

They had been making good time along one of the reservation's many service roads, using the map Bonniker carried to direct them back to the base camp. Still more than half an hour away on foot, though, he knew there was a good possibility that they would run into another patrol still engaged in the war game.

Dammit, Gardner thought. *Here we go again.* Technically, as they had been declared casualties in the earlier ambush, he and Bonniker's squad were not even supposed to be participating in this engagement. According to the rules of the game, he was just supposed to sit out any further firefights until the exercise was over or until he made it back to the base camp, whichever came first. It had sounded silly when the Marines had been briefed before the start of the exercise, and it was positively ridiculous now that the game was actually underway. After all, how was anyone to know who was and was not a casualty?

Not to mention that simply sitting around and letting the others play the game was damned boring. Bonniker had agreed. If they had to spend all night trouncing around the forest, they might as well have a little fun along the way.

"Over here!" he called out, pointing into the trees where he had seen the movement. There was no sign of anyone now, but Gardner was sure they were still close. He knew that their opponents, whoever they were, were already assuming their own positions among the concealment offered by the forest and the darkness.

He heard footsteps over his right shoulder and turned to see Bonniker moving to crouch down beside him, his weapon already pointed in the direction Gardner had indicated. The sergeant's eyes were wide with excitement. Gardner knew that the evening's activities were probably old hat to Bonniker, who at one time had served on active duty as an infantryman. Working these days as network administrator for one of the larger banks in south Kansas City, Bonniker was probably having fun compared to his normal workday. Helping stuffy bank employees to access their electronic mail when they forgot their password or chasing down the latest virus foisted on the network by a loan advisor downloading porn from the Internet simply could not compete with running around the woods and playing war.

"Where are they?" Bonniker asked.

Gardner indicated with a wave of his hand where he had first seen the shadowy figures. "Maybe twenty yards in." He frowned as several seconds passed with no signs of activity from their supposed ambushers. "Shouldn't they have started shooting by now?"

Bonniker nodded. "They had us cold on the road."

True enough, Gardner decided. If the other group had run a textbook ambush, everyone in Bonniker's squad would probably be "dead" already.

So what the hell were they doing in there?

"Check it out," he said, pointing to his left where he saw Melendez directing the movements of squad members into the forest.

"They're spreading out," Bonniker noted. "Trying to pin down the other group." Looking into the forest again, he tapped Gardner on the shoulder. "If we go this way, we might be able to surround them."

Gardner considered the idea. They still did not know exactly where their would-be attackers were, who had no doubt taken the last few minutes to establish defensive positions. With the moonlight filtering down through the trees and illuminating the dirt road, anyone approaching from that direction would provide a nice silhouette for targeting. Still, even with just the seven of them, Gardner figured that if he and his companions moved quickly they should at least be able to catch a few of their opponents before any momentum shifted away from their sudden counteroffensive.

"Let's do it," Bonniker said, and the two of them set off at a jog deeper into the trees. As they moved, Gardner kept his attention on the area of the forest where he had last seen signs of activity. There was no mistaking the feel of other eyes on him, watching him as he ducked behind trees and bushes. He felt like one of those targets in a carnival shooting gallery, moving along a track until someone shot him and forced him to change direction.

It's only a game, dude, he reminded himself. *Jesus.*

So why had the others not started playing yet?

To his left he saw other figures among the trees, Corporal Melendez and the other members of the squad, all of them moving in an ever-expanding semicircle in an attempt to envelop the other patrol. If the other group maintained their position, confrontation was certain.

Something snapped to his right, a twig or branch or pine cone, the sound as loud as a gunshot in the near silence of the forest. Gardner swung his rifle in the direction of the noise but saw nothing.

No. A bush was moving. Something had disturbed it.

"Gotcha," he said, smiling in triumph. "Tony, over here!" He heard Bonniker heading in this direction as he ran toward the bush, weapon out in front of him as he searched for a target. Surely the other patrol knew he was coming now, so why were they not shooting at him? For a fleeting moment he thought he might be stumbling headlong into a trap.

Screw it, I've already died once tonight.

Using the barrel of his rifle to clear a path, Gardner pushed through a thicket of vines. He felt dozens of tiny thorns grabbing at his clothing and equipment but he ignored them. As much as he might not want to admit it, the excitement of the war game had overtaken him. The heat, the bugs, the endless walking all over the base, all of it was forgotten as the adrenaline rush overtook his body. Even though this was all make believe, Gardner could sense that this is what it would be like in a real combat situation, with his body providing him the energy he would need to overcome fear or anxiety and to simply carry on. He had read about such sensations in books written about various wars, but he had never expected to experience anything even remotely resembling such emotions himself. After all, he was a payroll clerk, and how many of those went to war?

Left!

Sensing it rather than seeing it, Gardner caught a rustling of branches in the corner of his eye. He aimed his rifle toward the source of the movement, expecting to see a fellow Marine lying in wait.

But that was not what he found.

"Holy shit . . ."

Makoquolax had been caught off guard by the arrival of the creatures. For that he was angry at himself, as he should have been more careful to guard against just such an occurrence.

Since arriving through the portal only a few cycles ago, they had observed many representatives of what were apparently the higher order life-forms on this strange planet that was unlike their own world, yet at the same time so very comparable. These life-forms, which Plysserian medical officers had learned referred to themselves as "humans," also bore as many similarities to him and his fellow Plysserians as differences. They were noticeably smaller, true, and weaker as well. While they did not possess speed or agility on par with his people, the fact remained that they were native born to this world. Makoquolax thought it foolish to assume that physical disparities such as smaller size and lesser strength would give him or his companions any sort of guaranteed advantage.

There was still much to be learned, and with that in mind they had been forced to proceed with caution. All soldiers who had made the journey through the portal had been directed to avoid contact with any indigenous inhabitants of this planet. Should such contact prove to be unavoidable, under no circumstances was any Plysserian soldier to harm or kill any human encountered. They were to be captured instead.

Adhering to the directives had been easy enough at first. This area had proven to be largely unpopulated, just as the scientists responsible for creating and operating the portal technology had promised. The region was an ideal location for their purposes, and Plysserian military leaders had wasted no time ordering troops through the portal. Here they were able to seek respite from their enemies, the Chodrecai. Sightings of humans had been sporadic and uneventful, so much so that it was probably inevitable that laxness would take over and an accidental contact would occur.

Makoquolax just had not believed that he would be the one to let it happen.

The humans that appeared on the road were unlike any that he or other Plysserian scouts had covertly observed since their arrival. This group carried weapons and moved with a military precision. Makoquolax was sure that they were soldiers of some kind, which his leaders had warned to be on the lookout for. Contacting any sort of organized group on this planet now, when the Plysserians were still so vulnerable, could be devastating.

He moved to conceal himself with care, but Makoquolax knew he had been spotted when the humans began to call out in their strange alien tongue and spread out, heading in his direction.

Zanzi!

He barely managed to keep from uttering the curse aloud as he plunged through the forest, away from the approaching humans. While he knew that he could outrun his pursuers, that much could not be said for the armaments they carried. Makoquolax had no idea how much damage the weapons were capable of inflicting, and he had no desire to find out. His only option, therefore, was to hide.

Unfortunately, when selecting a place of concealment, Makoquolax made the mistake of not choosing his footing wisely, catching a small branch and stretching it away from the bush until it snapped. The sound created by the breaking wood echoed in the forest, advertising his position with the same clarity as if he had ignited a flare.

Makoquolax held his breath, listening for the impact of the misstep. For an instant his mind filled with the image of his initial training instructor and the reaction he would have had at the idea that he could make such a careless mistake. In any other circumstances, the vision would have been humorous.

At first he thought he might have gotten away with the grievous error, but then he heard one of the humans cry out. Already very near to his position, there was no way the creature could have missed the sound of the snapping branch.

Then the human was crashing through the underbrush, its weapon held out in front of it and trained on the center of Makoquolax's chest. It was yelling something at him in its own language, and as unintelligible as it was there was no mistaking the intent behind the strange alien tongue.

Do not move!

"What the hell is this?"

Gardner heard the question before he saw Bonniker break through the bushes and come up alongside him. He risked a glance in his friend's direction and saw the expression of utter shock on Bonniker's face before returning his full attention to the thing lying on the ground before him. The creature had remained still since Gardner had discovered it, moving to hold its arm away from its body, evidently to show that it was not a threat.

"Get your flashlight out," he told Bonniker after several more seconds passed. Bonniker grasped the green, curved head flashlight from the front strap of his patrol harness and, pausing only to remove the light's red lens, directed the bright beam upon whatever it was they had found.

"Jesus," Gardner whispered as the light illuminated the creature. While it at first resembled a man, or perhaps an ape, upon closer inspection Gardner saw that this was not the case at all. The thing was all muscle, like an Olympic weight lifter. Each of its arms was easily bigger than his own legs, and its skin was either a white or light gray, though the creature's face and body seemed to be dominated by a myriad pattern of shapes and designs rendered in a dark blue or black paint or ink. They reminded Gardner of the tattoos he had seen on bikers and other people who partook of body art.

Bonniker raised the light to the creature's face. A massive head topped the thing's muscle-bound torso, with large dark eyes that were somewhat oval in shape. Its mouth was large, with dull ash-colored teeth that looked big and sharp enough to bite through a steel bar. There were no ears or nose that Gardner could identify, only small holes set into the skull in the approximate locations where such features would normally be found on a . . .

. . . on a human.

"A fuckin' alien?" Bonniker exclaimed, giving voice to the insane thought already crossing Gardner's mind. Where they really looking at a visitor from another planet?

Get outa here.

Bonniker leveled his own weapon on the creature, indicating it with the barrel of his rifle. "It's wearing some kinda body armor."

Indeed, Gardner recognized what looked to be close-fitting plates covering the creature's torso, leaving its arms and legs free save for an assortment of different bands and straps affixed to its wrists and ankles. The chest plates looked thick and unyielding, even more so than the Kevlar vests normally issued to U.S. military forces, and the creature also wore a type of belt about its waist, replete with pouches and oddly shaped items attached to it. What looked to be the muzzle of some type of weapon extended up behind the creature's left shoulder, the weapon itself appearing to be strapped to the thing's back.

Gardner recalled a movie where an invisible hunter from another planet chased Arnold what's-his-name through the jungle. That bastard was huge, too, just like the thing sitting right here in front of him. He seemed to remember that the alien in the film wore some kind of mask or helmet to breathe, though, whereas this creature did not. Did this mean that wherever this thing was from, the air was similar to that here on Earth?

This was the stuff of dreams, right?

Unfortunately, Gardner's ruminations were overwhelmed by his current desire to run like hell and get as far away from these things as humanly possible.

"Do you think it can understand us?" Bonniker asked, still holding his flashlight on the creature. Gardner could hear the fear in his friend's wavering voice, though Bonniker was managing to keep himself remarkably calm given the circumstances. That made Gardner feel better. *Good, there's two of us who are scared shitless.*

"I sure as hell hope not," he replied. "Otherwise it's going to hear me tell you how stupid I think we look holding guns with blanks in them right now." Gardner had not seen the creature make anything resembling a hostile move, but it could only be a matter of time before it figured out that neither he nor Bonniker posed any sort of serious threat.

He'll probably know when you finally piss yourself.

Voices in the forest around him distracted Gardner. Of course, he realized, the rest of the squad could be encountering more creatures like the one here in front of him. How many friends did this thing have out here in the forest? That line of thought was only just beginning to assert itself when he heard the sounds of running feet. Someone was approaching through the trees. Gardner saw the creature's eyes grow wide in momentary fear as it heard the sounds, too.

Not friends, then, Gardner's instincts told him.

"Gardner? Bonniker?" Corporal Melendez's voice called out as he stepped out of the darkness, with the other members of his squad only a few paces behind him. "Whoever they were, they got away. Did you see . . . ?" The rest of his question died in his throat as his eyes tracked the beam from Bonniker's flashlight to see what it was illuminating.

"Fuck me," he whispered, his mouth dropping open in unabashed shock. "What the . . . what is that?"

Bonniker waved his rifle at the creature. "It's an alien."

"We don't know what it is," Gardner snapped, though his gut had already told him the same thing and his head was rapidly coming to terms with that initial assessment. Oddly enough, the more he found himself accepting the incredible idea, the more he could feel his initial fear beginning to diminish.

"It's carrying some kind of weapon," Bonniker added, indicating the object strapped to the creature's back. "Maybe it's like those laser guns on . . ."

"Jaq neltwok lehshak zu!"

The heads of all three Marines turned at the sound of the high-pitched shrill to see the creature staring at them.

"He sounds pissed," Melendez said.

Gardner shook his head. "I don't think so." Given the remarkable lack of facial features, eyebrows or noticeable wrinkles around its eyes or mouth, the alien did not seem capable of affecting a wide range of expressions. Despite this, and the unintelligible gibberish it had uttered, Gardner did not get the impression that the creature was angry.

"He sounds frustrated more than anything else." It was as though the creature was trying to tell them something, but the obvious language barrier between him and the Marines was proving a hindrance. If that was the case, what were they supposed to do about it?

This isn't one of those crappy movies where all the aliens speak better English than my college professor, he thought. *And it's not like we can call a translator.*

His attention attracted by the creature's movements again, Gardner saw that the thing was pointing to one of the pouches on its belt. What did it hold? A weapon?

Obviously sensing the same potential trouble, Melendez and Bonniker both took an involuntary step back. For a moment Gardner was afraid that the creature would see the opening his friends had given it and use that slip up to take advantage of the situation.

"Hang on a second," he said. The creature had ceased any movement at the Marines' reaction. Gardner was sure that if they had wanted to, the alien would have been able to defeat him and his companions with ease. Why had it not acted? There was something more going on here, he was convinced of it. "Let's see what he's after."

Making sure that he had the creature's attention, Gardner made a show of slinging his rifle across his back. Then, holding his empty hands out in front of him, he attempted to mimic the gesture he had seen the thing make earlier.

I just hope I'm not giving this guy the universal signal telling him to go fuck himself.

To his shock, the creature immediately returned the gesture, and its mouth moved into something that Gardner could almost take for a smile. There were still entirely too many teeth for his taste, but otherwise it was hard to take the expression as threatening.

"I'll be damned," Melendez whispered. "He understands."

Gardner frowned at that. "More like I understand. I don't think it's out to hurt us. I mean, look at him. Anybody here think that he *couldn't* kill all of us without breaking a sweat?" Still, despite the raw strength and power the creature's body seemed to project, Gardner continued to find himself growing more at ease in its presence than he would have thought possible mere minutes before.

"Jaq neltwok lehshak zu."

The strange words came out in a more subdued volume this time, but Gardner was sure he could detect desire, even pleading, behind the words. This thing wanted to communicate, he was sure of it. Could it sense his own diminishing fear? Gardner's hopes were buoyed somewhat as the creature repeated the gesture of pointing to the pouch on its belt, though it made no move to open the pouch.

He's asking for my permission?

"Think that's where he's stashing his wallet?" Bonniker asked, trying without success to inject a bit of levity into the tension enveloping the Marines like a heavy blanket. No one laughed, especially Gardner, who had arrived at his decision.

"I'm going to let him open it," he said finally, hoping that his voice was not telegraphing the lingering nervous tension that was still tying his stomach into knots. With no other idea on how to communicate with this creature coming to him, Gardner simply pointed at the pouch and nodded.

To his relief, the alien repeated its earlier expression that looked so much to the young Marine like a smile. Then, while keeping its left hand open and away from its body as it had before, the creature slowly opened the pouch and withdrew something. Gardner was surprised to see that it possessed an oddly familiar shape. He was not alone, either.

"Some kind of headband?" Melendez asked, and Gardner could tell from the tone of the corporal's voice that he had been expecting something otherworldly, as well.

Gardner noted that the band, if that was what it was, was actually a series of metallic sections connected together to form a circle. Two of the sections were slightly larger than the others and were connected together in sequence. Several of the other segments appeared to have varying numbers of small nodes protruding along their inner surfaces. He could not even begin to guess what the band could be used for, but it was an almost automatic reaction on his part to reach out and accept the mysterious object when the creature held it out to him.

"Wow," he said as he hefted it in his palm, "it's not heavy at all." Using both hands, he tested the band's elasticity and found none, nor was he able to break the circle it created with its connected components. "Whatever it is, it's made to last."

Bonniker tapped him on the shoulder. "Look." Gardner looked up to see that the creature had retrieved an almost identical band from the pouch on its belt. Holding it up for the Marines to see, the alien then proceeded to place the band on its own head, with the two larger sections on the front of its forehead just above its eyes. Then a transparent lens descended from the band to cover the creature's eyes, settling into place with a barely audible metallic *click*.

"*Kav joqweh nolz*," the creature said, making a motion to Gardner and the band he still held in his hand. The meaning was obvious: He was supposed to place the band on his own head.

Gardner cast a skeptical look at his friends. "What do you think?"

Shrugging, Melendez replied, "You seem to be doing okay so far, dude. No sense stopping now." Indicating the creature with a nod of his head, he added, "It's like you said. If he'd wanted to cap us, he'd have done it by now. I say go for it."

Gardner regarded the odd contraption in his hand. It seemed harmless enough, he admitted, but how could he be sure? What effect would it have on him?

I guess there's only one way to find out.

He took one last breath in a vain attempt to relax. "Well, here goes nothing," he said as, after making sure that the band was aligned as he had seen the creature do, he placed the strange device on his own head. Just as he suspected, it was too large to fit him, at least at first.

Faster than Gardner could react, the band tightened itself around his head and for an insane instant he thought it might continue to shrink until it simply crushed his skull. Then he realized that the band was actually resizing itself until it rested snugly around the widest part of his head. The nodes on the band's interior pressed into his skin as a transparent screen, identical to those on the creature's band, dropped down in front of his eyes.

He almost immediately became aware of an odd tingling sensation emanating from the nodes pushing into the sides of his head. The effect translated to an equally discomforting tickle coming from behind his eyeballs. All of this preceded a dull ache that was developing at the base of his skull. His first instinct was to rip the device from his head and throw it away.

And then, it happened.

"*Lejnak tuq wivrotdeh,*" the creature said. As if acting in response to the words, the lens covering Gardner's eyes darkened slightly before an image began to coalesce before him.

"It's some kind of heads-up display," Gardner reported for the benefit of his friends. He knew about similar technology used in military airplanes and he had seen it in some of the newer cars. Somehow, though, he doubted any of those displays were as technically advanced as what he was experiencing now.

For one thing, his display appeared to be reacting to the creature's voice. As it continued to speak, the image before Gardner's eyes changed to not only a graphic representation of the creature, but of himself.

"What do you see, Brad?" Bonniker asked.

"I think this is some kind of translator," he said as he watched the image of the creature begin a series of gestures with its hands, none of which appeared to be threatening. "It seems to be reacting to whatever he's saying." Though the uncomfortable sensations the band was producing were still there, Gardner realized he could ignore it easily enough by concentrating on the images. "I wonder how I can get him to understand me."

From behind him, Melendez said, "Well, if it works by talking to it, maybe you start with simple stuff and see how it goes."

That sounded reasonable enough to Gardner. Taking a

few seconds to consider what he might say, he thought about the obvious, shaking hands with the creature.

Instantly, that image appeared before his eyes.

"*Amleq!*" the creature shouted suddenly, and Gardner could see the now unmistakable smile on its face. Was it seeing the image as well? What did that mean? Could the alien device understand his very thoughts?

"What's going on?" Melendez asked, concern evident in his voice. "Brad, you okay?"

Gardner nodded excitedly. "Jesus. I think this thing can read my mind."

Success!

Makoquolax could barely contain his joy at the breakthrough he had made with the human. The translators had been an untested gamble, he knew, but it appeared that the confidence that the scientists had displayed when briefing him and his fellow soldiers had been well founded.

The devices had been in general use for quite some time, developed by an eager young linguist years before as a way to aid in the learning of the multitude of languages spoken by the various cultures on *Jontashreena*. The linguist had spent years working with a host of doctors, perfecting the complex series of sensors that enabled the translators to interpret signals sent by the brain and transform them into images and text representation that could be understood by anyone wearing the device. The translators had proven valuable in a wide variety of uses, from helping citizens born without vocal capacities to aiding police and even military interrogations.

He had been told that the translators had been modified to work with humans, based on research conducted by Plysserian scientists on captured specimens when the portals had first started being used. Makoquolax had not been convinced at first, but those doubts were gone now as he watched the images conjured by the human displayed before him.

It was an odd gesture the human was demonstrating, this grasping of hands. Makoquolax saw how it seemed to put both parties on equal terms, and with their bodies so close to one another the likelihood of being duped by a concealed weapon was slim. Agreeing to such an action required trust on the part of both individuals. Then he saw the human extend its hand to him and he decided that the only way to test his theory was to accept the strange offer.

He also had to concede the point that the humans could have already killed him if they had so desired. That they had not both relieved and confused Makoquolax, but it also filled his heart with hope, as well.

Reaching out to grasp the human's smaller hand, Makoquolax reminded himself to be careful not to crush it in his own undoubtedly stronger grip. As he did so, he wished his superiors were present to witness this event. They were naturally concerned that the planet's native inhabitants, should they become aware of the Plysserian presence here, would react with hostility toward what they might perceive as an invading force.

Perhaps there were humans who would view him and his fellow soldiers in that light, but there also had to be others here who would not take that stance. If that were the case, then surely it was in Plysserian interest to make contact and see if the humans were potential allies. This human certainly appeared to be one such individual. How many more were there like him?

Were there enough?

"This is unreal!"

Gardner could only agree with Melendez's assessment as the creature reached out and gently took his hand. Then it smiled again and he realized that his feeble attempt at communication had succeeded. The translator was doing the bulk of the work, of course, somehow scanning his brain as he spoke and formed the thoughts he wanted to convey to the creature. He imagined he could feel the band's nodes probing his mind, drawing out the information and restructuring it in order for the creature to understand him. What an incredible feat of engineering the translator must be, he decided.

He was no scientist, but given the apparent ease of interactivity he was enjoying with the device, just how different were these aliens from humans? How similar were their brains? There were countless questions he wanted to ask, with more presenting themselves with each passing moment.

"What are we supposed to do now?" Bonniker asked. "It's not like this thing's a stray dog, guys. We can't just drop it off at the pound or something."

Gardner was concentrating on conjuring images that reflected those very concerns. He harbored no illusions that he was even remotely qualified to be the ambassador for an entire planet, but who was? The government? Did they have people who worked to be ready for such an incredible eventuality as communicating with an alien species? Gardner tended to believe that such notions were confined to the realm of fiction, but the hand grasping his own was definitely challenging those assertions.

On his visor display, he saw new images, this time of other humans standing in front of his own representation. The faces of the newly conjured figures were older and more distinguished, and Gardner instinctively viewed them as people in positions of authority. Concentrating on the images, he modified them so that they appeared as officers in military dress, generals with gray hair and rows of multicolored ribbons on their chests.

"*Amleq*," the creature said again, nodding enthusiastically and continuing to smile.

"You think that's how he says yes?" Melendez asked.

That sounded right to Gardner. "I think he's telling me he wants us to take him to somebody in charge." He was sure that Captain Douglas would freak out when he saw what the Marines had found, but he saw no other choice. The reserve captain was still their superior officer, and Gardner would have to hope that Douglas would know enough to at least place a call to someone with the appropriate authority and expertise to deal with this matter.

"Well," he said finally, "this is definitely not how I expected to spend my Friday night, that's for sure."

7

Hiding in the dense thicket in which she had flung herself when the nightmare began, Lance Corporal Allyson Parker bit her lip to keep from crying out in pain as thorns and branches raked across her face, neck, and any other exposed skin. She felt the thicket grab onto her uniform and equipment, wrapping itself around her in a vicious cocoon and concealing her from view.

Terrified to the point of paralysis, she could do nothing but watch as agony and death erupted all around her. People she had lived and worked with, not just for the last two weeks but in some cases for a year or more, her friends, were dying and she was powerless to stop it.

Sergeant Thurman was flirting with her, and doing well at it, when he disappeared right in front of her, his body ripped apart by the invisible energy wave one of the monsters had leveled on him. For an insane instant the gruesome scene reminded her of pictures from a book about land mines she had once read. The photographs had been uncompromising in their depiction of the cruel wounds they could inflict on easily yielding human flesh, but even they could not compare with the force of the weapon that had killed Ronald Thurman.

Had Thurman suffered? She did not think so. At least, she was sure there could not have been enough time for him to feel anything.

The shooting and the screams continued for several horrific minutes, during which Parker tried to push herself deeper into the thicket. Her hiding place did not allow her to see any of the other Marines during the abrupt firefight, during which the night air was littered with the sounds of M-16s firing frantically at anything that moved, as well as more of the shrieking wails of the monsters' own weapons. She heard their cries for help, though. Some of them called for the carnage to stop. At least one person begged for his mother before all of the voices finally and mercifully fell silent.

Now that it was over, it took an extraordinary force of will for Parker to remain absolutely still where she had fallen, with the thorns continuing their assault as the things moved all around her.

What the hell were they?

Parker could only catch glimpses of the attackers as they passed into her field of vision, which had been compromised by the nearly facedown position she had ended up in after diving into the brush. Were they apes or bears? They moved unlike any animal she had ever seen, their bodies like stacks of coiled muscle. Their skin was pale in the moonlight, off-white or possibly ash. They wore a kind of garment about the waist, while what looked to be equipment belts and harnesses crisscrossed the things' backs and chests.

Then there were the weapons. Parker had never seen anything like them before, outside of a science fiction movie.

The things continued to mill about the area as they inspected the massacre they had unleashed on her friends. They were talking among themselves, at least that was what she thought they were doing. Some of what she heard sounded like spoken language, but it was laced with grunts and clicks and even some noises she could not recognize. Listening to the creatures communicate with one another only added to what was fast becoming a staggering realization.

Aliens?

"Oh my God," she whispered, the words escaping her lips before she could stop them. Realizing what she had done, Parker held her breath and listened. Had any of the monsters heard her?

Apparently not, as the things took a final look about the decimated campsite before moving away from the scene of utter human devastation they had wrought and fading into the dark forest undergrowth.

Parker silently counted to one thousand, then did it twice more before she dared to move a muscle. Removing herself from the thicket proved to be a challenge, with the thorns and vines continuing to rip at her skin and clothing. She gritted her teeth against the renewed pain, not wanting to cry out and risk discovery. Only after several moments of struggling was she able to pull herself from the hiding place that had somehow, miraculously, spared her from the same fate that had befallen her friends.

Her penance for having survived the attack, however, was to look upon those who had not been so fortunate.

The savagely mutilated bodies of the other squad members lay scattered about the area. Tree branches and bushes were slick with dark blood and shards of skin, bone, and clothing. Bile rose in Parker's throat and her stomach heaved as her mind replayed Thurman's death once more, reconciling it with the horror surrounding her. Tears welled up in her eyes and she angrily wiped them away.

Not now, she chastised herself. *See if there's anyone else.*

Taking several deep breaths to calm herself, Parker spent the next several minutes searching the area, hoping against hope that someone else had survived. Fearful that the things responsible for this massacre might hear her, she resisted the urge to call out to other members of the squad. Likewise, she opted not to use her flashlight to aid in her search, not that she really needed it. The moon was more than sufficient to illuminate her surroundings and provide even more evidence of what had happened here.

I'm the only one left.

The ghastly reality hammered home. Sergeant Thurman and the rest of the squad were dead, killed by . . . what? Aliens from another planet, moving through the woods and gunning down without mercy anyone they came across? Who would believe it?

Dear God, she realized with horror, *what about the others?* There were dozens of her fellow Marines scattered throughout the forest, all engaged in the mock war. None of them had any idea of the very real threat stalking the base, and none of them had a chance.

Unless she warned them.

"You're crazy," Parker told herself, still remembering to keep her voice low. What was she going to do? She was a twenty-three-year-old legal secretary who had joined the reserves for the extra money. Spending her one weekend a month and two weeks a year working with the unit's legal officer gave her enough extra cash to keep up the payments on her car. She had never seriously considered the idea of going off to war, even when the role of military reserve forces had been drastically reconfigured based on lessons learned in the years following the Gulf War.

Looking around one final time at the pitiful remains of what had once been her friends, Allyson Parker knew that she would have to bury her fear and her tears and her desire to crawl into a hole and hide until this nightmare was over. If she did not try to do something, more people would suffer the same fate.

From the seclusion of the forest, Raegyra watched as the creature staggered away from the remains of its companions and into the woods.

His first instinct had been to kill the creature the moment he had become aware of its presence, hiding as it was in the brush. Its death would have been quick, if not unsettling to his stomach. Even with the reduced power setting, the weapon's effects had still been horrific during the small impromptu battle moments before. Raegyra had not wanted to use their weapons on any more of the creatures that they might encounter, the appalling power of the pulse rifles on the smaller, weaker beings during his first skirmish with them still fresh in his mind.

Unlike the three animals they had come across earlier, it had quickly become apparent that this group posed a much greater threat. They appeared to possess some form of military training and weaponry, judging from the way they had reacted to the scouting party's approach. Rather than cowering in fear as the first animals had, these creatures had quickly responded by forming a defensive line and attempting to engage Raegyra and his companions. The fact that their weapons had proven to be even less effective than those the other creatures had employed was irrelevant. That they had acted in a more organized fashion made them a greater danger, one to be neutralized before more powerful weapons, if the creatures possessed them, could be brought to bear.

Despite the resistance offered by the animals, dispatching them had proven simple. Incredibly, neither he nor any of his companions had sustained any further injuries during the attack, though Raegyra was certain that one of the creatures he had killed had fired directly at him several times. Were their weapons that ineffective, or was the aim of their wielders simply that poor?

Was this the level of opposition they could expect from the planet's local inhabitants? Raegyra could not believe that. There was still a lot of world here to explore, after all.

It was this reason, more than any other, that convinced Raegyra of the virtue of allowing the lone remaining creature to live. One of his subordinates had disputed the decision, but only until the obvious tactical benefits of such an action became clear to him. In the face of the overwhelming defeat its companions had just suffered, the creature would surely flee back to where it had come from. Perhaps it would link up with more of its kind. That being the case, it provided Raegyra with an unparalleled opportunity to learn what they might be facing. Given their unfamiliarity with their new surroundings, any information they could collect for the Leadership would be advantageous indeed.

And somewhere, he reminded himself, *our true enemies*

still lay in wait. Where were the Plysserians he had been sent here to find? They had to be hiding somewhere in this forest, not too far from the portal that had transported them from *Jontashreena.* They would be biding their time, regrouping and preparing for renewed offensives against the Chodrecai.

Given what they had encountered so far during their survey of this alien world, Raegyra could not shake the notion that the Chodrecai's war with the Plysserians was about to become even more complicated.

8

Though Gardner did not know Sergeant Major Simon DiCarlo that well, he knew enough about him to form the opinion that he was a man who could seldom be surprised by whatever life might send his way. Given that he had served in the Corps for over thirty years and was fast approaching mandatory retirement, the man had to have seen it all, right?

Gardner watched as DiCarlo stood in the doorway to Captain Douglas's office, regarding the alien seated on the sofa. What thoughts were crossing the veteran Marine's mind? The sergeant major's expression offered few clues as he stood and studied the creature in silence, rolling the well-chewed tip of an unlit three-dollar cigar in his mouth. He had likewise said nothing as Gardner and the other Marines in his squad reported their encounter with the alien.

Once Gardner was finished, DiCarlo removed the cigar from his mouth and pointed it at the strange headpiece the younger Marine wore. "And that thing lets you talk to it?"

"Yes, Sergeant Major," Gardner replied. "It's a kind of translator." Indicating the creature, he added, "It's allowing me to understand Max here."

"Max?" DiCarlo asked, his brow furrowing. "You gave it a name?"

"His real name's a mouthful," Melendez replied from where he stood behind Gardner. "How do you say it again?"

"Mako-quo-lax. At least, that's how I think it goes." He smiled sheepishly. "I'm still getting the hang of this thing, Sergeant Major." Wincing in momentary pain, Gardner rubbed his right temple with his fingers. "It's also giving me a hell of a headache, but I'll figure it out." Only now, after having spent the past two hours during the walk back to base camp learning how to use the incredible device given to him by Max, was he beginning to realize just how taxing on him this undertaking was becoming.

The band around his head had at first merely translated simple images in concert with Max's voice. He and the alien had started out with simple exercises, pointing out trees, rocks, and articles of their own clothing and equipment and letting the translators help them to build a rudimentary communications bridge. As he allowed the wondrous technology to interact with his brain, Gardner began to understand that it was capable of so much more.

The translator seemed capable of "homing" in on those thoughts on which he concentrated hardest, interpreting them and transmitting them to the companion device Max wore. The process reversed itself in order for Gardner to understand his counterpart. His ability to communicate with the alien was growing faster, it seemed, the longer he kept at it, though prolonged contact with the translator was coming at a price. He could feel his fatigue and the pain of his headache continuing to grow.

I can sleep it off, later, he decided, though he did pause to rub his temples again. *This is too fantastic to pass up.* The things that Max had already conveyed to him were staggering on a number of levels and it was becoming apparent to him that his life, and quite possibly the lives of every living person on this planet, would never be the same again. That he was on the leading edge of events that would have such far-reaching implications was not lost on him.

From behind his desk, Captain Jeffrey Douglas could only sit and shake his head in disbelief. "This is incredible."

Gardner nodded, his expression growing somber as he realized that he could no longer put off revealing what he had been told. "Max has quite a story to tell, sir. Maybe we should think about getting in touch with somebody who can deal with something like this."

Melendez snorted derisively. "Who the hell are we gonna call? Men in Black? It's not like they advertise in the phone book or on the Web or anything." Stopping to consider what he had just said, the corporal shrugged. "Okay, maybe they do advertise, but I don't think we really want to call those freaks, do we?"

Douglas raised a hand to cut Melendez off. "There has to be someone we can call. We'll worry about that in a minute, but first I want to hear what Gardner's learned." He actually shrugged as he added, "It's not as if something like this happens everyday, right?" Gardner noted a growing confidence in the captain's voice, a quality that had not been there when the group had first arrived in his office. The initial shock had worn off, and now, like Gardner had done earlier, he was looking for information to help him fully understand what he was facing.

An information technology project manager in "the real world," Douglas's life was, as near as Gardner could figure, rather routine and ordinary. He had no doubt joined the reserve forces hoping that it would offer a periodic break from the regular, even mundane nature of his civilian life. Gardner could definitely understand the man's desire to make the most of the incredulous twist of fate this evening had visited upon all of them.

I wonder if he'll feel the same way five minutes from now.

"Okay then," DiCarlo said, his attention fixed on Gardner, "what has it told you?"

Gesturing toward the alien, Gardner replied, "Max is a soldier. It calls itself a 'Pliss-ear-ian' or something like that, but I haven't quite figured out if that's the name of its army or country or what."

"Is it here as part of some kind of invasion?" Douglas asked, making no attempt to hide the renewed alarm in his voice.

Gardner shook his head. "No, sir. In fact, if I understand Max correctly, they were never supposed to be here in the first place. They've been fighting a war, all right, but it's been against another army on their own planet." From the images provided to him through the translator, Gardner got the sense that the conflict raging on Max's homeworld was similar in scale to World War II, with numerous battles of varying scope taking place on multiple fronts. The technology was obviously different but from what he had been able to gather, many of the tactics employed looked to be very much like those used for centuries on Earth, especially with respect to ground troops.

"War broke out after years of political tension," he continued. "A lot like the Cold War, except that in their case the governments never found a peaceful solution. Max's side was winning for a while, but more recently, the enemy has been gaining the advantage. His army is suffering from attrition, and though the people in charge of his government aren't saying it in so many words, the scuttlebutt is that the whole thing could be over in a few months, with the Blues on the losing end of the deal."

Confusion clouded DiCarlo's features. "Blues?"

Pointing to the intricate network of tattoos decorating Max's exposed skin, Melendez replied. "A nickname, Sergeant Major." The corporal had coined the name during the walk back to base camp, attempting to generate a little camaraderie once it had become clear that the alien was not going to harm any of the Marines. As far as Gardner had been able to determine, Max did not seem to care one way or another how the Marines referred to him or his companions.

"The tattoos are something of a tradition among the soldiers of Max's army," Gardner continued. "They have different designs that describe rank and position, and even stories about the battles the individual soldier took part in. The artwork on each soldier tells a different and personal story." It was yet another fascinating aspect of these people that Gardner hoped to learn more about.

Douglas seemed satisfied with that. "Go on."

"According to Max, the Blue government was getting pretty desperate as the war dragged on," Gardner said.

"Their army was getting the shit kicked out of it by their enemies, which Max calls the 'Cho-dreh-sigh.' Blue leaders were looking for any kind of advantage. Every kind of concept, no matter how off the wall it sounded, was considered. Scientists were consulted in the hopes that some kind of new weapon could be developed and deployed before it was too late."

"This is the part where it gets crazy," Melendez said. "I still don't believe it."

Nodding, Gardner replied, "It's something else, all right. Apparently, some scientists working for a private group had been experimenting with a basic form of teleportation, sort of opening 'tunnels' or 'corridors' that could lead you instantly from one location on the planet to another. They had been preparing for their first test even before the war started, but some of the time they would have devoted to that project got taken up by helping with the more standard types of weapons research."

"But then the war starting going bad for them, and the government started looking for anything that might help them," DiCarlo said.

"Exactly," Gardner replied, nodding. "When the Blue government leaders got wind of the idea, they wanted to know more. The scientists behind the project were given the go-ahead to finish the preparations for their first test and then, with all the politicians and high-ranking brass watching, they flipped the switch."

"And instead of ending up someplace else on their own planet," Melendez cut in, "they opened a tunnel to here." Shaking his head, he added with a humorless chuckle. "Talk about your wrong turns."

Douglas was aghast. "You mean that these tunnels are connected to their own planet right now? That there are more of these things. . . ." He stopped short, his eyes falling on Max. Clearing his throat, he continued with, "Are you saying that more of Max's people could come through if they wanted to?"

Shaking his head, Gardner replied, "No, sir, it doesn't seem to be that simple. For one thing, the technology the scientists created was still in the experimental stage, so it had a lot of problems." Indicating Max with a nod of his head, he added, "He says that the portal, as he calls it, can only stay open for short periods of time, probably due to the amount of power it uses. At first, the Blue government thought the whole idea was a waste of time, but then somebody got a bright idea."

"What?" Douglas asked. "Invade Earth?"

Gardner could understand the captain's fear, as he himself had felt the same way at first, but Max had done a superlative job in explaining to him that the Blues had come to Earth motivated by self-preservation, not conquest.

"They decided that the portal technology, if it could be made more reliable and reproduced, could be used to transfer civilians, along with important political and scientific people and a good number of military personnel, through the tunnels to a safe hiding place. Once on the other side, the Blue forces would be able to regroup and rebuild as best they could, while the scientists that were brought along could continue working to perfect the equipment that creates the portals."

"And once they got their army restocked, they could go back through and rejoin the fight?" DiCarlo asked, shaking his head in apparent admiration. "Interesting tactic."

Gardner nodded. "Even better. The plan was that they could use the portals to transfer their soldiers right into the heart of enemy territory, hoping that a successful strike against their leadership might turn the war back in the Blues' favor."

"Pretty ballsy trick, if they could pull it off," Douglas conceded. "But if you ask me, it sounds like suicide."

"They seem to think it has a chance, sir," Gardner countered. "They've been using the portals to transfer people and supplies to Earth for weeks. It takes time to do that, as the only way to determine if the other end of the conduit is safe for transport is to send someone through, and it doesn't always work out for the volunteer, by the way."

Shaking his head, he forced that unpleasant image away as he continued. "They've also been spreading their resources out, in case the Chodrecai learn about the portals or even capture some of the equipment." Max had told him that in the time since the initial plan had been put into motion, thousands of Plysserians had come through the portals to Earth, hiding out in some of the most isolated regions on the planet. If Max's information was correct, his people were hiding deep within the most inhospitable deserts, jungles, and forests, among the highest mountains, and even in the harsh cold within the Arctic and Antarctic circles.

"But it sounds as though the equipment was giving them fits," Gardner added. "According to Max, the portals can only be generated from the starting point, which means that once they crossed over to this side and the tunnel was closed, Max and whoever else came through with him were stuck here."

"They didn't bring the equipment to open them up with them?" Douglas asked.

Gardner shook his head as he recalled the first images of the portal equipment Max had given to him. "It's too big to come through without being taken apart first. They've done that, and they have the technicians with them to put it all back together, but they have to wait for instructions before they use it, or else they risk the Chodrecai finding out about the technology. The only way that's going to come is if the Blue leaders send somebody back through one of the original portals as a messenger."

"Jesus," Douglas breathed. "What we're saying is that these people are using our planet as a staging ground for the next battle in their war." His features screwing up in sudden anger, the captain regarded Max and the younger Marine. "Has anybody stopped to think what might happen if the other guys find out about this and use it to come through?"

"Yes, sir, they have," Gardner replied. "In fact, in some cases it was necessary to destroy some of the original equipment to prevent its discovery by the enemy. That's what happened while Max and his group were transferred. As a result of that, only several dozen Blues are hiding out in this area. They've been staying hidden, mostly underground." Max had described the region where he and his people had secreted themselves, a small network of limestone caverns of the type that were abundant in Missouri.

Douglas was still clearly uneasy with this new information. "But there's a chance their enemies could find out about all of this, right?"

"Yes, sir," Gardner said. "But Max thinks that he and the rest of the soldiers hiding out here will be called back to the fight before that happens, though."

"Captain Douglas!" a voice called somewhere outside, interrupting their conversation. "Come quick!"

Everyone, including Max, ran from the office and exited the small two-story building that was the compound's lone permanent structure. Though darkness still enveloped the encampment, spotlights mounted on the walls of the building helped to illuminate the asphalt surface surrounded by an eight-foot high chain-link fence encircling the camp's perimeter.

Gardner saw three Marines just inside the fence surrounding the compound where the reserve unit had set up their base. One of them was calling out for Douglas and from the tone of the voice, Gardner sensed that something serious had happened.

One of the three, a woman, looked disheveled. She was not wearing a helmet or uniform cover, and the cuff of her right trouser leg had come out from where it would normally have been bloused down over the top of her combat boot. The woman looked to be out of breath and, more worrisome, extremely upset.

"Hey," Melendez said, "that's Allyson Parker. She looks like she's been in a fight or something. Wasn't she part of your squad tonight, Brad?"

As they approached the trio, the moonlight allowed Gardner to see that it was indeed Allyson Parker, and that she looked to have been the victim of assault. Her hair was matted with thorns and leaves, and her exposed skin was dirty and covered with bloody scratches. Her uniform was ripped in several places, including one sleeve that had almost torn away at the shoulder. A mixture of sympathy and rage washed over Gardner as he beheld the woman's bedraggled appearance.

"Christ, Allyson," Melendez said. "What happened? Are you okay?"

Though she was still out of breath and obviously distraught, Parker nodded shakily. When she did not say anything, Gardner noted the confused, distant expression on her face. Whatever she had encountered earlier, it was still very much in the forefront of her consciousness.

"Where's the rest of your squad?" DiCarlo asked gently. "Sergeant Thurman and the others? Didn't you come back with them?" Even as the sergeant major spoke the words, Gardner's mind filled with vile images of what might have happened to Parker out in the forest, and he steeled himself for her response.

What he had not expected to hear was what she finally said.

"They're dead."

Then, before anyone could react to that stunning announcement, Parker added, "We found some campers in the forest, college kids drinking and partying, you know. We didn't think it would hurt to hang out with them for a while, but then . . ." She paused again, her expression growing haunted and tortured as she remembered . . . what?

"Allyson?" DiCarlo prompted. "Then what?"

When the response finally came, it was almost too fast for her mouth to actually form the words. "This pack of . . . of . . . things . . . they showed up and started shooting everything. I don't know what they were . . . monsters with guns that just ripped everything apart. We never had a chance. They . . ." Her words caught in her throat for a moment before fading away entirely, replaced by heaving sobs as the tears came and Parker covered her face, crying into her hands.

"Creatures?" Melendez whispered, turning to Gardner. "Does she mean like Max here?" Turning to stare angrily at the alien, the corporal took a determined step toward it. "What the fuck is that about?"

"Dan," Gardner called out, grabbing his friend by the arm. "He can't understand a word you're saying, remember?" Looking in the alien's direction, Gardner tried to conjure images of what Parker had described for the translator he was still wearing. His efforts were complicated by anger and shock over the woman's condition and the story she had told, not to mention the fact that he was becoming increasingly aware of the pain behind his eyes and temples from the device's effects, making it difficult for him to focus.

He was ultimately defeated when he heard Parker gasp from behind him. "Oh my God . . ."

Turning, Gardner saw the dismayed expression on her face, brought on by the fact that she had finally seen Max. She started to draw away, but DiCarlo reached out to grasp her by the shoulders.

"No, Allyson, wait. It's okay, I promise." Trying to calm the woman down, he looked to Gardner. "Right?"

Gardner nodded hesitantly. "I think so. That's what I'm trying to find out."

Tearing his arm from Gardner's grip, Melendez pointed an accusatory finger at the alien. "Then ask him what he knows."

After taking a few moments to calm himself and relay

what Parker had told him, Gardner frowned when he received the response from Max.

"He wants her to describe the attackers."

"They looked just like him!" Parker screamed abruptly. "Huge, muscles, gray skin! They had these giant weapons that ripped people apart. I saw Sergeant Thurman shredded right in front of me!"

Passing that on, Gardner asked, "Did they look exactly like him? Did they have the same kind of markings as he does?"

"I don't know!" Parker was nearly on the verge of breaking down completely, with tears flowing freely and her breathing racked with sobs. After several moments she wiped her eyes and composed herself long enough to take another look at Max. She spent nearly a full minute studying the elaborate imagery drawn across the alien's arms, chest, and head. Then she slowly began to shake her head as she said, "Wait. They didn't . . . I don't . . . I don't remember, but I don't think they had any kind of tattoos."

"What does that mean?" Melendez said, anger evident in his voice. "So they didn't have tattoos. Big fucking deal."

"Don't you get it?" Gardner snapped suddenly, the purpose behind Max's questions now obvious to him. "Only the soldiers in his army have them."

It took several seconds for the meaning behind the words to sink in. Douglas tried to be the first to speak. "Are you saying . . ." before the words died in his throat.

Gardner nodded in response to the rest of the unspoken question. Unable to form any words of his own at first, he regarded Max, whose expression was unreadable as he stood quietly and watched the humans talking. Was the alien feeling guilt? Did he blame himself for what had obviously happened? Oddly, though the translator did not seem to want to convey that information, Gardner was able to discern that feeling readily enough.

"It's the Chodrecai," he said, with a touch of what he might later describe as finality in his voice. "They've found their way to Earth."

"They're here?" Captain Douglas repeated, alternating looks between Gardner and Max. "The ones you've been fighting?"

"Max figures they must have found the location on the other side of the portal where its generator is hidden," Gardner replied, glancing over to Max for confirmation, and the alien nodded solemnly.

Allyson Parker, a near nervous wreck mere moments before, had regained some of her composure. "Those things killed my friends. They hunted them down like animals and tore them apart!"

Douglas wiped his face, his eyes wide as he struggled to process this latest revelation. It was easy to sympathize with the man, Gardner knew. After all, nothing in any of the normal, humdrum, everyday lives the Marine reservists usually led could have prepared any of them for the nightmare unfolding around them.

"What the hell are we supposed to do now?" Melendez asked, his eyes darting to each of his companions. "How many more of these things are out there, anyway?"

Looking at Max, Gardner said, "I don't think he knows." Then pain stabbed at his temples. Rubbing the sides of his head, he sighed tiredly. Wearing the translator device was definitely taking its toll on him, but there was no way he could stop now. Max was trying to tell him something else.

Concentrate, he scolded himself as he fought his mounting fatigue. As he focused on what the alien was trying to tell him, though, pain and exhaustion were forgotten.

"Gardner?" DiCarlo asked, his expression one of concern. "What's wrong?"

Indicating the Plysserian with a nod of his head, Gardner replied, "Max says that although the Chodrecai are here looking for him and his people, they won't think twice about killing any humans they encounter to ensure their presence here remains a secret." The report only served to reinforce what Parker had told them about her fellow squad members, guilty of simply being in the wrong place at the wrong time as Chodrecai soldiers had slaughtered them.

"Jesus," Melendez said. "We've got people running around all over this fucking forest. They won't stand a chance in a fight with those things."

DiCarlo turned to Melendez. "I want every Marine recalled and accounted for. Get to the comm shack and have Sergeant Russell start making the calls." To Captain Douglas he said, "Sir, I think we should break out the live ammo and post sentries around the camp perimeter. If those things are out there, they might find their way here."

Gardner nodded in agreement, thankful that DiCarlo was already thinking ahead and treating their current circumstances like a potential combat situation. The sergeant major was a combat veteran of Vietnam and the

Persian Gulf and his knowledge, like that of the other seasoned veterans among the group, could prove invaluable if things turned nasty.

A sudden chill gripped him as he envisioned masses of alien warriors rushing the camp, the Marines fighting bravely yet vainly to repel an assault they had no hope of stopping.

"Jack's Pizza Shack. Can I take your order?"

Pulling the cellular phone away from her ear, Sergeant Belinda Russell looked at the device with growing contempt. What was wrong with the damned thing?

"Still screwed up?" Corporal Rebecca Sloane asked, resignation clouding her features more than confusion or frustration. After wrestling with the radios all night, a malfunctioning cell phone was par for the course, so far as she was concerned.

Russell tried to keep her own emotions in check in front of her two subordinates. They, like the majority of the Marines in the unit, still had no idea as to what was going on around them, and Captain Douglas wanted it kept that way for the time being, at least until he had the chance to brief the entire group. For now, only she knew why she was desperately trying to make one lousy phone call.

"Four times I've dialed the number already, and I get someone else every time." In addition to the pizza place, she had connected with an elderly lady who had been none too happy about being awakened in the middle of the night, an automated customer service hotline for a bank in Virginia, and an adults-only chat line. "I knew I should have gone with that other company's phone. Piece of shit."

Russell turned to survey the room's interior once more, including the row of radios on the worktable. Despite the problems she and her team had been having with the communications equipment, they had succeeded in recalling all of the teams that were still out in the forest, participating in the war games. With luck, everyone in the unit would have safely returned to base camp within the hour.

Almost everyone, she reminded herself.

Despite her love of science fiction and her general open-mindedness regarding the possibility of life on other planets, Russell had at first been skeptical of Dan Melendez's story about the aliens they had found in the woods and the others that had killed some of her fellow Marines.

That doubt was replaced with awe upon seeing the alien sitting in Captain Douglas's office, and Lance Corporal Gardner interacting with it through the use of that incredible translator device.

Nothing would have pleased her more than the idea of spending however long it might take to learn as much as she could about this Plysserian, its home planet, and how it had come to be here, but the stark reality of the situation forced itself upon her as she heard the report of what had happened to Allyson Parker's squad.

Now Russell found herself immersed in a scenario that could have been born from one of her stories, with her and her fellow Marines preparing to defend the camp against an alien attack. Even as Sergeant Major DiCarlo and Sergeant Bonniker were establishing a security perimeter and distributing live ammo, she had been tasked with contacting the base's headquarters and having a call placed to the Marines' own commanding officer back in Kansas City. Captain Douglas had decided that the best course of action at this point was to inform higher authority of their astonishing discovery.

It was a good idea, though putting it into action was proving difficult.

"I don't believe this," Russell said as she began to pace the room. "The radios are acting weird. Phones don't work. What the hell is going on around here tonight?"

Sighing as he leaned back in his chair, Eshelman picked up his coffee cup and took a long drink. Regarding the remaining contents of the mug for a moment, he finally said, "What about something with the weather? A system moving in, or something in the upper atmosphere?"

Russell shrugged. Her years in the television business had certainly shown her how weather conditions and other atmospheric anomalies could affect electrical and communications equipment. "There wasn't a cloud in the sky tonight, and I didn't hear anything on the radio about any storms moving in." No unusual solar activity that might explain their problems had been reported, either. In short, there was nothing that could account for the havoc being wrought on their gear.

Or was there?

"Of course," she said, her eyes growing wide as realization dawned. Leaving Sloane and Eshelman to offer one another similarly puzzled stares, Russell charged out of the comm shack.

She found Gardner and Max, along with DiCarlo and Douglas when she opened the door to the captain's office.

"Gardner," she said without preamble, "ask him about that tunnel they came through. Did it have any weird effects on its electronic equipment? Its radio or whatever else he brought with him?"

Gardner had certainly been rattled, aided no doubt by the young man's already exhausted condition, he blinked several times in confusion. "What? I don't . . ."

"Do it," Russell prompted again. "I think it's important."

She watched with no small amount of fascination as Gardner spoke with Max. Despite the man's extended contact with the strange creature and the translator it had given him, he was still having some difficulty bridging what had to be a tremendous language barrier. That he had progressed as far as he had in such a short amount of time was a true testament to the abilities of the alien technology, and to Gardner himself.

As Gardner and Max conversed, DiCarlo turned his attention to Russell. "What are you thinking, Sergeant?"

"The power source they used to create that tunnel is screwing up our comm, Sergeant Major." Pausing a moment to wipe away the perspiration that had given her ebony skin a brilliant sheen, she added, "No luck with cell phones, either. Something is jacking up electrical impulses in this area, and it's nothing we can find."

"She may be right, Sergeant Major," Gardner said, stepping closer to DiCarlo and Russell. "Max says that the portal generator could account for the problems we're having with our equipment. They experienced the same kind of problems when the portal opened to allow more of their people to pass through from his home planet. But he remembers it lasting only for as long as the portal was open, which was only for short periods due to the limitations of the technology."

Russell frowned. "But we've been having problems all night with the radios. Does that mean the portal is staying open now?"

"If that enemy army he's talking about has captured the equipment that opens this portal," DiCarlo said, "then they may be keeping it open to send through their own forces. If what he's told us is true, they could be staging personnel and equipment right now."

"Those things could be setting up base camps all over the world," Douglas said. Russell saw that the captain appeared to be addressing no one in particular. "We have to get out of here, tell someone about what's going on." The man's voice was shaking slightly. Russell thought it understandable given the circumstances, though it certainly would not do to have the captain breaking down in front of the troops. She figured that DiCarlo would talk to him in private at some point in an attempt to stave off any such potential deterioration.

Despite that, the captain was right. Someone in authority needed to be told about what they had found here.

"No radio, and no cell phone, and we don't have any land lines going out," Russell noted, referring to the lack of established phone lines in the building.

"We're leaving," Douglas said in a less than completely confident voice. "If we stay here, those things will find us. We won't stand a chance."

"It's a fifteen mile march to our pickup point, Captain," DiCarlo said, his voice remaining calm. "We'd be vulnerable moving en masse like that."

After debarking from the buses that had brought them here, the Marines had marched more than fifteen miles into one of the reservation's more remote training areas, accompanied by a five-ton supply truck and two "Hummers," one of which had been configured to be an ambulance. The vehicles were not enough to move the entire unit, and he did not like the idea of splitting up for the time it would take to move them in groups.

Russell's attention was drawn to Max, who looked visibly agitated. "What's wrong with him, Gardner?" she asked, indicating the alien.

"He's worried about the Chodrecai," Gardner replied after a moment. "He wants to be sure that his own people know they're here. There's still a chance that the Chodrecai advance through the portal can be stopped, or at least contained." Swallowing hard, his expression fell as he added, "the odds of success are better if we help."

Douglas's anxiety nearly consumed him upon hearing that. "Is he crazy? We don't stand a chance against them. You heard what Parker said they did to her squad. They'd tear through us like toilet paper."

No one said anything for a moment, the only sound in the room that of DiCarlo chewing thoughtfully on the end of his cigar. Russell knew that he tended not to smoke the cigars when he was around others, not so much concerned about offending the sensibilities of any nonsmokers in the room but rather preferring to wait until he could actually enjoy the cigar.

"He's right," he said finally. "We'd be walking targets if we tried to hike out of here, and I'd rather shoot than be shot at."

"Are you suggesting we stay here and try to hunt those things down?" Douglas asked, nearly aghast.

Shaking his head, DiCarlo replied, "No, sir, but we need to think about defending ourselves until we can get the word out to someone and have reinforcements sent to us. Sergeant Bonniker is already establishing a security perimeter around the camp, but we need to augment that plan. We've got fifty-three Marines here, so we put as many of them as we can on the line." Looking to Gardner, he said, "Find out if they can help us fortify our position here. If the Blues have got weaponry on par with those . . . whatever the hell he calls them . . . then we'll stand a better chance of living through this."

Apparently having realized that he had come close to losing his bearing, Captain Douglas stepped closer to Di-Carlo and when he spoke this time, it was in a more controlled tone of voice.

"We can send someone to Mainside," he said, using the term that commonly referred to that area of any military installation where the base's headquarters, main billeting, and personnel support services might be located. "Have them call back to Kansas City. The C.O. will know what to do." The 24th Marines commanding officer, Colonel Arnold Hawking, needed to be informed of the situation, anyway, but he would also be the best person to raise the attention of anyone higher up in the authority food chain to the bizarre events transpiring here.

Russell said, "Maybe they should contact the local sheriff, too. They deserve to know what's going on here, too."

"I don't think that's a good idea," DiCarlo countered, "at least not right away. Let Colonel Hawking decide who to let in on this."

Frowning, Russell said, "But civilians have been killed, too. Local law enforcement needs to know what's going on here." She wanted so say more, but stopped herself as DiCarlo held up a hand.

"I understand your concerns, Russell, but remember that according to Max and Gardner, those people were probably killed to preserve the secrecy of the aliens' presence here. We can take advantage of that, at least until we can get the word out and get reinforcements here. I don't want to make a call that might incite a panic." Noticing Gardner turning toward him again he looked in the young man's direction. "What have you got?"

The visibly exhausted Marine nodded toward Max. "He says that if he can get to where his people have established their camp, he can convince them to help us fortify our positions here."

"Tell him to go," DiCarlo said. "The sooner he's out of here, the faster he gets back with his buddies." Looking around the room at Douglas, Russell, and Gardner, he added. "As for the rest of us, we've got a lot of work to do, so let's get to it."

10

Teri Westerson's ass was sore.

Despite her death grip on the handlebar bolted to the passenger side of the Humvee's dashboard, she was unable to keep from jostling about as the vehicle sped down the poorly maintained service road. The vehicle struck yet another rut and she once again bounced up and slammed back down onto the inadequately padded seat.

"Dammit," she whispered, her curse inaudible over the sound of the Humvee's diesel engine and the notable lack of soundproofing in the vehicle itself.

The High Mobility Multipurpose Wheeled Vehicle, or HMMWV, had replaced the famed Jeep in military motor pools beginning in the mid-1980s. Since then the "Hummer" or "Humvee," as it was more commonly known, had become the military's general-purpose vehicle to support a whole host of roles in combat operations. Some police departments had taken to using the versatile vehicles as well, and even civilian versions, their lush interiors packed with the latest high-tech toys, became available in the early 1990s to celebrities and others who could afford the steep sticker price.

On the battlefield, Humvees transported troops or

acted as offensive weapons when equipped with turrets for either machine guns or antiarmor missile systems. Still others operated as ambulances. The creators of the vehicle, AM General, continued to update the Humvee and the variety of configurations it could assume in response to ever-evolving military needs. It was a popular vehicle with the troops, tough and versatile and capable of operating in a variety of harsh environments.

None of which made Teri Westerson's ass feel any better.

"Yo, Alan, I think you missed a pothole back there," came the voice of Lance Corporal Charlie Hudson from the Humvee's back seat. "What say you go back and take another shot at it?"

In the driver's seat, Lance Corporal Alan Guber did not divert his attention from the road ahead of them. "Sorry," he said, the word wrapped in a thick Texas drawl. "I don't remember the road being this shitty on the way in."

"How about slowing down just a bit," Westerson advised Guber. "It's hard enough to see anything in the dark like this."

Like Westerson, Hudson and his companion, Corporal Matthew Shane, were also holding on for dear life in the rear passenger area. Up front, Guber gripped the steering wheel with an intensity normally reserved for incensed rush hour commuters and NASCAR drivers. He kept his eyes on the uneven road ahead of him, difficult enough to see with the vehicle's headlights extinguished and the moon providing the only illumination. Long shadows from the trees crisscrossed the trail, making it difficult to see anything that might pose a hazard to a moving vehicle.

Keeping from being tossed about the interior of the Humvee was even more difficult for Hudson and Shane, who were also acting as security for the vehicle. The barrels of their M-16s protruded from windows on either side of the vehicle and they were struggling to keep a watchful eye out for any potential threats from the surrounding forest. The weapons no longer sported MILES laser emitters attached to their muzzles and they now held live ammunition instead of blanks in their magazines. Each of the Marines wore helmets and protective vests, another change from the way they had been operating earlier in the evening.

Likewise, Westerson knew that the Marines themselves were not as they had been earlier in the day.

Now, they were scared.

"I still don't believe it," Guber called out over the whine of the Humvee's engine. "I saw it with my own eyes, but I just can't believe it."

Westerson regarded the corporal, nodding in understanding. "That's okay, Guber," she replied. "I'm not sure I believe it, either, and I was standing in the same room with you."

The meeting that Captain Douglas had ordered after all of the Marines had returned to the camp still seemed surreal to her. First there was the roll call and the conspicuous absence of several personnel. Then there was the captain's incredible tale of alien soldiers, running about the forest, having brought their civil war here after passing through some kind of tunnel connecting their planet to Earth. Douglas's words had gotten laughs at first, but the humor faded when the captain had informed the Marines that these same aliens had killed members of their unit.

And then there was Max.

This entire situation was unbelievable, yet the obvious visual evidence was hard to ignore. Captain Douglas had certainly been convinced of Max's sincerity and, more than that, so had Sergeant Major DiCarlo. The veteran Marine did not seem like a man given to flights of fancy, in Westerson's opinion, and he was treating the events unfolding around them with deadly earnest. While she and the Marines with her had been sent to the base's headquarters, DiCarlo was directing the rest of the unit in their preparations to defend the camp against possible attack by the Chodrecai.

The Humvee hit another rut, a deep one this time, and the jarring impact forced Westerson to throw one hand up to avoid being slammed headfirst into the ceiling of the vehicle's cab. Her stomach lurched as they became airborne for a second before crashing back to Earth and continuing on.

"Easy on the gas, Guber," she growled, more than a bit of menace in her voice. "I want to get there in one piece, all right?"

"Sorry, Lieutenant," Guber replied, not taking his eyes from the road. After driving in silence for several moments, Westerson saw the corporal cast a tentative glance in her direction. "So, what's supposed to happen after we call back to K.C., ma'am? Sit tight and wait for the cavalry to show up?"

It was a good question, and one that Teri Westerson, First Lieutenant, United States Marine Corps, could not answer. As a financial systems officer working at the Defense Finance and Accounting Service location in Kansas City, she was one of the few active duty Marines who had come down to Camp Growding with the reservists to complete her required stint of annual combat skills training. In that regard she was more experienced, militarily speaking, than most of the Marines in the small training unit, with the notable exception of Sergeant Major DiCarlo and a few others, though her daily duties were far removed from anything resembling a tactical environment.

For that matter, the majority of the active duty Marines stationed in the Kansas City area did not possess combat arms specialties or assignments. Though every Marine in uniform was required to demonstrate proficiency in a variety of infantry skills, those stationed in Kansas City were firmly entrenched in the supporting arm of the Corps. Their duties were important, yet they were not the sort of activities normally depicted in high-energy television commercials or enticing recruiting posters.

Not even the Marines who were with her in the Humvee were experts in combat tactics. Guber was a mechanic in the unit's motor pool, a mirror of his civilian job working in the service department of a major automotive dealership. Shane, if Westerson recalled correctly, was a supply clerk. It was Hudson, a small-arms repair specialist assigned to the unit's armory, who held the most expertise with the group's various weapons.

"I don't know what the hell they expect us to do," Shane said from the back seat. "We're not cut out for this kind of stuff. Did you see the size of that alien or whatever the hell it was? It was huge. Wanna bet these popguns of ours ain't gonna be worth a shit if we try to shoot any of those things?" He tapped the stock of his rifle for emphasis.

Next to him, Hudson countered, "Hey, these babies

will do fine up close." He held up an extra magazine that he had pulled from a pouch on his belt. "One of these things hits you inside of thirty meters, you're going down. I don't care who you are."

Westerson nodded in understanding. The armorer had to know what he was talking about, and she had fired the rifles enough in the past to be familiar with their capabilities. The M-16 service rifle, in its various incarnations, had been in use by the United States military almost since the beginning of the Vietnam War. Though initially plagued by malfunctions caused in no small part by the harsh environment of the Vietnamese jungle, coupled with a design that favored simplicity of operation almost to a fault, the M-16 eventually earned its rightful reputation as an accurate and reliable weapon. The rifle possessed formidable stopping power, with a rapid rate of fire and a muzzle velocity of nearly one thousand meters per second. Such characteristics had proven invaluable in the chaotic close-quarters battle situations many American troops found themselves in against Vietnamese soldiers.

"Still," Hudson said, his expression falling somewhat, "if what Parker told the captain is true, I don't think I want those bastards getting that close. Hopefully they'll send in the heavy artillery."

"It'll be up to the brass," Westerson replied. "Colonel Hawking will know who to contact." Westerson's orders were to apprise Hawking of the situation and allow her to decide how best to proceed. The colonel would in turn contact her own commanding officer as well as someone at the Marine Corps' headquarters in Washington, but beyond that she had no idea how anyone in the chain of command would react to the news she would give them.

She turned her attention back to the trees speeding past the Humvee's passenger window. The forest here was particularly dense, the moonlight unable to penetrate more than a few feet beyond the boundaries of the road. Above the trees, the moon cast its full glow down upon them. On any other occasion the scene would be serene. If she closed her eyes she could almost picture herself riding down a moonlit road, seated in the passenger seat of the 1966 Mustang convertible that her boyfriend, Jerry, had lovingly restored over the course of two years.

Westerson could almost feel the wind in her hair, and her mind conjured an image of the last getaway she and Jerry had taken. Driving down to the Lake of the Ozarks in southern Missouri, they had spent three days sunning on their friend's boat and three nights nestled together in the romantic environs of the small cabin Jerry himself had built. Yes, she decided, it would be quite easy to forget where she was and lose herself in the grips of that fondly remembered weekend.

Then Guber hit another bump in the road and another jab of pain jolted her ass.

Her face flushing with anger, she turned in her seat, poised to verbally eviscerate the corporal. "God damn it," she hissed, her next words dying in her throat as something beyond the Humvee's windshield caught her attention.

Something darted across the road, perhaps fifty meters ahead of them. Moving from left to right, it was gone in little more than a heartbeat as it bounded into the trees on Westerson's side of the Humvee. Though she only got a fleeting glimpse of the shadowy figure, her gut told her what it was.

"What the hell," Guber said, pointing out the windshield. "Did you see that? Something just ran . . ."

"Step on it," Westerson ordered, her right hand already moving for the pistol on her hip. "Get us out of here."

Behind her, Shane was shifting in his own seat. "You saw one of those things? Shit. Where?"

As if in response, a shrieking whine erupted from the forest on Westerson's side of the road, followed almost instantly by something slamming into the Humvee. She heard metal tearing and plastic shattering as the vehicle rocked from the impact. The Humvee's rear end jerked to the left and Guber fought to retain control, twisting the steering wheel in a frantic attempt to keep them from crashing into the trees. What the hell had hit them?

She felt the front left tire leave the road and the Humvee tilted in that direction as the shoulder fell away. Only the vehicle's extra wide wheel base, nearly equal to that of the tanks whose tracks it was designed to follow in, kept them from rolling over as Guber jerked the steering wheel to the right. The Humvee bounced back onto the road with a lurch, fishtailing for several seconds before the corporal could bring it back under control.

"Holy shit!" Shane shouted from behind her. Turning in her seat, Westerson felt her jaw drop open as she saw that the entire upper half of the panel making up the rear wall of the passenger compartment was gone along with part of the roof. She now had an unobstructed view of the forest and the night sky behind them as the Humvee continued to career down the road.

Then she saw them, three huge muscular figures exploding from the forest behind them, their skin almost the color of ash in the glow of the full moon. They carried long, dark objects that Westerson knew could only be weapons, the same weapons that had torn through the metal shell of the Humvee. Now out on the road, they were covering ground in long, bounding strides as they gave chase.

And they were gaining.

"Jesus Christ," she breathed. How fast were they that they could keep up with a moving vehicle? How much faster could they run?

What if they were faster than the Humvee?

"Step on it, Guber!" Finally managing to pull her pistol free of its holster, Westerson racked the weapon's slide to chamber a round. She looked into the backseat and saw that Shane and Hudson were already twisting their bodies and their rifles to cover the vehicle's open and now quite exposed rear.

Hudson wasted no time taking aim and firing in a series of three-round bursts as fast as his finger could pull the trigger. Shane followed suit and the inside of the Humvee was awash with the sounds of weapons fire and spent shell casings ricocheting off the sides of the vehicle's interior. Westerson had no idea how the two Marines could possibly be hitting anything as the Humvee continued to bounce violently now that Guber had given up any attempts to avoid any ruts or holes in the road. Nevertheless, her ears rang in protest against the violent cacophony as the acrid stench of burnt gunpowder assaulted her nostrils. Within seconds the firestorm faded as both rifles emptied their magazines.

"I think I got one!" Hudson called out as he fumbled for another magazine. Looking behind them, Westerson could see that one of the hulking gray aliens had fallen behind its companions. The other two had slowed their pursuit somewhat, no longer gaining but still keeping pace with the Humvee.

Then one of the aliens raised its weapon.

"Incoming!" was all she could blurt out as she heard the piercing whine again. Behind them, the air rippled and roiled as something passed through it. Energy? A compression wave? That was as far as the thought proceeded before the energy burst slammed into the Humvee.

Everything on and in the vehicle, from the frame to the seats to the fillings in her teeth, shuddered under the impact. Westerson was thrown into the passenger-side door as the Humvee's rear end lurched, nearly forcing it 180 degrees about. The view outside the windows twisted and swerved in her vision before the road fell away and the Humvee plunged down into tall grass. Frantically spinning the wheel, Guber rose out of his seat as he nearly stood on the brake pedal.

"Watch out!" she yelled when she saw the gigantic oak looming beyond the windshield.

11

Move. You need to move. Now.

Fog shrouded Teri Westerson's mind and her body protested every movement. Had she lost consciousness? She did not think so. Only seconds could have passed since . . . since what?

"Are you okay?" Guber asked, his voice shaky and weak. Looking over at him, Westerson saw that the Marine cradled his left arm.

She nodded slowly, the action bringing with it an intense jolt of pain behind her eyes. "Yeah, I think so. You?"

"I think I wrenched my shoulder," Guber said. "Hurts like a son of a bitch, but I think I'll be okay. We need to get the hell out of here, ma'am."

He's right, her mind scolded. *They're coming.* How much time did they have? Not much, she figured. For all she knew the three aliens were standing just beyond the crumpled hulk of the Humvee, targeting it with their weapons.

Move move dammit goddammit move move move your ass!

Her head still throbbed and there was a dull ache in her side. A bruised rib, maybe. What other injuries did she have? Not that any of that mattered at the moment. Right now the pain was a good thing: It reminded her that she was still alive.

For the next few seconds, at least.

"Everybody out!" she snapped. Lance Corporal Guber was already pushing open the driver-side door and scrambling out, his rifle in hand.

It took her three tries to kick open her own door, which had jammed in the crash. She fell more than stepped from the vehicle, realizing as she did so that the trunk of a massive tree stood mere inches beyond the frame of her door. Westerson guessed it to be nearly four feet in diameter, towering up into the forest canopy and with limbs larger than many of the surrounding trees branching off in many directions. Huge chunks of bark had been torn from the oak's enormous trunk, but otherwise the tree had withstood the collision quite well.

"Jesus, that was close," Guber said from the other side of the Humvee, seeing the tree for himself. He had somehow managed to avoid a head-on collision with it, but the right side of the vehicle had crumpled on impact with the tree, trying its best to wrap itself around the mighty oak.

Westerson heard sounds from inside the wreckage and looked up to see Hudson crawling out of the Humvee from the driver's side. He had discarded his helmet and she saw blood coming from a gash on the Marine's forehead, a red line running down the right side of his face and neck. It added a glistening sheen to the young man's dark skin. How badly had he been injured?

He's alive, she scolded herself. *That's good enough for now.*

She bent to recover her pistol from where it had fallen

to the floorboard of the Humvee, the crash having pried it from her grip. A quick check reconfirmed for her that the weapon was ready to fire. Flipping the pistol's safety off, she looked to where Guber was performing a similar check on his M-16.

As he took up a defensive position at the rear of the demolished vehicle, Westerson turned to Hudson. "Get the radio. Call back to base camp and tell them what's happened." She knew that there was little chance of anyone being sent out to help them. If Sergeant Major DiCarlo and that Blue alien were right, the rest of the unit would have enough to worry about in short order. She had accepted that she was on her own for this mission, as had the three Marines who had volunteered to accompany her. Still, DiCarlo needed to know how the situation had changed and that he might be faced with sending out a second team of messengers in the event that Westerson and her group failed.

Her pistol gripped in both hands and arms extended out in front of her, Westerson stepped around the front of the Humvee. She scanned the forest from left to right, searching for threats. The three aliens were still close, she knew that much, though nothing moved among the trees, which surprised her. The aliens had not been that far behind them when they had crashed. They had to be here, somewhere.

"Lieutenant."

The voice was quiet, subdued, so much so that Westerson almost did not hear it. Looking over her shoulder she saw that the call had come from Hudson. The young Marine was standing to the side of the Humvee, his rifle seemingly forgotten in his right hand as the weapon's barrel drooped toward the ground. Westerson felt her blood chill as she saw the horrified expression on the man's face. As she stepped closer, Hudson pointed to the interior of the vehicle.

The collision with the tree had buckled most of the Humvee's passenger side, warping and twisting the metal and savagely rending the interior compartment. Feeling bile rise in her throat, Westerson saw that the area behind the front seats had been compressed to barely a third of its previous size, and within that abruptly reduced space, hard plastic and metal had pushed itself into and around comparatively soft flesh and bone.

Shane.

"Dear God," Westerson breathed. Her stomach heaved and she was nearly overwhelmed by the urge to vomit, but she found herself unable to move. Instead her eyes traveled over the sight of the young Marine, wedged among the wreckage. There were no movements, no cries of pain. It appeared that Shane had mercifully died on impact.

Turning away from the scene, Westerson drew several deep breaths in an attempt to calm herself. Still, her mind tortured her with images of the crash and how Matthew Shane's last seconds of life had played out. Had he even seen the tree that had killed him, or had he been so engrossed in trying to engage the enemy pursuing them that death had found him unaware? As a supply clerk, he had probably never considered that he might die in combat, at least not seriously. Westerson herself had certainly not thought about it, until tonight at any rate.

Behind her, Guber had extracted the PRC-77 radio from the wreck of the Humvee. The unit's rugged casing, deliberately designed to withstand harsh environments common to the battlefield, had helped it to survive the crash. Leaving the radio attached to the transport frame that allowed it to be carried like a backpack, Guber placed the unit on the ground to attach its antenna.

"*Base camp, this is Runner One,*" he called out as he keyed the unit's handset, using the call sign Captain Douglas had given Westerson and her group. The only response was a burst of static that made Guber pull the receiver from his ear. Adjusting the volume, he attempted the call once more but received the same result. Looking up at Westerson, he shook his head. "Lot of squawk, ma'am, the same kind of crap that's been screwing with us all night."

Nodding, Westerson replied, "Keep trying, Guber." Whatever she might have said next was forgotten, though, as the hairs on the back of her neck prickled. It was the only warning she had before a hum of energy erupted from the forest to her left.

"Get down!" Hudson yelled. Then the air was filled with the shriek of assaulted metal as another energy burst crashed into the front of the wrecked Humvee.

Even as she dropped to the ground and threw her arms up to protect herself, Westerson saw the effects of the attack as the wave tore into the Humvee, shredding part of the hood and engine compartment. Bits of tiny shrapnel struck her helmet and flak jacket and she gritted her teeth in momentary pain as something sharp and hot knifed into her thigh.

Rolling to his right, Hudson came up to one knee and brought his weapon to his shoulder, firing wildly in the direction from which the attack had come. It took him only seconds to empty the rifle's thirty-round magazine, swinging the weapon from left to right to cover as wide an area as possible.

"Ten o'clock!" Westerson called out as she heard running footsteps to her left. She raised her pistol and fired three quick rounds into the trees, not really expecting to hit anything. As the echoes from her shots faded, she listened for signs of movement in the forest but heard nothing.

"Do you see anything?" she asked Hudson, who merely shook his head. His attention remained riveted on the forest around him, the barrel of his rifle sweeping from left to right and back again in search of a target. Behind her, she heard Guber frantically trying to raise someone on the uncooperative radio.

Sounds to her right. As one she and Hudson swung their weapons in that direction and fired. This time they were rewarded with a cry of pain as their bullets struck something. Buoyed by apparent success, Westerson fired into the trees until the slide on her pistol locked to the rear. As she dropped the empty magazine and dug into a pouch on her belt for a replacement, Hudson fired his rifle dry, dropping to one knee so he could reload as well.

Both of them were holding empty weapons when the Chodrecai soldier broke through the forest undergrowth and into the open and aimed its own massive rifle at the two Marines. Hudson cried something unintelligible even as he fought to finish loading his M-16, and Westerson steeled herself for the effects of having her body filleted by the staggering power of the alien weapon.

Click.

The alien soldier's features clouded in obvious confusion when the rifle did not fire. Growling in what Westerson guessed to be frustration, the Chodrecai warrior tossed the weapon aside and drew a knife from a scabbard on its leg. The knife was nearly as long as Westerson's arm, the blade gleaming in the iridescent glow of the moon.

Before it could take a single step, Hudson finished reloading his rifle.

"Trick or treat, mother fucker," he hissed as he pulled the trigger.

At this distance it was impossible to miss and the alien staggered back as the first three-round burst took it full in the face. Blood or something akin to blood spouted in all directions as Hudson kept firing. Then the rifle's bolt locked to the rear as the Chodrecai soldier crashed in a heap to the ground, its head and face a shapeless mass of bloodied flesh and bone.

Rising to his feet, Hudson ejected the M-16's spent magazine and pulled another from the ammo pouch on his belt. "My last one," he said, holding it up for Westerson to see before inserting it into his weapon. Once reloaded, the Marine moved forward to inspect the unmoving body of the alien. Keeping his rifle aimed at what remained of the Chodrecai soldier's head, Hudson kicked its foot. There was no movement in the oversized gray body.

"Somebody up there loves us," Westerson said as she tapped the dead alien's weapon with the toe of her boot. Had the rifle jammed? Other than the snippets of information she had gleaned from Gardner's friend Max, she had no idea how the thing operated, but she decided to take the weapon with her anyway. Someone would be able to scrutinize it later.

"I'd rather not push our luck, Lieutenant," Hudson said

as Westerson picked up the alien rifle and slung it over her shoulder. "I say we get the hell out of here."

Westerson nodded as she adjusted the strange weapon across her back. It was similar in size to a SAW machine gun, though it did not possess that weapon's weight. "Good idea. Let's grab our stuff and get moving."

"Help us!"

The scream came from behind them, and Westerson turned to see Guber, still holding the radio handset and sounding as if he had descended into near hysteria. Seeing the panic in the man's eyes, she realized that the Marine had been nearly oblivious to the latest alien attack as he had vainly continued his attempts to contact anyone on the radio.

"Guber!" she snapped, having to repeat the summons twice before he acknowledged her. His eyes were wide with fear, but he appeared to calm somewhat when he saw her. "We have to get out of here, now."

In response, Guber pointed to the radio. "I . . . I can't . . . nobody will answer me."

"I know," she replied. It was hard not to want to sympathize with the man, but there were more pressing matters to attend to, such as the possibility that at least two more of the alien's buddies were still running around in the nearby forest.

Hudson emerged from the Humvee once more and Westerson saw that the armorer had another M-16 and a bloodied ammo pouch in his hand. "Shane's," he said simply. "I figure he'd want us to have them." Shrugging, he added, "You know, make a fight of it, or something."

Nodding soberly, Westerson took one last look into the wreckage of the vehicle, and something inside her clicked as her eyes came to rest on Shane's body. For his sake, they would make it out of here, she decided, and they would get to a phone. Her gut told her that she would not be able to prevent any more young Marines from dying tonight, but damn it, she could at least make sure that somebody knew what was happening here.

Matthew Shane deserved no less.

Confusion, horror, concern, frustration.

These were just a few of the emotions running through Raegyra's mind as he regarded the body of Cuuran. He had known the dead soldier only fleetingly, but long enough to form the bond that all warriors forged when thrust into battle together as well as anguish at the loss of a comrade.

It was becoming increasingly obvious that this group of creatures possessed military training. They had proven capable of defending themselves, and that they could react successfully against an ambush. They had managed to repel the assault staged against them even after losing control of their transport. They were on foot now and would be easier to pursue, he knew, but he was not ready to send his squad after them just yet. Weak as they may have appeared at first, these animals were certainly not to be underestimated. Before he committed his soldiers to another battle, he wanted some of his questions answered.

Around him, the remaining members of his squad were inspecting the area where the animals' vehicle had crashed, looking for anything that might provide them with useful information about their newfound enemy. The creatures had left little behind, though, and Raegyra could not begin to guess the function of the articles that were still here.

"Raegyra," a voice called out from behind him and he turned to see Albakor, one of his subordinates, kneeling next to what remained of the wrecked vehicle. The soldier indicated the open access panel leading to the vehicle's interior.

Moving closer, Raegyra saw how the impact with the tree had crushed and deformed the inside of the compartment around the soft yielding form of the body entombed within. It was obvious that the creature was dead, with its neck and extremities skewed at unnatural angles and a dark fluid that must be its blood oozing from a number of lacerations.

"It appears that he died on impact," Albakor said. Shaking his head he added, "A pity. We may have been able to interrogate him."

Raegyra suppressed a frustrated sigh. After following the lone animal that had survived their earlier skirmish back to their base camp and reporting their findings back to his superiors, he had been given instructions to capture one or more of the creatures for questioning. The Leadership was anxious to learn as much about the local inhabitants as possible. Were they allying themselves with the Plysserians? What level of resistance could Chodrecai forces expect to encounter? These were only the most immediate of many questions that still needed answering.

As if sensing his leader's concern, Albakor asked, "Should we not set out after the others?"

Though he nodded in response to the question, Raegyra did not give the necessary order. He had been prepared to give such instructions even as the ambush was still unfolding, in the event the creatures were able to fend off the initial attack and flee into the forest. As the vehicle crashed into the tree and its occupants spilled out onto the open ground, Raegyra had been ready to give the order to finish the creatures off.

Until his weapon and those carried by his subordinates had malfunctioned, that is.

The pulse rifles had been working at peak efficiency as the ambush developed, inflicting massive damage to the creatures' vehicle only to fall victim to malfunction moments later as he and his companions had closed the distance on their prey.

"Why did our weapons not work?" he asked no one in particular. He regarded the rifle in his hands, inspecting it with a practiced eye. The battery still held most of its original charge and he could find no sign of other damage as he aimed the weapon at a nearby bush and pressed the firing stud. His irritation was exacerbated as the shrub exploded in a flash of energy, the echo from the rifle burst fading into the forest as easily as whatever it was that had caused the malfunction in the first place.

Albakor repeated the test with his own weapon, and Raegyra's frown deepened as it functioned flawlessly.

Had the operation of their rifles been plagued by something employed by the animals? Raegyra did not understand how that could be possible, based on what he and his companions had seen of their technology since arriving in this strange land. Something unique to this world, then? A quality of the atmosphere? That made little sense, either.

Shaking his head, he tried to dismiss the questions and the doubt that accompanied them, leaving them for the Leadership as he had been taught to do. He was a soldier with a simple mission: Stop the creatures from escaping. Capture if possible; kill if necessary. They were all the instructions he needed to function.

Though as he gave the order to move out, Raegyra found that the questions and the doubts remained to taunt him.

For the third time in fifteen minutes, by his count, Simon DiCarlo heard the distinctive sound of a magazine being dropped from an M-16. He listened with growing annoyance as the rifle's owner went through the motion of checking the magazine's contents and reinserting it into the weapon.

"Is it still loaded?" he asked quietly, an edge creeping into his voice.

To his left, Lance Corporal Marcus George replied sheepishly, "Yes, Sergeant Major."

"Then stop fucking with it."

George nodded. "Sorry. I guess I'm just nervous."

Refraining from saying anything else, DiCarlo instead chose to gnaw a little harder on the end of the unlit cigar hanging from his mouth. He had managed to chew its immediate predecessor down to a nub earlier, and he realized that a similar fate was in store for this current specimen if he was not careful.

The thought of lighting the cigar never entered his mind, of course, as that would have been an unforgivable breach of the most basic tenets of stealth in a combat environment. A lit cigar or cigarette at night may as well be a flare advertising their position to an approaching enemy. It was a lesson he had learned long ago, as a know-nothing private on his first tour in Vietnam, when he had made the unfortunate mistake of firing up a cigarette while on night watch. The knot inflicted on his skull by the heel of his sergeant's boot remained swollen for nearly a week afterward, much longer than it had taken for Simon DiCarlo to give up cigarettes.

Of course George would be nervous, DiCarlo knew, if not outright scared. After all, the young Marine had never before seen combat. Hell, he was nervous himself, and not just because he knew he was sitting in what could soon be a war zone. He had been in those before, from the jungles of Vietnam to the deserts of Saudi Arabia and Iraq to the mountains of Bosnia and Afghanistan. DiCarlo had spent his share of time in firefights, and an even greater amount of time waiting for such engagements to commence.

As much as he dreaded the actual fighting, it was the waiting that he truly hated. Whether it was standing by for the order to launch an attack or manning a defensive position in preparation to repel an assault, waiting for the action to commence was something he had always loathed. How much time had he spent like that, with only the breathing of the buddy sharing his fighting hole or maybe the chirping of insects to keep him company as he waited for the enemy to make its move? Too much, he knew.

It was the main reason he had stopped wearing a watch years ago.

"Nervous is good, George," DiCarlo said, trying to reassure the young Marine. "Nervous keeps you alert." There had not been time for those feelings earlier, as the unit

rushed to prepare their defenses in the likely event that
the aliens would find them. It had been an exercise in im-
provisation and innovation, considering the limited resources at their disposal. While most of the Marines in the
unit had been detailed to digging fighting holes in a circle
around the camp's perimeter, Sergeant Bonniker had seen
to it that their supply of live ammunition was distributed.
Though the unit had brought several thousand rounds for
weapons training during the past two weeks, fewer than
two thousand rounds remained of that original allotment.

They had been able to augment that, though, by raid-
ing the ammunition storage bunker located less than a
mile from the camp near the firing ranges where the
base's National Guard unit had recently stocked the
bunker for an upcoming training exercise of its own. Bonniker had found a few crates of M-16 ammo as well as
some for the unit's four larger M-249 Squad Automatic
Weapons, or SAWs. DiCarlo had ordered the quartet of
machine guns positioned on the roof of the two-story
building at the center of the compound. With their
greater range and firepower, the SAWs would be able to
provide covering fire in a hurry if the aliens, "Grays" as
Gardner and other Marines had already taken to calling
the Chodrecai, attacked from multiple directions as he expected them to do.

The Marines had set out the remainder of their training flares and other incendiary and explosive devices in
the nearby forest surrounding the camp. With any luck,
none of the aliens would be able to approach the defensive perimeter without setting off one of the devices. Bonniker had also found and parceled out three dozen
fragmentation grenades, but had found little else that

might be of use to the Marines. DiCarlo would have preferred a dozen M-203 grenade launcher attachments for
their M-16s, but the armory had lacked those.

Can't do shit about that now.

"Sergeant Major," George said, his voice barely a whisper, "do you think Lieutenant Westerson and the others
made it out?"

"They should have reached Mainside by now," Di-
Carlo replied as he wiped sweat from his brow. Like every
other night they had spent here during the past two weeks,
the heat had refused to abate even now, only a few hours
before dawn.

The heat's the least of your problems, pal.

The headquarters building near the reservation's main
gate was at least thirty minutes away using the unimproved
roads on this part of the base. Even if Westerson had made
it there already and made contact with someone back
home, DiCarlo figured that any sort of reinforcements
was hours away, and that was if whoever picked up the
phone in Kansas City believed the story Westerson would
tell. Hell, it was hard enough for him to believe, and he
had seen the alien with his own eyes.

What he did believe was that he and the other Marines
stood almost no chance of holding their positions here
until anyone arrived to help them.

How long had it been since Westerson and her team
had left? An hour or more? It had taken the remaining
Marines nearly that long to fortify their defensive positions. Broken down into teams of two and three, the reservists had hastily dug shallow fighting holes, situated
thirty to forty feet from one another in a circular perimeter with the encampment itself at the center. Most of the

holes were not as deep as DiCarlo would have liked, and few of them possessed sandbags, logs, or anything else that might form a protective barrier. His gut had told him that they were working on borrowed time as it was, though, and he had wanted the Marines under some kind of cover as quickly as possible.

Max, the alien Gardner had befriended, had returned to the camp while those preparations were underway, bringing with him a contingent of twenty other Blues. With Gardner helping him to translate his plan, DiCarlo and Max had managed to brief the other soldiers on their role.

During the briefing DiCarlo had noted that nearly half of the aliens appeared to be female. The idea of women in combat was one that had troubled him earlier in his career, but in the last decade he had seen women moving ever closer to the front lines of the battlefield. Though most combat arms billets of the American military were still closed to them, women currently served aboard naval combat vessels and in a variety of support elements in all branches of the service. The nature of modern warfare had made it such that rear echelon units, where most female service members would normally be found, were as much a target as infantry troops in forward areas.

And of course there was the reservists' own situation, unfolding at this very moment. DiCarlo had not hesitated to place the women Marines, who made up nearly a third of the unit, on the defensive perimeter alongside their male counterparts. Similar rationale had guided his strategy to deploy the Blues among the ranks as well. Dispersed along the perimeter and mixed in with the other Marines, the aliens' superior night vision abilities as well as their more advanced weaponry would, he hoped, serve to augment their defenses and perhaps increase their chances of repelling the coming assault.

Yeah, from none to slim.

He hated to entertain such a negative thought, and would never even think of giving voice to it in the presence of the younger Marines who were looking to him for leadership and confidence, especially now, even though the realist in him knew the true score.

Other than himself, Bonniker, and a few of the other sergeants and corporals, none of reservists possessed any real combat experience. How would these Marines react when the first shots were fired and it became frighteningly apparent that an enemy force was rushing them with the intent to kill?

DiCarlo felt his gut twinge at the knowledge that he would have his answer all too soon.

Elsewhere along the defensive perimeter, Brad Gardner turned his attention once more to the forest around him, listening and looking for signs of movement. With only a few hours until dawn, the forest was quiet, almost tranquil. It reminded him somewhat of the wooded area behind his apartment complex in Kansas City. With a view that was free of other buildings, roads, or people, it was his habit to sit on his balcony in the evening, enjoying the serenity offered by the forest before going to bed.

"Your world is somewhat like our own," Max said in a quiet voice, echoing Gardner's thoughts as he lay next to Gardner and Captain Douglas at the forward parapet of their fighting hole. The alien's words were stilted and somewhat hesitant, but it was obvious that his command of the language had improved even in the two hours or so that had passed since he had left the camp to retrieve his friends.

"Really?" Douglas asked as he adjusted his position in an attempt to get more comfortable. "To be honest, I was hoping you'd tell us how different your planet was from ours."

"There are differences, of course," Max replied, shaking his head. "But many more similarities than you might imagine." Indicating the forest with a wave of a massive hand, the alien added, "Despite the War, there are a few regions similar to this which remain largely untouched by devastation. They are treasured by our people and provide a way to escape the reality of our everyday lives, if only temporarily. As a child, I would often venture from the city where I lived so that I could lie out under the stars and dream of one day sailing among them."

Gardner still could not help but be impressed with the alien's quick grasping of English. The translators were obviously designed to allow the transferal of language skills, and after just a few hours of exposure to the device, he realized that he was starting to understand the alien's own tongue, though he was still a long way toward being able to speak it or to follow a conversation. In addition to their evident physical superiority, it appeared that the Plysserians mental acuity exceeded that of humans as well.

Still, he was able to smile at the image Max's words painted as he continued to regard the surrounding forest and the illusion of peace it offered. It would be easy to forget that somewhere out there, beyond the perimeter of their camp, their enemy was approaching.

Our enemy?

It was a question demanding resolution. Were the Chodrecai the enemy of Earth? Certainly Max believed it to be true, given what he had told Gardner, not to mention the subsequent actions of Max and the other Plysserian soldiers that he had brought with him back to the encampment.

That, of course, had caused quite a stir.

There had been a wide spectrum of reactions from the Marines in the unit when Captain Douglas had briefed them on the situation and the presence of aliens in the surrounding forest. That had changed when Sergeant Major DiCarlo introduced Max and the other Blues to the group. The veteran Marine's no-nonsense approach to laying out the facts, mind-boggling as they sounded, had been enough to replace any doubts lingering among the group with varying degrees of excitement, awe, apprehension, and fear.

"I knew when I joined the Reserves that I could go to war," Gardner said. "But I figured they would send me to Afghanistan." He had been a reservist for almost two years when the terrorist attacks in New York City and Washington, D.C., had taken place and was surprised when he had not been called to active duty to support military operations in the Middle East. Never in his wildest dreams had he ever thought he would find himself thrust into the center of an alien civil war.

It had been surreal as they prepared their defenses, with the Blues standing by to assist them. They were forced to wait as Max, working with Gardner and the translators, had discussed with DiCarlo how best to use the alien soldiers, but in short order they had been distributed among the ranks along the perimeter. Also at

DiCarlo's direction, the Marines had dug their fighting holes inside the tree line surrounding the camp to better conceal their positions among the foliage. All exterior lights had been extinguished, plunging the entire encampment into darkness.

"I knew from childhood that I would be a soldier," Max said. "The War had begun while I was still in school, and it was a foregone conclusion that any able-bodied citizen would enter the service when they came of age. Like anyone else I hoped it would end before my time came, but that did not happen." Pointing to one of the tattoos on his left bicep, he said, "This image recounts my first battle. It began much like this night, quiet and peaceful. I will never forget how quickly that tranquility was destroyed."

What's it like to grow up in a world where war is a way of life? The thought echoed in Gardner's mind as he studied the intricate illustration. Like most people he knew, Gardner had never come closer to experiencing the horrors and adversity of war than watching news coverage on television. As a student, he had imagined living as a child in embattled countries like Israel or Kosovo, where war and violence were daily realities of existence. What Max had described, though, seemed even worse by comparison.

Situated between Gardner and Douglas, a crackle erupted from the PRC-77 radio and a faint voice emanated from the unit's handset. Reaching for it, Gardner brought the handset to his ear.

". . . Hole seventeen," the voice said. "We think we've got movement in the woods in front of Hole sixteen."

Each of the fighting holes had been given a number, starting with Gardner and Douglas's own hole as number one and continuing in a clockwise manner around the camp's perimeter up to twenty-two. There had not been enough radios to put one in each hole, so they were distributed to provide comm for three or four holes each. Anyone seeing anything was to report it via the radio net.

Picturing the layout of the camp in his mind, Gardner looked to his left in what he knew was a futile effort to see what the Marines in Hole sixteen might have detected.

"They're coming," Douglas said, bringing his rifle around to face down the leftmost boundary of their assigned field of fire. "Get ready."

Gardner could feel his pulse beginning to race as he moved his eyes from tree to tree, searching for any signs of movement, and feeling very vulnerable lying here in this shallow hole. What kind of range did the aliens' weapons have? Would the Marines even get the chance to see their enemy approaching before the alien rifles found them?

Then the familiar sound of an M-16 firing from somewhere to his right shattered the near silence of the forest.

"There!" a voice shouted out in alarm before being drowned out by another round of rifle fire. Gardner could only begin to swing his weapon in that direction before the glaring white light of a flare illuminated a spot among the trees perhaps fifty meters from his position. The darkness was chased away and long shadows stretched into the forest as the flare's glow intensified.

And some of the shadows were moving.

Figures darted between the trees in the already fading light offered by the flare even as another booby trap was triggered and another flare lit up the forest, this one closer to their own position. Now Gardner saw the massive forms of Chodrecai warriors scrambling away from the booby traps they had triggered. Some of them were moving farther into the forest.

Others were not.

"Here they come!" he called out even as he raised his rifle to his shoulder, searching for a target.

From elsewhere the sound of a grenade exploding ripped through the trees, no doubt the result of another of Bonniker's improvised traps. The sergeant had taken a handful of their grenades and cut the fuses down to near nubs before attaching them to tripwires strung in the trees. Once triggered the grenades would detonate only an instant or two later, hopefully catching one or more of the enemy within the five meter kill zone projected by the explosive if not inflicting injury on anyone or anything within the weapon's larger casualty radius.

Silence returned as the firing stopped, the only thing audible to Gardner being his own breathing as he strained to listen for signs of the encroaching enemy aliens.

"On the right!" Douglas yelled, already bringing his rifle around as a flash of light erupted from the forest and dirt and rock exploded not ten meters from them. The two Marines and Max rolled away from the fighting hole's parapet as dirt and pieces of rock shrapnel rained down upon them.

His ears still ringing from the blast, Gardner almost failed to hear the sound of more rifle fire, along with something else. It was a deep, resonating hum of power and he realized that Max was selecting targets from the approaching enemy force and firing his own strange weapon. Air rippled and distorted as the energy pulse launched from the rifle, followed by a scream of pain as the weapon found its mark.

It was hard to make out anything in the tree line as colored dots danced in Gardner's vision from the brightness of the tripped flares, but the sounds of running feet trampling through the underbrush were unmistakable.

Something moved to Gardner's left and he spun in that direction, shock freezing him in place as a figure broke through the foliage. Its hulking form was almost a blur as it charged directly at him.

13

"Jesus!"

Gardner's blood ran cold at Captain Douglas's exclamation even as the alien let loose a bellowing war cry, its mouth a yawning black maw as it bore down on him. Muscles rippled and dim moonlight reflected off its pallid gray skin and the metal of its chest armor and the weapon held in one massive hand.

Shoot, goddammit!

Even as the thought screamed in his mind he brought the M-16 to his shoulder and pulled the trigger. The weapon bucked in his hands as the first three rounds exploded from its barrel. Two of the shots missed and the third one struck the immense gray alien in the chest armor before Gardner was pulling the trigger again and again.

The alien stumbled in the face of the attack but did not go down. It snarled in evident rage as it leveled its own weapon in Gardner's direction, the huge muzzle searching for its target.

Gardner felt himself pushed aside as Max stood up in the fighting hole, his weapon raised and pointed at the oncoming alien. Then the rifle pulsed again and its ball of

energy slammed into the Gray warrior and knocked it off
its feet. The alien crashed to the ground, twitching in reaction to the rifle shot even as Max lunged from the hole,
his weapon firing again at the enemy soldier and catching
it full in the chest with a second round.

"Take his weapon!" Max ordered as he swept the area
in front of him with his own rifle, looking for other
sources of danger.

Gardner scrambled forward to where the pulse rifle lay,
scooping it up before diving back into the relative safety of
the fighting hole. Obtaining more of the alien weapons
had been a secondary objective of DiCarlo's, hoping to
pick them up from fallen enemy soldiers if and when they
were dispatched. Max and his companions had given a
crash course on the operation of the weapons, which were
reportedly not that much different from the ones the
Blues carried. Examining the hefty rifle he now held,
Gardner's confidence was buoyed as he realized that
Max's report was indeed correct.

"Incoming!" Douglas shouted and Gardner's ears rang
with rifle fire as the captain let loose with several bursts
from his M-16. Gardner looked up to see another Gray
rushing at them, so close that he could hear the bullets
striking the armor it wore as well as the dull punching
sounds of rounds tearing through the alien's dense hide.
The Gray staggered from Douglas's assault, halting its
movements long enough for Gardner to bring the pulse
rifle up and press the firing stud.

The weapon's recoil forced him back a step as its barrel
bucked up and to the right. It was enough, though, as the
bullet of energy spat forth and took the looming alien full
in the face. The Gray's head snapped back and its entire

body was thrown to the side, falling to the ground in a limp heap. It had not even come to rest before Douglas was clambering from the hole, his sights set on the alien's own weapon.

Then something moved to Gardner's right and there was no time to even shout a warning as an energy pulse tore through the air and slammed full force into Douglas. The Kevlar vest he wore was useless against the onslaught as the captain's torso instantly shredded in a shower of blood and tissue fragments, his body separating cleanly at the waist. Gardner's jaw dropped in horror at the sight of Douglas's legs continuing to stagger forward for several more steps before falling to the earth.

"Conserve your ammo! Wait for your shot and aim for the head!"

Simon DiCarlo shouted the order into the radio's handset, hoping to be heard over the escalating sounds of battle. It had become apparent in the first moments of the attack that the Gray soldiers were resistant to small arms fire, at least at greater distances. Bullets bounced off the chest armor they wore, but their heads and extremities were vulnerable, at least close up. DiCarlo knew that the Marines would have to show courage and resolve if they were to have any hope of repelling the Chodrecai assault.

A Gray broke out onto open ground to his right and DiCarlo swung to see the alien already bringing its weapon up, the massive muzzle aimed directly at him. Even as he tried to turn his own rifle toward the new threat, the alien had him cold.

Click.

DiCarlo watched as the soldier held its weapon up to inspect it. Why had it not fired? Had it jammed?

Giving thanks for the reprieve he had been granted, he fired at the alien, figuring as he did so that the bullets would not be very effective at this range.

They were not, but they did succeed in doing what Di-Carlo had wanted anyway by denying the Gray the chance to figure out what had gone wrong with its own rifle. The monstrous alien growled menacingly in Di-Carlo's direction, dropping the weapon and drawing a massive knife from its belt as it charged forward.

"Sergeant Major!" George called out as he saw the Gray running at them. DiCarlo ignored the warning as he heeded his own advice, sighting down the barrel of his M-16 as the Gray warrior closed the distance between them.

Twenty meters.

Fifteen.

The creature's face filled the weapon's rear sight aperture before DiCarlo finally pulled the trigger.

Keeping the weapon steady he watched as the trio of bullets plowed into the Gray's face just below its left eye. The alien cried out in agony as it stumbled to its knees less than ten meters in front of DiCarlo, who tracked the creature with the rifle's muzzle before letting loose with another burst into the enemy soldier's head. The Gray collapsed to the ground and remained still.

Beside him, Marcus George was firing, too, tracking another alien as it moved toward one of the fighting holes to their left. The combination of his fire with that of the Marines in the other hole was enough to bring the Gray down after several shots.

All around DiCarlo, the sounds of battle were raging,

sharp reports of M-16s and the SAWs contrasting sharply
with the high-pitched whines of the alien weapons. There
were also the screams of pain, many of them human,
telling DiCarlo that the enemy attack was already beginning to take a toll on the Marines along the defensive line.

It amazed DiCarlo that the Grays were not taking advantage of their superior weaponry and simply hammering the line from the safety of the trees. Many of the
enemy soldiers were even rushing the line with their rifles
held as clubs instead of firing on the run. What kind of idiotic tactic was that?

Looking to his right, he was startled to see one of the
Blues leave his fighting position, tossing his own rifle
aside as he charged an oncoming enemy soldier. The
Gray had likewise discarded his own weapon and as the
two aliens met the Plysserian lashed out with a savage attack that took his opponent in the throat. The Gray staggered under the assault, swinging its own arms wildly in
an effort to land a counterattack but the Plysserian had already stepped outside its reach. Feinting to his right, he
instead ducked back the other way and kicked out with a
massive leg, striking the Gray in the side of the head with
such force that DiCarlo heard the alien's neck snap even
from this distance. The melee had taken only seconds to
complete, after which the Plysserian scanned the forest
around him for new threats before returning to the safety
of his fighting hole.

Did the aliens' concept of warfare include needlessly
sacrificing large numbers of foot soldiers to secure their
objective? At first it reminded DiCarlo of the firefights in
Vietnam where chaos had seemed to reign supreme, even
though the Vietcong were almost always operating within

the framework of a thoughtfully laid out and executed plan.

This was different, somehow. To DiCarlo it felt as if the aliens were improvising in the face of unexpected difficulty.

"Get on the radio," DiCarlo ordered George. "Put another SAW on this tree line before we get overrun." Their only chance, he knew, was to hit the encroaching aliens hard and fast to keep them from establishing a foothold inside the Marines' defensive perimeter. If any of the Grays broke through the lines and the fight deteriorated to anything up close, DiCarlo knew his people were doomed.

Given a choice, Anthony Bonniker would much rather have been holding a weapon than a radio.

"McLanahan, get over to the southeast corner," he called out to the Marine manning the weapon on the building's south side. "They need more cover fire on that flank!"

Situated on the roof of the compound's main building, the sounds of war surrounded him. Rifle fire, shouted orders, cries of desperation and agony all filled the air. The steady chop of the four SAWs drowned out most of the clamor coming from below, though. Positioned one to each side of the building, the machine guns and their crews had been given the task of providing suppressing fire toward the forest in an attempt to keep the attacking aliens at bay.

Reports were coming in a flurry, with Marines on the line calling for fire support from the SAWs or for help from other fighting holes as the Grays continued their probing action. Tasked with coordinating the machine-gun teams, Bonniker was continuing to move from position to position, the radio strapped to his back keeping him in constant contact with the Marines on the ground and in the command center. There was still the constant static and interference that had been plaguing radio transmissions all night, but Sergeant Russell had assured him that everyone in the unit was close enough that maintaining contact would still be possible.

White light flashed along the wall of the building and the aluminum roof shuddered beneath his feet. Bonniker crouched down to minimize his silhouette as another shock hit the side of the building. Having seen the effects of the alien weaponry once already, he imagined the damage the energy bolts were inflicting on the building's paltry aluminum walls and anyone who might be seeking cover inside them.

"Bonniker!" the voice of Gunnery Sergeant Jackson Shelby barked into his ear from the radio's handset. *"I need more fire on the north side!"* The senior Marine was manning a point on the north end of the camp, Hole eleven if Bonniker remembered correctly, which was almost directly opposite from Captain Douglas's position. Though Shelby had served in Desert Storm, Bonniker knew that as a supply and logistics specialist, the man had never seen action on the front lines of the war. Still, his leadership experience was valuable as he helped to coordinate defensive actions on the perimeter.

"On the way, Gunny," Bonniker replied, already signaling for the two-man team working the west flank to adjust their fire to the north end of the compound. In response the two Marines grabbed the SAW and its belts of ammu-

nition and scrambled to the new position, the bipod attached to the barrel of the machine gun providing stability for the weapon as it was moved from spot to spot.

So far the defensive strategy put into play by DiCarlo seemed to be working. With the aid of the Plysserian soldiers the Marines were managing to hold the line. Bonniker heard the radio reports from different points along the perimeter being fed to the command center, where Lieutenant Stakely had been given the responsibility of being the captain's eyes and ears for the entire battle. Bonniker had at first been confused by the choice, thinking that Douglas would have elected to coordinate their defensive effort from the CC himself. He had to give the captain credit for choosing to place himself on the line along with the Marines in his charge.

Machine-gun fire from the south end of the building drew his attention and Bonniker turned to see McLanahan and his assistant gunner lying flat near the edge of the roof. McLanahan's body bucked from the recoil of the machine gun, the other Marine lying on his left and feeding the ammunition belt as fast as the SAW would take it. The weapon's barrel was aimed downward at a drastic angle.

"They're inside the perimeter!" McLanahan shouted between bursts of fire.

Bonniker had discussed the potential for this turn of events with DiCarlo earlier and they had concluded that if the Grays accomplished that, the battle was as good as over. With nowhere to retreat to, the Marines would be forced to engage the aliens hand to hand and Bonniker held no illusions about how such a skirmish would turn out.

We have to keep the bastards out!

*　　*　　*

"Why isn't this fucking thing working?"

Still reeling from the shock of Captain Douglas's death, Gardner's frustration with the Chodrecai pulse rifle he had liberated from its now dead owner was also mounting. It had worked when he had first picked it up but now for some reason the weapon was inert. Max had experienced the same strange problem with his own rifle and had already discarded it in favor of Douglas's M-16. It had only taken Gardner a moment or two to instruct the Blue on how to use the comparatively primitive weapon and now Max was employing it with deadly accuracy.

All around him, Grays were continuing to emerge from the forest, charging toward the defense perimeter. Several of the aliens had been gunned down by Marines or Plysserian soldiers, but he could also hear the sounds of fighting coming from behind him, telling him that at least some of the enemy had penetrated the line and gotten into the camp itself. There were shouts of alarm and more M-16 fire as some Marines were forced to retreat from their fighting holes. Under cover of the quartet of SAWs stationed on the command center's roof, they were trying to keep the attacking aliens in front of them as they fell back to the imagined safety of the building.

"*Lieutenant Stakely,*" he shouted into the radio handset as he brought the unit to his ear, "*Captain Douglas is dead! They're breaking through all over the place and they're in the compound. We need covering fire down here!*"

Any reply Stakely might have given was ignored as Gardner detected movement to his right. Max saw it, too, raising his M-16 and firing at a pair of Grays as they appeared from the tree line. Neither of the aliens was carrying a pulse rifle, though. What was with that? The alien weaponry was far superior to anything the Marines had, and there had to be more of them than what the Plysserians had brought to the fight.

Could the enemy weapons be suffering the same kind of weird malfunction that was plaguing the rifle in Gardner's hands?

The louder, more authoritative reports of a SAW rang in his ears and Gardner saw the bright orange streaks of the machine gun's tracer rounds raining down from above and behind him. The bullets struck the ground in front of the Gray soldiers, chewing a path in the dirt up to the aliens and cutting into them before they could react. Within seconds they both fell under the hailstorm of bullets, dropping limp to the ground.

As he grabbed for his M-16, Gardner heard footsteps behind him and turned to see Sergeant Major DiCarlo rushing at him from inside the camp perimeter. What was he doing here? Had he been forced to retreat as his position was overrun? Were the aliens behind him?

"Come on!" DiCarlo called out as he ran past Gardner on his way to the next hole on the line. "They're breaking off the attack and we've got them on the run!"

Could that be? Had the Marines succeeded in holding the line and forcing the Grays to turn tail and retreat?

As if in response to his unspoken questions Gardner heard the sounds of running feet to his left. Gray soldiers were moving through the trees, dashing headlong through the forest and away from the camp. Behind them more figures followed and Gardner made out the shapes of Marines giving chase, moving through the woods without the speed and grace of the aliens but providing enough impetus to drive the Grays' withdrawal.

"Over there!" he called out, pointing in the direction of the retreating aliens. "They're pulling back!"

A pair of the Grays saw the two Marines and Max and changed direction toward them, apparently deciding that one last skirmish was in order. One of the soldiers was still carrying a rifle and as the alien drew closer it raised the weapon to fire.

Gardner heard the whine of power and felt the violent rush of air being pushed aside as an energy bolt hurled past his right shoulder. He dodged to his left, ducking into the nearby foliage in a frantic attempt to conceal himself.

Jesus, he implored the fickle alien weapons, *make up your fucking minds.*

More M-16 fire ripped through the forest as DiCarlo and Max took up hasty defensive positions behind trees and opened fire, catching the Grays in a storm of bullets. Many of the rounds bounced off the aliens' armor but several found soft flesh instead. Not enough damage to incapacitate the two enemy soldiers, they were still sufficient to make the Grays abandon their attack and rejoin their fellow soldiers in their flight from the camp. Gardner could scarcely believe the sight of the aliens fleeing. Were they afraid or simply exercising the better part of valor with a strategic retreat since their weapons were acting so erratically?

Hey, who cares, just so long as they're getting the hell out of here.

"Sergeant Major DiCarlo!" a voice called out from the forest, one Gardner recognized as belonging to Daniel Melendez. The corporal was crashing through the foliage, approaching their position at a dead run. He was carrying a radio on his back, and he held the handset for DiCarlo.

"They're in full retreat," he said between labored breaths. "Lieutenant Stakely is getting reports from all around the perimeter. They're buggin' out."

It was a simple statement, but one that evoked a sigh of relief from Gardner. He sagged against the trunk of a thick oak, allowing the tree to support him as the aftershock of the battle washed over him. How long had they been fighting? Glancing down at his watch, he was stunned to see it was 2:20 A.M., barely ten minutes had passed since the first booby trap had been tripped.

Ten minutes? That's it?

"Some shit, ain't it?" DiCarlo asked, a knowing yet humorless smile gracing his craggy features as he regarded Gardner.

As the sergeant major relayed his report to Lieutenant Stakely, Gardner noticed Max standing nearby, a frown creasing his narrow mouth. "Max? What is it?"

Indicating the direction the Grays had fled, the Plysserian soldier shook his head slowly. "We may have won this battle, my friend, but do not be mistaken: This is not over."

14

Beyond the building's thin aluminum walls, Sergeant Belinda Russell could still hear muffled victory cries over the occasional round of M-16 fire as the Marines and their newfound friends continued expediting the withdrawal of the Gray soldiers. Radio traffic was constant as the latest developments from the perimeter came in. The enemy aliens were on the run, putting up little to no resistance as they were driven from the scene of the battle. No doubt the Marines' focus was already shifting to ensuring the camp was secure and that no Gray stragglers might be hiding within the compound's perimeter.

From the radio traffic, she knew that a sweep of the area was in progress to determine how many casualties they had suffered. Though Fate had for some reason seen fit to smile on her and her companions and allow them to repel the enemy aliens' attack, the Marines had not gotten away unscathed. She had heard Gardner's report on Captain Douglas's death, and other scattered details had come in all during the battle of other Marines being injured or killed. An official count was still being tallied, and Russell feared how large that number might be.

"I thought they had us," Rebecca Sloane said as she

propped her M-16 in the far corner of the room before dropping her protective vest, helmet, and equipment harness onto the floor. As she removed her camouflage uniform blouse Russell saw how her brown undershirt stuck to her torso, soaked through with perspiration. Her blond hair was matted with sweat as well. Reaching into her pile of gear, Sloane retrieved a canteen.

Keith Eshelman turned away from the worktable and its collection of field radios to regard his friend. "You okay?"

Downing most of the canteen's contents, Sloane wiped her mouth and nodded. "Tired. And scared and relieved and . . ." the words faded and she waved the rest of her answer away.

Russell thought she could understand the rush of emotions Sloane was feeling. Though she herself had been detailed to the command center along with Eshelman and a handful of other Marines during the battle, she had been privy to the happenings thanks to the array of radios she had been tasked with overseeing. Chaotic frenzy almost reigned supreme as her friends along the defensive perimeter sent in harried reports describing the progress of the fighting. It had been all she could do to keep some semblance of control over the comm net so that real calls for support to either Lieutenant Stakely or Sergeant Bonniker could get through.

"If it hadn't been for the aliens Gardner found," Sloane said between sips of water, "we never would've had a chance. The Grays would've run right over us."

Grays. Russell had heard other Marines using the term to describe the Chodrecai in obvious reference to the aliens' pallid skin color and their distinct lack of body art like that employed by the Blues. She knew the term from elsewhere, though, most notably as a common name for aliens that hundreds of people had reportedly seen since at least the 1940s. The descriptions she had read of those aliens often portrayed them as thin and weak, rather than possessing the muscular physiques of the Chodrecai, to say nothing of lacking the Chodrecai's apparent aggressive disposition.

How long would the battle have lasted without the assistance of the Plysserians? Would there have even been a battle, or would the enemy aliens have simply annihilated the Marines with little or no effort? The reservists, without doubt, owed their lives to the Plysserians.

Sloane said, "Before the Grays came, when we were just sitting in our holes waiting for them, I was terrified and just wanted to run away. Then it just started, and there was no time to be scared. I mean . . ." She paused a moment to gather her thoughts, her eyes cast down toward the floor. "I was terrified, but I knew I couldn't run. I had to stay there and fight." Shaking her head again she added, "I don't know how to describe it. Surreal, I guess."

"You described it perfectly."

The three Marines turned at the sound of the voice to see Sergeant Major DiCarlo standing in the doorway. Dirt covered his uniform as well as his face and hands. He carried his M-16 slung across his back and held what looked to be one of the Plysserian's energy rifles nestled in the crook of his right arm. Though he was carrying himself with the typical military bearing he displayed around subordinates, Russell could see the fatigue in the man's eyes.

"Sloane," DiCarlo continued, "you just explained what

every grunt who's ever waited for a battle to start has felt. People often wonder how soldiers can stand the pandemonium that war brings, but the simple truth is that most of the time, they're happy when the fighting starts because when the waiting's over, they don't have time to think about being scared shitless."

Russell heard the weariness in DiCarlo's voice. Was it simply a result of the skirmish with the Grays, or was it something else? She knew that he had seen action in many places over the years, if the array of award ribbons she had seen him wear on his duty uniforms were any indication. Approaching the end of a long and distinguished military career, the sergeant major had no doubt taken his current assignment in Kansas City as a "twilight tour," his last official posting before retirement. It was, naturally, one of the last places anyone might expect to be thrown into a combat situation.

So much for expectations, Russell reminded herself. Here they were, REMF's or "rear echelon motherfuckers" as Sergeant Bonniker and other infantry types tended to call Marines assigned to non-combat duties, and they were neck deep in a tactical situation unlike anything a fighting force on this planet had ever faced.

She nodded at the alien rifle DiCarlo held. "Are our new friends handing out extra weaponry now?" she asked. Looking at it again, though, Russell noticed that it was also different from the energy rifles the Plysserian soldiers had brought with them. She had been unable to shake the idea of examining technology from another planet since first laying eyes on the Blue soldier that Lance Corporal Gardner had befriended, even though there had been no time for that as the reservists set about preparing the camp for the coming alien attack.

"One of the Grays," DiCarlo replied. "He didn't need it anymore." Holding up the weapon, he looked at it in derision. "Isn't worth a shit, though. From what I saw during the fight, it kept jamming up. A lot of their weapons were having similar problems. That's the main reason we were able to hold the line like we did. I'm going to have Max look at it. Maybe he can figure out what's up."

Leaning forward in her chair, Sloane said, "You know, we saw that, too. One second they'd be shooting at us, the next they'd act as though there was something wrong." She frowned as she regarded the alien rifle. "In fact, I think the Blue in the hole next to mine was having the same kind of problem, and I know I saw at least one or two of them running around with M-16s. I didn't really think much of it at the time, figuring the batteries or whatever powered those things had worn out."

"From what I overheard Max telling Gardner," Eshelman said, "their rifles don't fire bullets. We're not talking about a regular jam here."

Holding up the rifle, DiCarlo said, "There's nothing physical that gets ejected, like a spent round. I don't see any moving parts, either, at least on the outside." Shrugging, he added, "Besides, if what Sloane says is right, several weapons were affected, on both sides."

Russell's brow furrowed as she listened to the exchange. What would cause all or most of the alien weapons to experience malfunction at more or less the same time? She had heard the report Gardner had given on behalf of the soldier that had become the reservist group's benefactor. As if drawn from one of the science fiction books, movies, or television shows she had enjoyed since childhood, the rifles carried by the Blues and their enemies fired energy bursts instead of physical projectiles. According to Max, the weapons employed a type of built-in electronic fire control computer that saw to targeting, power levels, and operating temperature among other vital processes.

Electronic?

"Something had to interfere with the rifles," she blurted out to no one in particular. "Something in the air or nearby or . . ."

Her voice faded as her eyes fell on the comm shack's worktable and its row of field radios.

"Holy shit."

Gathering Max, Gardner, and Lieutenant Stakely, Russell and the others moved out into the clearing behind the camp's main building. Outside she heard someone, it sounded like Sergeant Bonniker, issuing a string of orders as, all around them, Marines and Blue soldiers continued the process of securing the compound. The three Navy corpsmen had their hands full assessing and treating the injured, some of whom had already gathered near the back of the Humvee which acted as the unit's ambulance. The scene served to remind her of the grim reality of their current situation.

Putting that aside for the moment, Russell returned her attention to the pulse rifle she held. It took her a few moments to familiarize herself with the weapon's unusual handgrip before pulling the rifle into her shoulder. Bracing for the weapon's recoil, she pressed the firing stud.

White light flashed as the energy bolt exploded from the rifle and air screamed in protest as it was rudely pushed aside. The bolt crossed the distance to a fifty-five-gallon metal drum sitting twenty meters away in less than a heartbeat before tearing into the container's side, the drum's cylindrical exterior shredding and collapsing under the force of the assault.

"Okay," she said, "key the radio."

Behind her, Corporal Eshelman stood with one of the PRC-77's nestled in his left arm. Holding its handset, he pressed the transmit button and held it down.

"Go for it," he said.

Nodding in reply, Russell raised the pulse rifle and took aim again, this time at a nearby tree. She was not surprised when, as she pressed the firing stud this time, nothing happened.

"Son of a bitch," Sloane said. "The radios. All this time, it was the damned radios."

Russell lowered the weapon as she turned back to the group. "Maybe it's the frequency, or just the power output of the radios themselves, but whatever it is, it's obviously jacking with their gear in a major way."

Stepping closer, Max indicated the rifle in Russell's hands. "Your communications equipment is not that powerful, at least in comparison to our own. Given that the internal fire control mechanisms of our weapons are shielded, I suspect that your equipment's ability to interfere with them is limited to short distances."

"That makes sense," DiCarlo said. "During the battle the Grays were shooting at us until they got within maybe fifty feet or so."

Standing beside him, Stakely asked, "Can we use this somehow? Maybe provide some kind of blanket or shield for us while we get everyone out of here?"

"I do not see how that would prove effective," Max

said. "If the effectiveness of your radios' ability is indeed limited, then you are still vulnerable to attack from a distance."

DiCarlo added, "And on the move that would be even worse than defending from an established position."

"We'd never make it out of here on foot," Stakely said, shaking his head. "At least here we have some chance of defending ourselves."

Russell noted a new quality in the lieutenant's voice. The arrogance that had permeated Stakely's demeanor before was gone, replaced by a quiet introspection that added to the newfound air of authority he had been forced to undertake in the wake of Captain Douglas's death. She felt more than a little sympathetic toward the lieutenant, as there was no way he could have predicted being thrust into command in this manner.

"Our best option," DiCarlo said, "at least for now, is to stay put and wait for the cavalry."

Gardner asked, "Do you think Lieutenant Westerson and the others made it out, Sergeant Major?"

"Of course they did," DiCarlo replied, his expression neutral as he retrieved another of his prized cigars from a pocket in his camouflage jacket.

Frowning, Russell regarded the veteran Marine skeptically. "How do you know?"

"Because if they didn't," the sergeant major said as he lit the cigar, "then we're screwed."

3:42.

Looking at the clock on the convenience store's far wall, Brian sighed in mounting frustration. At this rate, there was no way he was going to last until six o'clock without beating the shit out of Jeff.

I'm not even supposed to be here tonight, he scolded himself. *Why the hell didn't I fake sick when I had the chance?*

"Come on," Jeff said from where he stood in front of the coffee machines, wiping down the counter with a sponge, "you know it makes perfect sense."

Leaning on the counter next to the cash register, Brian shook his head. "JFK was assassinated because he threatened to go public about how the space program was a big hoax? How is that supposed to make sense?"

"Easy," Jeff said as he finished with the coffeepots and moved to clean the soft drink fountains. "Everybody knows that none of the Apollo astronauts ever really left Earth's orbit. The whole thing was bullshit from Day One. NASA scientists knew that the Van Allen radiation belt would kill anybody who tried to pass through it, but instead of just admitting that the Russian space program, pile of shit that it was, was still better than what we had, the government opted to keep the scam going. Kennedy didn't want that, and he sure as hell didn't want to give away money on a project that would never work, so they had him killed."

"That's ridiculous," Brian said, dismissing his coworker's theory with a wave. Though Jeff had started working here less than a month ago, it had taken him substantially less time to become annoying as hell.

Before Jeff's arrival Brian had enjoyed the quiet and mostly mundane atmosphere of the twenty-four-hour convenience store without a partner, but a series of holdups and robberies at other Neosho area stores in recent weeks had prompted this shop's owner to assign a second employee to the graveyard shift. While Brian worked the main counter and handled most of the store's customers, including working the gas pumps and selling lottery tickets, Jeff took care of the store's small deli and video rental departments. In this capacity he dispensed movies along with hot dogs and pizza slices, all packaged with his own peculiar and oftentimes irritating viewpoint on whatever topic tickled his fancy on a given night.

The conspiracy theories had started out simple and even amusing at first, with the usual topics that Brian had already heard about, such as UFO sightings or Elvis being alive and running a strip joint in New Orleans or some other such crap. If nothing else, the lively conversations that often ensued when Jeff revealed one of his theories helped to while away the early morning hours.

The fun had faded quickly, however, as Jeff's outlandish speculations branched out to include everything from the government murdering key witnesses in mob trials to aliens trying to control the populace by masking hypnotic messages in the soundtracks of pornographic movies.

"Of course, the reason that hasn't worked is because the aliens don't realize that everybody fast forwards through most pornos," Jeff proclaimed one memorable Saturday night.

Having finished cleaning up the store's self-service beverage area, Jeff moved toward the line of coolers along the store's far wall. "Think about it. The government puts up this massive smokescreen to make it look like we're pushing for the moon. Congress approves billions of dollars for research and development over a span of years, money that goes into the pockets of greedy government contractors who know they'll never be able to build anything that'll make it to the moon in less than twenty years." He stopped long enough to pull a pint-sized container of chocolate milk from the dairy cooler.

Rubbing his temples with his fingers, Brian said, "Let me guess. Kennedy's all against it, right?"

"Bingo," Jeff replied as he took a swig of milk. "He can't support this boondoggle, not with all the problems we have with poverty and disease and racial tension, but it's too late. Backs have been scratched and promises have been made, and too many dirty politicians stand to be embarrassed if Kennedy starts running his mouth. So, in a fit of self-preservation, Congress gathers in a secret session in the fall of 1963 and votes to give the C.I.A. approval to carry out his termination. They take him out, and spend the next seven years setting up the biggest fairy tale in the history of the world."

Brian rolled his eyes. "I saw that stupid special on TV showing how they supposedly faked the moon landings. You do know that the people who made it are the same ones who did that bogus alien autopsy tape, right?"

"Ah, you fell for the ruse," Jeff countered as he made his way back to the front of the store. "The government put out that hoax special to throw people off the track of the real proof that it was all faked."

"Where do you get this shit?"

"The Internet, mostly," Jeff said as he moved back behind the counter, sporting a thin line of chocolate milk above his upper lip. "It's amazing what you can find out there if you know where to look."

Ignoring Jeff's reply, Brian turned to see headlights flashing through the store's row of front windows. He looked up to see a white sport utility vehicle bearing the logo of a television station from the nearby town of Joplin, Missouri. The SUV pulled into one of the several empty parking spaces close to the store's doors before the driver killed the engine and extinguished the vehicle's lights.

Thank God. Rescued at last. His relief dissipated, however, as he got his first look at the man in the truck's passenger seat. *Fuck me. Why can't I be lucky and just get robbed like everybody else?*

Brian turned to the door as it opened to admit the man and woman from the SUV. Jake Simpson, asshole reporter for Joplin's Channel 12 News, did not hold the door for his camera operator, Stephanie Maguire. Both were regular customers during Brian's shift, like him preferring the night hours to working during the day. More often than not they were the first news people to arrive on a scene whenever something happened to disrupt the comfortable, humdrum atmosphere that typified life in this part of southwestern Missouri. More often than not their travels to and from the events they covered brought them by the store in search of coffee and, in Jake's case, cigarettes. While Brian was happy to see Stephanie, having admired the brunette's trim, athletic form for months ever since she started working at the station, he would be thrilled if Jake, all 280 flabby pounds of him, were abducted and probed by some of Jeff's aliens.

"Hey," Brian said as the pair stepped into the store. Both of them were sweating, Jake very much so, and dirt soiled their jeans and shirts, testament to the fact that they had been out on assignment. Despite her disheveled appearance, Stephanie somehow still managed to look attractive.

Jake still looked like an asshole.

Though Jake said nothing in the way of greeting, Stephanie smiled at him as she walked past on her way to the coffee machines. "What's up, Brian? I didn't think you were supposed to be here tonight."

"Oh man," Brian replied, glancing over to where Jeff sat, engrossed in the pages of a *Hustler* magazine while continuing to sip on his chocolate milk. "Don't get me started. What's going on with you? You covering that wreck tonight?"

"The one on Highway 60?" Jake asked as he poured himself a cup of coffee. "Yeah. Couple of kids in a Mustang crossed lanes and went head to head with a beer delivery truck. Didn't work out too great." He shrugged as he took a drink of his coffee. "Oh well. Looks like two more parking spaces for me next time I go to Wal-Mart."

Brian grimaced at the reporter's casual disregard for the lives that had ended in senseless tragedy. "Nice. Be sure to include that when you write up your report for the morning news."

Looking up from his magazine, Jeff said, "We heard about it here." He pointed to the counter in the rear of the cashier's area where his Radio Shack police scanner sat, as it always did during his work shifts. "Some of it, anyway. It's not working worth a damn tonight, though."

"Yours, too?" Stephanie asked as she poured her own coffee. "The scanner in the truck is acting all screwy, too, and the station's been reporting problems with their satellite feeds. Even the cable company's been getting calls all night. Pay channels that should be scrambled are coming in crystal clear, and vice versa. Parents are pissed off because their kids are turning on cartoons and getting the Playboy Channel. Radios, cell phones, everything's on the fritz and nobody knows why."

"Gee," Brian said as he cast a mocking look in Jeff's direction, "maybe it's a government plot."

Jeff wagged a finger at Brian without looking up from the centerfold of *Hustler's* Honey of the Month. "The truth is out there, dude."

Stepping up to the counter, Jake set his coffee down and reached for his wallet. "Well, it's irritating the shit out of me. Can't hear a damn thing, either from the cops or the station. Our remote feeds aren't working, either, so we had to tape our stuff from the crash scene. I've got about an hour to get it edited and ready for the five o'clock show."

"Oh come on," Stephanie said. "It's not as if there's going to be a line to get into the editing room. You've got the one interesting overnight story in this whole damned town, so quit playing the martyr. Jesus."

Jake glared at her. "It's a good thing you're the best camera jockey at the station or I'd fire your ass."

"You can't fire me, and besides, I'm the only one who's willing to put up with your shit," Stephanie retorted. "Now pay for my coffee. It's the least you can do for me making you look good."

When Brian and Jeff both chuckled at her response, Jake directed what he probably thought was a withering gaze at the pair of clerks. "What's so fucking funny?"

"Nothing but the wondrous ongoing saga that is the human condition," Jeff said, holding up his milk carton in a mock toast.

Jake scowled as he tossed a rumpled twenty-dollar bill onto the counter. "Smart ass."

Though listening to his coworker could be irritating at times, Brian actually smiled at the idea of having a front row seat as Jeff unleashed one of his patented verbal assaults on the hapless reporter. Journalism degree or not, Jake never stood a chance whenever he made the unfortunate mistake of entering into a vocal sparring match with the clerk. The one positive effect it did have was that it almost always made Jake leave the store in a huff, and that's what would have happened this time if Jeff's police scanner had not chosen that particular moment to blare to life.

"*Mayday Mayday Mayday! To anyone who can hear*

me, this is Lance Corporal Alan Guber! We've been at-
tacked and one of our people has been killed! We're on the
run and we . . ."

The frantic call abruptly stopped, but it was enough to
freeze Jake and Stephanie in their tracks. Jeff jumped
from his perch on the counter and rushed over to the
scanner to adjust its volume, but there was only static.

"What the hell was that?" Jake said, turning around
and heading back to the counter.

Jeff shook his head as he fiddled with the scanner's tun-
ing and volume knobs. "Got me. Whoever it was, they're
gone now. I don't know if it's because of whatever's mess-
ing with everything tonight or what."

"Was that a cop?" Stephanie asked.

"No," Jeff replied. "He said his name was 'Lance Corporal' something. That's a military rank. Marines, I think."

Brian nodded. "Yeah, it is. Remember? A group of
them are over at Growding this week. War games and stuff
like that." Several of the Marines had come into the store
the previous weekend, looking for ice to fill several large
coolers. They had told him about the training they were
undergoing. It had sounded almost fun to Brian, though
not enough for him to run out and enlist.

"He sounded like he was scared shitless," Jake said.

Frowning, Stephanie replied, "If they're doing war
games, then he could simply be acting out a part or something."

"What if he wasn't acting?" Jeff said, still attempting to
bring some kind of signal in over the scanner.

"Oh jeez," Brian said, sighing in dread of what might
be coming next. "Please don't."

Jeff looked up from the scanner. "Don't what? Who

knows what those jarheads are up to, hiding out in the woods like that? Could be anything."

"Gimme a break," Brian replied, for the first time actually considering one of the pint bottles of cheap whiskey shelved behind the cash register as a possible defense against having to listen to his seemingly borderline psychotic coworker.

Could he be right, though? Were the Marines, some of them at least, in trouble? The guy had said he was under attack, but by whom? Who would be stupid enough to pick a fight with a bunch of Marines in the middle of the forest?

He saw that Jake was nodding in agreement with Jeff, too. "He didn't sound like he was faking, and even if he was, it might still be worth checking out. Even if they are just pretending for some game, it could make a quick filler piece." Clapping his hands for emphasis he added, "Throw me the keys. I'm driving and you're getting your camera ready just in case."

"What about the crash scene footage?" Stephanie asked.

"We'll drop it off on the way," Jake replied, waving her question away as he headed for the door. "Gail or Gregg will take care of it," he added, referring to the two line producers for the weekend news broadcasts.

As he pushed the door open and headed for the SUV, Stephanie looked over her shoulder at Brian. They exchanged small smiles before she said, "Here we go again. Talk to you guys later."

"Be careful out there," Jeff offered as she left. Then, as the door swung closed he added, "At least he's gone. God how I hate that prick."

"Not as much as he hates you, I'll bet," Brian countered as he tapped keys on the register, the cash drawer popping open in response. He counted out eight dollars and seventy-one cents and put the money in his pocket before extracting the same amount and handing it to Jeff. "But on occasion, there is some small justice to be found."

"What's this?" Jeff asked.

"The change from Jake's twenty."

16

A nervous breakdown by one of her people was the last thing Teri Westerson needed.

"*Mayday Mayday Mayday!*" Guber suddenly said, shattering the near silence of the forest. "*To anyone who can hear me, this is Lance Corporal Alan Guber! We've been attacked and one of our people has been killed! We're on the run and we . . .*"

That was all the man could manage before Hudson grabbed the radio handset away from him. "Shut up, you idiot!" he hissed.

His eyes wide with panic, Guber said nothing more as all three Marines remained still, listening for any sign that they might not be alone. Westerson scanned the forest while sighting down the barrel of her M-16, the one that had once belonged to Matthew Shane. She had opted to carry the weapon after observing the limited effectiveness of her pistol against the alien soldier back at the Humvee.

When nothing hell bent on killing them erupted from the trees after two or three minutes, Westerson allowed herself to breathe as she wiped sweat from her forehead.

"What the hell is wrong with you?" Hudson said, glaring at Guber.

Shaking his head, Guber replied, "We're going to die out here."

Westerson grabbed the Marine by the arm, jerking him to face her. "Not if we keep our heads, Alan. We're almost to the road, and we're bound to run into somebody once we get there."

They had been making decent time moving through the forest, having seen no sign of their alien pursuers since the encounter at the Humvee. Though Westerson held no illusions that their luck would hold out forever, she was not about to question their good fortune to this point. Her gut told her that the Chodrecai soldiers would have attacked them within moments of leaving the wrecked vehicle. Perhaps they had stopped to pay some form of final respects to their fallen comrade. Whatever the reason, Westerson had no problem taking advantage of the respite, no matter how temporary it might turn out to be.

Behind her, the first faint hints of light were beginning to filter through the trees. None of them were wearing watches so she had no idea of the time, but she figured that they had been on the move for close to an hour. Though she had only been able to guess at their exact location based on where the Humvee had crashed, Westerson had spent several minutes examining her map of the reservation and getting their bearings. Unable to correlate any prominent landmarks as they moved through the forest, she had finally decided that their best option was to head due west until they reached the closest paved road according to the map. From there her plan was simple: Hitch a ride in the first car or truck they could stop and find the nearest phone.

While on the move she had heard the sounds of distant

gunfire and what sounded like the reports of the alien rifles coming from the direction where the camp should be. It appeared that the predictions of the Chodrecai attacking the reservists had come to pass and she tried not to dwell on how such a battle might have gone for her companions, even with the limited assistance of Max and his fellow Blue soldiers.

Turning back to her two companions Westerson saw that Hudson had taken the PRC-77 from Guber, slinging the field radio across his own back and clipping the handset to the strap of his equipment harness near his right ear.

"Ready when you are, Lieutenant," he said, his voice quiet and confident. Once again Westerson gave silent thanks for the young Marine's calm and controlled demeanor. She had seen the fear in his eyes that mirrored her own, but he had kept his head throughout the attack and their flight through the forest. Like her and for the sake of carrying out their task, Hudson was suppressing what he had to be feeling at the idea of being hunted by the alien warriors.

The next several minutes were spent in silence as the trio of Marines moved through the forest, taking care not to step on anything that might snap or push through any thickets or other foliage that could make noise and give away their position. Around her Westerson could see the shadows beginning to recede as dawn approached. In another hour the sun would be up and it was her fervent wish that they not be in this forest when that happened.

A sharp short hiss sounded behind her and Westerson froze, holding her breath as she listened. The sound was repeated and she turned to see Hudson, his M-16 up and pointed to his left. Using two fingers on his free hand he pointed first to his eyes and then into the forest where his rifle was aimed.

Enemy spotted.

There was no time to plan, no time to react as the first energy pulse destroyed a dense thicket less than four meters from her. The light from the blast nearly blinded her as she threw herself to the ground and scrambled for cover behind a large oak tree. She heard other whines of energy and was relieved when she turned to see Hudson and Guber had also found concealment.

"Shit," she heard Hudson say in a low voice. "I knew it was too good to last."

The next round of energy bolts tore through the forest in search of targets. How far was the road now? Not very far, Westerson guessed, but it might as well be on the other side of the planet if they had to fight their way through a gauntlet of alien weapons to get there.

Or maybe not.

Peeking around the tree she tried to see where their attackers might be. She did not hear any sounds of movement in the forest. Did that mean that the Chodrecai had taken up positions and were waiting for the Marines to reveal themselves?

Let's see about that.

"Hudson, Guber," she called out in as quiet a voice as she could muster. "Get ready."

Casting a quizzical look in her direction, Hudson replied, "Get ready for what?"

"Just follow me." Reaching into her pocket, Westerson extracted her cell phone. Damaged in the Humvee crash, the phone was useless to her now, good for not much else besides what she was about to do. Looking for some place free of obstacles, she cocked her arm and tossed the phone away. It struck a pine tree thirty feet away, bouncing off the bark and creating a racket as it landed heavily amid the dry leaves at the pine's base.

As expected an energy pulse exploded from the forest, aimed where the phone had landed and chewing into the soft bark and wood of the tree. More important to Westerson though, was that she saw where the shot had come from.

"Go!"

Rising from her crouch behind the tree Westerson let loose with a burst from her rifle. She did not even pause to see the effect of her shots as she charged forward. Firing sporadically as she ran she darted from tree to tree, never offering herself up as a target for more than a second or two each time. To her left she heard the sounds of heavy footfalls crashing through foliage and the sounds of other M-16s firing as Hudson and Guber mimicked her movements.

When she had first been taught the concept of charging through an ambush, she considered the idea to be little more than a suicide tactic, a last-ditch measure born of desperation when all else had failed. It was the wizened instructors at the Basic School in Quantico who had quickly set her and the other recently commissioned officers of her class straight.

The lessons had come back with startling clarity, too. She had already established the location of the enemy's position and gotten herself as well as Hudson and Guber out of the kill zone. Now her priority was leading her people in an attempt to counterattack. Westerson was counting on the Chodrecai aliens having selected a static position from which to launch their ambush. With luck it was a location that would be difficult to move from without exposing themselves to incoming fire.

A flash ahead of her made her drop to one knee. The now familiar whine ripped through the air as an energy bolt tore through a small tree to her right, the attack crossing barely three meters in front of her. If she had not halted her forward charge she would have run full on into the blast.

On her left and somewhat ahead of her she saw Hudson and Guber continuing to press forward, firing intermittently as they moved. They had pinpointed the aliens as well and were laying down suppressing fire as they maneuvered to thwart the Chodrecai ambush.

Westerson saw something rise up amid the bushes twenty or so yards ahead of her. The huge dark form could only be one of the alien soldiers. Leveling her rifle at the figure she pulled the trigger twice, sending six rounds screaming toward her newfound target even as she rose and started forward once more.

"They're pulling back!"

It was Hudson, calling out as he pushed forward with his own attack. Though she doubted that their bullets did any real damage, their attack was having the effect she had been hoping for. The alien soldiers had obviously not expected the Marines to stand up in the face of the ambush to say nothing of actually mounting an active counterassault. She could see first one then another of the Chodrecai abandoning their positions and turning to seek other cover deeper in the woods.

They were close enough that she could hear the aliens' breathing, four of them turning to run away as she and her companions pushed forward. Westerson took aim at one of the enemy soldiers and fired, the three-round burst taking the Chodrecai high in the back. One of the rounds hit the warrior in its right arm and the alien grunted as its weapon fell from its hands. It tried to retrieve the rifle but Westerson fired again, this time striking the alien in the leg. The creature's growl was a mixture of pain and anger as it turned and plunged deeper into the cover offered by the forest. Regarding the scene around her, she realized that the other aliens had fled into the woods as well, leaving only the Marines to look askance at one another.

"Everybody okay?" she asked, to which both Hudson and Guber nodded in reply. Running to where the alien had dropped its weapon, Westerson dumped the one she had been carrying since recovering it back at the Humvee and exchanged it for this new one. So far as she had been able to tell, this particular model had not experienced the same malfunction as the one she had picked up earlier.

"I don't believe this shit," Hudson said even as he continued to watch the surrounding forest for signs that the Chodrecai might be returning. "Somebody tell me I'm dreaming."

Hudson had a point, Westerson decided. How long would this turn of the tables last? Surely the aliens would regroup within minutes, but she had no plans to be here long enough to find out.

Stephanie Maguire was sure she was going to die.

"Slow down!" she snapped, holding on for dear life as Jake Simpson guided the SUV down the narrow, unlit service route encircling Camp Growding's outer perimeter. The reporter had apparently failed to notice that they had left pavement behind miles ago, decelerating only slightly as the truck moved onto the service road's unimproved dirt and gravel surface.

Getting onto the Camp Growding reservation had been simple enough, with no gated fence or guard checkpoint to pass through. Even with the heightened state of alert that had come with the terrorist attacks of 2001, bases like Growding simply had no real military value, other than as training locations. Any sort of sensitive military property or information was instead confined to more secure bases used by the active forces, leaving reservations like Growding to act as little more than members-only recreational parks.

Heeding her pleas, Jake eased off the accelerator and Stephanie heard the truck's engine throttle back. Beyond her passenger-side window the trees no longer whipped past them in a chaotic blur. "Sorry," Jake said. "I guess I got carried away."

"What the hell for?" Stephanie asked, making no effort to disguise the irritation in her voice. "The way you're driving you'd think we were on our way to cover an assassination or a plane crash or something. You know how shitty the roads are here. You want to blow out a tire?" Looking up from her camera and leveling a menacing glare at Jake she asked, "For your sake I hope you're not thinking of pulling what you tried the last time you brought me out here."

Jake blinked several times, glancing over at her for second or two before returning his eyes to the road. "Don't worry. I haven't forgotten what happened last time."

Good, Stephanie thought, smiling in satisfaction. It had been over a year since Jake and Stephanie had come to the National Guard reservation, supposedly for Jake to spend some time shooting a feature piece about Army reservists and their preparations for deployment to Afghanistan.

The assignment had been a scam on Jake's part, his real motivation being his desire to spend time with Stephanie herself. She had not taken kindly to the unwanted advances and she had made Jake aware of that in no uncertain terms. According to his own disconcerted testimony, it had taken three days for the pain to fade after she had done her best to kick his testicles to Mars.

She allowed herself a marginal sigh of relief before turning her attention back to the bulky video camera lying across her lap. The unit was fine, save for the fact that she had not been able to transmit any of the footage she had shot earlier in the evening back to the station. The same strange interference that had rendered the truck's police scanner useless had also affected the camera's remote video feed capabilities. If they did find anything out here, they'd have to transport the tape back to the station for editing, as they had done earlier with the footage from the car wreck.

"Something in that kid's voice," Jake said, changing the subject as he steered the SUV around a rut in the road, "he sounded scared, and I don't mean pretend scared." He shook his head. "I've heard 911 from people who were terrified, and that's exactly what he sounded like."

Though Stephanie had only heard the same snippet of the mysterious call picked up by Jeff's scanner, she had to agree with Jake's assessment. The voice of that man, Lance Corporal Alan Guber, had been laced with terror. In fact, she thought, he had sounded almost hysterical.

Checking her camera once more, she said, "I would've liked to have heard more, you know, just to be sure." The police scanner installed in the SUV had not picked up any more transmissions by the mysterious Alan Guber. She had no idea whether that was due to the strange interference that had been plaguing the unit all night or the simple fact that the man had stopped transmitting.

"Any luck getting through to the station?" Jake asked.

Stephanie shook her head. "Nope. My cell phone's screwed up just like the scanner." Could some kind of sunspot activity be to blame for the rash of problems affecting the different types of electronic signals? It had to be something like that, she knew, for radios and television and cellular phones to be affected all at the same time.

"Shit," the reporter said. "Well, we'll just have to go without a remote linkup. We'll tape whatever we find and hope we can make it in before the morning show's over."

They drove for a while in silence, with only the static of the useless scanner and the wind whipping past the truck's windows. Off to the east the darkness was beginning to pale, with an orange glow just visible through the trees. The sun would make its first appearance within the hour, she knew. Back at the station, the anchors for the Saturday morning news broadcast were having their makeup applied and their hair styled in order to look their best as they greeted Neosho's early risers. The question on her mind now was: Would she and Jake find something out here that would be worthy of pushing aside the normal fodder which passed for much of the morning's alleged "news" stories?

The sensation of deceleration made Stephanie look up and she saw that the truck was indeed slowing down. In fact, Jake was bringing the SUV to a halt.

"What?" she prompted.

Jake held his forefinger to his lips, signaling for her to be quiet. "Listen," he whispered.

At first she only heard the sound of the truck's running engine through the open windows, but then there was something else. Popping noises, interlaced with something else. Some kind of high-pitched whine, sounding off in short disjointed beats.

"That sounds like gunfire," she said, "at least, some of it. I can't make out the other thing."

"Me neither," Jake replied, "but it's over there somewhere." He pointed into the forest ahead of them and on his side of the road, the side that led deeper onto the base. "Sounds like some kind of firefight, if you ask me."

Without thinking about it, Stephanie positioned the video camera on her shoulder and let the unit's lens hang out the passenger-side window, a quick glance telling her that the camera was ready to record as soon as she pressed the button. "It could be the Marines playing their war games," she offered.

Jake said nothing as he eased off the brake pedal, allowing the truck to coast forward. His attention was focused beyond the confines of the road, watching the trees that were becoming more distinct with each passing moment as dawn approached.

"There," he said suddenly, pointing again. "See that?"

Following his finger, Stephanie peered into the forest. She saw flashes of light amid the trees, swearing that they were in sync with the odd whines she was still hearing. There was more gunfire, too, a lot of it.

Jake stomped on the gas. "They're coming this way. Hang on." The trees raced past the window again as he guided the SUV, keeping only part of his attention on the road as he continued to watch the trees. He was right, the strange lights, and the sounds of gunfire, were getting closer.

The trees on the left side of the truck fell away as a clearing opened up in the forest. Wasting no time, Jake spun the steering wheel to the left and the SUV careened off the road and into the clearing. Once again Stephanie held on as the truck bounced across the uneven terrain, with Jake steering frantically to avoid holes, rocks, or any other obstacle that loomed in the vehicle's headlights.

"Start taping!" he shouted as he guided the truck in a circle so that within seconds the forest was on her side. Needing no further prompting she aimed the camera through the window again and let the unit autofocus on the forest before it. The clearing was perhaps fifty yards deep, with three-foot tall grass filling out most of the open area.

More of the flashes lit up the forest, and then Stephanie saw movement. Figures dashed through the trees in her direction. Seconds later she saw the first of the figures, a person wearing a camouflage uniform and carrying what looked to be a rifle. The soldier, if that was what he was, halted as he broke into the clearing and looked right at her, or rather toward the truck. She saw him wave in her direction before turning back to the forest.

"This way!" she heard him yell. "Hurry!"

Seconds later two more camouflaged figures appeared from the forest, one of them a woman, and then the trio was running for the road. They each looked over their shoulders and one of the men even turned to fire his rifle back toward the trees.

"Jesus!" she heard Jake exclaim. "Are you getting this?"

Stephanie was all set to unleash a sarcastic reply to the idiotic question, but her response was forgotten forever as she caught sight of something else moving from the cover of the forest in obvious pursuit of the three soldiers.

"Oh my God."

17

As she ran, Teri Westerson felt her heart pounding in her chest and thought her lungs were on fire. Even though she exercised regularly, scored the maximum number of points on the Marine Corps' semiannual physical fitness test and considered herself to be in damn fine shape, the extended exertion of sprinting through the forest was beginning to take its toll.

Guber was several yards in front of her and Hudson was bringing up the rear. If either one of the Marines was feeling similarly exhausted, neither one of them was saying anything. How much longer could they keep this up? The question taunted her but she felt a surge of hope as, ahead of her, she thought she saw a break in the trees. Could that be the perimeter road?

It has to be, her mind screamed at her.

"Come on!" Guber shouted over his shoulder. The now familiar sound of a Chodrecai pulse rifle punctuating his call, and Westerson heard him cry out in reaction to the shot. Fear was evident in the young Marine's voice, the stress of the running firefight eating away at Guber's nerves. For all she knew he could be on the verge of a total breakdown. If that happened then the

Marine stood almost no chance of surviving even the next few minutes.

Westerson heard M-16 fire and turned to see Hudson taking aim at one of their pursuers. Three bursts echoed through the forest before she heard the telltale click of the rifle's bolt locking to the rear.

Uh-oh.

"I'm out," Hudson called as he dropped the weapon and turned to run toward her again. Like Westerson he still had his nine-millimeter Beretta in its holster on his hip, but both Marines knew that the pistols' stopping power was much less than an M-16. It only accentuated just how desperate their situation was rapidly becoming.

Behind her, she heard the sounds of unrelenting pursuit. The quartet of Chodrecai warriors were bounding through the forest with uncanny speed and agility, but Westerson had noted how they kept their distance, not daring to venture too close even though they pushed the chase forward. Could the aliens be spooked by the Marines' ability to endure to this point? It was easy to sympathize with that feeling, because Westerson herself had no idea how they had managed to make it this far. The question now was how they would make it the rest of the way.

One possible answer, she realized, was bumping against her shoulder blade right now.

"Here," she called out as she tossed her M-16 to Hudson. The Marine caught it on the run and immediately turned to face their pursuers as she pulled the alien pulse rifle from where it was slung across her back. Studying it in the dim illumination offered by the moon, she saw that it featured an elaborate sighting mechanism that Westerson knew she had no time to figure out. The only thing she needed now was to know how to fire the damned thing.

Something flashed ahead of her on the right and she jerked her head up in response. Had one of the Chodrecai managed to get in front of them somehow? Then she saw the twin points of light moving on a straight line beyond the trees.

A car!

"This way!" she heard Guber yell again. "Hurry!" Looking in the direction of his voice Westerson saw that the Marine had indeed broken through the forest and onto open ground, some kind of clearing that teemed with overgrown grass. Beyond him, she saw the headlights of the vehicle careening off the road as it turned and came to a lurching stop.

Alien rifle fire erupted behind her again and she turned to see Hudson dodging for the meager cover offered by a medium-sized oak tree. All around the Marine energy pulses tore into the forest undergrowth as he huddled for protection near the base of the tree. The aliens were getting bolder, she decided, almost certainly having seen the arrival of the car out on the road and wanting to prevent the Marines from escaping.

Over my dead body.

Locating what passed for the trigger on the alien rifle in her hands was not difficult, and she hefted the weapon to rest it on her hip as she aimed it in the direction of the Chodrecai attack. Bracing herself for the anticipated recoil, she pressed the firing stud.

The rifle bucked against her hip but Westerson managed to keep it steady enough as the first energy pulse ripped through the foliage. She kept her finger on the trigger as she swept the muzzle of the weapon back and forth, laying down a deafening blanket of suppressive fire that Hudson used to abandon his meager place of concealment.

"Get to the road!" she shouted over the cacophony the rifle created as she began to step backward, retreating toward the clearing.

Instead of heeding her order, though, Hudson instead stayed alongside her. Holding his M-16 in his right hand he grabbed onto her equipment harness with his left. Westerson felt herself pulled first in one direction and then another and realized that Hudson was guiding her around trees so she could keep her full attention on their attackers. Much to her relief the Chodrecai seemed to be reacting to the violent barrage she had unleashed by taking cover, at least for the moment.

"Okay," she said to Hudson, "let's get out of here." Both Marines turned and sprinted for the clearing.

Guber, surprisingly, was there at the tree line as they emerged. Though his expression was one of near panic he had waited for his companions, his rifle out in front of him as he scanned the forest for signs of pursuit.

"Go go go!" she shouted to him as they cleared the trees, forcing herself to run faster now that she was out on open ground. Ahead of them the lights of the vehicle, a white SUV, beckoned to them. She saw a woman leap from the passenger side of the truck, holding something on her shoulder.

A camera? Are you shitting me?

Hope rose within her, though, as she saw the woman toss the camera to the ground and run for the rear of the

SUV. Throwing the vehicle's rear door open she turned to wave to the Marines.

"Come on!"

Weapons fire exploded from the forest and Westerson ducked, hunching over as she continued to run. Dirt spouted in all directions as the ground to her right exploded. Risking a glance over her shoulder, she saw movement behind her. The aliens were making a final push.

"Get in the truck!" she called to Hudson and Guber as she turned toward the attack once more, firing the pulse rifle as she spun about. Energy ripped through the tall grass and again the Chodrecai soldiers scattered. She hit one of the aliens in the chest, knocking it off its feet and sending it crashing to the ground. It was enough for Westerson as she turned to run for the truck once more. She saw Hudson and Guber waiting for her at the SUV, both men trying to cover her escape with their own weapons.

"Let's go, Lieutenant!" Hudson called before something caught his attention. He jerked to his right as another of the alien warriors emerged from the grass, no more then twenty feet in front of him. Hudson fired two quick bursts, the bullets striking the Chodrecai in the head and the alien went down.

Westerson hit the truck at a full run, diving through the open rear door and landing heavily on the SUV's carpeted interior. Her knee slammed into the door jam and pain jolted through her leg but she ignored it, scrambling inside the truck as Guber, Hudson, and the woman followed suit.

"Go!" the woman yelled even as the driver stomped on the gas pedal and Westerson could hear grass and dirt spinning out from beneath the truck's tires as it surged forward, its engine whining in protest.

Then gunfire boomed through the SUV's interior as Hudson fired through the still open rear door. "Get down!" he yelled between shots as the truck itself rocked under the impact of an energy bolt. Westerson heard glass shatter and felt the vehicle pushed to one side as the pulse slammed into it. Both Guber and Hudson fired their rifles dry as the SUV picked up speed and hurtled down the service road, leaving their remaining pursuers behind.

"Somebody tell me what the fuck is going on!" the man behind the steering wheel barked.

Trying to catch her breath, it took a moment before Westerson could respond.

"Believe me," she said between ragged breaths, "you're not gonna believe me."

No!

Raegyra could barely contain his rage as he watched the vehicle speed away, hopelessly outdistancing his ability to give chase.

The creatures had, once again, succeeded in eluding him. How was this possible? Everything he had observed about these beings since first setting foot in this strange land had convinced him that they were inferior by any sense of measurement, but there was no denying their tenacity, will to survive, or simple good fortune. That much had been evident throughout this entire pursuit.

Has the Leadership underestimated these creatures, whatever they are?

Have I?

His own poor judgment had already cost him three of

his subordinates, two of them with one of their own weapons. That alone proved that the creatures were capable of adapting quickly in the face of adversity. Experience had taught Raegyra long ago that such a trait was not to be dismissed out of hand. It was not uncommon for an enemy who found themselves fighting for their very survival to accomplish far more than if they initiated the battle themselves. He had seen similar resolve displayed by his own people countless times since the War had begun.

But are they truly our enemy?

It was a question that had no place in the mind of a soldier, but it was also one that Raegyra could not ignore. He knew that any concern regarding the creatures should be contained to assessing their threat potential and their ability to aid the Plysserians. Having engaged them in battle, he was certain that they presented more of a hazard to Chodrecai interests here than first believed. Was that because they truly posed a threat, or simply because they were defending their homeland? What if the bulk of the inhabitants here harbored the same instinct for self-preservation that this small group had displayed? What if there were others who possessed even more, along with the weapons or physical prowess to carry out their will?

What then?

18

"Come on, lady," Jake Simpson growled again as he guided the SUV down the road, "you gotta tell me something. What the hell were those things? Why were they shooting at you? What kinda rifle is that you're carryin'?"

"Like I told you before," Westerson replied, "I really don't know who they were." She tried to adjust her sitting position in the back of the SUV, though it would not do to get too comfortable. Given the events of the past several hours and the fact that it had been more than a day since she had last slept, the hum of the truck's engine and whine of the road beneath its tires would have no trouble lulling her to sleep.

The mission's not over yet, she reminded herself.

"Not *who*," Simpson countered. "*What*. Whatever the fuck those things were, they weren't human, so what were they?"

Exchanging looks with Hudson and Guber, she shook her head at the two Marines, a silent reinforcement of her earlier order for the men not to answer the reporter's questions. She had managed to deflect Simpson's line of questioning throughout the fifteen or twenty minutes they had spent in riding in the truck, so she figured she could continue to do so until they reached the headquarters building at Camp Growding's main post. The last thing she wanted to do at this point was discuss what might be lurking in the forest surrounding Neosho with this reporter. God only knew how Simpson would react, and she did not want to risk the reporter doing anything that might plunge the small and ultimately defenseless town into widespread panic.

Still, though, Westerson knew she should tell him something, if only to secure his cooperation long enough to get them to the base headquarters. Simpson and his companion, Stephanie Maguire, had saved her life and the lives of Guber and Hudson. Guber certainly seemed to think so, as he had thanked the TV station employees no less than two dozen times in the past fifteen minutes. For her part Westerson was happy to see that the young Marine's panic seemed to have abated somewhat. She had been genuinely worried that he might crack under the unrelenting pressure of the chase.

"They were aliens, weren't they?"

It was Maguire, who until now had confined most of her inquiries to checking up on the Marines' condition. She had asked about the strange altercation they had stumbled across but for the most part had deferred to Simpson and his own pathetic attempts at interrogation.

"It has to be, right?" she continued. "Those guns they had . . ." She pointed to the pulse rifle laying beside Westerson. "Where did you get that one?"

"She shot its owner and took it," Hudson replied, stone-faced. Westerson glared at him even as he added, "So I wouldn't screw with her if I were you."

Maguire shook her head, her expression one of astonishment. "Incredible. I wouldn't believe it if I hadn't seen them with my own eyes."

"We wouldn't have to worry about your eyes if you hadn't dropped the fucking camera," Simpson snapped, growling as he guided the truck down the road. "The story of all time dropped into my fucking lap and I don't have any fucking evidence because my fucking cameraman dropped her fucking camera." He smacked the steering wheel with the heel of one meaty hand. "Fuck me."

"Listen, you idiot," Maguire countered, "in case you missed it, those things were shooting at them, and us. How great would the story be if somebody else got to report how the aliens torched your fat ass?" The look on her face told Westerson that there was most definitely a history here between these two people, probably something along the lines of Simpson trying to get into her pants and Maguire not appreciating such overtures.

"It doesn't matter, anyway," Simpson said, talking more to himself than to any of the truck's other occupants. "We'll get Johnny and that goddamned news chopper over here, find those bastards, and light them up in time for the noon newscast."

Moving forward so that she was directly behind the truck's front seats, Westerson said, "I don't think that's a good idea. If you go on the air reporting about aliens shooting up the woods around town, people are either going to think that you're crazy or else they'll panic. Somebody could get hurt if that happens."

Simpson snorted. "This is news, lady, and as soon as I have footage of those freaks I'm going on the air. People have the right to know what's going on in their town. Besides, can you imagine the press coverage we're going to get once this gets out? Shit. I'll be able to write my own ticket. This time next month I could be anchoring a desk in New York. Probably get my pick of networks." Casting a wry look at Maguire he added, "You start treating me nice, and I might convince them to let you come along with me."

In response Westerson drew her service pistol from its holster, made a show of pulling the weapon's slide back and letting it slam forward with a loud metallic snap, and placed its muzzle behind the reporter's right ear.

"I don't think so."

Maguire's gasp of surprise made Westerson regard the camera operator with a sympathetic look. The lieutenant had not wanted to take such drastic measures, but the simple fact of the matter was that she was tired and hungry and most of all terrified at the idea of what the Chodrecai presence here might mean. It was also obvious to her now that Jake Simpson was becoming a liability to the accomplishment of her current mission. He seemed to be just fool enough to incite chaos in the name of bolstering his own obviously mediocre existence by telling the people of Neosho that their sleepy little midwestern town was the new home of an alien invasion force.

Guber sat up straight in response to her action. "What the . . . ?"

"Lieutenant?" Hudson asked, uncertainty clouding his own features.

"Hey now," Simpson said, holding one hand up in a gesture of surrender even as he continued to guide the SUV down the road. "I'm not looking for trouble here. I'm just doing my job, you know." Westerson felt the truck starting to slow down, no doubt an involuntary reaction on Simpson's part to having a gun put to his head. She could sympathize with him and probably would, but later. For now she indicated to the reporter to keep driving.

"Look, I know you're only doing your job, but you don't have a clue as to the magnitude of what's going on here. To be honest, I'm not even sure that I do. I'd like to tell you more but I don't really know enough about what's going on myself. My orders right now are to report my unit's situation and get instructions while attracting the least amount of attention possible, so that's what we're going to do. Understand?"

"Yeah, yeah! I get it!" Simpson replied with no small amount of fear in his voice.

I hope he's not going to have a heart attack, Westerson thought, *or wet himself.* While the reporter seemed to be battling panic, Westerson noted how his partner, Maguire, appeared to be enjoying the reporter's predicament. The small, satisfied grin on the woman's face spoke volumes.

Sighing, Westerson added, "Look, you took a risk when you hung around that clearing long enough to save us. I'm grateful for the risk you took. Believe me when I say I don't want to hurt you. I'd rather you continued to help me instead."

Simpson was nodding so fast it appeared for a moment that his head might fly off and ricochet around the SUV's interior. "Okay, okay. Deal. I just want one thing."

Frowning, Westerson replied, "What?"

"An exclusive."

Built in 1941, Camp Growding's heyday had come during the latter years of the Second World War, when it played home to nearly fifty thousand U.S. Army troops. In addition to providing basic training for soldiers who would thereafter be sent to Europe to fight, the base had also been the primary training center for the Army Signal Corps. Growding also had the distinction of being one of thirty-two such camps scattered throughout Missouri that had collectively held thousands of German and Italian prisoners of war.

In addition to the National Guard presence here, the Marine Corps Reserve maintained a training detachment as part of its ongoing military education program for enlisted reserve personnel. A good portion of the base's "mainside" acreage had long ago been sold to local businesses eager to modify existing buildings or replace them with their own more modern facilities. In fact, the civilian presence dominated this part of the once bustling Army installation. Only a small cluster of five buildings near the post's main gate, all painted the same uniform white with gray trim and situated in a semicircle around a flagpole that as of yet boasted no flag, even hinted at a military presence. None of the buildings appeared to be occupied.

"Where the hell is everybody?" Hudson asked as Jake Simpson pulled the SUV up to the main headquarters building. No civilian vehicles occupied spaces in the parking lot. Only a lone Humvee sat in a space marked for TACTICAL VEHICLES ONLY.

Westerson shrugged. "Well, it's not even 0600, and it's a Saturday. There's really no reason for the place to be packed with people. On the other hand, somebody is supposed to be on duty around the clock when any of the training ranges are in use." That had been made clear at the initial briefing for the training exercise even before the reservists had left Kansas City. The duty office in the headquarters building possessed a field radio in order to keep in communication with those training areas that did not have phone service. In the event of any sort of emergency, procedure called for the National Guardsmen on duty to be notified.

Wait until they hear about our little problem, Westerson mused.

Leaving Hudson to watch over a supportive Maguire and a still whining Simpson, Westerson and Guber entered the lobby of the headquarters building. The lights were on and a check of a directory hanging on one wall told them where the duty office was located. As they made their way down the main corridor of the two-story building's first floor, the heavy footfalls of their boots echoed on the dingy black and white linoleum tile, further accentuating the feeling that the place had been abandoned. No lights shone beneath closed doors. No one appeared in any doorways to greet them or wandered the hallway in search of early morning coffee.

"This place is like a tomb," Guber said as they approached the door to the duty office. Like all the others along this corridor it, too, was closed, though a handwritten sign on a piece of yellow legal-sized paper proclaimed that the room's occupants would BE BACK @ 0730.

Westerson tried the handle, confirming her suspicion that the door was locked. "Shit."

"Maybe they went to Denny's for breakfast," Guber offered. "The hell with them, Lieutenant. Let's just find a phone and get on with it."

Nodding in agreement, Westerson drew her Beretta. "You're right." She fired two rounds into the metal handle of the doorplate, shattering the lock as the echoes of the gunfire washed over the confines of the passageway.

"Well," Guber said, "that's one way to go."

Westerson kicked the door and it swung open, revealing the office's sparse contents. A single battered gray metal desk with three equally drab chairs, a single military style bed with plain white sheets and an Army-issue green wool blanket constituted the room's furnishings. Papers lay scattered across the desk, several of them sporting a brown ring no doubt imparted by the stained coffee cup currently sitting atop a pale green notebook. Occupying one corner of the desk was a computer, its screen saver a scrolling starfield simulating the viewpoint of a spacecraft in flight. A multiline phone sat next to the computer.

"Lieutenant!"

Westerson and Guber turned at the sound of running footsteps to see Hudson and Maguire coming down the hallway, towing a red-faced and huffing Simpson along with them. Hudson had his pistol in his hand and a worried expression on his face.

"It's all right," Westerson said, holding up a hand to reassure them as they ran up to them. Indicating the now open door with a nod of her head she added, "I had to pick the lock."

Hudson smiled appreciatively at the unorthodox tactic. "Whatever works for you, ma'am."

"There's nobody here?" Maguire asked.

Westerson shook her head as she stepped into the office. "They left a note that said they'd be back, but I don't feel like waiting."

"Who are you calling?" Simpson asked, still gasping for air after the exertion of running from the parking lot.

"Our superiors back in Kansas City," Westerson replied as she pulled a slip of paper from the pocket of her uniform; Lieutenant Stakely had given it to her and on it was written the number to the duty office for the 24th Marines. "Hopefully they'll know who to talk to about all of this." Being a Saturday, the unit's administration and other offices would be closed and she would need the reservist on duty to patch her through to the home of the commanding officer, Colonel Arnold Hawking.

She dialed the number and listened to three rings before the phone on the other end was picked up and a voice said, "24th Marines. Corporal Bridges speaking." Westerson quickly identified herself and explained her need to talk to the commanding officer. Thankfully, Bridges seemed to grasp the urgency of her request, placing her on hold while he made the call to the colonel's home number. Nearly a minute passed with her listening to nothing before there was a click followed by a gravelly voice.

"Hawking." That was all the man could get out before Westerson began to lay everything out. Who she was, the unit to which she was attached, and of course the reason for her call.

It was as she was trying to complete a sentence that began with "We've been attacked by . . . well, we think they may be aliens of some kind . . ." that it happened.

Click.

"Colonel Hawking?" she said, but received only dead air in response. Then she heard a rapid staccato refrain of clicks. She repeated her call to the reserve colonel but heard nothing else.

Then she heard a new voice.

"Lieutenant Westerson," it said, its delivery cold, serious, and full of authority. "Your call has been transferred. You will make your report to me."

Westerson pulled the receiver away from her ear and frowned at it for a moment before replying. "Transferred? Transferred to where? Who the hell is this?"

The voice on the other end of the phone did not waver in tone, volume, or intensity. "Your call has been transferred to an office better suited to dealing with your problem. Colonel Hawking is being notified of this as we speak. Right now I need you to tell me everything that you know about your current situation."

"How the hell did that happen?" the question was out of her mouth before she could rein in the emotional outburst. How had her call been redirected? What the hell was this all about? Was somebody screwing with her? If so, how?

"All that will be explained to you at the proper time, Lieutenant," the voice said, maintaining that now infuriating cool demeanor. "For now, you will concern yourself with making your report to me and answering my questions."

A sudden chilling thought washed down Westerson's spine as she listened to the speaker on the other end of the phone.

They already know?

How?

Declaration
of
War

19

Ktrol watched as the pair of guards guided the prisoner to the chair that had been placed before his desk in the office that he had made his own. He said nothing, as no words were necessary. Everyone in the room, including the prisoner, knew why they were here.

Motioning for the guards to leave and ordering the door to be closed, *Nomirtra* Ktrol regarded the Plysserian scientist for several moments, saying nothing. To his credit the scientist returned the scrutiny without flinching. His eyes did not wander, his hands remained clasped and idle in his lap, and he did not offer any other sign that he might feel nervous or even fearful. Considering all that had happened since the Chodrecai arrival here, this reaction was a testament to the Plysserian's courage. Ktrol could not help but smile in admiration.

Not quite ready to begin this latest round of questioning, he once again allowed his eyes to scan the office's interior. It, and the laboratory it was contained within, had only been the property of the Chodrecai military for a few cycles now. He was not fond of the bland color schemes and useless personal effects dominating the room, but that hardly mattered to his current mission. His priority and attention lay with what else had been discovered in the depths of this once secret facility.

"Are you comfortable?" he asked finally. "Would you like something to drink?" The prisoner shook his head. Ktrol knew that other officers had not employed such courtesies since the Chodrecai had captured this installation and began interrogating those that had been found working here, but he was not concerned about the actions of his peers. War was messy enough, he had long ago decided, without deliberately doing away with simple acts of civility and even compassion when the opportunity to display such traits presented itself. That included, so far as he was concerned, the benevolent treatment of prisoners whenever possible and practical.

"This is our first interview, Dr. Hjaire, is it not?"

The scientist nodded. "Yes, *Nomirtra*, that is correct." Ktrol bowed his head in appreciation at the use of his proper rank. Hjaire was, according to the information obtained during earlier interrogation of other Plysserians, one of the lesser-experienced members of the science team who had been captured along with the wondrous equipment Ktrol and his soldiers had found. While Ktrol did not expect to learn anything new from him about the technical workings of the machinery, he had decided that spending some time with Hjaire and the others who had not yet been interrogated might elicit some unexpected bit of otherwise useful knowledge.

"The technology you and your colleagues have created is astounding," he offered. It was not a lie. He had watched in awe as Chodrecai scientists, brought in after the area had been secured, pored over the equipment and determined its purpose. "These passages that you have created, if they truly work as our scientists believe they do, could make all other forms of public transportation obsolete, to say nothing of their obvious military value. Certainly an accomplishment to be proud of, yes?"

Hjaire swallowed before replying. "We created the portals as a means of retreat to a safe haven for our soldiers. They needed a place to regroup and reorganize that could not be reached by our enemies." He swallowed before adding, "By you. Many such regions exist across the planet, but it would be next to impossible to get there by conventional means." He shrugged. "Our task was to create an unconventional means."

"Oh come now, Doctor," Ktrol said, smiling as he leaned forward in his chair. "Surely you realized the immense tactical potential of what you had wrought? The ability to deposit your forces into the most vulnerable areas of our territory in the blink of an eye is an offensive weapon we would have no hope of defending against." Seeing the troubled expression on the scientist's face he added, "There is no need to be fearful. You and your colleagues are to be commended for what you have created here. Considering how the War is going, it is only a matter of time before our enemy falls completely under our control. As you said earlier, it is a time for unconventional thinking."

It was a statement Ktrol would have made in total confidence prior to the capture of this complex. Now though, he secretly admitted to feelings of unease at the staggering turn events had taken with their discovery here. According to the information gleaned during earlier interrogations, the Plysserians had possessed the ability to create these portals for many cycles now. What he and his fellow officers had so far been unable to learn was just how many of these portal generators existed, and where they might be. How many Plysserian soldiers had successfully fled through the portals, and how long until they had reorganized and were prepared to set the next stage of their bold plan into action? Even as he sat here, talking amiably to Hjaire, Chodrecai forces were at this moment searching for more facilities like this one in a harried and even desperate bid to answer those burning questions.

"It must have been heart wrenching for you when the decision to destroy your creation was made," Ktrol said as he rose from his seat and made his way around the desk. He pointed out onto the laboratory's main floor, where the mammoth portal generation equipment took up much of the available floor space.

Hjaire and his fellow scientists had been in the midst of attempting to dismantle the machinery when the facility was captured, and had succeeded in destroying several key components. "We were duty bound to keep the technology from falling into enemy hands."

"Oh I understand the necessity of the action from a military standpoint, of course, but surely you must have felt almost betrayed at the idea, especially considering that your attempts have ultimately proven fruitless." It had taken most of the cycles since the installation's seizure for Chodrecai engineers to understand the equipment well enough to be able to supervise the repair efforts and to ensure that the Plysserian scientists did not attempt any further sabotage while being directed in their work.

Once the generator had been restored to full operational capability, Ktrol had wasted no time selecting teams of soldiers to travel through the portal and reconnoiter what lay beyond. If, as he suspected, the Plysserians had used these wondrous passageways as a last bastion of refuge, then his plan would be simple: Find their refuges and relay that information back to the Leadership. Perhaps fortune would smile upon him and he would be given the opportunity to lead an attack through the portal that would, if all went well, signal the inevitable end to the War.

It was a thought that brought a smile to Ktrol's face.

There was a knock on the office door and it opened to reveal one of the guards standing at attention.

"*Nomirtra* Ktrol," the guard said, "*Zolitum* Raegyra has returned and is anxious to make his report."

"Send him in," Ktrol said, waving the soldier into the office. As Raegyra entered the office and saluted, Ktrol was struck by the young battle squad leader's tired appearance. Dirt and scratches covered his body and his arm had sustained some sort of injury.

"Are you well, *Zolitum?*" he asked. "You appear wounded."

"It is a minor injury, *Nomirtra*," Raegyra replied. "I will tend to it after I have finished here. The information I bring cannot wait."

Ktrol nodded, admiring the soldier's dedication to his duty. "Very well. Raegyra. What have you learned?"

"There is more to these portals than we first believed, *Nomirtra*, much more. I do not believe that they simply lead to other parts of our world, but to another world entirely." As the young *zolitum* continued his report, Ktrol felt a mixture of doubt, apprehension, and excitement.

"Another planet?" he asked. "Is that possible?" It sounded too outrageous to be true. Such ideas belonged in tales of fantasy, did they not?

"The sky looks nothing like that above our world," Raegyra continued. "Vegetation is different, as are some of the animals we encountered, including a type of being like nothing I have ever seen here. They possess weapons and technology, and though it is somewhat lacking compared to our own, it is not ineffective." He went on to describe the casualties he had suffered at the hands of the strange creatures and their odd weapons.

It was an incredible report, to say the least. Part of Ktrol wanted to dismiss it out of hand as the ramblings of someone who had taken leave of their senses, but he knew that Raegyra was a competent soldier not given to such flights of fancy. It was one of the reasons he had been selected for the reconnaissance mission in the first place. Still, could Ktrol believe such a story?

Then he looked at Hjaire. The scientist was fidgeting now, obviously uncomfortable with Raegyra's report. Had he and his colleagues unleashed a power even greater than first imagined?

Ktrol turned his attention back to Hjaire. "What of this, Doctor?"

Slowly, Hjaire nodded. "It is true, *Nomirtra*, though it was not our original intention to accomplish such a feat. We truly were attempting to create a way to transport our soldiers from one location to another, it was only meant to do so on this planet." Sighing in resignation, he added, "Our miscalculation, while a wondrous achievement, has served only to embroil an innocent people in what should be our conflict alone."

That set a whole new line of thought into motion for Ktrol. With his own sense of agitation growing he turned back to Raegyra. "And you say these creatures have allied themselves with our enemies?"

Raegyra shook his head. "I am not certain, *Nomirtra*. They could simply be defending themselves against a threat to their own land, much as we once did. I do not wish to cast a summary judgment upon this people until more is learned about them."

Waving the observation away, Ktrol began to pace the width of his office, barely able to restrain his composure. "Such issues are not for soldiers to resolve, *Zolitum*. Our duty is to see to the protection of our people against the Plysserian threat. If that duty extends to protection against enemies of other worlds, as astonishing as that may sound, then so be it." Defending the Chodrecai people against aggressors from another planet? What a campaign that would be, and at the end, what then? Surely, there would be rewards beyond imagination for anyone who could engineer such a staggering victory.

His mind awash in the possibilities, Ktrol began to mentally compose the report he would make to his superiors, while at the same time contemplating how best to turn this uncanny situation to his own advantage.

Sunrise, along with the beginnings of a new day, had also brought with it a stark realization to Simon DiCarlo: Once again, he was at war.

He walked the compound, observing silently the aftermath of the battle that had taken place here mere hours before and seeing how the chaos had been replaced with a new kind of intensity. Marines and Plysserians stood watch at various positions around the camp, while others labored to reinforce the fighting positions hastily constructed prior to the previous attack.

Yeah, that's right. The previous attack, he mused. *Because you can bet your ass they'll be coming again.* DiCarlo knew that the Grays had been caught off guard by the stroke of good luck that had befallen the Marines, but there was no way he was going to count on something so arcane as radio traffic interfering with the aliens' weapons to aid them again. In addition to the preparations underway inside the camp itself, remote observation outposts were being established in the forest around the compound. With any luck they would provide the rest of the unit advance warning if the Grays or anyone else approached again.

As he continued his survey of the camp DiCarlo came upon one of the Navy corpsman, Petty Officer Lyle Acavedo. The medic was treating a Marine wounded during the fighting. DiCarlo felt his heart sink as he saw where the man's leg had been amputated below the knee, and Acavedo had placed a large dressing over the ghastly wound. The Marine, thankfully, was unconscious.

"I gave him a sedative," Acavedo said as he looked up at DiCarlo's arrival. "The wound was cauterized almost instantly by whatever it is those Gray guns shoot. Good thing, too, otherwise he probably would have bled to death." Grabbing his medical pouch, he rose to move to his next patient.

"How bad is it?" DiCarlo asked.

Shaking his head, Acavedo replied, "Sixteen dead. A few of them were hit so bad they can't be identified, so I've already got a detail getting a headcount and accounting for everyone in the group." He pointed to another Marine sporting a bandaged arm. "About two dozen injuries, none fatal but a few critical like his leg back there. He and a few others are going to need a medevac, Sergeant Major. There's only so much we can do for them here."

DiCarlo nodded in agreement. As bad as the casualty list was, he knew it could have been much worse. He held no illusions that only the Blues' aid had saved the reservists from total annihilation.

"I've got Russell trying to get us some comm," DiCarlo said. "Now that we know what's screwing the radio traffic all to hell she thinks she might be able to come up with a workaround. Between her and Westerson, somebody's going to find out we're here." He smiled reassuringly at the corpsman. "Believe me, I don't want to spend another second here, but right now our best option is to hang tight. If we try to move now, especially with our wounded, we'll be sitting ducks if the Grays come back."

"I'll tell you what," Acavedo said as he waved to a cluster of Marines seeing to their injured comrade, "when I was in Afghanistan, I treated more sprained ankles during Operation Anaconda than anything else. You have no idea how many guys lost their footing on those fucking mountain trails." He shook his head. "But at least then we were on the offensive, not like this shit here."

As Acavedo moved toward the group of waiting Marines, DiCarlo's attention was drawn to the sound of someone calling out from the camp's perimeter. He turned to see one of the Marines assigned to the cleanup detail running in his direction. Behind him came three Plysserian soldiers.

No, he realized, *not three.* Only two of them were Plysserian, but the third alien was in fact a Gray. Its hands had been secured with some sort of manacles, and DiCarlo could see that the dark viscous substance that passed for their blood stained its upper chest and most of its right arm.

"Sergeant Major!" the Marine called out as he drew closer. "We found him during our cleanup sweep. He's injured, but," he indicated the Blues with a wave of his hand, "they don't think it's serious, and they say he should be interrogated."

DiCarlo regarded the approaching aliens, his mind already racing with the possibilities. How much intelligence value did the captured Gray possess? Did he know anything or was he a grunt, given just enough information to carry out his immediate mission and nothing more?

There was only one way to find out.

"Find me Gardner and that alien buddy of his."

After the Gray soldier was secured to a cot inside the camp's main building, DiCarlo saw to it that one of the Plysserian medics had the chance to examine and treat its injuries. Satisfied that the alien's immediate needs had been tended to, he looked over to where Lieutenant Stakely stood observing the proceedings.

"We're ready to go, sir."

Stakely nodded. "Thanks." DiCarlo noted the look in the other man's eyes, seeing that the man continued to exude some measure of bearing and self-control. His private talk with the lieutenant appeared to have done some good. Stakely seemed to be projecting the proper calm and poise as befit his newfound position of authority.

He, and DiCarlo himself for that matter, could not afford the luxury of allowing themselves to lose sight of their responsibilities to the Marines in their charge. With Captain Douglas gone, it fell to Stakely to lead with confidence and surety, even if he truly did not feel it himself. It was DiCarlo's job to make sure that the lieutenant had the support he needed to carry out his duty, and that was precisely what he intended to do.

"Ask him why they attacked us," Stakely said to Max, who with Gardner had been standing by waiting for instructions. Max turned to the Gray soldier to repeat the question in the alien's own tongue.

DiCarlo noted that Max had fitted the prisoner with the same type of odd prosthetic that he and Gardner had been wearing, remembering how Gardner had explained that one of the primary military applications for the translation devices lay in its ability to facilitate interrogation with the enemy. As it was reasonable to assume that the Gray would not willingly submit to their questioning, why not dispense with the inherent difficulties of such a task and use the translator to get right down to it?

Gardner was still wearing the device that Max had given him, probably so that he could keep tabs on the progress of the interrogation. Given what he had been led to understand about the alien contraption and the demands it made on the young Marine, DiCarlo figured that Gardner had to be nearing the point of exhaustion by now. Still, though, he pressed on. There was no arguing the kid's sense of duty, DiCarlo decided.

"His name is *Zolitum* Djeltik," Gardner said. Seeing the look of confusion on DiCarlo's face he added, "From what I've been able to figure out, *zolitum* is rank for a soldier in the Gray army. It's sort of like being a sergeant."

After several moments spent talking to Djeltik in the Gray's own language, Max turned back to the group. "It is as you suspected," he said, his speech somewhat halting and indicating that his grasp of English was still a work in progress. "The scouting party that attacked you earlier reported your presence to their superiors. They fear that you have allied yourselves with us, and that you might alert others of your kind to our presence here. As far as they are concerned, the only way to preserve their security is to ensure your silence. You can be sure they will return."

"Of course they'll be back," DiCarlo said. "They may have been spooked by what happened to their weapons before, but that won't keep them away for long." He shook his head. "I wonder if Westerson and her team made it out okay."

"Maybe we should send another runner team out," Stakely suggested. "Just in case they didn't make it."

DiCarlo started to pace the room. "I don't think that's a good idea, sir. If the Grays know about us, then they know we'll be trying to get help. When they come we're going to need everyone we have to mount a defense." He sighed in resignation. "Like it or not, we're going to have to put our faith in Westerson to bring the cavalry."

His attention was drawn to where Max and Gardner were continuing to question Djeltik. "What are you asking him?"

Gardner turned from the Gray soldier. "He's trying to learn more about their primary mission here. After all, they came here looking for Max's people. They didn't expect to find us. Max says that the Grays captured the laboratory which created the portal that brought them here, and that several units were sent to determine how many Plysserians are here."

"Reconnaissance," DiCarlo replied, nodding. "Of course. Once they know your troop strength, they'll send that information back to their leaders on the other side of the portal. They'll send reinforcements, enough to wipe you out." He paused before adding, "I wonder what they'll do when they get a better idea of how many people are already living here."

Max replied, "Their discovery of you will certainly be part of their report. If they believe that you have befriended us, then they may very well decide to mount a campaign against you as well."

"They might find that easier said than done," Stakely said. "There are six billion of us on this planet, and most of us won't take kindly to somebody coming to fuck with us."

What passed for Max's brow wrinkled in confusion, the alien obviously not sure what to make of the lieutenant's words. "If by that you mean that the majority of your world's population will resist any attempts at invasion, that is a noble sentiment, but it may be futile. You forget that Chodrecai technology and weaponry, like ours, is superior to yours. If they are successful in capturing enough of our portal generator locations on *Jontashreena*, they will have the ability to transfer as many soldiers and weaponry as necessary to take over this planet."

"But you said they had only found one portal generator," DiCarlo said. "The one that brought you here."

Max nodded. "That is correct. So far as this soldier knows, ours is the only one that the Chodrecai have discovered. No doubt they are scouring our planet in search of others. I do not suspect that they will take any overt action until they can secure more of the portal generators, especially if they suspect that they might face considerable opposition by you humans."

"A sound tactic," DiCarlo offered, "if a bit on the conservative side. If it were me, I might be tempted to get a large enough force through the portal to ensure a foothold on this side. I'm assuming your armies have even larger and more powerful weaponry than the stuff carried by your soldiers."

"Yes," Max replied, "but they would face the same problem transporting it through the portal as I told you before. Much of it is too large to move through without first disassembling it."

Absorbing this, DiCarlo started pacing the room again. If what Max said was true, then they were facing only a small Gray force, and a tentative one at that.

How much time did they have before reinforcements arrived? Could the Marines here afford to sit idly by and allow the Grays to fortify their positions? He did not think so.

"We have to do something," he said. "As I see it we have one chance, and that's to prevent them from establishing a toehold on our side."

"That's insane," Stakely retorted, his air of self-control slipping somewhat. "How the hell are we supposed to do that?"

"The same way we defended ourselves earlier," DiCarlo replied. "With the help of Max and his friends."

Stakely's eyes widened in disbelief. "We got lucky, Sergeant Major, you of all people should be able to understand that. If we try to go head-to-head with these things, we'll be slaughtered. I think we need to wait for Westerson to call in reinforcements before we try anything like that."

Drawing a breath to make sure he remained calm, DiCarlo replied, "We may not have the time to wait, sir, and that's even if Westerson made it out. Until somebody shows up, we have to move forward as if nobody's coming. That means taking action now." Truth be told, DiCarlo did not fancy the idea of risking the lives of the reservists on such a daring plan. Their training simply was not adequate for such an undertaking and he feared that he was consigning more of them to the same fate as those who had died during the last attack.

They'll die anyway, if we wait for the Grays to come get us, he reminded himself.

"Max and his people know where the portal opening should be," he said. "We need to reconnoiter that location and find out how big of a force we're dealing with. If it's small enough, then we can launch our own offensive and capture that position."

Slowly, Stakely shook his head. "I still think it's a crazy idea, but it's better than waiting around for those things to come and finish us off." He exhaled audibly, attempting a weak smile. "I'm guessing you're thinking the same thing, right?"

"Pretty much," DiCarlo conceded. Turning to Gardner he said, "We're done here. Have Max tell his buddies to secure the prisoner. I imagine they'll know how best to do that."

"Aye, aye, Sergeant Major," Gardner said, rubbing his temples with his fingers, and DiCarlo got the sense that the young Marine was troubled. As Max led the two Plysserian soldiers and Djeltik out of the room, DiCarlo moved closer to Gardner.

"Something wrong?" he prompted.

Frowning, the lance corporal shook his head. "I'm not sure." He paused, casting a look in the direction of the aliens before continuing in a quieter voice. "It's just that I get the feeling that we're not hearing the whole story."

DiCarlo did not like the sound of that. "Whole story about what? From which one? The prisoner, or Max?"

"That's just it, Sergeant Major," Gardner replied. "I'm really not sure. There seemed to be a lot more talking going on between them but I couldn't keep up with all of it." He removed the alien translator from his head, breathing a sigh of relief as he did so. "Damn this thing hurts after a while. Maybe that's it. I'm tired and this thing is screwing with my head."

It sounded plausible enough to DiCarlo. He could only guess what kind of strain Gardner had been under these past several hours as he struggled to learn the aliens' language. Could that explain the man's unease, or was there still something more to this already bizarre situation that they did not know about yet?

21

Belinda Russell frowned as she studied the contraption that had once been one of her PRC-77 field radios. She had watched the unit's slow transformation over the past hour or so as the Plysserian soldier, who possessed a name that sounded as if it was eight or nine syllables long and had made her decide to shorten it to "Kel" for her own sanity, worked.

"Are you sure you know what you're doing?" she asked.

Looking up from the worktable he hunched over, Kel replied, "Yes, I believe I will be ready to test momentarily."

Assigned to help solve the problems plaguing the Marines' comm gear, Kel had wasted no time setting to the task. With Corporal Eshelman guiding him the alien had disassembled the PRC-77 in only a few minutes and had spent nearly half an hour inspecting its various parts. Russell was more than willing to let Kel work at his own pace, as it gave her that much more time to examine the interesting set of tools and components he had brought along to assist him. Though most were unrecognizable to her, she thought that given the opportunity to experiment she could discern the function of most if not all of the implements.

It made a sort of sense, as Russell had learned that Kel was the Blue equivalent to a comm tech. Like her, one of his primary functions was to ensure the operational efficiency of field communications equipment. Using his tenuous command of English, Kel had described Plysserian communications concepts well enough for Russell to be confident that their technology, while more advanced than anything on Earth, appeared to be governed by many of the same principles as the equipment she was familiar with. This allowed Kel to tinker with the PRC-77's innards with only moderate coaching from her and Eshelman.

"So how is this supposed to work?" asked Rebecca Sloane from where she sat at the comm shack's main worktable. The remainder of the radios sat atop the table behind her, silent and as useless as the one Kel was working on.

The alien did not look up from where he continued to make adjustments on the hybrid radio-whatever it was, constructed from some of its original parts along with several components Kel had provided. "The energy emitted by the portal's generation is more than enough to scramble any transmissions you attempt due to your equipment's comparatively weaker power output. We encountered similar difficulties ourselves, though not to the same degree." He pointed to the squat metallic box, no larger than a phone book, sitting beside the PRC-77's outer casing. Russell saw a length of thin cabling connecting the box with the radio, its nearly transparent exterior shielding an even thinner wire that glowed a warm blue.

"I have taken the power cell from one of our weapon

recharging units," Kel continued, "and modified its output so that it will operate your radio without overloading it. The unit's transmission output should be sufficient to overpower the portal's interference."

Russell smiled, shaking her head in amazement as she listened to the alien speak. "I can't get over how easily you're able to understand us. I know the translators you're wearing are helping, but still. It usually takes us weeks to even begin to understand the most basic conversations in another language." It was a far cry from most of the stupid movies and shows on television that showed every alien speaking better English than the actors playing the part of human characters. She recalled how long it had taken her to become conversant in a second language while in college and shook her head in envy at Kel. *Where the hell was that gizmo of yours when I was busting my ass in French class?*

Kel indicated the translator band he wore on his head with one massive finger. "As you say, our translators help a great deal in this regard. Makoquolax . . . that is, Max . . . has transferred everything he has learned about your language to us, but I confess that I was never very good at academics." Picking up one of the odd tools he had brought with him, he added, "I much prefer to learn by doing."

"On-the-job training," Russell replied. "Nothing beats it, that's for sure." Once more she smiled at the idea that despite their obvious physical differences and advanced technology, the Plysserians appeared to share many similarities to humans as well.

Listen to yourself, her mind teased. *You sound like one of your stories.*

And why not? Her mind had been conjuring the possibilities since first laying eyes on Max, and she had been both excited and fearful during the past few hours. There had been little time to write down any of the thoughts jumbling about in her head in her notebook before the attack, and afterward such frivolous ruminations had been forgotten.

Things were quiet now, at least for a little while. Though Russell knew that their current situation was still perilous, Russell found herself imagining the opportunities that encountering the Plysserians presented. What was their planet like? What kind of cultures defined their civilization? Every question begat uncounted others, and it took an almost physical effort to remain focused on her duties. Despite that, one thought continued to tantalize her.

Imagine the book you could write about all of this. Her mind wasted no time with a sobering response: *If you don't get killed, that is.*

A voice drew Russell from her reverie, and it took her several seconds to comprehend that it was not coming from either Sloane or Eshelman, or Kel for that matter. It was coming, she realized, from the speaker that had been attached to the jury-rigged PRC-77.

"What's that?" she said, turning back to the table where Eshelman was adjusting the radio's squelch and volume controls. A frown creased the corporal's face as he leaned closer to the speaker, working with his eyes nearly closed.

"I heard somebody," Eshelman said. Opening his eyes and looking to Kel he asked, "Is the mike reconnected yet?"

By way of reply the alien picked up the hard plastic handset and the twisted length of cord attached to it. He took the blunt, unpolished metal connector at the cord's far end and despite his massive hands plugged it into the radio's proper socket with a deft touch Russell found surprising.

Nodding to Eshelman he said, "You should be able to transmit now."

The Marine gave the radio's volume another small adjustment before keying the mike. *"Unidentified speaker, this is Corporal Keith Eshelman, United States Marine Corps. Do you copy?"*

Unlike what they had experienced with their radio traffic all throughout the night, the response that erupted from the speaker was so clear that the person talking may as well have been standing next to them.

"Corporal Eshelman: Be advised. We are inbound to your position, ETA four minutes. We have been apprised of your current situation and are here to assist. Have your commanding officer standing by."

Elation erupted in the comm shack as Russell and the others cheered in response.

"It appears that your companions were successful in summoning assistance," Kel offered, the alien's narrow mouth contorting into what passed for a Plysserian smile. Russell nodded in reply, a wave of relief washing over her. Eshelman for his part could barely contain himself long enough to answer back.

"You have no idea how glad we are to hear your voice. We're in some pretty big trouble here, and we . . ."

A burst of static from the speaker cut him off. *"Don't say another word, Corporal. This frequency isn't secure. Just have your C.O. standing by when I get there. Out."* Another squawk of static followed the terse response, leaving no doubts to anyone in the room that the conversation had been terminated.

"Who the hell was that?" Sloane asked. "And how the hell did he cut you off in midstream like that? You can't do that with these radios."

"I do not know," Kel replied. "But they are close to our position, judging from the quality of the transmission. While I was able to improve the ability of your equipment to operate despite the interference from the portal, I was not able to increase its range."

Further discussion was interrupted as a faint sound made its way through the thin aluminum walls of the building. It was a deep, rhythmic thumping, and it was growing louder.

"Helicopter," Eshelman offered, his smile widening. "The cavalry's here. I just hope it ain't the Air Cav. My father will never let me live it down."

Still looking at the radio, silently reviewing the curt exchange that had just occurred between them and whoever was coming, had their situation improved, or just become more complicated?

Outside, the attention of DiCarlo and everyone else in the compound was drawn to the sounds of the approaching helicopter, the steady thrum of its engine growing in intensity with every passing second.

"Think they're looking for us?" Lieutenant Stakely asked as he stood next to the sergeant major. "Maybe Westerson made it."

Nodding, DiCarlo replied, "Could be. I certainly hope so." He had been concerned for the safety of the lieutenant and the Marines who had accompanied her on the trip back to Mainside in search of a phone. Though he had been uncomfortable with the idea of risking such a small group to the dangers lurking in the forest around them, he knew that a daring course of action had been necessary for the possible survival of the entire unit. Westerson and the three Marines who had gone with her understood that as well, for they had been the first to volunteer for the mission.

And from the looks of things, they may very well have succeeded.

The very air was vibrating now and everyone looked up to see a large helicopter appear over the tops of the trees to the north of the compound. DiCarlo recognized it as a UH-1N Huey, the workhorse chopper that had been in the military inventory for decades. Though it had seen extensive use during the Vietnam War and for much of the 1980s, the various service branches had been gradually phasing the model out for years in favor of the heavier CH-53 assault helicopter and its variants. There was no disputing the reliability of the Hueys though, at least so far as DiCarlo was concerned, as he had taken more than his share of rides in them.

"The thing's armed to the teeth," Stakely said, and DiCarlo nodded in agreement. Configured for combat, it was carrying what looked to be either a SAW or a fifty-caliber machine gun mounted in the doors on each flank, as well as what he thought he recognized as nineteen-shot 2.75-inch rocket pods mounted forward of each side door.

"Yeah, but whose is it?" DiCarlo asked. Unlike most of the helicopters in the U.S. military arsenal, this one was not painted green or gray but rather a flat black, with no external markings of any kind. "It ain't a Corps bird, or Army for that matter."

He caught a glimpse of two men sitting inside the cockpit as the helicopter came in low, passing almost directly over the compound. Another man sat just inside the right-side passenger door, strapped in behind the machine gun stationed there. Whoever they were, DiCarlo decided, they meant business. The Huey continued on past the tree line to the south of the camp, heading for a clearing that the reservists had used to park their vehicles. It slowed but did not come to a hover, instead arcing down toward a fast landing in the knee-high grass. The pilot at the controls had to be a cowboy, or more likely someone with experience flying in and out of hot landing zones.

After taking the precaution of having Max keep the other Plysserians back at the compound for the moment, DiCarlo led the way to the clearing. He, along with Stakely and a group of curious Marines emerged into the clearing as the helicopter was powering down its engine. The door on the left side of the chopper opened and three people emerged wearing black combat fatigues and carrying an assortment of individual gear and weapons. All three men looked as though they spent a good deal of time in their local gym, including carrying themselves with that arrogant swagger DiCarlo had always found humorous. The man who was obviously the leader of the group had close-cropped blond hair and wore a pair of wraparound sunglasses with mirrored lenses. He was also chewing gum, an action that only added to the overconfident air he was affecting.

DiCarlo hated him immediately.

The three strangers took their time, sauntering through the grass to stand a few meters away. None of the men offered a handshake or any other form of warm greeting. The one who appeared to be in charge regarded Stakely, his cold expression enhanced by his sunglasses.

"Where is Captain Douglas?" he asked without preamble.

"He's . . ." Stakely began, but stumbled on the words. "He's . . ."

DiCarlo finished for him. "Dead. The lieutenant here is in command."

The new arrival appeared to accept the report as if being informed of a restaurant's daily special. "Very well," he said. "My name is Nichols, and I've been sent here to investigate your situation."

The blunt statement made DiCarlo blink. Where was the skepticism he had expected from anyone who might be briefed on the events of the previous night? Hell, he had been here and he could hardly believe it himself.

"Who sent you?" he asked.

Nichols turned his attention to DiCarlo. "The Pentagon." A small smile creased the man's features as he added, "I'm happy to report that we're here because of your Lieutenant Westerson."

"She made it?" Stakely asked, as cheers erupted from the other Marines.

Nodding, Nichols replied, "I haven't been given all the details, but I do know that some of our people are debriefing her and her team right now. They'll be returned to you once that's finished."

"Your people?" DiCarlo asked, frowning at that. "And who might that be?"

"Believe it or not, there's a group tasked with preparing for the sort of encounter you seem to have had here. We're not very big, and we tend to keep a low profile."

"You got here from D.C. pretty damned fast," DiCarlo said.

"We've been tasked with gathering as much on-site intel as we can get," Nichols replied, "and provide a tactical appraisal of the situation for possible military action." DiCarlo noted how the man neatly sidestepped the issue of how he had come to be here in such a short amount of time.

D.C. my ass.

Nichols continued. "According to Westerson you've

made friends with some of the aliens. I'm going to want to interview them and add any pertinent information to my assessment."

Stakely spent the next few minutes detailing what they had learned about both the Plysserians and the Chodrecai. He recounted the battle, particularly the details regarding the effects of the reservists' radios on the alien weapons.

When the lieutenant was finished DiCarlo asked, "What sort of action did you have in mind?"

"That'll depend on what other intel we can gather, but two mechanized infantry divisions are making preparations to head this way from Army bases in Kansas, and we've got stealths on standby from Whiteman." DiCarlo was familiar with the Air Force base east of Kansas City and the squadron of B-2 Stealth bombers headquartered there. During military operations following the terrorist attacks on the World Trade Center and the Pentagon, the bombers had flown directly to Afghanistan from Whiteman, refueling in midair along the way before attacking their targets. Afterward they continued on to an island base in the Indian Ocean where the pilots rested before making the long flight home.

"That's an awful lot of hardware on such short notice," DiCarlo said, an unpleasant thought beginning to tease the back of his mind.

Nichols shrugged. "I've been placed in command of this situation, Sergeant Major, and I've been authorized to utilize whatever assets I need to accomplish my mission," Nichols said. He looked to Stakely. "That includes your unit, Lieutenant, at least for the time being."

"Now wait just a damned minute," Stakely said, "My

people aren't qualified for this kind of thing. Shit, we're not even active duty."

"Seems to be that you've done well enough, judging from what you've told me so far," Nichols replied. "You should be proud of the way you've handled things to this point, and you're my best source of information right now. Besides, the less people who know about this right now, the better. Before I risk drawing public attention to a massive influx of military personnel and equipment, I need to be sure of what it is we're facing. My authority comes directly from the Pentagon, and your respective commanding officers are being notified as we speak. Like it or not, you're my starting lineup, at least for the short term."

Giving Stakely a moment to let that sink in, Nichols turned to the two men who had accompanied him and instructed them to begin inspecting the alien technology the Marines had so far recovered. Then he directed the still quite stunned Stakely to take him to see the Plysserian soldiers. As the group began to move off in the direction of the compound, DiCarlo remained where he was. Sergeant Bonniker, who had been part of the group silently observing the conversation, saw this and turned to step back toward him.

"Sergeant Major?" he prompted.

Frowning, DiCarlo exhaled audibly. "Something's not right here. There's no way they could have gotten here from D.C. and gotten all those assets mobilized as fast as he says he did, unless they knew something was up beforehand."

"Does seem kinda fast, now that you mention it," Bonniker replied. "You think they know more than they're letting on?"

DiCarlo nodded. "If they're government, then you can count on it. They could've been preparing for something like this for years. Maybe they're reacting to some kind of elaborate scenario." He shook his head at that thought. Conspiracy theorists had long suspected the government of covering up the existence of aliens visiting Earth, but it was something DiCarlo himself had never taken seriously.

"If somebody knew about any of this," he said, "that means they could've prevented the deaths of Captain Douglas and the others. Assuming I live past today, I'm going looking for that somebody, and God help that asshole when I find him."

Other than the long narrow table and the set of twelve chairs situated around it, the conference room lacked much in the way of aesthetic features. Most of the chamber was cast into shadow except for the area directly above the table itself, illuminated by a row of track lighting that cast a harsh glare over its polished surface. There was no artwork on the walls, and no useless trinkets or other decorations cluttering up display shelves. General Bruce X. Thompson preferred the sparse decor, for it tended to focus the attentions of anyone entering the room on the one thing he cared about: Getting answers to his questions.

"Where are we, Tommy?" he asked, glancing at his watch as he took his customary seat at the head of the table. It had barely been an hour since his last briefing, but he knew that several key events had transpired since then.

Sitting to Thompson's right, his second-in-command and friend Brigadier General Thomas Brooks leaned forward in his chair and consulted a file he had brought with him, the manila folder looking tiny in Brooks's massive ebony hands. Like Thompson himself, Brooks was an imposing man, his impeccable Air Force uniform tailored to fit the trim yet muscular physique he had maintained since his earliest days as an officer. A vast array of multi-colored ribbons above his left pocket rivaled Thompson's own collection, bearing mute testimony to a long and distinguished military career.

"Our operatives have been on site for just about forty minutes, sir. Mr. Nichols and his team have spent most of that time getting briefed as well as inspecting the extraterrestrial specimens and their hardware. From his preliminary report, what he's found is consistent with intelligence we've gathered from other locations in recent months."

Thompson shook his head. "It looks like those reservists stumbled into a shit pot full of trouble, didn't they?" Still, he and everyone around the table knew that the Marine reserve unit's discovery of an alien presence on Earth had given his group the best opportunity to date to study the potential threat they faced. "And you're telling me what they found down there jives with the other leads we've been following?"

"Yes, sir," Brooks replied. "The same type of disruption in electronic transmissions and the descriptions of the aliens themselves are consistent with sightings in Russia, China, and Great Britain, as well as recent reports from Tel Aviv, Seoul, and Eugene, Oregon. They fit the profile we've been building during the past twenty-eight days. With the overwhelming amount of information coming out of Missouri, I think it's safe to say that we're looking at some type of coordinated effort on the part of an alien species attempting to establish a commanding presence on our planet."

There was a quiet consensus from the other military officers and civilian advisors sitting at the table, the leadership caste of the small group known by its authoritative yet otherwise undistinguished title of United States Space Command, Operations Section 04-E.

Officially assigned as an assistant director of the Space Command, Thompson was second only to a civilian appointee who answered directly to the secretary of defense. In actuality, he was the director of Op04-E, or "4-Echo" as members referred to it, the top secret subsection of Space-Com tasked with investigating reports of visits to Earth by beings from other planets and the development of strategies on how to deal with such situations. Conspiracy theorists were certain that the "E" in the section's designation stood for "extraterrestrial," but like the group itself, it was a notion that had never been confirmed or denied by any government official.

Active for only three years, 4-Echo was in fact the latest incarnation of an organization that had existed since the creation of Project Sign by President Harry S. Truman in 1947, beginning its life as an impoverished and disrespected investigative arm of the United States Air Force. It continued to exist for decades as fodder for jokes and contempt by cynics and politicians who saw numerous other uses for the tax dollars being spent on such a ludicrous endeavor as hunting down little green men from Mars.

Nevertheless, 4-Echo and its predecessors persevered, rebuffing doubt and scorn all while quietly and meticulously gathering enough hard evidence of extraterrestrial existence to eventually convince ardent skeptics and, more important, elected officials who approved the group's funding. Working in shadow under a variety of names and missions, with teams of operatives located at military installations and hidden within the infrastructure of private corporations around the world, the group had evolved over the decades to become the leading authority on extraterrestrial activity.

In the bowels of the vast subterranean complex hidden deep beneath their Pentagon conference room, evidence and information detailing the reports of unidentified flying objects and strange beings filled entire rooms. Much of that vast storehouse of knowledge, itself only a portion of the total collection of data and artifacts recovered in the more than fifty years of the group's existence, had never been seen by anyone outside of 4-Echo.

Much of it never would.

"Teams are being dispatched to those locations for follow-up investigations," Brooks reported, "and our regional control centers are being activated as we speak. Military assets are being deployed to provide support as well. So far we've been able to move troops and equipment under the guise of normal repositioning or training exercises. That'll change if the situation continues to escalate, though."

Nodding at the report, Thompson looked toward the far end of the table where Nancy Spencer, one of his most trusted aides, sat. "Nancy, what's the story on how they got here? Is it true that no sort of ships have been found?"

"According to the report we obtained from the Marine lieutenant," Spencer said, "the first group of aliens, which Westerson called 'Plysserians,' arrived here via what they refer to as an interdimensional tunnel connecting their own world with ours. No ships or vehicles have been seen by any of the Marines, as far as she knows. The second group, known as the 'Chodrecai,' arrived via the same means, after apparently capturing one or more installations where the portals are generated on the aliens' own planet."

Spencer, a civilian, had been assigned to 4-Echo even longer than Thompson himself. Though she was only in her early forties, she carried herself with the confidence of someone much older and wiser. She was an attractive woman by any accepted standard of measure, dressed as she was in her dark pants suit and cream-colored silk blouse. Her brown hair had never, to the best of Thompson's knowledge, ever been seen by anyone outside of the taut, functional ponytail she preferred.

Not that any of that nonsense mattered to Thompson, who had long ago come to appreciate the woman's wide range of talents and expertise. It was her job to keep him updated on anything having to do with recovered alien technology. Under her tutelage he had learned more about extraterrestrials than anyone hoping to live a care-free life should know. She treated her enormous responsibilities with earnest, which was why Thompson valued her counsel second only to that of Tommy Brooks.

"From the lieutenant's report," Brooks said, "it looks as though these two groups are fighting each other. The Plysserians used the tunnels to seek sanctuary, a place to regroup. Westerson said that the aliens' intention was to be able to move to other locations on their own planet, not connect to a completely different one." The general shook his head and made no attempt to disguise his amazed expression. "One hell of a mistake, if you ask me. Kiss rush hour and airport security screenings good-bye." Nods of agreement from around the table greeted the flippant remark.

Leaning forward so that his forearms rested on the

table, Thompson said, "If this report is accurate, then we'll have to revise our contingency planning from the ground up, and pretty damned quick, too." He did not need to remind anyone in the room that none of the tactics developed over the decades in response to possible extraterrestrial attack dealt with anything resembling what they might now be facing.

First off, there was the revelation that the aliens spotted in Missouri and the other locations Brooks had given bore no resemblance to the majority of descriptions obtained by witnesses to alien activity dating back to the 1940s. Many of those statements portrayed extraterrestrials as diminutive and perhaps even fragile, rather than the robust and dangerous specimens described by Lieutenant Westerson and her subordinates. These aliens, by comparison, appeared to be unlike anything previously encountered.

Then there was the simple notion that the majority of strategies devised over the years involved defending against assaults from space. Thompson knew that many of those plans had even been created with the assistance of leading writers of speculative fiction, whose imaginations had fueled countless ideas for dealing with just such a situation. No one, with any degree of seriousness at least, had ever envisioned a scenario where aliens would simply appear out of thin air, arriving from their own planet via a cosmic gateway as easily as he might walk through the conference room doorway.

As if it really makes any difference, Thompson scolded himself. Most of the scenarios for dealing with an alien attack usually ended with Earth on the losing end. It was yet another snippet of information that 4-Echo had wisely chosen, in his opinion at least, to refrain from disseminating to the public.

"What about satellite imagery?" he asked. "Can we get any pictures of this tunnel, Nancy?"

Spencer consulted her notes before replying. "I've already requested a flyover, General. It should be in a position to give us something in about twenty-seven minutes. If something can be identified, it'll hopefully be enough to task all of our recon birds to look for similar openings, or whatever the hell they are, elsewhere."

"Given what we know so far, who wants to bet that there'll be something in the same areas Tommy listed earlier?" There were no takers, of course. "It's not what we know or what we're reasonably sure of that's bothering me right now, people. The reports we're getting are coming from areas that have at least a minimal human presence, but the world is a big place, and there are plenty of areas where humans can't or don't go. How many more of these tunnels are popping up for every one we know about? Just how many of these aliens are we talking about here?"

It was early enough that unchecked speculation was dangerous, Thompson knew. He and his people could do nothing except wait for the more detailed reports from Nichols and field operatives who had been sent to other locations around the world where trouble seemed to be brewing. From Westerson's statement, though, they could discern that the one group of aliens, the Chodrecai, seemed to be driven more than anything else by their desire to finish their war with the other group, the Plysserians. For the moment, the Earth appeared to be nothing more than the latest battlefield for these two armies, with humans apparently caught up in the conflict as unwilling bystanders and, in some cases, ill-fated victims.

Westerson's report indicated that the one alien race, the Plysserians, was benevolent, but would that last? If the situation became desperate enough as their war progressed, would these aliens turn on any humans unfortunate enough to be caught in the wrong place at the wrong time?

And what about after the fighting was over? Would the victor, whoever that turned out to be, be an ally or an enemy of the human race?

Brad Gardner sat up in his cot, awakening from troubled sleep. Glancing at his watch, he saw that it was nearly noon. He had been sleeping for almost seven hours, but it had been anything but a peaceful slumber.

Looking around, he saw that he was not alone. Marines occupied more than a dozen of the cots that had been arranged in two double-tiered rows in this, the large open room that comprised the main building's second floor. All of the Marines in the room save for him were bandaged in some manner, and a few had bottles of medication being fed intravenously into their arms as they slept. These were the fortunate few who had been wounded by the awesome power of Gray weapons and survived. Some of the Marines, he noted, were looking at him with various expressions of confusion and even unease.

What's going on?

Movement to his left attracted his attention and Gardner turned to see Max sitting on the edge of an adjacent cot. The rack's mattress and frame sagged under the alien's massive gray bulk as he regarded Gardner with what the Marine had figured out was what passed for a Blue expression of concern.

"Your companions were beginning to worry," Max said. "You were talking in your sleep."

Gardner frowned, shrugging as he replied. "I guess that makes sense, since I was dreaming." He shook his head. "Weird dreams, too."

"You were speaking in my language."

That made Gardner sit up straighter. "What?" he asked as he swung his legs off the cot and let his feet drop to the floor, the soles of his boots thudding on the concrete. He had been so tired that he had simply collapsed in the rack without even bothering to undress.

"Only some of your words were Plysserian, but it was enough to grasp my attention. It seems that your sleep is burdened by what you have learned about us."

Blinking away the last vestiges of sleep, Gardner nodded in reply. The dream had been more vivid than any other he had ever experienced, much of it born, he was sure, from the onslaught of imagery provided by the extended use of the translator Max had given him. The visions of life on the alien's home planet, of the war he and his fellow Plysserians had fought for so many years, were even now continuing to replay themselves in his mind. This, despite the fact that he had removed the translator hours ago and placed it with the rest of his discarded equipment at the foot of his cot. Were the images plaguing him simply a by-product of his exhaustion, or an actual side effect of the alien technology?

More so than the visions themselves, it was what they might represent that truly troubled him.

"Max," he said in a quiet voice as he leaned closer to his friend, "during the interrogation, I got the sense that the prisoner was afraid of you."

"That is a normal reaction for a prisoner to have," Max replied. "Would you not agree?"

Gardner frowned. "There's more to it than that, something you haven't told me." He shook his head, looking to the floor as if the answers to the questions nagging him might have secreted themselves between his feet. "This war of yours, there's more to it than you've told us, isn't there?"

Several seconds passed as human and alien stared at one another. Finally, though, Max nodded and Gardner thought he saw what might be an expression of resignation on his friend's face.

"My people started the War."

Though the simple statement was one Gardner had been half-expecting to hear, the words still drilled into him and his mind reeled with the implications of their meaning. He was speechless as he struggled to comprehend how this staggering revelation changed everything he knew and understood about the aliens that had, until now, been viewed as their friends and protectors.

"What happened?" he asked.

Max drew a breath, looking about the room to ensure that no one could overhear the conversation. Gardner saw that most of the injured Marines had settled back down, though a few still cast glances in his direction. No doubt they were still somewhat in awe at the sight of an alien sitting among them.

"You must understand," Max said, "that the War has existed on my world since I was a child. Even before it started the relationship between my people and the Chodrecai was a strained one. Our nations had been at odds with one another for generations. There was competition in industry, the discovery and refining of natural resources, and of course the inevitable political posturing as both sides endeavored to convince the peoples of smaller nations to accept their way of life.

"Most of the strain between the governments was due to the vast differences in our respective cultures. Whereas the Plysserian way of life focuses on the rights and freedoms of the individual, the Chodrecai government is much more monolithic, especially in the way it treats its people. Individuals are expected to sacrifice all for the greater glory of the society, regardless of the personal cost."

"Communism," Gardner said, though he shook his head as soon as the word left his mouth. He did not consider himself a student of political science by any stretch of the imagination, and knew that his comment was a gross oversimplification of what Max was trying to explain.

"While our government used diplomacy and the promise of mutual trade and cooperation to attract the support of smaller nations," Max continued, "the Chodrecai preferred the employment of military force to achieve their goals. They used their might to extend their influence across the world, annexing smaller nations and absorbing them. Smaller skirmishes ensued as our own armies tried to defend the independence of those who lived in the affected areas. Relations deteriorated as time passed, to the point that many believed war between our peoples was unavoidable. Our armies were poised to engage one another at the slightest provocation. I am told it was a very frightening time."

Gardner nodded. "Just like us and Russia." Whereas his parents' childhood had been one where nuclear war between the United States and the U.S.S.R. existed as a constant threat, the Cold War had been little more than a chapter in a history book for Gardner himself. The global conflict that many experts and futurists predicted would come before the close of the twentieth century had never materialized, and the ties between the two nations were stronger now than they had ever been.

"In that regard, your people have proven to be wiser than mine, my friend," Max said. "Your governments saw fit to exhaust every option in search of a peaceful solution, whereas ours saw things very differently. Fearing that the Chodrecai would one day launch an offensive against us, our leaders authorized a preemptive strike. A massive coordinated attack was launched against numerous Chodrecai military installations that were in positions to threaten sensitive Plysserian targets. Our soldiers were sent in with the information that the enemy forces were no match for ours." Pausing, Max exhaled audibly. "The information was wrong. The Chodrecai army, though not as advanced as ours, was still enough to hold back the brunt of the assaults due to superior numbers. What should have been a series of quick strikes against vulnerable targets soon devolved into all out war."

Gardner was only half-listening, but it was enough. Instead he was concentrating on the images that had been all but burned into his mind by his extended use of the translator. Scenes of battle flashed in his vision, with alien soldiers thrust into the chaos of a war they probably did not even fully understand.

"Days dragged into weeks," he heard himself whisper, "and months into years. War erupted all over your world." Horror engulfed his expression as he looked at his friend once more. "Dear God."

Soberly, Max continued. "Smaller nations, defenseless people that my government had wanted to befriend and protect against what we had been conditioned to believe was the Chodrecai menace, were crushed under the boots of both our armies. Whatever meager resources they offered were absorbed as the War raged. We fought the Chodrecai almost to a standstill, but at enormous cost. Everything we valued as a culture was abandoned." The last sentence came out as a tortured whisper. Gardner saw the pain etched in Max's face and thought he detected moisture at the corners of the alien's eyes. Did Plysserians cry like humans did, and for the same reasons? It seemed likely, he decided.

"Then the Grays started winning," Gardner said, "didn't they?"

Max nodded quietly. "After a period of fighting that caused massive Plysserian casualties on several fronts, the Chodrecai launched a series of daring yet highly successful campaigns on positions made vulnerable by the sustained battles. They broke through our lines with ease, and we soon found ourselves struggling to retain and defend territory that had been hard to win in the first place."

"They had you on the run," Gardner said, scenes of brutal warfare once again flashing in his mind. He winced in reaction to the savage imagery of soldiers dying in every possible horrific manner assaulting his vision. "But they didn't stop with just beating you back, did they?"

Max started to reply but stopped himself as footsteps echoed in the hallway outside the barracks room. Both he and Gardner looked up to see Petty Officer Acavedo enter the room and begin to check up on the wounded Marines resting in their cots. Once satisfied that the medic could not overhear them, Max returned his attention to his friend.

"The Chodrecai continued to press their advantage, exploiting our vulnerability and overwhelming any chance of a regrouping effort. Time passed and soon the entire tide of the War changed as they went on the offensive." He shook his head before continuing. "We underestimated our enemy's resolve and thirst for vengeance, my friend."

"Vengeance?" Gardner asked.

Instead of Max replying, it was another quiet voice from behind him that said, "Vengeance is a powerful motivator, especially in war."

Both Gardner and Max looked up to see Sergeant Major DiCarlo leaning against the nearby wall. His muscular arms were crossed in such a manner that Gardner could see a faded tattoo of the Marine Corps emblem adorning the tanned skin of his right forearm. The stub of a cigar hung from the man's mouth, unlit no doubt out of consideration for the Marines convalescing throughout the room. The sergeant major had entered the room and approached without either him or Max detecting his presence, proving once again that age had done as little to diminish the man's stealth talents as it had the rest of his tested combat skills.

Pushing away from the wall, DiCarlo pulled the cigar from his mouth as he stepped closer. "From what I've heard, the Grays definitely seem to have a case for retribution."

Both Gardner and Max rose from their seats at DiCarlo's approach and Max bowed his head formally in the sergeant major's direction, as much a gesture of respect as a salute would have been had DiCarlo been a commissioned officer. Gardner noted that Max let his eyes remain cast downward even after they had greeted the veteran Marine.

"So let me guess," DiCarlo said. "Months pass, then years, and all the while the war continues, except now it's about the Grays getting even with your people for all the trouble you've caused. After all, a war that went on as long as yours did before the tables were turned probably means that cities were destroyed and thousands if not millions of lives were lost, on both sides, right?"

Max nodded. "As battles waged back and forth, with each side repeatedly gaining and losing the upper hand, even the reasons for why the War began seemed to lose any sense of meaning. There was simply the fighting, only now it is not about ideologies or which way of life is better or even dealing with perceived threats by the other side. All of that was lost even before I became a soldier. Now it is about one thing: survival. With each passing year resources are becoming sparser. Food, fuel sources, even places to live that are free from the contaminants of weapons. There are areas of my planet, Sergeant Major, that have been rendered uninhabitable by the War, and will remain so for generations."

"Jesus," Gardner said, his voice barely a whisper. The scenes of such destruction had played in his mind, mostly during the dreams that troubled his sleep. To hear Max actually give voice to the visions that had haunted him sent a shiver down his spine, especially when he imagined just how close his own planet could have come to falling into a similar abyss of war and devastation.

Continuing to chew on his unlit cigar stub, DiCarlo

said, "The Grays have chased you here because they thought your armies had found places to hide and a new way to maneuver with those portals of yours. How long will it take them to figure out that they've found an entirely new world, ripe for the taking? We've done a fair job of screwing up this planet without a lot of outside help, but I'd bet that after years of war it's still more inviting than your home. What will they do then?"

Max was shaking his head slowly, and Gardner could almost sense the anguish radiating from the alien. "I honestly do not know," he replied. "Even as a simple soldier, pledged to obey the orders of my superiors, I realize now that what we have done here is wrong. You have to believe me when I say that your involvement in this affair is accidental. I would like to think that the Chodrecai would understand that as well, but I fear that the War has robbed them of their pride to such an extent that the only way they feel it can be restored is through our total defeat, and the defeat of anyone who might ally themselves with us."

The first tendrils of fear reached out for Gardner as another thought gripped him: Had the Marines allied themselves with the wrong side? Max and his fellow Plysserians had helped defend against the Gray attack, but was it because they truly regretted the humans' involvement in their affairs? What if the gesture had been made simply because befriending the Marines now meant the Plysserians would be in a better position to exploit the relationship later for their own gain, if and when the Grays were defeated? Earth would still be here, perhaps defenseless against the designs of whichever alien army emerged victorious from their war.

And what kind of war would that provoke? Earth was

composed of many nations and peoples whose cultural and political beliefs did not always mesh, but Gardner found it incomprehensible that such differences would not be set aside in order to deal with a common enemy that threatened the safety of the very planet. Such a war, he imagined, would be larger in size and scope than every conflict ever fought on Earth combined, with the stakes equally staggering: the possible extinction of Humanity.

"Why didn't you tell us this before?" he asked.

"Would you have been as willing to befriend us if I had?" Max countered. "I saw the fear in your eyes when you found me, and in the eyes of your companions. How would you have reacted to the knowledge that we were hiding from a war that had been started by our own government?"

It was DiCarlo that responded. "Before he answers that, I want to know something. If your side wins your war, Earth will still be here. For better or worse, those portals your scientists created have linked us together. So what happens to us if you win?"

Max nodded in understanding. "It is true that my people could also benefit from what your planet has to offer. Do not think that the thought has not occurred to me, or to my companions. Your world is lush and fertile and beautiful, much in the way our planet once was, I am told, but my people are not tyrants, Sergeant Major. We have been given strict orders not to harm any of your people, ever. I have to believe that such a directive also extends to after the War has ended. There is also the matter that you have come to our aid, just as we have come to yours. That will not be forgotten, you have my word on that. I can see my government coming to you for assistance, certainly, but not to conquer you. If that were to happen, then it would be against everything I've been taught to believe my culture holds dear."

"And what about the Grays?" DiCarlo asked.

The expression on Max's face turned worrisome again. "I cannot imagine the Chodrecai passing up the potential salvation to be found here. There is also the unfortunate fact that in their eyes, you have allied yourselves with us. After being victimized by us for so long, they will see you as simply another threat to be dealt with before they can enjoy final peace."

Gardner felt his blood chill at the words. The fates of Humanity and the Plysserians had been intertwined, regardless of what might happen, from this point forward.

The only question now was: Would the people of Earth stand by and allow fate to be dictated to them, or step up and make their own fate for themselves?

As he pressed the firing stud and felt his rifle's recoil, *Zolitum* Volaquiln pictured the effects of the energy bolt as it washed over the Plysserian warrior. In his mind's eye the power of the weapon tore through the enemy soldier's body, disrupting the flow of blood to vital organs and short-circuiting the nervous system and brainwave activity. The actual result of the attack was not as spectacular as his imagination depicted it, of course, but it was satisfactory nonetheless. The Plysserian fell to the ground, the last of the battle group to do so and signaling the end of what had turned out to be a woefully short battle.

"That was too easy," another soldier said, one whose name Volaquiln could not remember, though he had no trouble recognizing the cockiness and overconfidence of youth. He himself had displayed such traits during his early days of military service, but those feelings of arrogance had been tempered soon enough, ground out of him by the stark reality of the War.

Still, the young soldier was correct, the battle had been won far too easily. The Plysserians dispatched by Volaquiln and the other soldiers of *Lutna* Squad had displayed none of the prowess that their warriors were renowned for. Perhaps fleeing to this strange land had given them cause to grow complacent with the belief that they could not be hunted and had allowed their fighting edge to dull. If that was the case, then it stood to reason that other Chodrecai battle squads would enjoy similar success when they routed other enemy soldiers from the holes in which they had secreted themselves.

And what of this place? The landscape surrounding Volaquiln was unlike any place he had ever visited, even given the extensive travel he had undertaken as a soldier. Dense clouds blocked nearly all of the sun's rays, and the cold damp air chilled his skin, telling him that this area received frequent and inordinate amounts of rainfall. The ground, mostly dark soil interspersed with sparse and pathetic vegetation, was soft and gave slightly with each step he took, but not so much as to be treacherous.

During the briefing he and his fellow soldiers had received prior to entering the portal, Volaquiln had at first been incredulous at the idea that another world waited on the other side of the conduit. Even after arriving here and taking in the unfamiliar surroundings that stretched off in all directions as far as he could see, he still remained skeptical. While it was true that he did not recognize the plant life struggling to thrive in this uninviting terrain, there was still grass and the occasional shrub that looked similar to foliage back home. Further, his group had encountered no animals or higher forms of life that would provide more conclusive proof of what the Leadership claimed awaited them here. Though he was not as yet convinced of that, Volaquiln was open-minded enough to at least acknowledge the possibility.

We will find the proof, he mused. *Sooner or later.*

Footsteps behind him made Volaquiln turn to see his trusted second-in-command, *Kret* Nokal. Volaquiln noticed that his friend was wearing the combination earpiece/microphone component of his communications device. The unit's transceiver components were, like his own, cast into the ruggedized chest armor all of the Chodrecai soldiers wore, protecting the fragile units from the harsh environment of the battlefield.

"I have already sent out patrols to sweep the area," Nokal said. "No signs of other enemy activity have been reported yet." Indicating his headset he added, "You know that *Nomirtra* Padrijan will be waiting for us to send in a status report."

Volaquiln was unable to keep a sigh of resignation from escaping his lips. The officer in charge of his and four other battle squads would be breathless with anticipation for something that he could forward on to his own superiors. Padrijan was a slave to politics, a glaring truth made evident from the first day Volaquiln had reported to him for duty. The problem with Padrijan, Volaquiln had decided at that first meeting, was that the *nomirtra*'s priorities were focused on advancing up the ladder of authority and power at any cost rather than properly leading the warriors in his charge. As a common infantry soldier, Volaquiln was not concerned with such matters, but as a leader himself it was his duty to see to the welfare of those he commanded. So far, Padrijan's political agenda had not interfered with Volaquiln's ability to carry out his own duties, and with that in mind he was content to leave the officer to his higher aspirations.

Nodding to his friend he replied, "Let us not keep our master waiting." Regardless of how he felt about Padrijan personally, it was still prudent to update the *nomirtra* as quickly as possible. While Volaquiln and his companions had been out searching for proof of the Plysserians' presence here, Padrijan and his other battle squads had been hastily constructing a temporary headquarters at the mouth of the portal in preparation for the arrival of even more of their fellow soldiers. Defensive positions were being constructed at this very moment, including heavier weaponry in the event their enemy had managed to bring their own larger armaments and vehicles through the tunnel. Given the somewhat restricted size of the portal itself, it had been necessary to disassemble the larger equipment and rebuild it on this side of the conduit. Such procedures were long and tedious, and Volaquiln was thankful that Padrijan had chosen *Lutna* Squad to conduct the security sweep.

Retrieving his own headset from its storage compartment on the side of his chest armor, Volaquiln activated the comm transceiver when something else begged for his attention. "Do you hear that?" he asked but realized that Nokal was not listening to him.

"Something's coming," Nokal said before pointing into the sky. "There."

Definitely something mechanized, Volaquiln decided as his own eyes locked on a pair of dark spots among the gray clouds, moving on a straight line in their direction. The objects were approaching with great speed, growing in size with each passing moment. Already he could make out the narrow, tubular shapes with angular projections on either side. Though they were similar to aircraft he was familiar with, Volaquiln could tell that they were unlike anything in the Chodrecai military arsenal, or the Plysser-

ian air forces for that matter. He doubted they were reinforcements for the enemy soldiers he and his squad had
just decimated.

So who were they?

Even as he and his companions dropped to the sodden
ground, their only option for cover on the otherwise barren terrain, Volaquiln activated his comm and spoke into
the microphone near his mouth. *"Prime Base, this is
Lutna Squad Leader. We have unidentified aircraft approaching our position."* He realized that if the craft continued on their present heading they would fly over the
area where the portal opening was located, and passed on
that information as well.

"Acknowledged, Lutna," a voice sounded in his ear just
before the two strange craft screamed past overhead. Even
at the speed they were moving Volaquiln could still make
out various markings on their hulls, though he recognized
none of them. The brief look was also enough to confirm
that the craft were not anything possessed by any military
force he was familiar with.

A pulse rifle whined nearby and Volaquiln jerked his
head to see the young soldier, the one whose name he
could not remember, with his weapon pulled into his
shoulder and firing at the passing craft. Volaquiln had no
chance to react before Nokal pulled himself from his
prone position in the mud and ran to the subordinate, dispensing with niceties as he tackled the younger soldier
and sent both of them crashing to the ground.

"Idiot," Nokal hissed. "You risk giving away our position firing like that. Did you really think you could hit
something traveling so fast?" He slapped the subordinate
across the side of the head to emphasize his point.

Volaquiln was not so concerned with their inability to hit the unidentified craft as he was with the greater threat of disclosing their location to a potential enemy. With that in mind he concentrated on following the flight paths of the craft as they continued on toward where he knew the portal and Prime Base to be. What were their capabilities? Were his comrades at the new base ready to defend against this potential threat?

His questions were answered moments later as criss-crossing energy beams that he recognized as coming from mobile armaments dissected the gray clouds. One of the craft disintegrated in a massive fireball that lit up the dull sky. The explosion faded as quickly as it appeared, replaced with metal shrapnel that began to rain down to the earth below.

"Our friends appear to have finished their preparations," Nokal remarked as the remaining craft banked away in what Volaquiln recognized as an evasive maneuver. The pilot was obviously skilled, for he managed to avoid the second barrage of weapons fire tearing through the sky in pursuit.

Briefly.

The pilot never stood a chance, Volaquiln would realize later when he replayed the scene in his mind. As the odd vehicle came out of a turn in a desperate attempt to climb for greater altitude, two of the mobile pulse cannons traced its trajectory and fired once more, succeeding this time in catching the aircraft in a deadly crossfire. Like its companion moments earlier, the second craft succumbed under the force of the merciless onslaught, the remaining wreckage falling to the ground out of sight beyond one of the distant knolls.

"Whoever they were," Nokal said as he pulled himself from the mud, "they certainly did not put up much of a challenge."

Volaquiln was not so sure, though. Prime Base had almost certainly had the advantage of surprise. "They appeared to be a reconnaissance patrol of some kind," he said. "Assuming they follow protocols similar to our own, the pilots would have been in contact with their superiors. Those superiors are no doubt aware that the pilots are no longer transmitting, and it will take them little time to ascertain that their ships have been destroyed. They will return, and in greater numbers." That was a problem for *Nomirtra* Padrijan, and one that did not take away from Volaquiln's more pressing concern: the search for Plysserian fugitives.

Of course, what if it was discovered that the Plysserians had befriended whoever lived in this strange land?

What then?

Controlled chaos enveloped the atmosphere of Op04-E's Situation Center as Bruce Thompson entered from the door leading to his private office. All around the general both military and civilian personnel worked at the computer stations arranged in three tiered rows and situated in such a manner that anyone seated at the stations had an unobstructed view of the large map of the world dominating the room's far wall. Some of his people wandered the room, their eyes not focusing on anything as they carried on conversations via the wireless phone headsets they wore.

Other supervisors or directors might require a briefing to keep them apprised of the current situation every time they entered the realm where their people dwelled and toiled, but not Thompson. Years ago he had learned that the best way to do his job was to simply let his people do theirs. He preferred to stay out of their way while they worked rather than hover over them like some mother hen, knowing that they would come to him when they had something worth reporting. The current situation, regardless of its scope, was no different. Now more than ever, he realized, it was vital that his people knew they had his confidence in their abilities.

Surveying the floor, Thompson's attention moved to the map wall, which was in actuality a series of flat sixty-inch video screens linked together and configured in three rows of four. A map of the world was digitally rendered across the span of all twelve screens in multicolored vector lines across a dark background. Fiery red indicators illuminated various areas on the map, some of them having been added since Thompson had last looked at it. He noted that in addition to highlighted areas in southern Missouri, Tel Aviv, Great Britain, and eastern Russia, portions of South America, New Mexico, Australia, and even Skagway, Alaska, were now marked as areas of suspected alien activity.

"Satellite imagery coming in from Russia," Tommy Brooks said as he stepped around a computer console near the map. "Bruce, you need to see this." Nodding to the Army lieutenant operating the computer station, he indicated the map with his thumb. The lieutenant tapped several keys into her console and one of the screens toward the center of the map changed to display an image of a snow-covered landscape taken from high altitude. Without further prompting from Brooks the picture began to zoom in, depth and detail coming into focus with the aid of computer enhancement.

"The bird picked up signs of a portal opening in this region," Brooks said as Thompson moved closer, descending the stairs linking the tiers of computer stations until he stood next to his friend before the bank of screens. "Lucky break for us. The bird was originally supposed to take pictures of suspected mobile missile launch sites in Chechnya and its flight path brought it down from over Siberia. We had to get it retasked in order to get updated intel. This is its third pass over the area, and look what we came up with."

On the screen the quality of the image had been improved to the point that Thompson could make out rocks and trees contrasting against the snow. He could also see individual figures, more than he could easily count, deploying in what looked to be military defensive formations, though the configurations themselves were not ones he immediately recognized. The figures moving with speed and agility were not human, he knew, without having to hear the report from Brooks or his people.

"More weapons emplacements?" he asked, pointing to a group of six oblong shapes arranged in a semicircle several dozen meters from where the computer had designated the portal opening to be. Even if he had not already seen satellite photos of similar equipment being deployed at other locations, Thompson had studied enough high-altitude pictures of enemy and allied defensive positions to recognize antiaircraft weaponry when he saw it.

Brooks replied, "Looks that way, sir, the same as what we've seen in the Brazil and Australian locations. At this point we don't even know which side they're on."

"I don't care which side they're on," Thompson said. "Just get me detailed pictures of those weapons. I want to see the pimples on the ass of the alien sitting behind the damned things." In his mind, it was a prudent measure to learn as much about their newfound allies as well as their enemies. After all, he reminded himself: Today's friend could be tomorrow's adversary.

"Already got Imaging on it," Brooks replied, "but it'll take a few minutes." Shaking his head he added, "Preliminary estimates place almost thirty thousand troops on the ground, just in the locations we know about, and from the looks of things the numbers are continuing to increase. It's not just grunts, either. We're talking matériel, too. Crates, equipment, all sorts of shit we can't identify. More stuff is showing up with each pass a bird makes over a target area. They're digging in, Bruce."

On the screen the image began to break up as the satellite's orbital arc carried it out of range of the alien staging site in Siberia. Thompson paid it no mind, instead moving to the next item on his mental checklist that was growing with each passing hour.

"Tell me about England."

"RAF has scrambled a squadron of fighters," Brooks replied, "and they're en route to the target zone right now. ETA six minutes." He consulted the clipboard in his left hand before continuing. "This one started with two American hikers backpacking on the British moors. They reported seeing what they called a 'tear in the air,' and strange creatures emerging from it. They made a call to local authorities from a pub in one of the small towns scattered across the countryside there, which was intercepted by operatives in our British office. At our request, the RAF sent a pair of Tornados out to investigate, but the pilots reported they were taking heavy fire before all contact was lost." He gestured once more to the lieutenant at the nearby computer station. He added, "They did manage to get some good recon photos of the target zone, though."

Once more the center display shifted, this time to show a still photograph of another landscape. Unlike the imagery from Siberia, the terrain here was dark and foreboding. Often enshrouded by rain and fog, the moors were a stark contrast to the lush forests and farmlands that dominated much of the English countryside. The weather, though not nearly as unforgiving as that found in northeastern Russia, was still harsh enough that few people ventured out onto the desolate rolling hillsides. Long a source of fodder for stories intended to frighten small children and curious tourists, the moors had played fictional home to ogres, werewolves, and, perhaps most famous of all and the one Thompson remembered from his childhood reading, the Hound of the Baskervilles.

Wonder what Holmes and Watson would think about the moors' latest visitors?

"Damn," he whispered as the picture was replaced by another and then another, the image shifting every five seconds in a preprogrammed rotation. The pictures varied in angle and detail, mostly because of the velocity at which the planes taking the photographs had been traveling. Still, the digital imagery was superb enough that Thompson and the others in the room could easily make out the figures of alien warriors moving about the barren landscape.

Pointing to the screen as the picture changed again, Brooks called out, "Hold that one." Thompson did not have to turn around to know that the eyes of everyone in the room were now riveted on the image before them, which showed a trio of aliens. Their gray bodies were hardly distinct against the sparse pale vegetation which was all that thrived in the harsh weather of the moors. The aliens had been photographed in the act of firing their weapons, presumably in the direction of the two British fighter planes.

"Look," Thompson said as he pointed to one of the aliens. "No blue tattoos or other skin markings. That means these are the . . . the Chodrecai." He stumbled over the name, again. Shaking his head he added, "However the hell you say it."

At Thompson's direction the rest of the pictures were displayed, and this time it was he who ordered the rotation halted as his eyes fell on something familiar. It was a large, squat construct, with a flat base sitting on the ground and supporting what looked to be a cannon barrel. An alien stood at one end and another of the strange distorted areas projected from the other.

"Weapons turret," he said. "Like the ones in the Siberian photos." Thompson could guess what had transpired. The Tornados, probably flying at something much less than their maximum speed in order to capture the reconnaissance photographs, had apparently been easy prey for the alien weaponry. The British pilots had, in all likelihood, never stood a chance. "That probably answers who's in Siberia, and Australia and Brazil as well. How many of those things do they have?"

Brooks shook his head. "No way to know, sir. The Tornados only got one pass before contact was lost. If this group is following the same protocol as those in the other locations, then there are anywhere between six and ten emplacements at each location."

As he began to pace the length of the area in front of the map wall, Thompson studied the polished linoleum floor tiles that reflected even the Situation Center's muted lighting. The illumination levels in the chamber were intended to soothe the personnel who spent long hours hunched over computer screens and poring over reams of cold data, but they did nothing to help ease the tension knot forming right now at the base of Bruce Thompson's skull.

The situation was escalating as the Chodrecai continued to solidify their footholds at various locations around the world. How many more staging areas were yet to be discovered? How many thousands of alien soldiers were still in hiding, preparing for God knew what? Soon this state of affairs would spiral beyond the ability of Thompson and his people, as well as the other agencies working with them, to contain it. How long before word began to spread about the aliens' presence? Even the resources he commanded would not be sufficient to keep that from happening.

Fortunately, there was help to be found. Since its activation, Op04-E had enjoyed a mutually beneficial relationship with various intelligence agencies around the world, particularly Great Britain's MI6 or Secret Intelligence Service as it was otherwise known. In recent years accounts of UFO sightings had been on the rise in England and the surrounding regions, prompting intelligence officials to respond with the dedication of more resources to investigate the reports. Information was exchanged at regular intervals between the British and American agencies as new data came to light. Thompson was grateful now more than ever that the barriers between the intelligence assets in America and other countries that had been in place at the time of his assignment to 4-Echo had been removed. It did not take a genius to figure out that the current atmosphere of collaboration was their best bet for dealing with the alien threat.

"General Thompson," a voice called out from behind him and he turned to see a Navy chief petty officer standing up behind one of the consoles on the uppermost tier of computer workstations. "Sir, we're getting a call from MI6. The fighter squadron they've dispatched is approaching the target area. Contact in just under a minute."

Brooks looked up from where he had been conversing with a female Marine captain seated at another station. "We'll have telemetry for this. MI6 is piping us the transponder data from the planes." He nodded to the Marine officer and the digital image of the world map zoomed in to an area of southwestern England that Thompson knew represented the moors. Most of the area depicted on the twelve screens was black, but now a group of thirty-six red dots depicting the squadron of British fighters was superimposed across the graphic. The dots moved rapidly across the screens toward another grouping, this one a collection of gray indicators that had been rendered to illustrate the location of the aliens.

"Each plane is carrying twin twenty seven millimeter cannons and Sidewinder missiles," Brooks reported. "They'll make a parking lot out of that hillside."

On the map wall the group of dots representing the British fighter planes began to disperse, assuming what

Thompson recognized as standard attack formations. The gray dots were not moving, of course, their positions depicted in accordance with the latest satellite photography. Unlike the approaching fighter squadrons, no transponder, satellite imagery, or other means of intelligence gathering to update the computer-generated map was in place to monitor the aliens' actions.

One of the red dots abruptly disappeared.

Another quickly followed.

"What's happening?" someone asked, but Thompson already knew, a ball of ice forming in his gut as he watched three more red indicators wink out of existence.

"The weapons turrets," he said. "They're picking off the fighters like they're standing still." As a young pilot in Vietnam, Thompson had flown through hell storms of antiaircraft fire, emerging from all but one of those missions unscathed. What he was watching now was more effective than any kind of defensive barrage he had ever seen. Even as the remaining lights on the map began to scatter, another half a dozen of them vanished. Nearly a third of the Tornado squadron had already been neutralized, and the battle had been underway for less than a minute.

Behind him, Brooks stood at one of the computer stations, his attention divided between his console and the map wall. Thompson knew that his friend was monitoring transcripts of the comm traffic between the fighters and their base, which were being automatically generated via a computer recording the transmissions and sent to Op04-E via Internet connection.

"They're pressing with the attack," Brooks said. "The squadron commander is giving orders to regroup." Brooks looked up from the console and his eyes locked with Thompson's. "They haven't gotten off the first damned shot yet."

Thompson felt the grip of helplessness tightening around him, his breath quickening and his pulse pounding in his ears. The red dots silently winking out of existence could not begin to describe what was truly happening at the moment as, an ocean away, brave pilots were being killed as easily as an exterminator might kill a host of insects. Not only was he horrified at the massacre currently unfolding, but fear also clutched Thompson's heart at the thought of how any resistance to the alien threat would be answered.

Would even the efforts of Earth's combined military force meet with outcomes similar to or even more devastating than what was happening in England? All over the world the Chodrecai were at this moment continuing to fortify their positions, and the force being unleashed at the British fighters was the result of a mere few hours work. What would their defensive capabilities be like after a day?

A week from now, the aliens could be all but unstoppable.

It was that thought which continued to taunt Bruce Thompson as, on the map wall, the last of the red indicators faded away.

Simon DiCarlo had experienced several combat situations in the years following Vietnam, and during most of those engagements he had been on the side with the clear tactical advantage. On those occasions the opponents of the United States had usually been outclassed in nearly every military sense, from their weapons to their training to the morale of their soldiers. America had never been in the habit, at least so far as the public was concerned, of sending its sons and daughters into harm's way without more than reasonable belief that most if not all of those children would return safely. Naturally that had not always been the stark reality, but such proclamations generally made for good sound bites on the evening news, especially when uttered by politicians seeking the favor of a voting audience.

This time was different, of course.

How long had it been since he had maneuvered deep inside the territory of an enemy with the upper hand? Not long enough, DiCarlo decided. Still, the surrounding forest with its stifling humidity that caused sweat to run freely down his body and soak his uniform brought back memories of the hot, fetid jungles of Vietnam with a clarity he had not experienced in years. The thoughts brought others with them, though, recollections of sights seen and friends lost that he had no wish to revisit.

Though they had been the superior force on paper, American troops in Vietnam had taken little time to learn that statistics served little use in that country's hot, fetid jungle. The Viet Cong had proven to be more than a competent adversary, employing audacity and resolve instead of state of the art weaponry and tactics. What should have been a textbook case of establishing military dominance had devolved into years of near chaos, with guerrilla skirmishes taking the place of organized battle plans.

Whether it had been a simple matter of fighting on someone else's home turf or a case of massive underestimation of their enemy had been the subjects of debate for years following the end of the war. DiCarlo had always preferred to keep the matter in perspective: They had gone in overconfident, gotten their asses kicked early on, and had rallied enough to bring the war to a draw. With that in mind, he had been content to bury those experiences and move on, knowing that he was forever a changed person, and hopefully a better one, thanks to the stark lessons imparted to him in that faraway land.

Enough of that, DiCarlo chastised himself. *You've got work to do.*

With the alien Max and Gardner on point, DiCarlo along with Sergeant Russell as well as the mysterious Mr. Nichols had set out for the portal that had brought the aliens here. While finding the conduit was not a problem, getting there without being detected was something else entirely. Moving with stealth, the group had managed to avoid three Gray patrols, due in large part to Max's superior hearing, eyesight, and whatever other senses the alien employed to remain aware of his surroundings. DiCarlo did not care what the alien used, just so long as it worked. And it had.

"I'll be damned," Nichols whispered as he and the others looked down from their concealed position, giving the humans their first look at a doorway to another world. Though he had never considered himself a philosophical man by any means, DiCarlo still appreciated the magnitude of this moment. How would historians discuss the significance of this day years from now? How would they regard it? Would they lament, as he did right now, that it had come under such dire circumstances?

There was no denying that the portal was remarkable, though it still did not seem as impressive as DiCarlo imagined it might look. "It can't be more than three, maybe four meters wide," he said in a quiet voice while continuing to study the opening through a pair of field binoculars. "I can understand now what Max was talking about. There's no way they could get anything of any size through there without taking it apart first." As he watched, he saw another in a series of rectangular-shaped cargo containers they had observed appearing in the portal's aperture, simply materializing as if out of the very air. More matériel had arrived from the aliens' planet.

As for the portal itself, DiCarlo could make out no details of what lay inside or beyond it. Only a frenzied swirl of colors was visible, hinting at the tremendous energies harnessed to create the conduit and link it between two planets. How many uncounted billions of miles separated Earth from the aliens' homeworld? That, more than the portal itself was a staggering question and served to remind DiCarlo just how very insignificant he and the planet of his birth truly were when compared to the rest of the universe.

And what about the mysterious Mr. Nichols? Since arriving at the compound the man and his companions remained a total conundrum. Concentrating on learning as much about the threat potential the aliens posed, Nichols had offered almost no information about himself or his team. The most DiCarlo had been able to get out of the man was that he represented a classified government agency.

DiCarlo had encountered enough people like Nichols in his travels to comfortably guess that the agent had spent at least some time in the military, probably in a special warfare branch. That had almost certainly been followed by a stint in one of America's more mainline intelligence organizations before joining the unnamed outfit he currently represented. Nichols looked to be close to his own age, which presupposed that the man had seen action in some or all of the same conflicts as DiCarlo had, though he did not bother asking when it became apparent from the man's demeanor that Nichols was not the sort to engage in idle conversation, especially about himself.

Typical spook, DiCarlo reminded himself. *Get over it.*

The trio, along with the rest of their group, had secreted themselves among a line of foliage that formed a natural parapet at the edge of the plateau they had found. The highest point in this area of Camp Growding, it offered a spectacular panoramic view of several hundred acres of the reservation including the small valley below them where Gray soldiers moved about no more than a hundred meters away.

Lying on the ground to DiCarlo's left, Russell said, "If the other portals Max described are like this one, that could be a huge break for us if we can take advantage of it."

"I count at least fifty troops, and a shitload of supplies," Gardner said from where he lay next to Russell. "Looks like they're planning to stay a while." He pointed to a series of structures that looked to be tents and other temporary-looking buildings. DiCarlo nodded at the assessment, smiling grimly at how similar the deployment of the encampment reminded him of several of the firebases he had pulled duty at during his tours in Vietnam.

Dismissing that thought, he instead took note that all about the camp, many of the aliens were occupied with the contents of various cargo containers, either unpacking them or passing off items to their companions who were busy assembling a plethora of equipment, much of it unrecognizable to him. There was no mistaking the concerted work effort currently underway. It had all the feeling of what the reservists had done back at their own compound nine or ten hours earlier.

"Marauder," Max said from a few meters away, his voice low and just audible as he pointed down to something DiCarlo could identify. "It is a light assault vehicle." Three Gray soldiers were working on the chassis of what most likely passed for an alien all-terrain vehicle. Larger than the Marines' Hummers, it appeared capable of carrying only two passengers in its cockpit, with some form of weapons turret taking up the bulk of the vehicle.

"No gunner's seat," Russell said as she scrutinized the vehicle through her own binoculars. "Probably controlled by whichever rider's not driving the thing."

DiCarlo noted two other such vehicles in varying states of assembly as well as parts and equipment for still more of the LAVs before a flicker of energy caught his attention. He turned his head to see that the portal was closing.

"Without a generator on this side," Max said, "the portal can only stay open for brief periods without risking an overload. I imagine that once the area is secure they will either find the technicians we brought with us or else bring a group of captured Plysserian scientists through to this side in order to assemble the portal generator equipment that we brought with us." Shaking his head he added, "Once that is accomplished, they will be able to bring more soldiers and equipment through. They may even eventually find a way to expand the size of the portal itself, allowing them to bring larger equipment here. We will almost certainly be defenseless if that happens."

DiCarlo was only half listening to the alien, his attention instead focused on the encampment as he envisioned various tactical possibilities. "They have a decent layout," he said, "but it's not perfect. Not even considering that they're in a low-lying area that can be exploited from above, it's a big area and a lot of matériel to defend."

"They must have something else up their sleeve," Nichols said. Pointing to something else that was in the process of being assembled beyond the line of tents and cargo containers. "And I'm betting that's it." He indicated similar devices in varying degrees of construction along the outermost perimeter of where the Grays had established their camp. "Look, there and there. Those have to be defensive positions."

"Computer-targeted weapons," Max confirmed. "They are designed to track the flight path of attacking aircraft;

they are capable of responding to airborne threats much faster than any pilot might react. I suspect that your pilots and their attack craft will be even more vulnerable to those weapons."

Nichols grunted in mild frustration. "It's the classic role of a landing support battalion. Establish a beachhead before you bring the rest of your assets ashore, all the while maintaining a full blown repair and resupply point while the main fighting force expands its sphere of control outward. While all that's going on, they're receiving fresh troops and equipment through the portal, cycling the entire process over and over again. It's damn near perfect, and if this is going on at locations all over the world . . ."

"Then we're in deep shit," DiCarlo finished for him. "Our only chance is to hit these sites before they can get their antiair defenses online." He leveled a glare at the mysterious government operative. "Nichols, you need to get on the horn and order in a bomber strike or whatever it is you have authorization for, but something big enough to neutralize that camp." He pointed down to the Gray encampment for emphasis.

Nichols shook his head. "There may not even be time for that. Remember that my comm gear is just as hosed by the energy that portal's putting out as yours is." Despite the best efforts of Sergeant Russell and the Plysserian who had helped her and her team, they had been unable to completely defeat the jamming effects of the portal generator on communications and other electrical equipment. It would still be necessary to travel some distance away in order for the effects to ease enough to get a call out.

"We still have short range comm," Russell said, indicating the radio strapped to her back. At Lieutenant Stakely's insistence she had brought it with her in order to maintain contact with him back at the compound. "You can call back to camp and have your team fly out of here with that chopper of yours. They can do it in couple of minutes."

"It will still take time for the bombers to get here, won't it?" Gardner asked. "And what about those ground units you said were coming? They're still too far away, aren't they?"

Glancing down at his watch, Nichols said, "You're right. They won't be here for at least another seven hours." The older man nodded approvingly at Gardner, obviously impressed with the younger Marine's grasp of the tactical situation. "But I do have one other ace up my sleeve." Motioning to Russell he said. "Hand me that mike, Sergeant."

Russell complied, breathing a small sigh as she did so. Nodding in the direction of Max she said, "It's a good thing they don't have any kind of that weird futuristic scanning hardware that could detect our transmissions. We'd be giving ourselves away."

"It is not that we do not possess such technology," Max said, "but rather that your communications traffic operates on frequencies that are below such equipment's normal detection thresholds." He affected what DiCarlo took to be a shrug. "In this case, your more primitive technology is working to our advantage."

As Nichols studied a map of Camp Growding he had brought with him and issued a rapid-fire series of orders into the radio microphone, DiCarlo gave silent thanks to whichever deity was charged with determining which aliens received weird futuristic scanning hardware and which ones did not.

*   *   *

Less than fifteen minutes later, the humans and Max watched from their vantage point as, down below, the Grays began to detect the faint noise of something approaching. DiCarlo could see from the reactions of several soldiers that they did not recognize the sound, though a few of them did point in the direction the sound seemed to be coming from.

Of course DiCarlo and his companions already knew what it was.

"*Roger that,*" Nichols said into the radio handset one last time before lowering the hand unit away from his ear. "They'll be here inside of thirty seconds. I figure this should be over in about ninety."

DiCarlo nodded at the report. Obviously the other agents had been standing by for just a call from their leader. Still, he frowned at the brash statement. On what was the operative basing his prediction? "This is a pretty ballsy plan you've got, Nichols."

The agent shrugged. "Not denying that, but it's the best move, all things considered. We've been pretty lucky to this point that the Grays have been taking a lot of time they should have spent fortifying their positions to screw with your unit. They seem to be bored with that for the moment, or maybe they're scared because they don't understand that you pulled that firefight out of your ass back there, and they've gotten back to strengthening their foothold on this side of the portal."

He nodded in the direction of the alien camp. "In a few hours those shitheads will probably be dug in so deep I doubt anything but a balls-out bomber strike will do any good. Unfortunately that would also attract a lot of unwanted attention at this stage of the game. We have to act now, while they're still vulnerable and there's a chance we can contain the situation." Apparently noticing the doubting expressions on the Marines' faces he added, "The hardware my chopper is carrying is more than enough to level that camp and everything in it."

Behind them, the sound of the approaching helicopter's engine was growing with each passing second. In the valley below, the Grays were beginning to react in a fashion DiCarlo would have expected from soldiers, taking up their rifles and moving for positions of concealment. He quickly counted at least thirty-five weapons being brandished by individuals, but thankfully no activity seemed to be coming from either the perimeter defenses or the LAVs that were still under construction. The odds would be somewhat in favor of Nichols's chopper crew, at least for the battle's opening moments.

"No matter what happens," he said to the group lying to either side of him, "maintain your cover. Don't give away your position." He held no illusions of surviving a ground fight between his small team and any aliens who might discover their presence here.

Any reply DiCarlo might have received was cut off as the helicopter announced its presence with authority. He recognized the sound of rockets launching a split second before twin contrails of smoke, one slightly ahead of the other, tracked across the late afternoon sky, the rockets producing them descending from somewhere behind him and heading directly for the alien camp. Two of the perimeter weapon stations disappeared in matching plumes of fire and shrapnel that exploded in all directions and littered the compound with debris.

"Here we go," Nichols said unnecessarily as a loud whine rushed by overhead. Then the Huey sailed past as it continued down on its attack vector. It flew in low and fast, seemingly selecting targets on the fly as it fired six rockets in as many seconds. Five of the rockets struck prime targets of three more weapons positions and one of the LAVs. The sixth missile sailed past another of the vehicles but continued on to explode as it struck a large cluster of cargo containers staged near one of the tents. All the while DiCarlo heard steady machine-gun fire as Nichols's men operated the door-mounted SAWs, covering the chopper's rear as it swung around for another run.

"That is one hot shit pilot," Russell said in a voice that DiCarlo barely heard. It was true, though. He had not seen flying like that since Vietnam, and maybe not even then. Whoever the guy was, there was no doubting his status as a tested warrior.

Nichols continued to issue orders into the radio, directing the chopper's attack and target selection. So far the agent and his pilot had been working in deadly tandem, with even the errant shot having caused some amount of valuable damage.

"He's gonna have a handful this time around, though," DiCarlo said. Even as the chopper arced around for another pass he could see several of the Grays readying themselves to return fire. Nichols saw it, too, because DiCarlo heard the agent relaying that same information to the helicopter via Russell's radio.

"Can their rifles really hurt the chopper?" Gardner asked.

Nichols replied, "According to your Lieutenant Westerson, Gray rifles tore the shit out of her Humvee. There's probably ten times that firepower down there."

Now aware of the situation on the ground, the chopper pilot's next attack run was even hairier than the previous ones. Dodging and careening in a series of maneuvers DiCarlo would have thought impossible for a helicopter, the Huey dove almost to the ground before leveling out and firing another rocket, with yet another following right on its heels. Explosions consumed two more weapons stations as the chopper darted away in yet another evasive move, the pilot taking advantage of the flight path to eliminate another pair of turrets in the process.

This time, the pilot's skills came up short.

The now familiar whine of pulse rifles echoed in the small valley as several Grays took aim at the bobbing and weaving chopper. The Huey lurched violently to the left and DiCarlo saw two ragged holes in the side of the chopper. Somehow the pilot was able to retain control, though the chopper's engine howled in protest as he steered the craft up and over a small rise at the edge of the valley.

"No!" Nichols called out, for a moment even forgetting to be mindful of maintaining the concealment of himself and his companions. DiCarlo also saw the end coming as the chopper maneuvered upward to avoid the rocky hillside. There was only one place for the helicopter to go and the Grays were aware of it, too. Another barrage of energy pulses ripped through the air and this time they caught the Huey with the full force of their attack.

There was no way to count the number of wounds the chopper absorbed before it exploded in midair.

"Good God," DiCarlo breathed as a monstrous fireball consumed the helicopter. There was nothing he or his companions could do as momentum carried the craft for-

ward for an additional several dozen meters before plummeting to the ground with an arcing tail of flames.

Triumphant cries echoed from the encampment and
DiCarlo looked down to see Gray soldiers emerging from
their defensive positions, their weapons held above their
heads as they danced in celebration of their victory. That
only lasted for a few seconds, though, before one of the
soldiers barked a series of orders in the aliens' language
and a small group of the Grays set out on foot for the spot
where the helicopter had crashed to the earth.

"Be thankful," Max said as the group watched the
Grays moving to where the wreckage of the Huey still
burned. "Your friends could have survived that crash long
enough to be captured."

DiCarlo turned away from the scene to see Nichols,
standing away from the rest of group as he stared at the
ground at his feet. Apparently feeling eyes on him, the
agent looked up.

"I've made a huge mistake."

Frowning as he regarded Nichols, DiCarlo silently
evaluated the man's comment before choosing to say anything. For his part, Nichols's expression was a mix of frustration and defeat, and for a moment the sergeant major
could not fathom the reason behind the man's words.

"Looks like about half the turrets are history," Russell
offered as she surveyed the alien camp through binoculars. "So are the vehicles they were working on, along with
a good chunk of their supplies."

Also scanning the area, Gardner said, "I count at least a
dozen bodies on the ground, too." Turning to face Nichols
he added, "Your team bought us some time, Mr. Nichols."

"Don't you understand?" Nichols asked. "That's just it.

They bought time, but what are we supposed to do with it? Losing my men and the chopper and all that hardware is bad enough, but we also lost the fastest way to go and get help. There's still plenty of those things down there, with a direct line to however many more they need, to say nothing of an undisrupted supply chain."

Stepping forward, Max said, "He is correct. So long as the portal remains open, this is nothing more than a setback. Equipment and personnel can be replaced within a cycle."

"Then there's only one thing left for us to do," DiCarlo said. "Close the portal."

It took several seconds before Nichols reacted to the Marine's simple statement but when he did it was with no small amount of incredulity.

"And just how the hell do you propose to do that?" he said, his voice rising enough that all three of the Marines in the group as well as Max looked in the direction of the alien encampment to see if the agent's words had been heard. Nichols noticed his lapse, though, and DiCarlo could see the transformation in the man's face as he regained control over his emotions and reasserted his focus on the mission at hand. "Sorry," he offered in a much lower voice. "Sergeant Major, are you considering what I think you're considering?"

"We're out of time," DiCarlo replied, "and we've only got one card left to play." He cast a weary look at Russell and Gardner. "We attack."

Nichols frowned. "The Marines in this unit are reservists, with little or no combat experience. They're not exactly trained for this kind of thing."

"They got plenty last night," DiCarlo countered. "And

unless you've got a platoon that's been trained to fight an alien army, then they're our best option." He had seen the way the Marines, most of them untested on the field of battle a mere twenty-four hours ago, had handled themselves during the defensive stand at the compound. Launching a counterattack was something else entirely, he knew, but with the assistance of the combat vets he did have as well as the Plysserians who had aided them, it was not an entirely outlandish proposition. He cast another look at the two very young Marines standing silently nearby, this one an expression of confidence. "They'll be all right."

The words seemed to mollify the government agent somewhat, though his tone was still doubtful as he asked, "Do you have a plan?"

DiCarlo shook his head, unable to keep a small smirk from his face. "Not yet.

27

Raegyra was tired.

He knew, though, that no rest would be forthcoming any time soon. All around him fellow soldiers and other specialists were hard at work repairing weapons emplacements and other equipment damaged or destroyed in the recent attack. Though he himself had not been detailed to any of the actual repair duties, he and other soldiers had been tasked with providing perimeter security for the base camp while the work progressed.

Despite the pace he and his scouting party had been keeping since their arrival here, it had been hard not to allow the beauty surrounding him to act as a distraction from the mission at hand. Lush trees and vegetation, a rarity on *Jontashreena*, existed in abundance here. It reminded Raegyra of the forests near his grandparents' home in the mountainous region north of the city where he had grown up, one of the few places on his world that had been spared the ravages of the War. The similarities were such that if he allowed his attention to wander to the nearby trees as he recalled those childhood memories, he could almost believe that his grandfather would soon be shouting for young Raegyra to come in for dinner.

Such recollections were quickly stifled by the reality of their current situation.

The creatures who lived here were receiving assistance from Plysserians who had fled here from *Jontashreena*, and it was obvious that they would not simply bow before the military might of an opposing force. They possessed a courage and spirit that Raegyra could admire. His earlier skirmishes with them as well as their attack on the base camp with their odd flying machine was evidence enough of that. It would take several cycles to restore the destroyed defensive systems as well as replace troops, supplies, and other equipment that had been lost in the attack. Though the officers would not say as much, Raegyra was experienced enough as a soldier to know that the camp could be vulnerable if the creatures mounted a larger offensive before repairs were completed.

Naturally, this new development was causing the Leadership great concern.

After being on the defensive for so long, many believed that the Plysserians' defeat was not only foreseeable but imminent as well. This was, of course, before the discovery of the technical marvel that had given them access to this, an entirely new planet. If this world possessed a large enough population willing to ally themselves with the Plysserians, it could just be the catalyst they had long been looking for to shift the balance of power back into their favor. With this in mind, the Leadership had issued directives to respond to this emerging threat.

Now that Chodrecai forces had captured the portal and controlled access to it at both ends, control of the priceless technology was required in order to continue bringing more of their fellow soldiers along with supporting equipment and weaponry. This required that the search for Plysserian hiding places as well as any further action against the creatures or their encampment be halted in order to concentrate on strengthening defensive positions at the portal opening. It was a sound decision in hindsight, given the recent attack on the camp, but it was nevertheless a duty that did not appeal to Raegyra. He much preferred being on the offensive rather than sitting and waiting for the Plysserians to attack. Once a secure base was established, he would be ready to continue looking for their enemies in order to eradicate them.

Of course, he realized that accomplishing such a goal would now be much more difficult with the creatures of this planet possibly aiding the Plysserians. Would the Chodrecai finish the War that had begun during Raegyra's childhood, only to find themselves at odds with these humans as a new enemy? Long exhausted from fighting and supporting a war they did not start, would their collective morale be enough to withstand another lengthy conflict?

Weapons fire from somewhere behind him jolted Raegyra from his reverie and he turned in time to see a fellow soldier fall the ground. No sooner had his brain registered the sound as coming from a Plysserian pulse rifle than a host of similar bursts erupted from the forest. Warriors collapsed all around him, trapped in a deadly crossfire coming from multiple locations among the trees.

We are under attack! Again!

Raegyra shouted out in alarm as he raised his own rifle and fired into the forest, more as an attempt to force the enemy to take cover than with any real hope of hitting a target. He fired on the run, dashing for what had once been one of the perimeter defensive turrets. Its scorched ruins were a meager source of concealment but it was better than standing out in the open, for even as he sprinted toward it he heard the sounds of energy pulses howling nearby, seeking him out.

Diving behind the wrecked turret, Raegyra turned back toward the forest even as more energy bursts exploded from the tree line. Cries of warning were coming from all over the camp as soldiers reacted to the attack and within moments, the air was filled with the ferocious cacophony of weapons fire. Energy shrieked in his ears as both sides exchanged salvos and Raegyra saw several of his companions fall in the face of the assault.

Movement registered in the corner of one eye and he turned to see the first wave of Plysserians break from the tree line. Their rifles spat pulse bolts as the enemy soldiers sprinted across open terrain, forcing Chodrecai warriors to seek cover from the vicious storm of firepower. Raegyra tried to retaliate but was repeatedly forced to drop down behind the turret wreckage to avoid being hit.

It had been a long time since he had been in a firefight of such intensity. Even the earlier attack on the camp had not approached this level of violence. In recent engagements the Plysserians had been a ragged force fighting with the desperation of an opponent who knew they were beaten but who were too stubborn to lay down their arms and surrender. It was one of the few traits he and other Chodrecai soldiers could admire about their enemy, regardless of the fact that it served only to delay the War from its inevitable conclusion.

The Plysserians continued to advance under cover of their brutal barrages of rifle fire, and as they drew closer it

was becoming increasingly problematic for Raegyra to select targets to shoot at while protecting himself behind the
destroyed weapons turret. It was then that he became
aware of a new sound coming from somewhere to his left.
Diverting his attention from the line of approaching
enemy soldiers was difficult at first, but as the strange
droning sound continued to increase in volume he could
not resist the urge to look for its source.

Raegyra turned in time to detect a dark object moving
among the trees, coming toward the perimeter. It was a vehicle of some kind, the sounds he was hearing obviously
emanating from its propulsion system. There were other
sounds as well, which he recognized as belonging to the
types of projectile weapons the creatures had been using
during the earlier battle. He could see some of the creatures as well as more Plysserians, running alongside and in
front of the vehicle, which was itself not much bigger than
their army's own single-seat assault craft.

Something slammed into his chest and Raegyra felt
himself thrown to the ground, the impact with the hard
soil forcing the air from his lungs. It took another moment
for the pain to register but when it did it shrouded everything else. He felt blood rushing in his ears as the heat in
his chest began to radiate outward to the rest of his body.
Through the agony that was already clouding his brain he
realized that he had been hit by a pulse rifle set to full
strength and that the effects of the weapon were wasting
no time wreaking havoc on him.

In all the time he had spent as a soldier Raegyra had
until this moment never been wounded in combat. He
tried to bring himself to a sitting position but failed. An attempt to retrieve his fallen weapon was also unsuccessful.

He lost feeling in his extremities and each labored breath he took brought with it a new wave of pain. He could only lie here, helpless as the battle continued around him and his body inexorably succumbed to his injuries.

Turning his head to look toward the new threat, Raegyra saw through blurring vision that the creatures and enemy soldiers were spreading out into a wedge configuration, with the vehicle at the formation's base, and as they did so he understood at that moment the reason for the ferocity of the Plysserian's initial attack.

Diversion.

As the sights and sounds around him began to fade away, Raegyra managed a weak smile that no one around him could see. It was a smile of admiration for his enemy. Not the Plysserians, whom he had waged war against for longer than he could easily remember, but rather the humans, who despite their apparent inferiority in every conceivable sense had still risen to the challenge of defending their home against invaders.

Raegyra's last thought was one of regret that he would not live to see whether or not their challenge would be successful.

28

"Here we go again."

His hands applying a death grip on the steering wheel, DiCarlo guided the five-ton supply truck from the concealment of the forest out onto the open ground less than a hundred meters from the Grays' defensive perimeter. Outside the vehicle the hellish chorus of the Marines' small arms and alien weaponry filled the air as the line of human and Plysserian soldiers pressed forward, clearing a path for the truck to follow. With the Blues' own weapons affected by the radios in the same manner that had disrupted those of their enemy, the aliens were forced to use extra M-16s that Sergeant Bonniker and his merry band of thieves had retrieved from the base armory.

"Again?" Russell asked from the passenger seat, casting a puzzled look at him. "You've done this before?"

Only then realizing he had spoken the words aloud, DiCarlo diverted his attention from the windshield just long enough to glance at her with a thin smile. "Actually I did drive through the fence of a Vietnamese POW camp once. It was a rescue mission. We hijacked one of their trucks and used it to approach the camp without being noticed. By the time we got there they had bugged out, though."

"Let's hope we have better luck," Russell offered. The truck hit a bump and she reached for the dashboard to steady herself. The barrel of her rifle rested on the door-jamb, though it was practically useless as the truck bounced on the uneven terrain. It was all she could do to keep herself from being thrown all about the vehicle's interior as DiCarlo attempted to avoid the larger ruts and holes perforating the ground ahead of them.

DiCarlo nodded grimly. The rescue mission deep into enemy territory all those years ago had been hazardous and the odds of success had been very slim, but that had not stopped him or his unit from attempting it. It had been a cakewalk, though, compared to what he and his Marines were attempting now.

After breaking into Camp Growding's primary supply warehouse, Bonniker had collected every field radio he could find, along with batteries to power the entire assortment. Sergeant Russell and Kel, the Blue soldier who had helped her and her team to work through their communications difficulties, had set every radio to the frequency the alien comm tech had determined would most effectively provide the jamming field Russell had discovered. The radios were then loaded onto the supply truck with the buttons of their microphone headsets taped down so that every unit continuously transmitted.

Russell had proposed the idea, theorizing that if enough of the units were used in sync with one another, it could be possible to create a larger area where the alien weapons would not function.

It was Kel who had taken the thought one step further.

The jamming field generated by the radios might be able to provide a means by which they could attack the Gray compound and possibly seize the portal. In fact, the alien had even postulated that enough of the radios, tuned to the correct frequency, just might disrupt the conduit itself if the generator powering the portal was operating on a similar frequency.

"Once we get inside their perimeter," DiCarlo said during his briefing of the Marines and Plysserians on the roles they would play during the mission, "the main objective is to get the truck to the portal in an attempt to disable it. Even if that fails, though, the portal cannot remain in enemy hands, and that includes the equipment the Blues brought with them to build a generator on this side. If we can't capture it, then it has to be destroyed."

The expressions of anxiety and fear that had permeated the reservists during the briefing served to remind DiCarlo that these men and women were in a situation for which they were not even remotely qualified. He had said as much to the group, though he had added the caveat that there was absolutely nothing any of them could do about that now. Maybe they were not Marines who served on active duty every day, but that no longer mattered. Just as he had done so many years previously, they had taken the same oath and undergone most of the same training. "If you remember what you were taught and trust in the Marine next to you," he had told them, "then you'll get through this."

His hopes had been buoyed somewhat when Corporal Melendez, obviously hoping to lighten the otherwise somber mood, had asked, "You think we'll get hazard pay for this?"

"Look," Russell said as she pointed at something beyond the windshield and DiCarlo could see the battle developing more than a football field's length away from them. "It's working. The Grays bought the fake out."

The diversionary action being unleashed by Max and several dozen Plysserian soldiers was proving to be most effective, thanks in no small part to the earlier offensive strike by Nichols's team on the chopper. Apparently nervous at the idea of another assault because of the heavy damage the helicopter had caused, most if not all of the surviving Grays were running frantically to defend against this latest onslaught. The result, of course, was that they were now vulnerable to attack from another flank, such as the one being launched by DiCarlo and his group.

"They're starting to get smart though," he said as he saw the first of the enemy soldiers reacting to the second phase of the audacious plan he had put into motion. With the Plysserians serving to draw as many of the Gray soldiers away from the portal as possible, DiCarlo had hoped to be able to cover most of the distance from the tree line to the portal itself before a resistance could be mounted in their direction. As expected though, the distraction had only bought them a few seconds and now some of the Grays were reacting to the new threat. His first instinct was to step on the gas, but he could not afford to outrun the Marines and Plysserians who were providing the truck's primary protection against enemy fire from a distance.

Russell had volunteered to ride with him, an offer that DiCarlo had resisted at first. He quickly dismissed his reluctance though, scolding himself for thinking of the sergeant as a woman instead of a Marine. She had already proven her mettle in the hours since they had first encountered the aliens, and it was her ingenuity that had gotten them this far. Besides, he needed the extra pair of eyes to watch for threats.

Additionally, Nichols and Kel were in the back of the truck, manning a pair of the unit's SAW machine guns to offer greater protection and ensure that no unwanted guests could climb aboard. DiCarlo suspected that Kel was motivated by the friendship he had struck up with Russell, while Nichols probably wanted nothing more than a simple chance at payback for the loss of his team.

"Here they come," Nichols called out from behind the truck's cab before DiCarlo heard the distinctive sound of the SAW firing. Whereas the M-16s had only proven effective against the aliens at close range, the larger machine gun's firepower was more than enough to keep them at bay. The Grays were respecting the weapon, hanging back and seeking cover as they attempted to juggle what had quickly become a two-pronged attack on their position. This gave the Marines and Plysserians accompanying the truck the opening they needed as they broke off into assigned groups. Each team laid down suppressing fire as they advanced on pre-selected targets of equipment or supplies, carrying out DiCarlo's directive that the enemy be left with as little as possible even if the goal of destroying the portal failed.

"There's the portal," Russell said, pointing again. DiCarlo could see it, too, perhaps another hundred meters or so inside the Grays' line. They still had to breach those defenses if they were to have any hope of getting to the conduit opening, but the veteran Marine could already see an area of the perimeter that might be exploited.

"Nichols!" he yelled over the din of the truck's whining engine. "Two o'clock! Clear the road!" Seconds later the sounds of machine-gun fire were rewarded with more of the Gray soldiers scrambling for cover, creating the breach DiCarlo needed. He stomped on the gas and the truck lurched forward, accelerating over the uneven terrain.

Risking a quick glance at Russell he said, "Time to see if your plan's going to work, kid. If we survive long enough for you to write a book about all this, remind me to buy a copy."

His pulse pounding in his ears, it took every scrap of self-control Brad Gardner possessed to maintain his position in the skirmishers line he and other Marines formed as they, along with a contingent of Plysserian soldiers, continued their advance toward the Gray compound.

M-16 and SAW machine-gun fire ripped through the air all around him, mixed with the telltale reports of alien rifles. Dozens of meters away he could see Gray soldiers, at first caught up in defending against the attack launched by Plysserians on the opposite side of the camp, now reacting to the new threat. Somewhere behind him the comforting grumble of the supply truck's massive diesel engine continued as it moved forward, with other Marines and Plysserians running blocker for it as Sergeant Major DiCarlo took on the formidable task of driving the truck to the portal.

The attack had started well, but Gardner could already see the focus of the battle shifting toward the truck and its line of defenders. The diversion had bought Sergeant Major DiCarlo the time he had needed to get the truck into the clearing without being detected, but now it would be little more than a footrace to get the vehicle and its precious cargo the rest of the way.

"Split off!" a voice shouted out over the sounds of battle. Gardner recognized it as belonging to Lieutenant Stakely just as he saw Marines and Plysserians to either side of him breaking away from the initial formation used to protect the truck during the opening moments of the assault. As dictated by the battle plan Sergeant Major DiCarlo had outlined, the group was splintering into smaller configurations as they switched to their secondary objective of destroying as much of the alien base as possible.

Almost immediately the battle began to take a turn for the worse. Plysserians fell under the onslaught of Chodrecai weaponry but it was the humans who suffered the most. Cries of agony reached Gardner as all around him fellow Marines were ripped apart by bursts of alien rifle fire, the body armor they wore offering no protection from the vicious power of the Grays' weapons. Though the precaution had been taken of distributing some of the PRC-77s among the ranks as a means of hopefully disrupting the Grays' ability to fire at the ground troops, the Grays themselves were still too far away for the individual radios to have any noticeable effect.

He detected movement to his left and turned to see a Gray rising up from behind the burned out ruins of a weapons turret. The alien's weapon was not trained on him, though he could see immediately who the intended target was.

"Lieutenant!" he shouted, too late to warn Stakely. One instant the officer was running and shooting at an enemy position and the next his body was shredded as the energy pulse ripped through it. Most of the lieutenant was reduced in the blink of an eye to a spray of blood and skin and bone along with fragments of uniform fabric and equipment, while what little of Stakely that had not been disintegrated fell to the earth in a wet heap.

There was no time for Gardner to even register the shock of the brutal killing, though, as the Gray soldier turned its weapon on him.

"Brad, look out!" Max shouted from his right, but before Gardner could respond there was a massive hand grabbing onto his right arm. Then he was yanked sideways just as the whine of an energy burst howled past his left ear, tearing through the space he had occupied the instant before. He stumbled to retain his balance and crashed into Max's left side as the Plysserian fired the M-16 he carried, the weapon looking like little more than a toy in the alien's huge hand. The rounds did not strike the Gray soldier but instead forced him to crouch under cover, allowing Max to pull Gardner out of danger.

As they continued across the compound, darting for cover and shooting at any enemy soldier who showed themselves, Gardner realized that he had not felt fear in the face of the near miss. Even the horror of Stakely's violent death seemed surreal, and all of these feelings were in direct conflict with the dread that had gripped him not even an hour previously.

Like many of the other reservists in the unit, he had been terrified at the idea of marching into a battle with the very real possibility that he might be killed in the action. DiCarlo's uplifting speech during the pre-attack briefing had been able to ease his fears somewhat, and now as the assault continued he found that his anxiety had been replaced by something else that he could not define. Unlike the excitement he received during simulated combat exercises, the feelings generated by the overwhelming demands of real battle were much more intense, in effect prohibiting him from being afraid as he and his companions pressed forward.

A Gray soldier appeared in front of him, rising from behind the cover of a large cargo container and aiming its weapon at him. Without thinking Gardner swung his rifle around, not realizing that he had even pulled the trigger until he saw the effects of the three-round burst on the alien. One of the bullets struck the Gray in the chest while another caught the soldier in the face, spoiling its aim and forcing it to stagger backward a step. This gave Gardner the opening he needed to lunge forward, firing again as he did so. Five of his next six bullets struck the alien in the upper chest, neck, and head. The alien fell to the ground and remained still.

Gardner did not see that as he was already pressing onward and searching for another target. Behind him he heard the sound of the truck's engine whining louder as DiCarlo pressed on the accelerator. They were moving into the final stages of this insane plan, and there was no turning back now.

Glancing down at the rapidly shrinking belt of 5.56-millimeter rounds feeding his SAW machine gun, Nichols saw that he was in danger of firing his weapon dry.

"Ammo! I need ammo!" he shouted to be heard over the sounds of the truck as he continued to shoot at anything that even looked like it might be trying to move in their direction. Beside him, Kel crouched down in the truck long enough to pull two replacement belts from the ammo box at their feet.

"Here," Kel said, offering one belt to Nichols before using the other to reload his own weapon. Nichols's experienced hands made short work of the reloading process, and he could not help but be impressed at the prowess the alien soldier showed as he repeated the task. Though he had learned the workings of the machine gun scarcely an hour before, Kel was operating the weapon with a proficiency the agent had only seen in the most experienced combat veterans.

That was fortunate for them. The fighting had intensified as the Grays seemed to realize that the truck was important to the success of the attack. While there was a threat from Grays who fired at them from a distance, those forces were still occupied by the first wave of Plysse-rians who had set this whole plan into motion. That left only those soldiers who were closer, who were quickly dis-covering that they were the ones who were in danger.

"It's working," he said, indicating one group of nearby Grays as he readied the machine gun to fire again. "The radios are screwing up their weapons." As the truck pushed deeper into the encampment it was becoming ob-vious that the jamming effect, created by the collection of nearly forty field radios they had brought along, was hav-ing the desired results. From his vantage point overlook-ing the driver's side of the truck, Nichols could see Gray soldiers trying to fire their weapons and examining them when they did not function. All of this happened in the space of mere seconds as the agent took advantage of the enemy's confusion to dispatch them with the SAW. Some of the soldiers discarded their rifles and ran toward the truck only to be met by a hailstorm of bullets as Nichols targeted them. He guessed from the sounds of machine-gun fire to his right that Kel was having similar success as he covered the area to the front and along the passenger side of the truck.

All around them Grays were reacting to the jamming effects, dropping their weapons and boldly wading into the advancing line of Marines and Plysserians. Within seconds dozens of small melees erupted all across the bat-tlefield as the fighting degenerated into hand-to-hand combat. Many of the Marines, physically outclassed and woefully unprepared for the harsh reality of fighting for their very lives, almost immediately began to fall victim to the superior skills of enemy soldiers despite the assistance of Plysserians trying to come to their rescue.

This isn't exactly what you signed up for, is it?

The firefight was unlike anything Nichols had faced, either as an Army Ranger or an agent for the Central Intelligence Agency. Even the first two years of his unusual reassignment to the Space Command's top secret Operations Section 04-E, bizarre as they had been, had done nothing to prepare him for the insanity he was experiencing at this moment. When he had first joined he had worried that Op04-E existed merely to salve the idiocy or unchecked paranoia of some government official who had watched too many *X-Files* reruns.

If I'd only known then what I know now, he chided himself. Of course, what he also suspected right now was that if this insane plan of theirs did not work, then any fate imagined for Earth in a movie or book would almost certainly pale in comparison to whatever the Grays had in mind. If the aliens who had befriended them were correct, then this planet stood as a beacon of salvation for the Grays if they won the day. If that happened, then Humanity's odds of survival were remote at best.

It may not have been our fight before, Nichols decided, *but it sure as hell is now.*

"Nichols!" Kel shouted just before the agent heard something moving behind him. He turned to see three Gray soldiers scrambling to climb over the side of the truck. One of the aliens wielded a nasty-looking knife, its blade easily as long as Nichols's forearm. It cleared the railing and began to advance but it only took two steps before Kel was able to swing his machine gun around and fire. A string of bullets ripped through the alien's chest and sent it tumbling back over the railing.

Then the SAW jammed.

Nichols heard Kel mutter something in his own language before the other two aliens dropped into the back of the truck and moved toward him. They were having trouble, though, keeping their balance as the vehicle bounced over the uneven ground, each of them grabbing on to the side railing in order to keep their feet steady.

There was no way Nichols could bring his own rifle around in time so he simply gave up trying. Instinct told him that he would never get his pistol cleared of its holster, either. His right hand moved as of its own free will to the combat knife taped to the shoulder strap of his equipment harness. The knife had barely cleared its scabbard before the agent howled a fierce war cry at the top of his lungs and charged forward.

The Grays had obviously not expected a weak human to launch such a brazen attack, as they hesitated for the briefest of instants before reacting. That indecision was all that Nichols required as he rushed the nearest enemy soldier and drove the knife into the alien's throat. He grabbed onto the soldier's chest armor as the Gray wailed in agony, and Nichols pushed the blade still deeper through the tough skin. Twisting the knife around, he tried to sever arteries or veins and anything else that pushed blood through the alien's body. In the corner of his eye he saw Kel fighting with the remaining Gray but he could not spare any time to see how that skirmish was going. It took everything he had simply to hang on to his own opponent.

Still possessing incredible strength, the Gray yanked Nichols off his feet, clawing at the agent's knife hand and fighting to get the blade out of its own throat. Dark liquid frothed from the alien's mouth and Nichols saw its eyes go

wide as it staggered backward, all while Nichols continued to hang on. Then the Gray began to arc backward
and Nichols felt his stomach lurch as he realized with
horror that he and his enemy were going over the railing
and tumbling from the truck.

No! Even as gravity took hold of the Gray and finished
pulling it over the railing, Nichols let go of the knife and
the alien's armor and scrambled for something to break
his own fall.

His hands closed around empty air.

"Nichols!"

DiCarlo heard Kel's frantic shout even as movement in
the driver-side mirror caught his eye and he saw something drop from the truck. Two bodies, one alien and the
other unmistakably human, had fallen in a tumble to the
ground, rolling away as the truck continued forward.
Looking out his window he saw three Grays turning to run
to where Nichols had landed.

Russell had seen it, too, watching the scuffle unfold
through the truck cab's rear window. DiCarlo risked a
glance in the rearview mirror and saw Kel battling with a
Gray soldier just as the Plysserian got the upper hand in
the fight and leveraged his opponent over the side railing.
Pausing only long enough to wave toward the cab, the
alien retrieved his machine gun and resumed his defensive position.

"What about Nichols?" Russell asked, but she caught
herself before DiCarlo could respond. She knew as well
as he did that if the fall had not killed the government operative, then surely the trio of Grays would finish the job.
It was an unpleasant thought to be sure, but there was

nothing he could do about that now. Other than those Marines in the unit who had faced combat before, Nichols better than anyone else had appreciated the risks of the assault. Destroying the portal was the top priority, and DiCarlo knew that the agent would want him to carry out that mission no matter the cost.

And that's what we're going to do.

The sounds of battle were fading as DiCarlo guided the truck deeper toward the portal, now less than fifty meters away. There seemed to be no signs of movement in front of them. Had their two-front assault been effective enough to draw all of the Grays into the battle and leave their most valuable asset exposed?

Kel's SAW barked again and DiCarlo saw figures running at them from the right. Hiding behind stacks of equipment near the portal opening, the Grays were forming a gauntlet that the truck would have to run in order to reach its goal. They were taking up positions nearly fifty meters away, and though he did not know for sure, DiCarlo had a hunch that the aliens' weapons would be effective from that range.

His suspicions were confirmed when the truck lurched under the impact of enemy rifle fire. The steering wheel bucked from his hands as the energy bursts tore through the vehicle's metal paneling and for a second DiCarlo feared a salvo would hit the truck's oversized diesel tank. He grabbed the steering wheel back and fought to keep the truck under control as Russell aimed her M-16 through her window and began firing. More SAW rounds echoed as Kel brought the machine gun to bear once more.

"Kel!" DiCarlo shouted above the truck's howling engine. "We're almost there! Get ready to jump!" Casting a sidelong glance at Russell he added, "You, too."

The plan had been to get the truck close enough to the portal to ensure that it would make contact before jumping clear, where he and the others would then take their chances on the ground. DiCarlo could see now that the uneven terrain would likely spoil the truck's trajectory if there was no one at the steering wheel. He had no choice but to remain behind.

Russell fumbled for the door handle but missed when another volley of enemy fire hit the truck. Something heavy fell behind them and DiCarlo realized that Kel had been knocked off his feet. There was no way he would be able to jump clear before . . .

"Jump!" he yelled to Russell, but then it was too late. The portal loomed in the windshield, then there was a flash of light and a deafening roar as the truck made contact with . . .

. . . *something.*

"Holy shit!"

Hearing Sergeant Bonniker's exclamation, Gardner at first thought that the truck had exploded, disappearing as it did in a furious eruption of light and energy blasting outward from the center of the portal. Even from a hundred meters away, he could feel the force of the conduit's unleashed power washing over his body. What must it be like for anyone standing closer? What about DiCarlo and the others in the truck? How could they possibly have survived the force of that detonation? Had the explosion carried back through the tunnel and, if so, what kind of damage had it caused on the other side?

As the blast faded, Gardner sat up and saw that nothing remained where the portal had once been, including any indication of wreckage from the truck. Had it been incinerated? There was no scorched earth or any other sign of an explosion. It was as if the portal, and the truck, had never existed at all.

"It appears that the battle is all but over," Max said from where he stood to Gardner's right. Around them a few scattered combatants on either side were still moving about and Max pointed to where small groups of Plysserians were charging the few remaining Gray defensive positions, firing wildly at anything that moved as they finished off lingering pockets of enemy resistance.

Glancing at his wristwatch, Gardner shook his head in disbelief just as he had done so after the firefight back at the Marines' base camp. "Just under eight minutes. Unreal." His astonishment slowly ebbed away, though, replaced by anguish as he beheld the dozens of bodies, alien and human alike, strewn across the battlefield.

When the battle had begun his fear was that the Marines would not be able to succeed against the Grays' superior weaponry and physical prowess a second time. The best they could have hoped for, in his eyes, would be to keep the enemy at bay long enough for DiCarlo to get the truck to the portal, most likely while sustaining massive casualties. His throat tightened at the thought of the number of Marines who had suffered the same sickening fate as Lieutenant Stakely, defenseless against the Chodrecai weapons.

He heard someone yelling and turned to see Petty Officer Acavedo calling out to assist in getting a handle on the casualty situation. Marines, far too few of them, were emerging from cover in order to help, assisting wounded buddies to the relative safety of the tree line where they could be treated by the Navy corpsmen. Once that was accomplished, the more grisly task of evacuating the bodies of dead friends would begin as those who had survived the firefight did their part to carry on the time-honored tradition of not leaving fallen comrades on the battlefield.

And then what?

What were they supposed to do now? Lieutenant Stakely and Sergeant Major DiCarlo, among uncounted others, were dead. Likewise, the agent Nichols and his team had also been lost. Those who had survived the battle had no way of knowing if their mission was successful. The portal seemed to have been closed, but had they simply shorted out the conduit itself, or actually destroyed the equipment that had created it in the first place? Had the Marines and their Plysserian benefactors ended the Gray threat, at least at this location, or simply thrown fuel on a fire that was already dangerously close to burning out of control?

Was this a victory, or simply a prelude to ultimate defeat?

30

Almost there.

That was what the digital readout of the Geographical Positioning System in her hand told Special Agent Alyssa Richards as the UH-1N Huey helicopter she was riding in descended over the forest of Camp Growding. Supported as it was by state of the art satellite tracking technology, the GPS was capable of pinpointing a pimple on a mosquito's ass, at least according to the technicians charged with maintaining the equipment. With that kind of accuracy, exaggerated or not, she knew that homing in on a set of known map coordinates was child's play for the techno-gadget.

The question now was: What was waiting for them there?

Richards had read transcripts of the reports submitted by Agent Nichols detailing what the Marine reservists had stumbled across. What they had found was astounding, there could be no disputing that, and it was difficult for her not to believe that the discovery had the potential for global consequences. Finding evidence that an alien civilization had visited Earth was one thing, but to learn that those aliens possessed a way to relocate their entire population, to say nothing of their military might, from their own planet to here with the same effort that she might cross the street? That was almost too overwhelming to think about.

"Agent Richards," a voice sounded in the headset she wore, and she looked up from the GPS and toward the helicopter's cockpit where its pilot, a Navy commander named Harbor, was waving for her to come forward. As she did so the pilot pointed through the windshield to where plumes of smoke were rising from the forest. "Right where we're headed," he said, drawing the last word out with that Texas drawl Richards had found irritating from the moment she had met the man.

"Is there enough room to land?" she asked.

Harbor nodded. "Plenty. We'll be down inside of a minute." Richards patted the commander on his shoulder before turning and heading back to her own seat, situated near the open passenger door on the Huey's right side and which gave her an unfettered view of the treetops as the helicopter skimmed over the forest.

What had happened down there? Was Nichols involved? Her instincts told her yes, but she had no way of knowing for sure, as he had stopped transmitting hours earlier. Communications attempts with the operative or members of his team had been unsuccessful, in fact. The coordinates leading her to this location were the last piece of useful information Nichols had sent prior to contact being lost. She, along with a trio of attack helicopters, a convoy of mechanized infantry, and a battalion of ground troops, had been dispatched to Camp Growding at his direction, presumably to support him and the plan he had seen fit to put into motion. It was also why a squadron of

B-2 Stealth bombers at Whiteman Air Force Base in northern Missouri had been placed on standby.

Richards had already directed the ground forces to move to the compound where the Marine reservists had set up camp, presumably as good a place as any to begin gathering onsite intelligence about the current situation here. The helicopters, in the meantime, would proceed on to the location specified by Nichols's map coordinates. According to his last report, the alien portal was located there, and she wanted to see it for herself. Besides, with Nichols out of contact, he had apparently left a puzzle for her to complete. Given the events currently developing all across the planet, there was damned little time in which to do it, too.

The reports coming from General Thompson at Op04-E were not promising. From the information conveyed by other operatives and various sources around the world, signs of alien encroachment were turning up everywhere. Several encounters had already occurred between the Chodrecai or "Gray" aliens and military forces of various nations, with mixed results. There had been minor victories, but none of them had come against established Gray positions near the strange portals connecting Earth with the aliens' home planet.

Other accounts contained details of how military forces around the world were scrambling to mount defenses in desperate attempts to contain the aliens. Most disturbing so far was the account of a British Air Force attack squadron decimated in southern England by what could only be described as alien antiaircraft weaponry. The defenses appeared capable of taking out fighter planes with ease, giving the aliens formidable protection while they continued to build vehicles and transport more troops and supplies through the portal at that location, further strengthening their foothold here on Earth.

What if that action was being mirrored at countless other locations around the planet? Was it simply the prelude to full-scale invasion? How did the other aliens, the Plysserians, factor into all of this? Some of them had allied themselves with the Marines here in Missouri, but no other similar reports had come in from anywhere else, not yet at least. Could the same be expected, or hoped for, by others of their kind? Even if the Plysserians did pledge their allegiance to Earth, would it be enough to fend off the Grays? There was no way of even knowing how many Plysserians had even made the journey through the portals, or how much of their advanced weaponry and other technology they had brought with them.

You're getting ahead of yourself, Al, her mind chided her. *One thing at a time.*

Richards could feel the helicopter slowing as it descended. Trees rose into her field of vision, filling the open doorway before the Huey bounced ever so slightly as its landing skids touched the ground. Richards was out of her seat, equipment bag in hand and jumping through the hatch even before the chopper's engine began to cycle down.

She stopped short, though, when she got her first look at what awaited her.

"Dear God."

As a field operative for Op04-E, Richards had been ready and waiting for an opportunity like this since joining the secret group more than three years earlier. Though the idea of participating in an event such as first contact with an extraterrestrial race was not spoken of openly within the organization's corridors, it was nevertheless one that she and many other agents harbored privately. Unlike some of the section's more skeptical members, Richards had come to the assignment with the belief that life did exist on other worlds and that in all likelihood representatives of that life had visited Earth. She was not a fanatic on the subject, but rather proceeded from the conviction that it was ludicrous for humans to be the only intelligent life in the entire universe. Once that notion was dismissed, the alternative was easy to accept.

Regardless of the open mind with which she had entered into her service with Op04-E and the training her employers had bestowed upon her, it was not enough to prepare her for what she saw as she exited the helicopter.

All around the clearing, stark testimony to the battle that had transpired here beckoned for her attention. The smell of death saturated the air. Smoke rose from scorched and ruined piles of equipment and what could once have been vehicles of some kind. Small fires still smoldered here and there, but it was none of that which caught Richards's attention. The field was littered with bodies and many of them, she noted, were not human. Some looked to have been felled by gunfire, others seemed almost to be lounging in peaceful repose. Many Marines lay with their bodies twisted at obscene angles, testament to brutal force employed without mercy.

"Ho-lee shit," a voice said from behind her, and Richards turned to see Commander Harbor standing several meters away, his eyes wide as he surveyed the scene. The pilot had shed his flight helmet and vest and had drawn the nine millimeter pistol from his shoulder holster, the muzzle of the weapon aimed toward the ground. A member of the military detachment assigned to Op04-E, Harbor had been cleared for the types of activities the unit was likely to engage in, though the commander had never actually seen any evidence of extraterrestrial life before today, so far as Richards knew.

Shaking his head, Harbor added, "I have to admit, I always thought a lot of the stuff we covered in training was crap, but this . . ." He waved the pistol around the battlefield, "This is unreal."

"This is as real as it gets," Richards said as she began to move about the area, recording everything she came across with the digital video camera she had retrieved from her equipment bag. Later she would transmit the footage by way of a high-speed wireless Internet connection, after properly encrypting it of course, to Op04-E for detailed analysis. "There were fifty-three Marines assigned to the reserve unit, but there aren't nearly that many human bodies here. What happened to the rest of them?"

Harbor pointed his pistol at the body of an alien soldier. "There looks to be more of them than of our people," he said. The pilot was right, Richards realized. She also noted that many of the alien bodies looked to be those of Plysserians, judging by the descriptions she had been given.

It was then that she noticed what was missing.

"Where's the portal?" she asked as she turned a complete circle while allowing the video camera to record the panoramic view. "Do you think Nichols opted to attack, hoping to destroy it?" Had the situation been so desperate that the agent thought it necessary to launch an offensive with nothing more than a group of inexperienced part-time soldiers? Of course, success would have meant severing the connection to the aliens' home planet, perhaps cutting off a vital supply route for the Grays.

"If that's the case," Harbor said, "then it looks like they kicked some serious ass here."

Richards could only agree, but at what cost had that victory come? And where were the survivors? Surely combatants from both sides had lived through the battle?

She suddenly felt very vulnerable standing out in the open.

Unlike the Gray camp, the compound where the reservists had established their base of operations was a hive of activity.

Richards's fellow Op04-E agent, Gary Tate, had accompanied the ground units to the compound and had already taken the step of deploying the mechanized infantry battalion's tanks and the accompanying troops in a large defensive perimeter. Nothing would be able to get within five hundred meters of the camp without raising an alarm. It was a prudent move on Tate's part for a number of reasons, not the least of which was the fact that it reduced the chances that any of the regular army troops might see who, or what, was waiting for them inside the compound itself.

After all, Richards was having a hard time getting used to what she was seeing, too.

The aftermath of battle lay around her. Three overworked Navy corpsmen were laboring frantically to assess and treat a variety of injuries sustained by both human and alien soldiers, with a handful of Marines pressed into service in an attempt to assist the medics. A quick conversation with the ranking corpsman, a harried petty officer named Acavedo, revealed that the situation was nearly under control but that she or anyone else in her group with medical training would be "fucking great" to have. Otherwise, the corpsman had informed her that she could "get her bony ass out of the way." Richards settled for a combination of both suggestions, calling on the Army unit's medical personnel before getting herself out of Acavedo's hair. She had pressing concerns of her own, anyway, such as figuring out just what the hell had happened here.

The answers came from an exhausted-looking Marine lance corporal named Gardner and his unlikely companion, a Plysserian soldier named Max.

She recognized the man's name, as well as that of the alien, from the report supplied by the Marine lieutenant, Westerson. Gardner had taken on the phenomenal task of learning the alien's own language with the help of a type of translator technology provided by Max. Whatever the gadget was that had facilitated Gardner's amazing accomplishment, Richards knew that it was far and away more advanced than anything that could be found on this planet. Would there be time, ever, to examine the technology, along with the alien weaponry and other assorted hardware the reservists had recovered from both alien armies? For now, though, she had to focus on getting as much information about the current situation as possible for her report to General Thompson.

"It's good to see you," the young Marine said to her at their initial meeting before attempting to answer the rapid flurry of questions Richards put to him about what had happened here during the last twenty-four hours.

Throughout the course of the interview she asked several questions more than once, not because of Gardner's inability to answer but rather the simple fact that she was having difficulty believing everything she was hearing.

"You're saying that simple radio transmissions were enough to disrupt their weapons?" she asked.

Max nodded. "That is correct, though I would advise against you becoming too reliant on that tactic. It will not take long for Chodrecai weapons specialists to devise a counteraction to this difficulty."

He was right of course, and after a moment Richards realized how odd and yet somehow comfortable it felt to take advice from this alien. "Still," she said, "you were able to make it work just with what you had here. It's a strategy that might prove valuable toward developing something more effective if better equipment was brought into play." This bit of information would be in her first report to Op04-E as soon as she was done here.

"You have Sergeant Russell and Kel to thank for that," Gardner said. "They're the ones who came up with the idea and gave us our chance. Sergeant Major DiCarlo and your Mr. Nichols decided to destroy the portal before the Grays could set up permanent defenses to protect it." He spent a few minutes describing how the attack had unfolded, with massive casualties inflicted on both sides. The descriptions of the alien weapons on fragile human bodies caused Richards to swallow a succession of lumps that formed in her throat.

Finally, Gardner explained how DiCarlo and Nichols, along with Sergeant Russell and Kel, had directed the truck to the portal, causing the strange conduit to overload and ultimately disappear, the truck vanishing without a trace as well. "If you'd seen the weapons the Grays were building you'd understand what made them do it."

Richards nodded. "Don't worry, Brad. I know all about the turrets." Very quickly she briefed the young Marine and his alien friend about the developments taking place around the world. Gardner's face paled appreciatively as he absorbed the information.

"Jesus," he whispered. "What do we do now? I mean, we got our asses kicked here. There's something like fifteen of us left, out of fifty-three. If we're getting beat that badly all over the world . . ." The words died in his throat and he was silent for several seconds.

"We're not there yet," Richards said. "Your unit has already proven that we can fight them. We just have to be smarter about it from now on, that's all." She looked in Max's direction. "I don't think you realize what a valuable commodity you've become. If we're to have any chance of getting through this, it's going to have to be with your help, along with your friends." Returning her attention to Gardner she added, "And as for you, your ability to talk to the aliens in their own language is something no one else seems to have. My superiors are going to want to talk to you."

Richards did not want to say anything more for the moment, so as to avoid placing too much undue pressure on the Marine. The truth was that in short order Lance Corporal Brad Gardner would almost certainly find himself and his newfound yet still unique skills at the center of the astonishing events unfolding around them and indeed all across the planet.

"I think Sergeant Major DiCarlo and Mr. Nichols understood that trying to close that portal was a potential suicide mission, but they did it anyway," Gardner said after several moments spent grappling to keep his emotions in check. The extra effort had no doubt been required because of lack of sleep, to say nothing of the tremendous strain he had been under since all of this had started. "The same with Sergeant Russell and Kel. They knew, didn't they?"

"Most likely," Richards replied. "Nichols was an experienced agent, and I have no doubt that DiCarlo was an old hand in combat, too. It was a brave sacrifice, as were those made by the rest of the Marines in your unit. Unfortunately, they were only the first of many that we'll probably need before this is all over."

Looking at Max once more, it occurred to her that his presence here, along with that of every Plysserian and the Gray soldiers who had pursued him and his kind from their world to hers, could very well symbolize a turning point for every human who lived on this planet. Sacrifices made by the Marines of this small reserve unit and the aliens who had come to her aid were only the beginning, she knew, and they would not be limited to this small town in Missouri either. Such battles as the one fought here would have to be taken to the Grays everywhere, no matter the cost, if Earth were to have any hope of averting the alien threat.

It would be a war unlike anything the world had ever seen, making all previous conflicts pale in comparison. Could the various peoples who made up the planet's many dozens of nation-states come together in this time of crisis and focus on the single enemy threatening them all? How could the countless battles that humans waged among themselves, most of which were fueled by variations of negative emotions like greed, envy, or intolerance, possibly be important in the face of total extermination?

Alyssa Richards felt an icy hand grip her heart as she considered one final question: Was Humanity capable of coming together to wage a war where the prize was Earth itself?

Battleground

31

Studying the scene laid out in stark infrared detail before him through the lenses of his wide-angle night vision binoculars, Staff Sergeant Angus Feder felt the final shreds of doubt about his current mission inexorably melt away.

"Holy Mary, Mother of God."

As a soldier with the Australian Army, Feder had seen his share of action. He had participated in peacekeeping operations in East Timor and later as part of Operation Enduring Freedom and the United States-led coalition tasked with fighting the so-called "War on Terror." Rooting out Taliban and al-Qaeda terrorist forces hiding in the countless caves and underground tunnel networks crisscrossing Afghanistan's treacherous mountain regions had been as demanding an assignment as any he had ever been given.

Along with the training his unit had undergone beforehand, Feder had prepared himself for the type of guerrilla warfare he and his fellow soldiers were likely to encounter by reading several books covering the history of the region. Most informative had been the texts detailing the Russian military's efforts to subjugate the tiny country during the 1980s, which had aided his understanding of the Afghan people's notorious tenacity.

None of that had been enough to prepare Angus Feder for what he was looking at right now.

"With my own friggin' eyes I'm seein' this, and I still don't believe it," he said as he regarded the large rock formation perhaps seventy meters in front of his unit's present position. Barely visible in the feeble light captured by the night-vision viewfinder, it was obvious from the way the rocks were aligned that they had been moved into their current positions to form an effective defensive perimeter. Feder could also make out what could only be weapons emplacements positioned equidistantly around the barrier. Hints of movement behind the stone barrier caught his eye.

"Look to eleven o'clock," said Agent Campbell, the Defence Department operative who had been with the unit since the previous evening, speaking in hushed tones. Lying to Feder's right, he along with Lieutenant Matthew Bartus, Feder's platoon leader, shared the cluster of rock and dried, brittle grass. The rest of the platoon lay scattered about in a line to either side of him, hiding amid the sparse vegetation and rugged topography which was all that passed for cover and concealment in the stark terrain that characterized so much of western Australia. Slowly raising his arm, Campbell pointed toward the leftmost end of the massive stone perimeter. "See him poppin' his noggin up over the wall there?"

Orienting his binoculars in the indicated direction, Feder looked again and saw what the agent meant. Just visible near the far end of the barrier, he could see what looked to be the shape of a head poking up above one large boulder. It was obvious that it was not the head of a man as he judged its size, the lack of any hair, and the pallid gray coloring of its skin.

Alien.

It still seemed so much cods wallop. Aliens, invading different locations on Earth by means of passageways connected to their own planet? Soldiers from another world bringing their war here? It had sounded ludicrous to Feder during the briefing he and his unit had received a scant few hours earlier, but it was hard to hold on to such disbelief as he surveyed the scene before him.

Scrutinizing the encampment through his own binoculars, Bartus said, "Yeah, I got him. Big bastard, whatever the hell it is."

The strange creature looked much as Campbell had described during his initial mission briefing, and it absolutely resembled similar figures in photographs the agent had supplied. Taken by intelligence agents in the United States, the photographs had shown the bodies of alien soldiers along with many American Marines. The images were blunt testimony to a fierce battle and the numerous casualties suffered by both sides. Other such pictures, taken from high-altitude satellites and low-flying combat aircraft, depicted alien activity in a variety of locations including the British moors, areas of Russia, and elsewhere in the United States to name but a few examples.

It was the Americans' initial success against the "Grays," costly as it may have been, that had moved others to action. With several points of infiltration already identified, military commanders around the world were being directed to conduct reconnaissance missions, like the one Feder and his unit were currently undertaking, in order to determine the aliens' strengths and weaknesses. Though much was still unknown, the information provided during Campbell's briefing about the aliens' weapons had of course been of much interest to Feder and his fellow soldiers. The chilling descriptions of the pulse rifles' effects on the bodies of those humans who had fallen victim to attack had done much to quiet the normally jovial platoon.

Definitely don't want to hang my arse out around here, that's for sure.

"There's plenty of movement down there," he said as he continued to study the compound. "I'd guess about two dozen of them moving about. Probably more, considering how big that perimeter is." Feder knew from the photos provided by Campbell that the portal opening was at the center of the encampment set up by the Grays to defend the conduit, apparently a tactic currently being employed with varying degrees of success around the world. The photos also showed a myriad of equipment being staged, with the aliens using components brought through the portal from their own world to construct weapons platforms and mobile assault craft. Feder could not see any actual evidence of that from his current position, though, the massive stone barrier protecting such equipment from view.

"It looks like these boys have been here a while," Bartus said. "It would have taken time to set all that equipment up if they had to put it together." Campbell's report had indicated that the portals used by the aliens were too small to accommodate large equipment or vehicles, necessitating the disassembly of such assets prior to transport through the conduit from the aliens' home planet. That alone was sufficient reason for Feder to give thanks to whoever might be responsible for such a quirky stroke of good fortune.

Unlike the camp first discovered by the Marines in Missouri, this group of aliens appeared to have remained undetected long enough to establish a solid presence. It would have been a simple enough feat, Feder conceded, here in the isolated Outback. People traveled these routes only rarely, and even then they were only doing so to get away from here and to kinder, tamer environs.

"Do you think they're here alone?" he asked, lowering the binoculars and wiping sweat from his brow. "What about aliens from the other side? The Plusserians or whatever you call them."

"Plysserians," Campbell corrected. "Though the Yanks have taken to calling them Blues because of their elaborate tattoos." He shook his head as he wiped his own face with a rag from his jacket pocket. "Blues and Grays. Typical American simplicity at work."

Feder shrugged. "Seems a might easier than wrappin' your tongue around whatever it is those things call themselves, mate." Besides, in this case, the monikers seemed rather apt, he decided. Though the war the two alien armies seemed to be fighting was on a much greater scale than the American Civil War, it only made sense that their brother soldiers in the States would draw parallels to battles from their own history, assigning appropriate descriptors to the situation they currently faced.

Looking at his watch, Feder noted that he could almost tell the time without the aid of the timepiece's luminescent elements. "The sun'll be up in less than thirty minutes," he whispered. "Time to get out of here." They had to get back to base camp in order for Campbell to contact his superiors with what they had found out here, and wait for directives on what to do next. Feder imagined that those directives would entail some kind of offensive against the alien camp, much the same way that the Marines in Missouri had done. Those mates, most of them not even active soldiers, had done as good a job as could be expected given their circumstances. More important, he knew, their hard won knowledge would serve other military units as they prepared to deal with the alien threat. For that, Feder could salute the Americans.

Bartus and Campbell both nodded at Feder's suggestion. "Right," Bartus said. "Let's make tracks." Using hand signals to communicate with the soldiers nearest to them, who in turn then passed the instructions on down the line, Bartus and Feder gave the silent order to withdraw back the way they had come. It would not be an easy process, especially if the aliens' ability to see in the dark and their superior hearing were as accurate as Campbell had indicated during the briefing. His men were experienced field operators, though, and would take the necessary precautions to keep from revealing themselves. That meant everything from not lying or stepping on any of the dry grass and thereby leaving an imprint to ensuring that no gear or trash was left behind. They would leave as they came, in stealth.

It was not until they had crossed back over the first ridge and achieved a better sense of concealment from the enemy camp, doing so at a slow belly crawl over the unforgiving rock and hardened soil, that Feder allowed himself to relax even the slightest bit. Now hidden from the camp, he pulled himself to his feet and adjusted his grip on his Steyr AUG A1 assault rifle. Set to "Safe" while he had been observing the compound, his right hand moved the weapon's selector switch to firing mode.

Around him, other members of the platoon were moving into column formation for the march out of here. Two of his men had taken up positions to cover their withdrawal, and Feder knew that Lance Corporal Peter Holland was already taking his preferred place on point, scouting out ahead of the rest of the unit in search of any possible threats from their front. If anyone or anything was waiting to ambush them, Holland would sniff them out.

"Let's move," Bartus whispered and Feder nodded in acknowledgment.

It was the last thing he heard the lieutenant say before an ear-splitting howl, like that of an airplane's engine, filled the air and something passed to Feder's left from behind. It struck Bartus in the chest and the lieutenant disappeared in a spray of blood.

"Christ!"

Feder dove for cover, scrambling behind a small stone formation jutting from the rock littered soil even before the few remaining pieces of Matthew Bartus finished splattering to the ground. Despite his protective armor, the officer had stood no chance in the face of the alien weapons.

"Behind us!" he heard someone shout. Maybe it was Campbell but there was no way for Feder to be certain as more enemy fire filled the air. All around him, he heard shouts of warning and cries of pain as the alien weapons found other victims. Machine-gun fire rattled off somewhere to his right, the MAG-58's sharp staccato bursts echoing amid the rolling hills. Had the machine-gunner seen their attackers, or was he merely trying to lay down cover fire?

Looking back the way they had come, Feder saw large, dark figures moving with incredible speed among the rocks and the grass, the same rocks and grass that he and his men had used for cover only minutes earlier. Intermittent small arms fire sounded among the rocks to either side of him as his men also saw and tried to engage targets, dueling with the alien weapons to tear the air apart in a chaotic hellstorm.

Campbell had taken up a similar protective position behind a large boulder to Feder's right. "They saw us," the agent hissed. "They had to see us pulling back."

"No way," Feder said as he sighted along the length of his rifle's barrel and pulled the trigger, missing the fleeting figure he had aimed at. "They would have sounded an alarm if they'd seen us." He could feel the hairs on the back of his neck standing straight up. Something about what was unfolding around them simply did not feel right.

Shaking his head, Campbell replied, "Doesn't really matter now, does it, mate? One thing's for sure, though. We can't stay here."

Rather than answer, Feder instead fired again, tracking the running form of a Gray who was firing its weapon as it bounded across the broken terrain. He could see more of the alien soldiers moving amid the rocks. They were advancing at a startling rate and not enough of them were falling under the onslaught of his men's counterattack. If the platoon remained in place they would be overrun in minutes.

"Pull back!" he shouted over the din of weapons fire, rising to his feet and shooting as he backpedaled away from the approaching aliens. Campbell did likewise and both men fell into a practiced rhythm of watching the other's blind side as they retreated. As he moved he could see alien soldiers taking up positions behind rocks and small hills in front of him as well as on both flanks, and he realized just how vulnerable he and his men truly were. He could see some of his soldiers withdrawing along with him, but there were far more dark stains on the rocks where many of his men should have been. How many of them had been burned down by the alien weapons already?

"They're trying to hem us in!" In seconds enough of the aliens would be in position to catch him and the remainder of his men in a deadly crossfire. How had things deteriorated so quickly?

That was when Feder heard the new sound behind him, a deep mechanical hum coming from several sources and growing in intensity. He pivoted around, his rifle tight in his shoulder and its barrel tracking along with his eyes as he searched for the new threat.

Both eyes and rifle barrel stopped as he saw the squat, dull metallic hull of the assault vehicle, looking very much like the one in the photos Campbell had shown him, right down to the massive energy cannon mounted on its roof. The difference between the pictures and the real specimen sitting in front of him, of course, was the presence of the hulking Gray warrior wielding the weapon, its considerable muzzle aimed directly at him.

His arms folded across his chest, General Bruce Thompson regarded the various images displayed on the map wall's twelve huge screens, and did not like what he was seeing.

"We have reconnaissance missions underway in Brazil, Australia, and Canada. Local intelligence agencies are heading up military operations and coordinating their findings with our satellite offices in those regions," Nancy Spencer called out in his direction, indicating areas of a global map displayed on one of the wall's lower monitors. "Authorities in Brazil have lost contact with their infiltration team, and we've received word that the op in Canada was a failure. Flyovers of that area reported the total loss of the ground unit, along with two of three planes sent to provide air cover." Aiming a laser pointer toward the bottom right quadrant of the map she added, "We're still waiting to hear from the team in Australia and should have updated intel within the hour."

"Containment?" he asked.

Spencer regarded her palm-sized personal digital assistant before replying. "So far we only have isolated reports of civilians encountering aliens, but those people have been taken into custody for debriefing, along with a handful of journalists and law enforcement officers who were contacted. There's also reason to suspect that missing persons reports filed in some of those areas could be for people unlucky enough to have run into Grays. So far we've been extremely lucky, if you want to call it that."

It was an understatement. Efforts to keep the truth behind the current situation classified had been successful to this point, mostly because the aliens themselves were proving adept at remaining hidden. With concentrated search efforts underway and with incidents of contact on the rise, Thompson knew that it was only a matter of time before the aliens' existence became public knowledge. Further, if events continued to unfold the way they had in England, Brazil, Canada, and most likely Australia, a widespread panic was inevitable.

Putting aside that unpleasant line of thinking, Thompson pointed to one target area of the map that Spencer had not highlighted. "What about China?"

Spencer shook her head. "No go, General. They're not heeding our advice and conducting any kind of recon mission. At least, that's what they're telling us. Satellite imagery shows significant activity in the mountains east of Guangzhou, but no noticeable movement by Chinese military forces. From the looks of things the Grays are in full-scale construction mode, the same as what we saw in northern Russia. This is obviously one of the areas where the Blues arrived early on and were able to remain undiscovered until the Grays followed them through."

"Damn," Thompson said. "Why can't they listen to us just once?" He knew the answer, of course. Political relations between the United States and the Republic of

China had long been strained, but most decidedly so in the past few years. The capture of a U.S. Navy spy plane forced to land after colliding with a Chinese fighter jet had fueled that tension, as had the United States' position on the longstanding dispute over Taiwan's wish to remain an independent nation rather than part of the ROC. So, naturally, both governments scowled at one another from their respective capitals and the Chinese leadership consumed itself with worry, as always, about saving face before a global audience. There was no way they would allow themselves to appear dependent on the United States for anything, even knowledge that might help their country avoid a serious ass kicking.

Many of the problems affecting the state of affairs between the countries could be traced to the current White House administration. How would the president react to this latest news when Thompson briefed him, along with his cabinet and the Joint Chiefs of Staff, in a little less than twenty minutes?

Politics really were not Thompson's concern at the moment though. The problem in China was symptomatic of the larger dilemma the whole world would be facing in the coming days. Detecting the Grays' presence around the planet was difficult and time-consuming, even with the balance of the United States' military reconnaissance satellites already retasked for the purpose. The aliens were proving to be anything but stupid, no doubt familiar with the concept of evading high-altitude surveillance on their own world.

What type of technology did the Blues, or the Grays for that matter, employ to perform that sort of reconnaissance? Thompson figured that, like their weapons, it was sure to be more advanced than anything created by a human.

Just be thankful they apparently couldn't bring all of that with them, he mused. *Otherwise, this thing would've been over before it even started.*

It was also obvious to Thompson from the results of reported engagements with the Grays that he and his staff had underestimated the aliens' abilities. This, even after reviewing every scrap of information relayed to them from various locations before disseminating that data to intelligence agencies around the world. Despite the plethora of technology and armaments at their disposal, human military units were being beaten back if not crushed outright time and again.

The difficulties experienced by ground forces were actually less depressing than the reports Thompson had seen detailing the effects of airborne assaults on the alien positions. The antiaircraft weaponry deployed by the Grays had proven to be devastating against assault aircraft as well as bombs dropped from high altitude and even long-range missile attacks. As had happened with the RAF squadrons in England, further assets had been lost in similar offensives around the globe as the alien weapons surgically removed incoming threats from the air with ease.

Spencer's report was but the latest addition to a list that included setbacks and defeats in northern Russia, Africa, and South Dakota. The victory in Missouri, meager as it might be, was their sole cause for celebration at this point.

So, what you're saying is that you need more help. Right, General?

Turning away from the map wall, Thompson searched the room until his eyes fell on Brigadier General Brooks.

"Tommy, what about the Blues our people rounded up in Missouri? Where are they now?"

Brooks looked up from where he was observing an Army captain scroll through pages of computer information detailing the alien encounters to this point. "They're being detained by Agent Richards and her people at the National Guard base there while the troops we sent there round up the remaining pieces of alien hardware." The Marine reservist unit had, through an action of sheer audacity laced with liberal amounts of luck, succeeded in closing the alien portal located there. Casualties had been prolific, including the loss of the unit's officers and senior enlisted personnel, but the Marines had also secured a treasure trove of alien weaponry and equipment.

Typical jarheads. Even their part-timers are balls to the wall. Thompson knew, though, that the Marines' tactical victory would not have been possible, though, without the assistance of the Blues who had befriended them. Was that an asset that could be counted on again? If so, to what extent? How far could this bizarre newfound relationship be expanded?

"Get them on a plane, Tommy," he said. "I want them and whoever's talking to them here, and I want 'em here yesterday."

33

"Listen to me! You tell that cocksucker client of yours that I don't give a damn if he got an Oscar for that bullshit art flick. He committed to two fucking sequels before he became the Academy's bitch, goddammit."

A car horn blared behind Diana Kraft as she changed lanes without signaling, and she pulled the one hand she did have on the steering wheel away long enough to give the horn blower the finger without looking. Then that idiot was forgotten as she guided her Audi convertible around the one that had made her switch lanes in the first place, a weak-looking man with wire frame glasses who was driving a Saturn in the fast lane with all the speed of a turtle walking through molasses.

When are they gonna install lanes for people who have shit to do?

Diana Kraft, Hollywood producer and the guiding hand behind a string of successful movies in recent years, including one that could almost be called a blockbuster, simply had no time for the rest of the world to meander through life at its own insufferable pace. She had not been clawing her way up the ladder of the show business power elite just to wait for people to kick their own asses into the proper gear, damn it. Her last picture had the studio execs buzzing with talk of sequels and perhaps even a full-blown franchise featuring the actor who had portrayed the star character. Kraft knew that if the sequel she was working on right now proved successful it would be the final rung of that ladder for her. She would join that small select cadre of uber producers, most of them men, with total control over the projects she worked on. Actors would beg to be in her movies, and studio suits would beg for her expertise and be willing to pay top dollar for it. She would be able to write her own ticket.

Assuming, of course, that the morons driving in front of her right now would get the hell out of her way and let her get to her office.

"Yeah, well if he thinks he can pull that holding up production shit so he can renegotiate his contract," she barked into her phone, "you tell him I'll make damn sure his next job in Hollywood is the assistant jizz mopper at a peep show on El Centro, understand?"

The applause had not even begun to fade at the Academy Awards ceremony before her star had begun his version of the now-accepted stalling tactic, using the golden statue's clout to demand more money for his work on the movie he was working on for Kraft. He saw himself as the champion of crossover appeal; his work on the low-budget independent film that had garnered him rave reviews and his first Oscar would most certainly be good for Kraft's studio and their more mainstream action extravaganza.

Renegotiations between the whiney asshole and the studio had already happened once in the months since the ceremony, but now it seemed he wanted even more money. Apparently, being guaranteed a disproportionate percentage of what was sure to be monster grosses was no longer enough. This had generated the rather spirited conversation Kraft was now having with the actor's agent, who had seen the dollar signs in the air the moment he heard his client's name announced after the words, "And the winner is . . ."

Conniving little prick.

A beeping sound from the Audi's passenger seat caught her attention, and Kraft switched the phone to her left ear with practiced ease and steered the car with her left elbow as she reached for the PalmPilot sitting atop her briefcase. As she did so she knocked over the open bottle of mineral water resting there, splashing its contents all over the seat and everything on it.

"Shit!" she yelled, dropping the phone into her lap and forgetting about the idiot on the other end of the line as she reached to rescue her purse and her PDA, taking her eyes off the road for a moment as she did so.

And then all hell broke loose.

Tires squealed somewhere ahead of her and Kraft jerked her head back to the front in time to see an ocean of brake lights flaring bright crimson as cars and trucks across all five lanes of southbound highway traffic swerved and fishtailed on the concrete roadway. Vehicles slammed into one another in an ear-splitting, gut-wrenching cacophony of splintering glass and crunching metal. Kraft stomped on her own brakes and jerked the steering wheel to the left but it was too little too late as the Audi careened into the back end of the SUV she had been tailgating.

White exploded all around her, the driver-side airbag deploying and enveloping her in its massive cushion of air as the passenger side of the car slammed into the truck.

Whooshing air from the bag drowned out everything else as her momentum jerked Kraft toward the impact, her seat belt tearing into her skin through the fabric of her clothes. She heard more tires screeching on pavement and she realized that other cars were driving headlong into the escalating pileup with each passing heartbeat.

As the airbag deflated and she fought to get it away from her face she detected movement to her left. Instinct made her claw her way toward the passenger side of the car as she turned to see a minivan sliding to stop next to her, coming to rest so close to her door that she could see the collection of bugs plastered on its radiator grill.

Around her the chaos began to subside. The acrid stench of burned rubber and smoke filled the air and she became aware of car horns blaring all around her and people calling out for help. What the hell had happened? A jackknifed semi? Punks dropping cinder blocks off an overpass? Snipers? Kraft had seen it all in the seven years since moving to Los Angeles from Nebraska in search of her dream career, so nothing really surprised her anymore as much as it simply irritated the shit out of her.

The driver side door was stuck and would not open so Kraft was forced to climb over the side of the car to get out, after first determining that she had not sustained any serious injuries of her own. Standing beside her own wrecked vehicle she could now see the extent of the accident. All around her cars and trucks of all sizes had piled up alongside and on top of one another. Some of the vehicles were on fire and people were running all about the area.

No. The people, all of them, were running toward her, screaming as if in the grips of panic. Rather than running to the scene of the greatest damage in an attempt to help, those people who could move under their own power had abandoned their vehicles and were running north, away from the central point of the pileup. *Dear God*, her mind screamed. *Had a chemical truck exploded or been damaged? Was it leaking poisonous crap into the air?*

Kraft was ready to take off running herself when she heard something else amid the screams. It was a kind of electrical whine pulsing sporadically from somewhere ahead of her. What the hell was that? Whatever it was, she realized, it was getting louder. And closer. Kraft turned at the sounds of lumbering footsteps and as she did so she froze in shock at the horrific vision approaching her.

Massive, gray, and muscled. Huge dark lifeless eyes that reminded her of the sharks she had watched on Discovery Channel documentaries. It was carrying something in its enormous arms and turning to aim one end of it at her. Long and shiny, it looked to be a rifle of some kind.

She recognized the gaping black maw staring at her to be the weapons' muzzle just before the shrieking whine sounded one final time.

34

You were right, Nicole, Thompson mused. *I should have retired five years ago and opened that fishing camp in Montana.*

His wife had always been the smarter half of his marriage, a fact to which he had comfortably conceded many years ago. It had been her suggestion that he retire upon reaching his thirtieth year of service, and the discussions of what they might do afterward had filled the air over many Sunday breakfasts. Moving to Montana was the one idea that had intrigued them both, along with the leisurely lifestyle offered by that beautiful state. Plans had been made and dreams had been refined in preparation for the next chapter in their lives together once his time in uniform was completed.

Nicole's untimely death from cancer six years previously had derailed those plans, and with her gone and his children long since grown and departed from home, there was no one with whom Thompson could share that new life. His lone alternative, he had decided, was to continue with the one thing that still brought him satisfaction: Putting on his uniform and carrying out his assigned duties.

And look what that got you, he chided himself as he watched the center screen on the map wall, where the one thing he had been dreading for weeks was now playing out for anyone with a television to see.

"You are watching footage provided by NewsChopper 5 from above the Hollywood Freeway," the voice of the female news anchor said, *"where something incredible is happening."*

The images provided by the helicopter showed a section of the normally bustling highway that was a major artery of Los Angeles traffic. A massive pileup of vehicles cluttered the road, clogging all of the southbound lanes. Some of the cars were burning where they had crashed into others or into the retaining wall dividing the highway. Figures moved among the wreckage, though to Thompson's dismay many of them were not human. Gray soldiers were spreading out in what he could clearly see was a combat formation, sweeping the area and shooting at anyone they encountered. The video feed from the helicopter captured the carnage without compassion as the alien weapons effortlessly carved through human flesh and bone.

"Holy God," someone said. Thompson did not recognize the voice, but he agreed with the sentiment. Even with the proliferation of real-time reporting that had accompanied military operations for the last decade, including ventures into combat zones, death was still something that most television producers chose to keep from the eyes of American television viewers. Occasionally a car chase that ended in tragedy or the climax of a shootout between police officers and criminal suspects made it to local newscasts, but for the most part showing human lives ending violently was still a broadcast taboo.

Except for today.

On the screen, the image from the helicopter shifted to show the focal point of the accident and the frenzied swirl of colors that Thompson now recognized as the opening to one of the alien portals. Larger than other portals he had seen captured by satellite imagery, Gray soldiers had established a defensive perimeter around it as a convoy of their assault vehicles emerged from the entryway. The vehicles were dispersing as soon as they cleared the portal,

"It's a turkey shoot down there," Tommy Brooks said as he moved to stand beside Thompson. "They've figured out a way to make the conduits large enough to get equipment through without taking it apart first."

On the screen the female anchor said, *"This footage is being carried via CNN to pretty much everyone around the world, and we have begun to receive reports from some of our sister stations of similar events unfolding in other cities around the country."* The image on the scene shifted to that of a pair of Grays moving through the wreckage on the highway, firing at anything that moved. *"Gigantic creatures carrying weapons that literally tear their targets apart are appearing out of thin air and attacking anything and anyone they see. We have attempted to contact local authorities about what you're watching right now, but so far they are not responding."*

"No shit, they're not responding," Nancy Spencer said as she stepped from behind one of the computer workstations and moved toward the map wall. "We're getting reports from all over the place, General. Los Angles, Toronto, Rome, Philadelphia, Sydney, and Seattle so far. It's as if the Grays aren't even making an attempt to sneak around anymore."

Thompson grunted at the report. "Why should they? They've got us by the balls." The incidents of encounters between humans and aliens had been escalating in the weeks since the initial contact in Missouri. All across the planet, military forces and equipment were being stretched to the limit in response to the increasing Gray threat. Efforts to keep the situation contained and secret from the eyes of the civilian populace had been mostly successful, miraculously, with only a few isolated incidents even making it to news organizations. Those occurrences had been treated with much the same disdain and annoyance as reports of UFO and alien sightings had always been regarded. The buzz on the Internet ran the gamut from people talking about what they had seen to full blown theories about how the Earth was experiencing the initial stages of total conquest at the hands of an alien army. Most of it, like a good portion of the "information" infesting the Web, could be dismissed as the delusions of those desperate for attention.

This latest development was the realization of Thompson's worst nightmare about what the Grays might try next. Apparently no longer content to exploit the portal openings that had already been established by the Plysserians for use by their own forces, the Grays had now seen fit to begin creating new conduits that could disgorge fresh troops wherever the mysterious technology saw fit to deposit them.

And they're making them bigger, he reminded himself. *Don't forget that.*

"What's the story in Texas?" he asked.

Consulting her PDA, Spencer replied, "A militia group based outside of Houston somehow found out about a

Gray contingent during one of their weekly meetings at a local gun range. They used a couple of pickup trucks loaded with homegrown explosives made from fertilizer and whatever the hell else those idiots find that will blow up, and drove them right into the Grays' camp." She shook her head and a small, humorless laugh escaped her lips. "Nice job, cowboys. Anyway, they destroyed the place and killed a number of the aliens, but captured a couple of survivors and delivered them to local law enforcement." Looking up from her PDA she added, "Not like those boys to trust the government, but I guess when aliens come to take over your planet you tend to reevaluate who you distrust, huh?"

"They didn't find the portal that's been pinpointed in that region, though," Brooks said. "Our agents in the area managed to keep the situation contained, so no media found out about it. Not that it matters much now."

Thompson absorbed the reports for a moment before saying anything. Everything happening right now was obviously part of some new strategy by the Grays, but to what end? The areas selected for these latest attacks were all dense population centers, but they held no strategic value that he could ascertain. Even if the cities being infiltrated did hold some military importance, how would the Grays have determined that?

"What else?" he asked.

Brooks exhaled a tired sigh before replying. "We have confirmation that the Grays have figured out our little trick of jamming their weapons with radio frequencies. It looks as though they're simply overpowering our transmissions with their own equipment, which puts out more juice than most of the gear we can move into position against them. The 'anti-jamming' equipment seems to be deployed at some of the camps we've found, especially those with portals, but not with any troops or vehicles that are on the move."

"Our guess," Spencer continued, "is that the equipment needed for the job is too big to move around easily, and they haven't built enough units to deploy to all of their camps yet." She shrugged at that part of the report. "Anyway, that's why we've had some success against a few of their groups. The Chinese took out one camp in the Philippines with naval bombardment, and we hit another with a squadron of Cobra gunships near Albuquerque, but these camps didn't have antiaircraft weaponry deployed yet. And don't forget those ballsy boys down in Texas."

Thompson smiled slightly at that last part. In the wake of what was being broadcast right now around the globe from Los Angeles and with the reports coming in from the other cities Spencer had cited, there was no way to keep the situation contained any longer. As encounters with alien contingents increased in frequency all around the world and the military forces of nearly every nation were called into service to combat them, incidents such as the ones in Texas would surely become more common in the coming days. A speech had already been prepared for delivery by the president of the United States in the event that something like Los Angeles occurred, with similar pronouncements to be made by other national leaders around the world as they saw fit. By this time tomorrow most of the planet's population would be aware of the aliens' presence.

As the situation continued to worsen, Thompson knew, partisan groups would begin to spring up everywhere.

These would in turn give rise to further grass roots skirmishes as citizens took up arms or whatever they could fashion into weapons to defend their communities, at least long enough for organized military forces to arrive and assist them. It was the same story that had been told in every war that humans had ever fought. Many of those people would fall victim to the Grays' superior firepower and technology, dying perhaps even before he and his group or similar organizations in other countries became aware of the aliens' presence in a particular area. Even if military assets could be directed to a point of Gray infiltration, chances are that they would be outclassed as well.

"What about finding more of the Blues?" he asked.

Spencer nodded her head. "The ones who survived the Missouri battle have been very cooperative, General. Their comm techs have been working with our people to adapt our communications technology to better interact with their own. We were able to send encrypted messages to several isolated pockets of Blue forces. Those who've come forward to help us say there should be more of them out there, but so far they haven't responded."

The number of Blue soldiers that had been located to date was not encouraging to Thompson. There were not enough of them to provide assistance as they had in Missouri, and a precious few other isolated locations on the larger scale that he knew would soon be required if there was to be any chance of repelling the growing Gray threat.

Sighing in exasperation, Thompson shook his head. "Why the hell didn't I retire?"

Qudamah ran.

His pulse hammered in his ears and his breath came in quick yet controlled bursts as Qudamah Abul-Fath sprinted across the uneven terrain, trusting his feet not to betray him to the unforgiving landscape. Swift and sure, he found the places between the rocks and across the ruts in the broken ground as he propelled himself deeper into the desert canyon along with the other soldiers who were all that remained of three platoons. As he ran, he prayed for Allah to guide them through the darkness.

"Fall back! Fall back!" Sergeant Yassin's voice sounded over the chaos surrounding Qudamah. Yassin was bringing up the rear, laying down suppressing fire to cover their retreat. Every few seconds Qudamah heard the sharp report of the sergeant's AK-47 as Yassin turned to fire back the way they had come.

This was most definitely not what Qudamah had expected when he had joined the army last year. In the aftermath of the Taliban's removal from power and the establishment of Afghanistan's provisional government, Qudamah and other men like him, each possessing the desire to defend their nation, had responded to the call for service in the country's new army. The promise of hot meals, warm beds, and a salary that would more than take care of his family's needs had been more than enough incentive for him to join. Like everyone else who stepped forward to serve, Qudamah figured that the enemies he would be fighting were those he was already familiar with during decades of conflict in his native land.

The enemy he fought today was something else entirely.

Taken on its own merits, the report of the strange creatures in the desolate region west of Kandahar had sounded like the ravings of a delusional mind, but Qudamah had seen the news reports in recent days and knew that the world was apparently in the grips of a new menace that threatened everyone. The creatures, Grays as they were being called on the American news channels, had established a camp of sorts here, the isolated expanse of mountains and desert offering them ideal conditions for concealment. It had only been due to one old man stumbling across the encampment that the army had been alerted at all. A trader in scrap metal scouring the uninviting landscape in search of debris left over from decades of war waged with all manner of enemies, the man had been blessed with the good fortune to get away from the area undetected so that he could inform local authorities.

The camp the old man had found was a small one, harboring perhaps two dozen of the creatures. The platoon leaders had theorized that this might be some kind of advance scouting party, and that other such groups were probably hiding out elsewhere in the desert. If what the soldiers had been told about the method of the aliens' arrival on Earth was true, then one of the mysterious doorways to their own planet was still out there, somewhere in the wilderness, waiting to be found. With this in mind, the officers agreed that the best strategic move would be to attack this smaller camp, confident in the knowledge that the number of soldiers they commanded would be more than sufficient to accomplish that objective.

The officers were wrong.

"Look out!" someone behind him shouted as the now familiar hum of energy echoed among the rocks behind Qudamah and his ears were assaulted by an agonized cry as yet another of his fellow soldiers fell in the face of enemy fire.

It was foolish to attack them without support, Qudamah knew, but as a lowly soldier in the army he was not in a position to do anything except obey the orders of those appointed over him. Yes, larger numbers and the element of surprise had been on the side of the Afghan soldiers in the battle's opening moments as they launched a three-pronged attack on the alien camp.

The Grays had taken no time to turn the tide in their favor thanks to the superior firepower they commanded. While perhaps half of the Grays had been injured or killed, the Afghan soldiers had incurred many more casualties including most of the officers, who had led the charge and were among the first to be exposed to alien weapons fire. Leadership of the surviving soldiers was now left to sergeants like Yassin, who had wasted no time determining the futility of direct action against the Grays and sounded the retreat.

Rifle fire to his left made Qudamah turn to see two soldiers, their forms illuminated in the pale light offered by the moon, firing back the way they had come. Then a large gray blur was bounding over the rocks, an alien warrior firing its own weapon as it came into view.

"No!" Qudamah cried in vain, freezing in his tracks as he watched for the first time the effects of an alien rifle as the energy it discharged tore through both the air and the two soldiers' bodies with equal ease. Blood and the shredded fragments of what had an instant before been two men sprayed everywhere, a sickening sight that was augmented by the sound it made as it splattered across the rocks and the parched soil.

How are we to fight something like this? His mind screamed the question at him, but he had no answers. Could anyone or anything on Earth stand up to the threat these aliens represented? Unable to answer that question, either, he instead did the only thing he could.

Qudamah ran.

"Fire!"

No sooner did Major Kung Jae Paik give the order, than the cacophony of his Russian-engineered T-72 tank's main gun hammered his ears and the familiar scent of expended gunpowder assailed his nostrils. He had waited as long as he dared before giving the command, hoping to catch the maximum number of enemy soldiers in the killing zone as possible.

Kung knew from the intelligence briefings about their adversaries that he and his troops would only get one chance to make a sizable dent in the opposing force before they reacted. It would have to be a good one if he and his men stood any hope of halting their enemy's advance, and he had chosen this flat, low-lying expanse of land between the rolling hills for just that reason. Flanked on all sides by thick forest undergrowth helping to conceal his mechanized forces in the predawn darkness, it was the one area along the route the aliens were taking toward the city of Sariwon that presented the best opportunity for an ambush.

He watched through his targeting viewfinder as the first shell impacted the target area, followed an instant later by a barrage of other rounds from the first wave of tanks as their commanders commenced firing on his signal. Dirt and rock hurtled into the air from the force of the explosions, the thick dust they kicked up not quite obscuring the scene of dozens of alien bodies being cast in all directions along with the wreckage from some of their own assault vehicles. The first volley was as devastating as Kung had hoped, his confidence buoyed as those aliens not affected by the initial attack scattered for cover.

Now that the attack was underway, the individual tank commanders were authorized to fire at will as targets became available. Kung nodded to himself in satisfaction as the battle unfolded and the officers under his command reacted in accordance with their training. He did not have to look to know that his own crew was reloading the main gun with practiced ease, ejecting the spent shell and replacing it with a new one as he and his assistant gunner went through the process of selecting a new target. It was a cycle they would repeat as many times as was necessary, with each iteration taking only seconds to carry out and employed with a near-perfect choreography honed from hours of intensive training.

"Move out," he called to the driver and the tank lurched forward, emerging from the concealment of the forest and accelerating as it broke out onto open ground. After seeing what the aliens were capable of in battle, he had no desire to sit still and wait to fall victim to their weapons.

The Grays were getting bolder since their initial discovery in America several weeks previously. As if realizing that stealth no longer mattered to their plans, the aliens had instead taken to launching brazen attacks on any humans they came across. They were expanding outward from the points where they had arrived from their own planet and continuing to capture territory as more of their soldiers emerged from the conduits. So far, they had stayed away from larger cities and towns, but Kung suspected that such targets would be the aliens' next logical step as their numbers continued to grow. Conservative estimates placed nearly three hundred thousand of the aliens now on Earth, at least in those areas where their presence had been confirmed. The idea that uncounted more of the creatures could be hiding out in places that had so far avoided detection chilled Kung's blood, though for now he could only concern himself with the Grays presently looming before him.

American, Russian, and Chinese satellites had detected both a portal and the presence of several thousand aliens in Korea alone. Military units like Kung's, on alert from the moment the first images of aliens had been transmitted around the world from the United States, had been deployed to protect the country's major cities from attack. Even now there were more sightings of Grays moving toward the larger population centers, which had prompted military leaders to provide protection and, if possible, launch preemptive strikes. It was not these heavily populated areas that concerned Kung, but rather the uncounted small villages, settlements, and family farms scattered across the Korean peninsula. There were more civilians spread out across hundreds of thousands of square miles than there were soldiers to protect them.

The cold, harsh reality of the situation was that the beleaguered North Korean military's best chance of protecting the greatest number of people was to defend the cities like Sariwon. With that in mind as he prepared for battle, Kung had broken regulations and dispatched a messenger to the village of Numai in the hopes of warning his parents and the other residents to evacuate the area before the aliens came. That he had not yet heard from his soldiers worried him, but he forced the troubling thought away as he focused once again on the situation at hand.

"Do you have a target?" he asked his assistant gunner, who answered in the affirmative and gave him the coordinates. Wiping sweat from his brow, Kung adjusted the viewfinder until he found the cluster of Grays spotted by his A-gunner and smiled in satisfaction. It was not one of their vehicles but it would have to do. "Fire." Another explosion flared in the targeting scope as the shell found its target, obliterating the group of alien warriors.

The enemy was rallying, though. Having broken away from the wedge formation that they seemed to prefer for ground movement, Gray soldiers now scurried for cover as assault vehicles that had not yet been damaged took evasive maneuvers. Kung could hear the high-pitched whine of alien energy weapons and then the hull of the tank shuddered around him. To his left he heard one of his men curse and he turned to see that a sizable dent had been pounded into the vehicle's armor plating. A tiny pinprick of light shone through at the center of the dent, testifying to the power of the Gray pulse rifle even against the tank's fortified exterior. He knew that the weapons carried by the alien ground troops were powerful, but it was something altogether different to see their effects for himself. Given the small demonstration he had just witnessed, it was almost certain that their assault craft were more than capable of defeating the tanks.

"Concentrate on their vehicles!" he barked into his radio headset, broadcasting his order simultaneously to the other tank commanders even as his own A-gunner fed him coordinates for one of the alien craft.

The next shell they fired only caught a glancing blow but it was enough to send the vehicle careening into a nearby hillside. In his headset Kung heard the reports of other commanders relaying similar success as they continued to engage targets as well as calls for assistance as some tanks took enemy fire of their own. So far he had heard two other commanders relay that their vehicles were disabled. Were there others? How much longer could his luck hold out?

Kung had no idea how much time passed before his A-gunner finally shouted, "They're retreating!" And it was true, too. In the viewfinder he could see alien soldiers turning away from the battle and retreating across the open ground, heading back the way they had come. He could only see two of their vehicles, one of them billowing smoke, and both of them were turning about to retreat as well. Amazing as the idea had sounded to him several hours ago, it seemed as though their ambush had been successful after all.

"We're going after them," he said, giving the order over the radio for his remaining tanks to give chase. Considering how few victories had been enjoyed against the Grays since their arrival, it would be ludicrous in Kung's mind not to press any kind of tactical advantage that presented itself.

It is time for us to take this fight to our invaders.

37

In the five years since she had first come to Norcross, Detective Angela Salinas had watched the suburb of northeast Atlanta evolve from a quiet, unassuming community to one plagued by the problems that had once been primarily the scourge of the inner cities. Gang activity, a growing element here over the past few years, had risen to such critical levels in recent months that the Gwinnett County Sheriff's Department had established a task force to deal with the increasing problem. Salinas and the other ten detectives who comprised the unit had been given only one assignment: Find a way to deal with the gangs.

It had always been easier said than done, of course. Hundreds of kids in this part of northern Georgia were reportedly immersed in the turbulent lifestyle. Whether they were black, white, Latino, Chinese, or Japanese, racial and socioeconomic backgrounds did not seem to factor into the decision to join a gang. Some of the groups were small and concerned themselves with little more than robberies, burglaries, and carjackings, while others were branches of larger gangs networked across the country and involved in all manner of organized crime from drug trafficking to gun running to prostitution and even child slavery.

Then there was the intra-gang warfare, of course. Dispute over territory was commonplace, and clashes between the various groups occurred with frightening regularity. Oftentimes innocent bystanders and other people unfortunate enough to be in the wrong place at the wrong time were caught in the middle of the skirmishes, compounding the dilemma Salinas and her fellow police officers faced.

Of course, she mused as she regarded the scene around her, *if we get more days like this one, I might just be out of a job.*

Her hands tucked into the pockets of her khaki pants, Salinas slowly walked the perimeter of the playground located at the center of Norcross Park, now designated as a crime scene. Yellow caution tape was strung between the trees surrounding the playground, warning spectators to remain outside the area lest they interfere with detectives and forensic scientists working to gather evidence. In this particular instance, Salinas found the sight of the yellow barrier almost humorous given the fact that even now, in the middle of the afternoon, not a single civilian had come to gawk at the goings-on. Recent events, including the news that one of the mysterious alien portals had been detected outside Atlanta along with a large contingent of Gray soldiers and their war machines, had conspired to drive people from the area in search of a safe haven from the alien invaders. That is, if indeed such a place existed anymore.

Looking down at the bodies of two Gray warriors Salinas took some comfort in the idea that the aliens were not indestructible. They could be defeated, and not even with sophisticated military weaponry. Each riddled with dozens of bullet wounds, the gang symbols sprayed across the aliens' armor and the ground around them was testament enough of that. Dark fluid had leaked in copious amounts from the multiple wounds, obscuring portions of the graffiti, but not so much that Salinas could not recognize the markings.

More bodies were scattered around the playground as well, at least two dozen, though almost all of them were human or the remains of what had once been human. Though she had seen her share of death and the different types of trauma that could be inflicted on a body, Salinas had not been prepared for the level of carnage that the aliens' weapons were capable of unleashing. The odor of spilled blood and ruptured organs hung over the playground like a blanket and it was all she could do to remember to breathe through her mouth.

"Weird, ain't it?" said the man standing on the other side of the two aliens at her feet. Shaking his head he added, "Tagged by gang bangers? I've seen a lot of strange shit in my time, but this ranks right up there."

He had identified himself simply as Agent Reynolds, dispatched by the Pentagon to investigate reports of alien activity in this area. At least, that's what her captain had told her when he had made the introductions earlier in the morning. It was all she had to go on, as Reynolds himself had so far not been inclined to offer much in the way of supplementary information. Based by his speech patterns and the way that he carried himself, the man was either active military or had recently left the service and the old habits were still ingrained in his system. The black combat fatigues he wore offered no insignia to indicate a service branch, though his close-cropped brown hair suggested either the Marines or Army.

"Any idea which gang did this?" Reynolds asked, indicating the alien corpses again.

Salinas nodded. "Two separate gangs, actually." She pointed to the two very different symbols gracing each of the dead soldier's chest armor. "This first marker is used by the Brownside Locos, and the other one belongs to the Latin Kings. They're both pretty big gangs in this area and rivals, too, at least so far as we know, which makes this even weirder than you think."

"How so?" Reynolds asked.

"The Locos and the Kings hate each other. They're always mixing it up in various pissing contests over who owns what street corner or park. They've had more than a few throwdowns in this general area." In fact, she had come here to investigate so many gang-related incidents in the past two years that she felt she almost knew every square inch of the park.

"Usually when one gang tags something that's already been marked by another gang," she continued, "they cross out or otherwise desecrate the first group's tag. It's a common way of showing disrespect." Pointing at the symbols on the dead aliens' chests again she added, "but these markings were made so as to deliberately avoid obscuring each other. The Locos and the Kings have joined together."

She nodded to where several human bodies were strewn about in the grass field that formed the perimeter of the playground. "Have you taken a look at the bangers lying out here? That is, the ones that weren't shot to shit by those alien weapons. They've got two different sets of colors on them, but not a one of them looks to have died by normal gunfire or knife or whatever else a banger would use to off somebody. And none of the bodies have been fucked with like we normally see when rival gangs mix it up."

Movement to her right made Salinas turn to see a man and a woman, dressed like Reynolds, working over the corpse of yet another Gray soldier. While the man took photographs with a digital camera, the woman was dictating something into a small voice recorder, though Salinas could not hear the words. The detective noted how easily the two agents went about their work, as if they might have had cause to examine the body of a dead alien before. That alone was an interesting thought, she conceded, but not one she could afford to waste time pursuing today.

"Gotta give 'em credit for balls," Reynolds said. "There're only the four Grays here. Must have been a scouting party or else maybe they got separated from a larger group." He shook his head. "The portal is about fifty miles north of Macon, way south of here, so I have to wonder what the hell they're doing this far north. There's been no other indication of activity in this area."

"Maybe they're probing," Salinas offered. "Checking for weak spots. There's plenty of places around this city to hide and stage your forces for an assault." For all they knew there could be a million more of the things surrounding Atlanta and preparing for an all-out attack. She paused as the vision took hold in her mind and the chill it brought with it ran down her spine.

"Something else," Reynolds offered as he pointed to

the dead aliens again. "Their pulse rifles are missing. The surviving gang members must have taken them." He frowned and shook his head. "Bangers with ray guns. The general's going to think I'm smoking crack when I call this in."

Sighing in exasperation, Salinas said, "Where the hell were these aliens five years ago when I started this shit?" It was a lame attempt at dry humor that fell flat, though Reynolds had the decency to chuckle anyway.

Her mission as part of her department's task force had been to find a way to rid the community of its gang problem. Part of that assignment had been attempting to get the various opposing gangs to at least stop killing each other long enough to reach some kind of temporary truce. From there it was hoped that they could move forward with lofty ideas of fashioning ultimate peace between the factions. There was no denying the stark irony that while every tactic her department had tried in order to accomplish even that fundamental goal had failed almost without exception, two of the fiercest gang rivals in Atlanta had apparently joined forces without fanfare in order to combat a common threat. Though their tactics had been horribly unrefined, they had been enough to take care of business against this small alien contingent.

Irony, Angela Salinas decided, was a bitch.

38

It was an effort for Wu Ailiang to control his hands, which had begun to shake during the past few minutes. The sensation appeared to be worsening the closer they drew to their target. With the duties of flying the strike bomber left to the capable hands of his pilot and friend, Bai Peitan, there was nothing for Wu to do except monitor the status of their payload and the plane's fire control system as he contemplated the action they were about to undertake.

"Range to target is seven hundred miles," he reported as he reviewed the bank of computerized status displays on the console before him.

In the plane's front seat, Bai nodded. "Arm the weapon." It was an order the pair had exchanged and carried out hundreds of times before, though each of those occasions had been as part of a training exercise. Today was the first time that Wu, or any other officer in the People's Liberation Army Air Force for that matter, would carry out the simple instruction in an actual combat scenario. He tried not to think about that as he moved trembling fingers over his control console.

Have we really come to this? The question, among others, raged in Wu's mind. Surely there had to be a better way to deal with this threat? Had those in authority truly exhausted every option available to them? Was what he and Bai were about to do really the only remaining viable alternative?

After the revelation of the aliens elsewhere in the world, every effort had been undertaken to locate the presence of invaders within China's borders. Some army units had already encountered groups of Gray soldiers in remote areas. In almost all cases those engagements had gone badly for the Chinese forces. The aliens, having apparently arrived here several weeks before the detection of their comrades in the United States, had established a base camp surrounding the gateway which connected their own world with Earth. While skirmishes against smaller Gray units were encountering mixed results, with some victories in addition to the defeats, action against the main camp was a different matter.

According to intelligence reports, the base was defended by an array of weapons emplacements that had already proven to be most effective against aerial assault. According to after-action reports submitted by those few pilots who had survived three separate assaults on the Gray camp, the weapons turrets had destroyed forty-seven of the fifty-two combat aircraft that had participated in the attacks. The alien weapons were formidable against ground offensives, as well. Large numbers of dead and wounded had been reported as foot soldiers and mechanized infantry had tried in vain to overtake the alien base. In short order it had become apparent to the generals coordinating the attacks that their forces, though decisively outnumbering their enemy, were by themselves not enough to combat the aliens and the more advanced technology they commanded.

Rumors were also circulating that a contingent of the other group of aliens, the Plysserians or "Blues" as they were referred to on American news channels, had been encountered near the Longgong Caves. It was believed that a few of these aliens had used their technology to communicate with Chinese soldiers. Was it this dialogue, which had apparently expanded to include exchanges between the aliens and the Chinese government, behind the mission he and Bai were flying today? Of course, the general who had ordered this mission had not seen fit to confirm the rumors or Wu's suspicions, and Wu had known better than to ask for details. Military protocol and discipline did not allow for such questioning of orders, after all.

Nor did they explicitly prohibit one from being terrified at the prospect of what carrying out those orders meant, and at the moment Wu found no difficulty in exploiting that particular loophole. What if their mission failed, or worse, succumbed to error? What if he made a mistake in the targeting or if a fault lay undetected in the embedded software that would guide the weapon once it was launched? The potential for loss of innocent life and heavy collateral damage was very real, and it was just one more factor that contributed to the now quite noticeable shake in his hands.

The status light he was waiting for on his fire control system's missile status panel switched from red to green and Wu felt a lump catch in his throat. The walls and overhead canopy of the plane's two-seater cockpit suddenly seemed to be closing in around him. He realized he was breathing in short rapid gasps and he felt sweat beginning to run down his chest and back.

You never felt this way during the training exercises, did you?

"The weapon is armed," he said aloud. Everything was in place now. The only thing left to do was for Bai to give the order to fire. Wu waited for that command, all the while pleading silently that it would never come. Though he was not devoutly religious, he nevertheless found himself praying that someone, anyone, would contact the plane and direct them to abort the mission.

Call us back, he prayed to anyone who might be listening. Abort. *There has to be another . . .*

No one seemed to be listening.

"Fire," Bai said, his voice flat and cold.

Wu's hand continued to shake even as he pressed the fire control.

"Detonation occurred at 23:47 eastern standard time. According to the Chinese government, the device used was a Dong Feng Model 15 tactical missile, fired from a Hong-7 strike bomber retrofitted to carry the thing. The missile was equipped with a five hundred kilogram nuclear warhead with an expected yield of somewhere between ten and twenty kilotons." Shaking her head she added, "We don't know exactly what type of warhead they fitted it with, and the Chinese aren't saying."

Bruce Thompson knew all about the DF-15 and its nomenclature, having seen the statistics on it and other weapons hundreds of times in intelligence briefings. It was the most widely produced model of nuclear missile in the Chinese arsenal, with somewhere between 375 and

425 of them being deployed throughout China at last count. Another fifty or so had been sold to Syria and a handful of others had reportedly made their way to Iran and Iraq.

"The explosion was detected by NORAD low-orbit surveillance satellites," Spencer continued, "as well as by astronauts on the space station. Seismic tracking equipment all around the world picked up the disturbances. Underground tremors pushing outward from ground zero reached the Chinese coast, causing tidal disruptions that flooded low-lying areas as far as thirty miles inland on Taiwan and several other islands in the region."

Thompson felt his blood grow cold as Nancy Spencer conveyed the report. She was maintaining her stoic bearing as she spoke, but Thompson thought he could detect the slightest wavering in her otherwise controlled voice. There was no faulting her or anyone else for having such feelings at this moment. No one in the room, not even himself or Tommy Brooks, had even been born the last time a nuclear weapon had been detonated in a combat situation.

Looking to his right, Thompson saw the bank of television monitors, each of them tuned to one of the world's numerous news channels. The coverage on all of the channels was essentially the same, with each network giving time to a different aspect of the current situation. Several of the networks had already fashioned garish "Alien Invasion" logos to accompany their coverage, making sure to inundate the screen with them as often as possible.

No doubt this latest incident would be added to the continuous coverage that had dominated all of the channels for weeks. The people of the world had, understandably, become transfixed with the continuing developments, remaining in their homes or other places of refuge and in front of their televisions to see what might happen next. If the world was going to end, then it would do so in front of one hell of an audience.

The atmosphere was much the same here. In stark contrast to the charged atmosphere that had permeated the Situation Center in the weeks since this entire unreal chain of events had started, activity in the room had come to a complete halt as the first reports of what had happened in China began to come in. First had been the preliminary notification from NORAD, which had been tasking satellite passes over areas of suspected alien activity for weeks now. That had soon been followed by the first images of the scene, captured by reconnaissance satellites, which succeeded in casting a suffocating pall over the entire room.

Wherever they happened to be at the moment, people throughout the room had paused in their work and turned as one to focus their attention on the map wall. All twelve of the computer screens had been configured to show a view of China from orbit. A dark blemish discolored a large portion of the landscape near the country's southernmost edge, extending almost to the coastline. Thompson had seen enough bomb damage in his lifetime to know when he was looking at it. The area of destruction he was studying now, plainly visible even from orbit, was huge, probably hundreds of miles across.

"What's the blast radius?" he asked.

Brooks replied, "Initial estimates give a diameter of almost three hundred miles." The general shook his head. Using a laser pointer he indicated the center of the crater.

"Ground zero looks to have been the portal at the center of a Gray base camp ninety miles northeast of the city of Fuzhou. We're guessing that no one within one hundred twenty five miles survived the blast. Satellite flyovers show that Fuzhou looks to have been leveled. The damage begins to taper off at that point, but there are reports of smaller buildings destroyed as far as four hundred miles away. Initial casualty estimates are everywhere between fifty thousand and three hundred thousand dead, but it could be months before we know for sure."

"We may never know," Spencer said. "There's no way a DF-15 did that. Hell, there's not a weapon on this planet that could do that kind of damage, Tommy."

Thompson grunted at the statement. "No weapon made by humans, you mean."

His two closest friends and most trusted advisors turned to look at him, their expressions skeptical. "You think the Grays did this?" Brooks asked.

"It was your people who caused this destruction, though they did not do so intentionally."

The new voice came from behind and above them, near the Situation Room's rear doors. Thompson and everyone else on the main floor turned to see four figures standing near the right side exit. Three of the figures were human, but the other one most certainly was not.

"I see our advisors have arrived," Thompson said, waving the new arrivals to join him, and all eyes in the room turned to watch as the two Marine sentries escorted another Marine and an alien soldier quickly down the stairs. The general understood the need to stare at the alien, its muscles rippling beneath gray skin decorated with an elaborate network of blue tattoos and its huge dark eyes scanning from

left to right and back again as it walked. Though there could
be no mistaking that the soldier would be a formidable opponent in battle, Thompson sensed the alien's underlying
peaceful nature as evidenced by the easy way it walked
alongside the Marine that fate had for some reason chosen
as its link to this world.

The two sentries assumed positions of attention and
saluted. One of the Marines announced, "Reporting with
prisoners as ordered, General."

Directing Gardner to relax, Thompson said, "Not prisoners, Marine, but guests. We must remember how important our new friends are." He saw the look of
nervousness in the eyes of the Marine accompanying the
alien and moved to dispel any anxiety he might have. Before the young man could even bring himself to attention
in order to render a salute, the general stepped forward
and extended his hand in greeting.

"Lance Corporal Gardner," he said with what he hoped
was a pleasant smile on his face. "Welcome. I've been looking forward to meeting you." Thompson noted the circles
under the man's eyes. He had not been sleeping well, it appeared. That was understandable, given the stresses of the
past weeks. Surviving a brutal firefight against enormous
odds only to find himself at the center of the storm that
had erupted in that battle's aftermath? It would be enough
to break many men, but aside from noticeable fatigue,
Gardner seemed to be holding up well enough. That was
good, Thompson thought, for what he had endured already was at best only a prelude for what was still to come.

Taking his eyes from Gardner, Thompson looked to
the alien accompanying him and nodded in greeting. "I
understand that they call you Max."

Max nodded. "That is correct, General."

"I want to thank you for the service you've both provided during all of this," Thompson said as he turned
away from them and back toward the map wall. "Lance
Corporal Gardner, your ability to communicate with
Max's people has proven especially valuable to us." It was
true enough. Very few people had been willing to subject
themselves to the alien technology in order to begin the
process of learning the Plysserians' language. Thompson
knew from reports he had received that interfacing with
the translator equipment had been taxing on Gardner and
those precious few who had volunteered to follow his
lead.

As for Max, he too had been an enormous wealth of information. He had willingly sat through hours of questioning on a plethora of subjects ranging from Plysserian and
Chodrecai military tactics to the aliens' weapons and
technology.

Turning to face the Blue, Thompson asked, "You think
you know what happened here?"

Max stepped forward as he replied. "Yes, General. I believe that the initial explosion set into motion a larger
chain reaction fueled by the interaction of your weapon
with the energy being manipulated by the portal generator on *Jontashreena*." Pausing, he added, "I am sorry. I
mean our homeworld."

"The yield from the missile acted like a battery jump,"
Spencer said, "and the energy released by the combined
reactions simply cascaded outward until it was exhausted."
Shaking her head she added, "The Chinese aren't admitting it, but from everything I've seen I think they were trying to target the portal itself in order to send the missile

through the conduit to the other side. I wonder if any damage was sustained there."

"Maybe there was an overload," Gardner said. When all eyes in the room turned on him, the young Marine paused, obviously hesitant to continue.

Thompson nodded in his direction, once more offering a fatherly smile. "Go ahead, son. What do you think?"

Swallowing nervously, Gardner said, "Judging by the damage here, could there have been some kind of feedback or something shot back through the portal to the other side?"

"That is quite possible," Max replied. "Given the amount of energy released, such feedback would certainly be enough to disable to the system." He turned his attention to Thompson. "It is quite likely that this particular portal is gone forever, along with the equipment that generated it and anyone working in the complex where it was stored."

For a moment, Thompson found himself caught up in the clarity with which the alien spoke in English. Though he continued to wear the translator headband that had initially allowed him to communicate with Gardner, the Blue soldier was speaking with a fluency sadly lacking in most of the people Thompson knew, himself included. How had he accomplished that feat?

There'll be time for this crap later, he reminded himself. *At least I hope there'll be.*

Frowning, Thompson considered Max's report. "So it appears that the Chinese effort had not been entirely fruitless, but it's not exactly a tactic I can endorse, is it?"

"Can you imagine the effect of a blast like that on Tokyo or Paris or New York?" Brooks asked. "The cost in innocent lives alone forbids it."

To that Thompson was forced to agree. The idea of using nuclear weapons had been floated around the Op04-E conference table, and the president had already been given a report detailing casualty projections in the event such attacks were forced to take place on major cities, though no one had foreseen anything like what had happened in China today.

"There may come a time when such action is unavoidable," Max said. All eyes in the room were once again riveted on him but the alien gave no indication that he either noticed or even cared about the level of scrutiny he was receiving.

"Are you saying that such action could be our endgame scenario?" Spencer asked, and Thompson could hear the tension in her voice. No doubt she was envisioning a series of blasts like the one in China tearing apart other cities around the world. Was she was imagining the destruction of her hometown, or the city where her family lived, just like he was doing?

Enough, he chided himself.

To Spencer's question Max replied, "The Chodrecai will continue to deploy more troops and equipment through the portals. They have begun to experiment with shifting the location of the portal endpoint, which means that they can shift insertion to areas that you have not yet detected. They may already be doing so. Even with the assistance of my people, it may not be enough to stop their advance." He nodded at the image of China and the huge wound that had been torn into it. "How long do you have left before such action, desperate as it may seem, is the only remaining option?"

The harsh question, unwilling as Thompson was to admit it, was valid.

Though, as Spencer said, accurate casualty figures might not ever come from China, it was very likely that more people had died in that single act than in any other dating back to the attacks on Hiroshima and Nagasaki. Like the massive conflict which had precipitated those events, the situation begun in Missouri was spiraling outward, moving to encompass the entire world. It was in some respects eerily similar to the days when his grandfathers had fought in Europe and the Pacific, with multiple fronts erupting across the globe, disparate yet all feeding into the same ultimate goal.

"What do you think the Grays are trying to do?" he asked.

"The Chodrecai are obviously experimenting with opening new portals," Max replied. "Though I am no scientist, my understanding of the process is that once a conduit has been established between two points, the exit portal can only be moved after a complex series of calculations. The scientists who devised the portals warned our Leadership against such practices, as determining the destination coordinates is not a static process and must be done each time a portal is redirected."

Gardner added, "I think it has something to do with the way the planets are always in motion." He shrugged. "I was never good at science, General."

Chuckling, Thompson patted the younger man on the shoulder. "That makes two of us."

Stepping forward from the map wall, Spencer asked, "But as long as a conduit is active, it's static, right? It's only when it's turned off and then back on that they have to recalculate where the exit will be?"

"That is correct," Max said. "Though it appears that

they have captured several locations where portal generators are housed, the Chodrecai are in all likelihood not comfortable with the technology. Even with the assistance of captured Plysserian scientists, Chodrecai leaders would have erred on the side of caution in the beginning. If they are branching out now, it is almost certain that they are doing so in attempts to find the centers of power here on your planet. They will seek these locations out with the intent to neutralize them, then continue on with the next most powerful forces, and so on until the remainder of your people simply surrender or are defenseless against them."

"That makes sense," Thompson said, and indeed he had already forwarded on similar opinions and information to the president along with the recommendation that military units be placed on alert at various strategic locations across the country. Similar actions, so he had been told, were also being undertaken across the world, just as they had done decades ago during the last war that had threatened to engulf the entire globe.

Whereas his grandfathers' war had been fought with liberty pitted against world domination, it was very possible that Thompson along with the people in this room and every other living thing on the planet could be fighting for their very existence. The Grays, if this new strategy of theirs was any indication, no longer seemed to be interested only in defeating the Blues. They had concluded that the inhabitants of this planet were a threat as well.

Perhaps the aliens saw Earth as a vast storehouse of resources that would aid them to rebuild their own war torn world, and the only way to avail themselves of those resources was to remove the humans first. They would stop at nothing to achieve that goal, Thompson decided. With so much at stake there seemed to be no other explanation for the growing ferocity and frequency of the Grays' military actions.

Would history regard this time as the beginnings of the next world war? For that Thompson had no answer. For such history to be recorded at all meant that humans would have to survive whatever obstacles still lay before them. One thing he did know, and feared, was that there could very well come a time for humans to realize that they could not save the entire planet. They could very well be forced to decide which parts of it needed to be sacrificed if they were to save anything at all.

Is this simply the next world war, or the last?

The only comforting notion Thompson could glean from the sobering thought was that, for the first time in its history, Humankind had been embroiled in a conflict not of its own making. Could this war succeed where others had failed, forcing people to reevaluate how they chose to coexist with their fellow humans from this time forward?

Assuming they lived through it, of course. For that to happen Thompson knew they would need help, and not just from those Plysserians who had already come forward and allied themselves with human forces around the world.

"Max," he said as he turned back to the Blue soldier, "what are the chances of either us or one of your people getting a message through one of the portals? Could we call for help to the other side?"

Shaking his massive head, Max replied, "That would be difficult, General, if not impossible. From my understanding, communications through a portal are only possible if both parties are in proximity to each of the conduit's openings. With Chodrecai forces seizing more and more of the portals and securing positions both here and on my homeworld, getting to one will prove most difficult indeed."

"So what you're basically trying to tell us," Brooks said as he stepped up to stand next to Thompson, "is that we're on our own?"

His features offering no emotion, Max nodded soberly. "I am afraid so, General."

39

So close, and yet so far.

The thought teased the back of DiCarlo's mind as he sat at the edge of the narrow, slow moving creek. The stream was only a few inches deep near the bank, allowing him an unfettered view of its bottom through the clear water. For a brief moment, he could almost forget where he was and imagine that he was a child again in Colorado, about to cast a fishing line into the creek in the hopes of catching a trout for dinner.

The peaceful image was a perfect compliment to the idyllic area he and his companions found themselves in, a forested ridge overlooking a sweeping valley that appeared untouched by war and the first such area they had seen since arriving on *Jontashreena.* This, after traversing the ruins of two devastated cities and the scorched remains of what, according to Kel, had once been a vast, breathtaking forest that reminded DiCarlo of the plains of the midwestern United States.

After making contact with the portal, DiCarlo and Russell had awakened in the wrecked cab of the truck to find themselves in a vast underground chamber filled with unfamiliar furniture and electronic equipment. The cavern had also been littered with the bodies of dozens of Grays, some of them soldiers and others dressed in civilian clothing, though that, too, looked odd to DiCarlo. It had taken the Marines only seconds to realize that they had passed through the conduit to arrive here, the planet that Kel called *Jontashreena*.

Their Plysserian benefactor had also made the trip, having fallen unconscious during his scuffle with a Gray soldier in the back of the truck during the battle back on Earth. With Kel leading the way, DiCarlo and Russell took their first tentative steps out of the cavern and onto the surface of an alien world.

Kel had then spent the next several weeks leading the Marines deeper into territory that had once belonged to the Plysserians but which was now occupied by Gray forces, all the while avoiding the numerous enemy patrols blanketing the region. At least, Russell was pretty sure it was weeks. She had been doing her best to keep track of the passage of the days with her wristwatch and the notebook she carried in her rucksack.

Needing none of that, DiCarlo only had to reach up to scratch his face and let his fingers brush through the beard he had grown. Years of military life had engrained in him the need to shave almost every day, and the feel of the soft hair beneath his fingertips was a reminder of just how long they had been here. Shaving and other luxuries of a comfortable lifestyle had been set aside, however, as much of the time in the weeks since arriving through the portal had been spent covering as much ground as possible.

Evidence of what had once been a prospering civilization—buildings, vehicles, roadways—abounded.

Decades of conflict had consumed much of it, though. The aftermath of destruction and its resulting desolation were far more intense than anything DiCarlo had ever seen in any of those postapocalyptic movies that had been popular with Hollywood filmmakers several years ago. According to Kel, in fact, the city they had skirted had been abandoned during his childhood, many survivors having long since left the pitiful remnants behind for scavengers to fight over.

DiCarlo heard heavy footfalls behind him and turned to see Kel returning from his exploration of the surrounding area. The Blue soldier's search appeared to have been successful judging by the two dark-colored spheres he carried in his massive hands.

"You found the snack bar, I see."

Kel regarded the Marine with a puzzled expression, his heavy brow furrowing over large black eyes. He shook his head after a few seconds, giving up his attempt to understand the comment and instead held up his find. "These are *paolas*. They are abundant in this region." By way of demonstration, Kel began to peel the globe's dark covering away, revealing a pale yellow interior that to DiCarlo resembled the inside of an orange or tangerine, complete with a thick juice that ran down the alien's hands. A not unpleasant odor drifted to his nostrils as he watched Kel work, and he was not surprised to feel his stomach grumble in response.

"That looks pretty good."

Holding out the second *paola*, Kel asked, "Are you sure you do not wish to try one?"

Reluctantly, DiCarlo shook his head. "I'll stick with those *acho* berries you found for us."

On their first day here, DiCarlo had been concerned about finding food and water. There was no way to be certain if any fruits or vegetables they might find during their cross-country hike would be edible without trying them, but after several days on the march he and Russell had eaten the last of the four energy bars he had carried in his rucksack. Those had been fortunate leftovers from the various training evolutions the reserve unit had been conducting before this entire bizarre adventure had started, and once they were gone the humans had been forced to experiment with the local cuisine. A few of the fruits Kel had selected for them had tasted like the sole of his combat boot, but otherwise no ill effects had manifested themselves. Still, DiCarlo was hoping to minimize any potential risks until they could meet up with Kel's fellow soldiers.

"Once we meet up with some of our forces," Kel said, "our doctors will be able to examine you and determine which of our foods are safe for you to eat." Holding up the *paola* again, he added, "Hopefully you will get a chance to try one of these. They have always been a favorite of mine."

DiCarlo nodded. "I hope so, too." Taking a moment to inspect the scene around him once more, he asked, "Are you sure you know where you're taking us?"

Pointing a finger sticky with *paola* juice toward the valley, Kel replied, "At one time the forest below was a rallying point for our battle groups. When the War began to go badly for us, our leaders established a series of remotely located camps to serve as regrouping areas. This was before our scientists revealed the existence of the portal technology. Even after we began to use the portals, though, our soldiers still used some of the rendezvous areas when needed, including the one down there. Once you and Sergeant Russell have had a chance to rest, we will continue on to the camp. With luck it will still be in use."

"Sounds like a plan," DiCarlo said. Leaving Kel to his meal, he turned back toward the stream, where he saw Russell sitting at the water's edge, having taken off her boots and allowing her feet to soak in the coolness of the creek. The humans had been relieved when Kel theorized that the water here would be fit for them to drink and bathe with, basing his hypothesis on the fact that he and his fellow Blues had sampled the water on Earth and found it quite refreshing, if somewhat odd-tasting. Though he had hesitated at first before trying the water himself, DiCarlo had finally shrugged off his concerns. Going without eating for a few days was one thing, but surviving without water was out of the question. It therefore seemed logical to find out sooner rather than later if the water was among the long list of things on this planet he was sure would kill him. The water did not seem to have any noticeable effects, though, though it did possess a perceptible metallic tang.

"Amazing, isn't it?" Russell said from where she sat as she noticed DiCarlo's approach. "This could almost be somewhere in Arkansas or Mississippi. That is, if the trees all had rusty-looking bark and their leaves were brown. And the grass was brown. And the sky was orange." Sighing, she added. "Okay, so maybe it's not Arkansas. Texas, maybe."

DiCarlo chuckled as he cast a look into the sky, which was more auburn than orange, and the pale sun hanging there. According to Russell's watch and notes, the Marines had been here nearly three weeks, though the sun had risen and set fewer times since their arrival than it would have on Earth. Russell believed it meant that the planet probably rotated on its axis at a slower rate than Earth did, or perhaps that it was simply larger than their own world. DiCarlo opted to take the young sergeant at her word, shaking his head at the faded memories of high school science courses that he had probably attended before Russell's first kindergarten class.

Almost immediately upon their arrival, the Marines had noticed that the gravity of this planet was somewhat stronger than on Earth while the air was a bit thinner. Even standing still the heavier gravity was noticeable, but its effects were readily apparent as they and Kel continued their overland trek. To DiCarlo it felt as though he were hiking through the mountains of Colorado or Washington, and despite their above average physical conditioning, both he and Russell had required frequent rest breaks. As he rested against a rock and waited for his breathing to return to something approaching normal, DiCarlo actually bemoaned his cigar habit for the first time in his adult life.

"This place reminds me of the southeast," he said. "But some parts look like they could have been pulled from California or Utah, with a bit of the New England area thrown in. The trees and plants are weird looking, sure, but you can see the similarities, just like you can in any forest or jungle back home."

Russell nodded. "Did you notice their technology? Their vehicles and other equipment are more advanced, and the buildings and such are designed with the aliens' physiques in mind, but like you said, the parallels are defi-

nitely there. They must have evolved a lot like we did."
She spent a moment moving her feet in the soothing
water before continuing. "Between the atmosphere and
the vegetation and terrain we've seen, it makes a sort of
sense. And what about that city? Hell, that could be what
one of our own cities looks like in a hundred years or so."

Looking over to where Russell sat, DiCarlo watched as
she scribbled something in the now familiar government-
issued logbook, complete with heinous pea-green cloth
cover, that she had been carrying in her own rucksack.
"How's the book coming?" he asked.

Russell smiled as she looked up from her work and indicated the scene around them with a wave of her hand.
"Have to write all this down. People back home are going
to want to read about this someday, you know."

DiCarlo chuckled at that as he lowered himself to the
ground and leaned his back against a tree close to the
water's edge. From this vantage point he watched as Russell returned her attention to the logbook, allowing herself
a moment of peace and contentment that the Marines
and their alien benefactor had been hard pressed to find
since setting out on their journey.

It took him nearly a minute to realize he was staring
at her.

Was it his imagination, perhaps even fueled by the idea
that they could very well be stranded here together for the
rest of their lives, that made DiCarlo ask himself if he was
becoming attracted to Russell? Yes, he decided. At least,
he was sure that what he was feeling were the initial stir-
rings of attraction. There was no denying the young
woman's beauty, and though he could not be certain he
thought that there might have been a few moments dur-

ing the past days where the feelings could have been mutual. No doubt, he figured, Russell had to be contemplating the same possible future. Marooned here on *Jontashreena* with him, possibly forever, it only made sense that they would turn to each other for support and comfort. And later? Could something more develop?

Yeah, you're the expert on romance. The closest thing you have to a relationship is that alimony check, remember?

DiCarlo's first and only marriage had come to an abrupt conclusion one afternoon five years earlier while he was stationed at Camp Pendleton in California. He had returned early from a three-week training exercise to find his wife sharing their bed with the young sergeant he had left in charge of his office. He had told himself over the years that he should have seen the end coming, but the reasons for why it had come about had faded years ago along with the pain.

The bright side, if there was one, was that he did not have to worry about anyone left behind on Earth. He had no children of his own, and his parents had died years ago in a car crash while he had been deployed to the Persian Gulf. An only child, he had been forced to endure the anguish of returning home just long enough to arrange for their funerals. That done, he had returned to Saudi Arabia in time for the attacks to commence on Iraqi forces as Operation Desert Shield gave way to Desert Storm.

Perhaps things would have been different if DiCarlo had not spent so many years traipsing around the globe. If he had been home more, his wife might not have been compelled to find solace in the embrace of another man. Maybe his parents would have stayed in New York for Christmas in 1990, awaiting his arrival for holiday leave, instead of driving to Virginia to spend the weekend with friends.

There was nothing he could do about any of that now, of course, but one result of the divorce and the loss of his family had been for him to resist committing to any kind of serious long-term relationship, at least so long as he remained in the service. For years that self-imposed strategy had served him well.

As he regarded Belinda Russell, quite possibly the last human he would ever meet or spend time with, all of that seemed so far away and irrelevant now.

DiCarlo's thoughts were interrupted as he noticed Kel, who had stopped eating his *paola* and was now sitting motionless. The alien's head was cocked at an angle, his brow creased in concentration.

"What is it?" the Marine asked after several seconds, his own eyes darting about the surrounding forest as he looked for what had spooked Kel. The Blue soldier did not reply right away, but instead rose slowly to his feet. Russell, also seeing his odd behavior, was already rising from her spot at the bank of the stream and moving to where her gear was staged on a nearby rock.

"Do not reach for your weapons," Kel said, holding his hands away from his body. "We are being observed."

DiCarlo felt his muscles tensing in anticipation as he rose to his feet, though he did not reach for the rifle slung across his back or the pistol in its holster on his equipment belt. "Where are they?"

"They have surrounded us."

Shit!

How had they allowed anyone to get so close to them? He chastised himself for the idiotic mistake, the kind made by inexperienced boots during their first week in the field, not to veterans with nearly two thousand days spent in combat zones across the world.

A sound in the trees behind him made DiCarlo turn to see movement among the trees. Five figures emerged from the undergrowth, Plysserian soldiers dressed and equipped as Kel, their bodies adorned with varying collections of the now familiar blue markings. "Friends of yours, I hope," he said to Kel.

Darkness had fallen by the time the Plysserian battle squad led Kel and the two Marines to the encampment hidden deep within the recesses of the forest.

The Blues had of course been shocked at first by the sight of the humans, but the surprise had turned to happiness when Kel told them the story of the wondrous land on the other side of the portal. That pleasure was repeated as other soldiers in the camp came to meet the new arrivals, and yet again as Kel and the Marines were brought to the camp's commander.

"So these portals work far better than their creators intended?" asked Javoquek, a Plysserian military officer who held a rank akin to a Marine captain or major, according to the description Kel had given him. The exact word had not translated, and it was all DiCarlo could do to keep up with the conversation as Kel described the events that had transpired since he and his group had traveled through the portal to Earth. Though the translator bands he and Russell wore allowed them to understand most of what the aliens said when they spoke in their own tongue, the language database that had been expanding since the Marines' initial encounter with the aliens still had many gaps to be filled. It did not help that DiCarlo was already feeling the same sort of intrusive headache that Lance Corporal Gardner had reported during his use of the alien technology.

"They work much better, it would seem," Kel replied. "With the proper battle plan in place, they could be used to attack strategic Chodrecai targets with total stealth. The process is invaluable if we are to seize back the advantage." He paused a moment before adding, "I am surprised to hear that you know about the portals, sir. The information was classified, and it was my understanding that only a few officers not directly involved with the project were aware of their existence."

Javoquek uttered a noise that sounded to DiCarlo like a humorless laugh. "I am afraid that much has happened here in your absence, my friend, and that the time for keeping secrets may have long since passed. Chodrecai forces have advanced quite far into our territory on several fronts, while our own armies have managed to rally, so much so that the War has actually stalled here. They could have pressed their advantage, but they chose not to and for a time we could not figure out why."

Shrugging, he added, "Of course, it did not take long for us to determine the reasoning behind our enemy's actions. Now that they know of the existence of the portal technology, they are using all available resources to seek out the locations of all the conduit generators." Javoquek shook his head. "If they succeed in doing that, they will be able to hunt us down and attack us with overwhelming force. It appears, however, that fortune is seeing fit to smile on us for at least a little while longer."

"Why is that?" Kel asked.

"Finding the portal origin points and controlling them long enough to make use of them is proving harder for the Chodrecai than they originally anticipated. Confusion is running rampant among their ground troops, who of course know nothing about the true nature of what they are searching for. In many cases they are being sent into areas to reconnoiter and are being overwhelmed by our groups assigned to protect the portals." He indicated Di-Carlo and Russell with a nod of his head. "If what happened to your group is any indication, the Chodrecai may very well be encountering even more difficulty with the humans they find."

DiCarlo could not help snorting as the translator relayed Javoquek's words. "Somehow I doubt they're encountering too much resistance, given the superiority of yours and the Grays' weapons and other technology."

"It may be enough that they're simply overextending themselves," Russell countered. "Think about it. The war fronts they had to worry about have multiplied tenfold with the portals. Just when they think they have the Blues on the ropes, they find out there's a whole secret stash of them, along with plenty of friends. If the Grays are stretching their resources thin to find the portals, that could actually work in the Blues' favor if they play their cards right."

Listening to the exchange between the two humans, Kel relayed the gist of the conversation to Javoquek. The Blue officer then directed his attention to the Marines.

"For what it is worth, human, I deeply regret that the people of your world have become involved in our affairs. Our mistakes should be ours to bear alone, but I am afraid that it is too late for such useless ruminations. Will your people help ours in the fight against the Chodrecai?"

DiCarlo shrugged. "We don't really have much choice, do we?" he replied, pausing for Kel to translate his comments. "People on my planet don't normally like others coming into our lives and causing trouble. Our history is full of wars that have been fought in the name of freedom and defense against tyranny. To put it as simply as I know how, you've involved us in your war and we won't be happy."

"Of course," Javoquek said, "from what Kel has told us, your people stand very little chance of mounting any type of prolonged resistance against the Chodrecai."

"Way to state the obvious," Russell muttered just loud enough for DiCarlo to hear.

To Javoquek DiCarlo said, "Eventually the Grays will get themselves organized, and with more of the portals coming under their control, they'll use them to bring the war to the heart of your remaining strongholds here. With that accomplished, your forces on my planet will be cut off from any kind of reinforcements, and the Grays will push through to the other side and wipe up any lingering resistance. If they can send through more powerful weaponry than they've already got there, my people won't stand a chance."

"Then it seems, human," Javoquek said, "that we need each other."

40

Running a finger along his collar, *Jenterant* Lnai Mrotoque knew that his discomfort did not truly stem from an ill-tailored uniform or even an improper setting in the command center's environmental controls. It was a feeling that gained credence as he regarded the faces of the officers clustered about the center's main briefing table and sensed the growing agitation infecting the well-being of his most trusted advisors. As the supreme commander of the Chodrecai military forces, the *Jenterant* could not afford his officers to harbor doubt or anything else that might undermine their effectiveness, particularly now.

Forcing the troubling thoughts away, he instead turned his attention to the immense computer-generated map dominating the center of the table. The map displayed the world on the other side of the portals, or at least those portions of it that had been surveyed so far. At this point the information at his disposal was sketchy, cobbled together from topographical scans conducted on the ground by reconnaissance troops as well as information gleaned from numerous humans taken captive in the cycles since the discovery of the portals and the planet connected to their far end. Still, many areas of the map remained undefined despite the plethora of information that had been accumulated.

Dangers, it had been discovered, lay in wait for those not expecting them.

"A scouting party was lost during transport to this location, sir," said one of the officers, *Nomirtra* Farrelon, as he indicated an area in the lowermost portion of the map. "It is a region that one human prisoner identified during interrogation as *An-tark-ti-kah*. The conduit opened into an underground cavern beneath tons of ice and the reaction of the portal's energy discharge melted a significant portion of the surrounding ice instantly, causing a collapse of the cavern and drowning or crushing any soldiers we sent through."

Mrotoque shook his head in disgust. "How was this allowed to happen?" He already knew the answer, though. The questioning of human subjects had been ongoing in the cycles since the first captives had been taken. A great deal about them and their planet had been learned in that time, though that information had come with great difficulty. Most of the human subjects had not even survived long enough to be of any use, an unfortunate effect of the Security Division's interrogation techniques.

The translator equipment employed by the unit to extract information directly from a prisoner's mind had proven most harmful to humans and their starkly different physiology, and the effects appeared to worsen in direct proportion to the amount of resistance supplied by the individual interrogation subject. Only a few hardy specimens had not only managed to survive the process, but had even on rare occasions succeeded in supplying misleading answers to questions.

"The prisoner who was questioned provided us with information which led us to believe that the region held a military installation of some significance," Farrelon said. "I must confess to a certain admiration for that particular human. He was very convincing during his interrogation, and even maintained a brave front as he was executed."

Mrotoque countered, "The human exploited the fact that until this moment we have underestimated him and his fellow creatures." The *Jenterant* paused, catching himself as he held up a hand. With a small humorless smile he added, "As you can see, I am guilty of it myself. We have allowed the initial reports of these humans to taint the way we think of them. Rather than regard them as animals which can be easily defeated, we must treat them as a cunning enemy that is, if given the opportunity, quite capable of defeating us."

He heard and allowed the rumblings of disbelief that filtered through the room. Another of the officers, *Malirtra* Curpen, looked at him askance. "*Jenterant*, from what we have seen, the majority of these humans are not armed, nor do they possess the means to defend themselves in a combat situation. Their military capabilities, if one could call them that, are limited in comparison to the technology we command."

Mrotoque shook his head. "Their level of sophistication may not be on par with our own, but they are by no means primitive. Have you forgotten your histories? The projectile weapons they employ are not all that different from those carried by our forefathers not three generations ago. They transport themselves in vehicles that use combustible fuels derived from the depths of their world just as we once did. I submit that we are more alike than different, my friend."

Indicating the map with a wave of his hand, he continued. "So far we have proceeded with our ventures into the new world even though our knowledge of the portal technology is still not complete. We have learned enough to create new exit points but as has been demonstrated, this can be hazardous even when the humans are not deceiving us." He chose not to revisit the report of one scouting mission which had ended in disaster when a newly created conduit discharged an entire battalion of soldiers and vehicles into midair, where they plummeted thousands of *cenets* to the ground below.

The map was programmed to react to touch, with selected areas illuminating in a series of bright colors. Curpen tapped several different locations on the map, which in turn lit up in bright red. "It's obvious that the Plysserians are helping the humans to find the endpoint of some of the portals." Using the map's control keypad to select another color, the *malirtra* tapped several additional areas which transformed into a warm blue. "We have also learned during interrogation sessions that even with their limited technology, which apparently includes orbital reconnaissance apparatus, the humans have found several other portals on their own. With this information at their disposal, they have been able to deploy forces to combat our own. In several cases they have launched attacks before our soldiers were able to erect proper defenses."

"They are causing problems in locations with already established conduits, as well," Farrelon said. "While they have suffered several defeats, they have also enjoyed a few key victories. Whether they are receiving substantial aid from the Plysserians or not, the humans are adapting to their situation very quickly."

Clasping his muscular arms behind his back, Mrotoque began a leisurely stroll around the command center. He said nothing for a time as he let his eyes wander over the banks of computer consoles, each of them displaying a menagerie of information supplied by forward units scattered across *Jontashreena*. Most notable, and troubling, among the constant updates he and his staff received were the ones detailing casualties and losses of equipment the Chodrecai military was continuing to endure.

It was all Mrotoque could do to rein in his anger at the lives which had been wasted because of his own eagerness. His desire to press ahead with the offensive on Earth, to pursue the Plysserians to the depths of their newfound hiding place and crush them, had blinded him to the threat the humans posed until it was too late. That misjudgment had cost him far too many soldiers and too much matériel lost in battles that had to be fought each time Chodrecai forces were sent through a newly discovered portal.

The level of attrition, he decided, was simply unacceptable.

"We cannot afford to continue with our present strategy," he said at last. "The only way we can hope to enjoy ultimate victory over the Plysserians is to begin dealing with the humans as the dangerous adversaries that they are. Their technology may be primitive compared to our own, but that gap can and will continue to be closed with the aid of our enemies." Looking down at the map once more, he added, "We must find a way to strike at the heart of this new threat, and we must do so quickly."

It was Farrelon who replied first. "*Jenterant,* according

to what we have learned during interrogations, their population is nearly double to that of our own. While their planet is fractured into a vast number of nations, governmental bodies and cultural identities, true power resides in only a handful of these components. If these major power centers can be vanquished, then the remaining populace will be relatively easy to conquer."

There were nods and murmurs of approval from the others around the table as Curpen leaned forward and cleared the highlighted areas from the map. He then tapped on three areas, the regions they represented fairly equidistant from one another on the map's surface. Each of the selected regions glowed a bright orange in response to the *malirtra*'s touch.

"Information taken from several different prisoners leads us to believe that these are the three most powerful entities on the planet, just as Farrelon suggested. The humans refer to them as *Bee-jing*, *Moss-koe*, and *Wosh-ing-tun*. Our technicians are already preparing the calculations to open portals in these locations. That itself is not an easy process."

Continuing to pace the room, Mrotoque nodded in understanding. He had already suffered through several tedious explanations by members of his scientific cadre about how difficult it was to determine new endpoint coordinates for the portals. As he understood the matter, it had something to do with the rotation of both the humans' planet and their own as well as the movement of both bodies through space. Even deactivating and reestablishing a connection with a previously used endpoint required the entire process to be repeated from the beginning. Mrotoque did not pretend to comprehend any of it, but instead simply relied on the expertise of those better qualified than he to carry out the necessary tasks. One did not reach the rank of *Jenterant* by distrusting those who served under him, after all.

"Our best option is a simultaneous attack," Farrelon said. "Strike all three targets in a massive, decisive action designed to bring them to their knees. Take them, and the rest of the planet will follow in short order."

It was a straightforward strategy, Mrotoque knew, but not one that would be simple to carry out. Such a bold offensive would require much in the way of troops and equipment in order to be successful. Just marshalling such resources would itself be a time-consuming affair. It was also not without risk. If these were the strongest governmental and military bodies on the humans' world, then it stood to reason that they would also be the most well-defended, did it not? He suspected that once the humans figured out that they were now the focus of aggressive action on the part of the Chodrecai, they would stop at nothing to defend themselves and their homeland.

He expected no less.

"Am I the only one not saddened," he said in a quiet voice and with his eyes locked on the map of the alien world, "that the humans have become involved in this mess? This is not their war, after all."

"They allied themselves with our enemies," Farrelon said. "Does this not make them our adversaries as well?"

Mrotoque sighed heavily. "You forget, my friend, that they were given very little choice. The humans you yourself have questioned believe the Plysserians to be the hunted and the victimized, while we are the vicious conquerors who will stop at nothing until we have achieved final victory. While that much is true at least so far as the Plysserians are concerned, I have no desire to harm any of the humans or their planet. I would prefer very much to simply forget that their world even exists at all, for they do not deserve to be made an unwilling part of the War."

That was impossible now, of course. The humans had, unfortunately, become pawns in what remained of the War between his people and the Plysserians, and Mrotoque had no choice now but to continue as he always had, with the interests and welfare of the Chodrecai as his primary motivating concern. Vast portions of *Jontashreena* had already become uninhabitable as the result of the unremitting conflict, and leading scientists were predicting that the entire planet would be incapable of supporting life even within the remainder of Mrotoque's own lifetime. Desperate measures were becoming increasingly necessary if the Chodrecai were to be saved from eventual extinction. With that in mind, it was impossible not to see this new planet as a beacon of salvation. Once the War was over, the portals would make the task of relocating his people to the lush, relatively unscathed new world simple enough.

But what of the humans? There would be survivors, of that Mrotoque was sure. How would they react to the idea of being forced to share their planet with those who would conquer them? He detested that thought, as it was not a course of action he wanted to take.

"No," he said after the few moments spent in silence, "the humans are not deserving of this fate. What we can do is find a way to end the fighting as quickly as possible in order to begin the process of healing and rebuilding. Perhaps one day they can be made to understand the reasons behind what we are being forced to do. Maybe they will even become our friends one day in the not so distant future. I know that I would like to live long enough to see that."

Indicating highlighted areas of the map, Mrotoque sighed in resignation. "For now, however, it is we who are without choices."

41

What I wouldn't give for a good cup of coffee.

As he finished lacing up his boots, the thought ran through Simon DiCarlo's mind much as it had nearly every morning since he and Belinda Russell had arrived here. The Blues might have the edge over humans when it came to physiology, technology, and weaponry, but their version of a preferred morning beverage left much to be desired. Kel had introduced him to *gangrel,* a thick sweet concoction that seemed to have the same effects as coffee, but it was no substitute for the rich Colombian blend that DiCarlo had become spoiled on long ago. Where the hell was Juan Valdez when he needed him?

Noise from behind him made DiCarlo turn to see Russell's still-sleeping form as she moved beneath the covers of their makeshift bed. The dark skin of one bare shoulder peeked from beneath the heavy woven blanket one of the Blue soldiers had provided. Her breathing told him she was still asleep, and he saw no reason to wake her. Unlike him, Russell had experienced difficulty sleeping on many nights since their arrival, so he was not about to disturb those infrequent opportunities she found for rest if he could help it.

After much fumbling and stalling, the two Marines had finally given in to their growing attraction for one another. DiCarlo suspected that their hesitation had been fueled by the idea that turning to each other for comfort somehow signified their acceptance about never returning to Earth. There was also the matter of his own misgivings about becoming romantically involved with a subordinate, not to mention how his feelings for Russell might affect him if and when they found themselves in combat again. There was also, he admitted, some guilt at the idea of his increasing desire for a woman who was several years his junior, and that he might somehow be taking advantage of any feelings of vulnerability or even loneliness Russell might be having.

Thankfully, his concerns had proven to be unfounded. As intelligent and confident a woman as he had ever known, including his former wife, Russell had picked up on his trepidation. The two had spent one memorable evening talking through the uncertainty they both shared, allowing what happened afterward to feel natural and giving DiCarlo a sense of closeness he had not felt toward anyone in quite some time.

"What are you staring at?"

The voice, still slurred by sleep, startled him out of his reverie as DiCarlo realized Russell was awake and regarding him with an amused expression. Rubbing his hand across his bearded chin, he said, "Just trying to figure out what you might see in an old man like me."

"I told you already," she replied as she tossed the blanket aside and rose from the bed. "You're the only game in town." DiCarlo watched in appreciation as she padded naked across the cave's stone floor to where her clothes and equipment lay, once more admiring her toned yet still strikingly feminine physique. As she pulled on her brown undershirt, she cast a mischievous grin in his direction. "Besides, I've always liked older men. Not as much training required in the important areas, you know." She wiggled her eyebrows suggestively as she said the last, eliciting a chuckle from him.

As she continued dressing, Russell cast a look about the dreary rock walls surrounding them. "Have I mentioned yet today how much I hate caves?" She shook her head as she reached for her camouflage pants. "I don't know how they can stand living down here day after day."

DiCarlo had to agree with her as he regarded the small niche that served as their quarters, connected as it was by one of several tunnels that formed the underground base camp for this particular unit of Blues. In more ways than he cared to admit the place reminded him of the vast network of mountain caves he had been forced to endure while searching for al-Qaeda terrorists in Afghanistan. With the possibility of danger lurking beyond every curve, navigating those claustrophobic passages had been nerve-wracking. At least here, he could be reasonably certain that they were among friends.

And friends they were. For the past two weeks the Blues had gone out of their way to help the Marines to familiarize themselves not only with their language but also with their weapons and equipment. As their learning had progressed, Russell made the observation that the level of technology here, not counting the obvious differences that took the Blues' disparate physiology into account, was somewhere between forty and fifty years more advanced than their own. Many of the things they'd seen so far, she had explained, were not unlike predictions made by science fiction writers of the 1940s and 1950s when postulating what the far off world of the year 2000 might be like. The rapid succession of training had only served to reinforce to the two humans that it was they who were the outsiders now.

Buck Rogers, eat your heart out.

Still, none of their new surroundings seemed to inhibit Russell's learning curve, as she had taken to the Blues' version of a desktop computer, for example, with surprising ease. No doubt she was aided by the translator device that both she and DiCarlo continued to wear when in the presence of other Plysserians besides Kel. Like Lance Corporal Gardner back in Missouri, both Marines had experienced the discomfort brought about by extended use of the alien technology but it was a necessity if they were to communicate here. The headbands had enabled both of them to pick up portions of the Blues' language, and while Russell had proven more adept at the process than he had, DiCarlo had learned enough to get by and let the translators do the rest.

Heavy fast-moving footsteps heading in their direction caught DiCarlo's attention and he looked up in time to see Kel ducking so that his massive form could pass through the low entryway into their quarters. The Blue's features were etched with concern and his eyes were wide with anxiety.

"DiCarlo, Russell," he said without preamble, "you must come at once. Something is happening that you need to be made aware of."

"What's wrong?" Russell asked as she finished pulling on her uniform jacket, beating DiCarlo to the question.

Both Marines knew that some kind of operation had been in the works during the previous several days, but Javoquek had elected not to fill them in on the details. Though the unit leader had made efforts to acquaint himself with the humans, DiCarlo had been able to sense the alien's unwillingness to trust them, at least not completely. The sergeant major could not fault Javoquek, of course. He was sure his feelings would be similar, were their positions reversed.

Kel shook his head. "Javoquek has sent for you. This is important, my friends." With that he turned on his heel and with DiCarlo and Russell following him he ran back up the tunnel. It only took them a moment to reach the unit's command post, itself an alcove cut into the rock of the mountain that was perhaps twice as large as the small hole where the two Marines shared their bed. It seemed smaller still, packed as it was with a plethora of communications and computer equipment along with stacks of packing crates.

Looking around the small chamber DiCarlo saw the pair of Plysserians operating their equivalent of a communications system, undertaking the grueling task of decoding encrypted message traffic being sent between the numerous Blue military units scattered across the world.

Further crowding the room was a large table, atop which DiCarlo could see a map or chart of some kind. Javoquek himself and a diminutive female Plysserian that DiCarlo did not recognize sat at the table. The new alien's physique and manner of dress told the Marine that this was not a soldier but rather a scientist or technician of some kind. She sported a collection of tattoos on the exposed portions of her skin, but they were not as numerous or varied as those worn by many of the military troops.

"Hello, DiCarlo, Russell," Javoquek said, looking up from the table. "Thank you for coming." Like Kel, the platoon leader had taken the time to learn the humans' language, hoping to glean from them information about the situation on Earth. He had wanted to know as much as possible about how his fellow Plysserians were faring on the other side of the portals, with an eye toward using that information in the formulation of battle plans here. DiCarlo had respected that desire, even though his own knowledge of alien movements on Earth was limited to what he had seen in Missouri.

Indicating the unidentified Plysserian, Javoquek said, "This is Dr. Yagen, a member of our scientific cadre. Until recently she was a prisoner of the Chodrecai forces that had taken control of Galantra, a small province two days' march from here."

"Was a portal generator located there?" Russell asked.

Yagen nodded, obviously impressed with the sergeant's astuteness. "That is correct. As I am sure Javoquek has told you, the locations of the portal generators are among our most closely guarded secrets. Only a small number of the Leadership possesses that knowledge, and most of them have been captured or killed. The information is classified and compartmented even among the scientific community, to preserve the locations of as many portals as possible should one fall into enemy hands. Now that the Chodrecai know about Earth, they are expending a great deal of resources to find the other generators."

"We must prevent that if we are to have any chance of winning the War," Javoquek added.

DiCarlo could not help himself. "A portal only two days from here? Were you able to retake the town?" He could feel his pulse racing at the idea of a way back home being so close.

As fast as his hopes had risen, they were just as quickly dashed.

"We did not have the resources to drive the Chodrecai out," Javoquek replied. "Our battle squad was outnumbered three to one, but they did succeed in their secondary objective, which was to destroy the complex where the generator equipment was located if they could not recapture it, as well as retrieve any prisoners being held there." He shook his head. "I lost twenty soldiers in that action, but it was necessary. Once we found out what Dr. Yagen knew, it was imperative that we not only destroy the portal but also make it appear that any prisoners being held there had also died in the explosion."

"But their sacrifice was not a vain one," Yagen countered. Looking in DiCarlo's direction she said, "There is now one less path that our enemy can use to travel to your world. Given what the Chodrecai are planning, this is a significant victory."

Despite his disappointment at the loss of the portal, DiCarlo understood the drastic action the soldiers had been forced to take and that there were larger concerns here than simply securing a ticket home for Russell and himself. From previous talks with Javoquek, he knew that Blue forces were in a vulnerable state at the moment. Resistance cells across the planet were slowly rebuilding and regrouping in preparation for a renewed push against the Grays, thanks to a sense of rekindled spirit among the Plysserians with the knowledge that humans were fighting alongside their comrades who had been sent to Earth. Several attempts by the Grays to gain territory on Earth

had been frustrated by humans working with what remained of Plysserians forces.

In an effort to assist from this side of the conduits, a
campaign had been put into motion to either retake those
locations with portal generators that had been captured by
the Grays or to ensure that they could no longer be used
by the enemy. It was hoped that once some of those locations returned to Blue control, reinforcements could be
sent to Earth to aid in the fight waging there. Timing was
critical, though, as it would only be a matter of time before the Grays advanced technology and their ability to resupply from the relatively safe havens of their own planet
tipped the scales of battle to their side once and for all.

Russell asked, "What are the Grays planning? Some
kind of attack on Earth?"

"That is correct," Yagen replied. "At least, that is what I
was able to learn during my time as their prisoner. They
are planning a major offensive against sensitive targets on
your planet."

Motioning for the Marines to step closer to the table,
Kel pointed to the map that he and Javoquek had been
studying earlier. DiCarlo realized he was looking at a
crude representation of Earth, as if the map had been
drawn using a variety of incomplete sources as reference.
Continents were out of scale with one another and several of the landmasses were not shaped as DiCarlo knew
they should be, though he had no trouble recognizing
the three locations on the map that had been highlighted
in red.

Neither did Russell. "Washington, Beijing, and
Moscow," she said. "Jesus."

"These are primary centers of power on your world,

yes?" Yagen asked. "I was among a small group of those ordered to determine coordinates for creating portal links between key locations here on *Jontashreena* and your planet. Large numbers of soldiers and equipment are being amassed at these locations in preparation for the assault, a simultaneous attack on these three locations. It is the largest of its kind that I have seen in my lifetime. The Chodrecai believe that if the leadership of the largest nations on Earth can be overthrown, the rest of the planet will be unable to mount any kind of sustained defense."

"They're right," DiCarlo said, his voice somber. "Even if the Grays don't get what they want right away, taking out the largest governments would throw most of the world into chaos. I can't see it taking much more than a year to take the whole planet. Hell, things have to be pretty screwed up right now as it is." As various images of what world conquest might look like flashed through his mind, DiCarlo had to release a humorless chuckle at one in particular.

Wonder what the stock market's doing right now? Jittery and fickle during the past couple of years, it always seemed to be teetering on the edge of oblivion in the wake of terrorist attacks and a rapid succession of corporate scandals. The traders on Wall Street were probably experiencing a collective stroke at what an alien invasion had to be doing to interrupt their never-ending quest to screw the middle class out of their life savings.

Good riddance, then.

"That is not all," Kel said. "If the Chodrecai succeed in taking your planet, it will be they who have the advantage of an entire world to retreat to, and they who will possess the ability to strike at us with impunity." He shook his head. "When I was but a child my father told me how he believed that by starting the War, my people had in fact engineered their own ultimate downfall. If he were alive today I wonder what he would have to say about how far we have come in order to make his prediction come true."

"It's not over yet," Russell said. "There has to be something we can do. We have to warn Earth at least, get word to them about what's coming."

"Now you can appreciate our reasoning in creating the illusion of the prisoners' deaths," Javoquek said. "If the Chodrecai knew that anyone with knowledge of this offensive had escaped to tell us about it, they would surely alter their plans. We now know where they are preparing for the attack, and where those attacks will be. We should be able to put that information to use against our enemies on both planets."

DiCarlo said, "Simply warning Earth isn't enough. The only way they'll stand a chance in the long run is to have access to intelligence from this side of the portals."

Kel regarded him with a puzzled expression on his face. "What are you suggesting?"

"If we could somehow get word back to Earth about where the portals are, that would be a good start. After that, well, we need to think about moving up the timetables on some of those offensive actions you've been planning. If we could do that, we could maybe find a way to disrupt their plans to get more troops and equipment to the other side."

He paused, considering the magnitude of what he had just said. The suggestion, simple as it was, did not reflect the massive, coordinated effort it would take to have any kind of decisive impact on the Grays' movements. It could very well mean escalating the War to an entirely new level, a task he was not sure the Plysserians were prepared to undertake.

"Notifying your people may not be as difficult as you imagine," Yagen said. "There are still a few portal generators under Plysserian control. If we can make contact with one of those locations, we can send information through to the other side. I do not think there is anyone among us who wants to see your people suffer any further for our mistakes." She paused, lowering her head and casting her eyes at the rock floor of the cave for several moments before returning her gaze to DiCarlo and Russell.

"I feel I must apologize to you," she said. "As I was one of those involved in the development of the portals, I feel personally responsible for what has happened to your world because of what we have done here. It was my people who started the War, and my colleagues and I were merely seeking a way to end it once and for all. We never dreamed that we would involve the people of another planet in the mess we had created for ourselves."

Russell replied, "There's no need to apologize, Doctor. We know that you're not to blame for what's happened on our planet."

"What we need to concentrate on now," DiCarlo added, "is the best way to use your knowledge and keep the portals from being the downfall of us all."

Easier said than done, pal.

42

Teri Westerson had never seen the Mall so quiet.

Flanked by the buildings comprising the family of Smithsonian museums, the expanse of lush green grass and towering trees carved a narrow line of tranquility through the heart of the bustling body of oddly controlled chaos that was Washington, D.C. This place had always been a favorite destination of Westerson's during her infrequent visits to the capital. Since the beginning of the twentieth century it had been a gathering place for locals and tourists alike, each year attracting as many if not more visitors than any of the city's numerous monuments and exhibits. Spring and early summer were her favorite times to be here, as the city teemed with life. Westerson smiled at the memory of the midday jogs she had taken here, watching people sunbathe or kids playing all manner of games. The Mall, to her at least, had always represented a microcosm of everything that was good about living in this country.

All of that was gone now.

Looking around her, Westerson saw the peace that this place had always symbolized shattered, perhaps forever, by the machinations of war. A network of trenches in a

concave formation now scarred the once pristine landscape along the west end of the Mall, five feet deep and
lined with sandbags. Each stretch of trench connected to
another by narrow passages cut into the earth in similar
fashion to allow fast and easy access to any point in the
massive defensive position while still maintaining cover
and concealment. Coils of jagged concertina wire ran the
length of the trenches, with claymore mines and other explosive antipersonnel devices strung amid that wire. In
front of the trenches sat a mechanized infantry battalion,
deployed here from Fort Stewart in Georgia. When the
battle commenced it would be the first line of defense
against whatever armaments the enemy aliens brought to
bear. The ground troops in their fighting positions were a
secondary measure in the event any Gray forces made it
past the tanks.

Poking her head over the parapet created by the sandbags, Westerson could see the helmets of other Marines as
well as soldiers from the three Army regiments that had
been brought in from bases in Virginia and North Carolina. To her the scene was reminiscent of images she had
seen of the battlefields in France during World War I,
with thousands of men pitted against one another during
one of the bloodiest periods in human history.

"How the hell did we get here?" she asked as she
strolled the section of the trench she and a platoon of
Marines had been assigned to, more to herself than anyone else. Still she did receive a few puzzled looks from
Marines manning positions along the trench wall as she
walked past them.

Since the first engagement in Missouri that she had escaped from in order to warn others about the alien threat,

several other battles had been fought in various locations around the world. Though the details of many of those skirmishes were unknown to the public, she and her fellow Marines knew that the Grays had won the majority of those battles and were continuing to strengthen their positions here on Earth. The only thing that stood in their way was the combined might of the world's military forces, called upon to defend against the threat of invasion on a global scale.

What a recruiting poster this would make, Westerson mused. *Join the Corps and fight aliens. Sure beats that "Army of One" crap.*

Beginning with their debriefing by officials at the Pentagon, Westerson and the two Marines who had survived their unlikely exodus, Guber and Hudson, had become de facto experts on the aliens. Though their knowledge was limited because they had been dispatched before the battles had unfolded there, they had spent long hours in the subsequent days offering insight on the situation in Missouri to the group of civilian and military personnel tasked with crafting a defense against the Grays.

Their information was soon supplemented by the handful of Marines who had survived that encounter. Westerson remembered the shock that had gripped her upon hearing the news of the battle at Camp Growding. Despite suffering massive casualties, they had been successful in beating back the Grays and closing the portal there. Though the reservists had received assistance from the Blues to accomplish that objective, her heart surged with pride at how the Marines had conducted themselves in the heat of that battle, exemplifying the Corps' philosophy that each Marine, regardless of job description, was a warrior first.

It was with that attitude that Westerson and Lance Corporal Hudson, the armorer who had made it out of Growding with her, had requested deployment to the front line when word about the coming attacks reached them. Officials at the Pentagon who had come to rely on their expertise, limited though it may be, had resisted at first but Westerson persevered. Many of her friends had been lost in Missouri, and she could not stand the thought of standing on the sidelines while still others went into battle. Relenting at last, those same officials had given their authorization for her to deploy with the 2nd Marine Division.

Based out of Camp Lejeune in North Carolina, the division had been mobilized nearly a month previously, preparing for what they believed would be deployment to the Middle East as part of yet another attempt to quell rising tensions in that volatile region. Westerson remembered the annoyance she had felt upon hearing the news of that assignment, frustrated at the idea that fellow Marines would once again be called upon to bring peace to an area of the world that had seemingly never known anything but war.

Considering what they currently faced, she had to admit that a stint in the Persian Gulf seemed rather appealing just now.

As she looked about the Mall and saw the troops and equipment arrayed here, Westerson took heart in the knowledge that when the enemy finally decided to attack, they would face formidable opposition. To the south in East Potomac Park, artillery crews waited for forward observers to feed them coordinates so that they could unleash the power of the massive guns under their control. On the grassy plain that surrounded the Washington Monument, squadrons of Apache and Cobra gunships were standing by for the command to lift off, the helicopters ready to swarm any advancing opponent at a moment's notice. Even more tanks, troops, and attack helicopters stood ready to defend the White House in the event the battle moved past the Mall's environs.

Off the coast, the aircraft carrier *John F. Kennedy* and her battle group awaited orders to support the fight with naval gunfire to say nothing of its own squadrons of combat aircraft. Westerson had at first found it incredible to believe that more engagements had not been fought using the numerous jet fighters in the U.S. military arsenal, but it had not taken her long to understand the reasons for this oddity. The Grays' encroachments on Earth to this point, with the covert nature of the portals driving their advance, had proven difficult to defend against with any kind of assets. It took time to deliver aircraft into an area where the aliens had been detected, and in the cases Westerson was aware of, the Grays had consistently thrived at employing weaponry to repel aerial assaults. From the reports Westerson had been given, the most success against the aliens seemed to be on the ground, harking back to the massive campaigns of previous generations.

As those battles had defined the world she now lived in, Teri Westerson knew that the next hours could well chart the destiny of Humanity.

She tried to keep such weighty thoughts at bay and concentrate on her immediate situation but it was proving difficult. The enormity of the events unfolding around her and across the entire world was simply too great for a single person to grasp, she decided, and such effort was further hindered as she regarded her surroundings. In the distance, Westerson could see the Capitol Building plainly visible in the fading light as the sun sank below the horizon to her back. It, like every other building in the city and indeed the entire area, had been evacuated at the same time the troops had been digging in.

Not everyone had left, though. The president had refused to flee in the face of the impending threat, electing instead to remain in Washington. That simple gesture was enough to fuel the motivation of every man and woman involved with this combat action, Westerson thought. Everyone here, on some level, realized the tremendous psychological impact that the loss of the nation's capital would have on a country now quite clearly beset by the spectre of war.

Westerson had been stunned at the general's briefing to learn of the message that had arrived through a portal located in Tel Aviv, warning of impending attacks on Moscow and Beijing in addition to Washington. According to the general, the message had come through a portal that had at one time been under Gray control and recently retaken by Blue forces. The encrypted message had required the expertise of Blue communications experts to decode it. Fortunately a few of those were available, survivors of the first group of aliens encountered in Missouri and taken along with the handful of Marines who had survived that battle from there to the Pentagon to act as advisors.

The Blue comm techs were able to decrypt and authenticate the message, the immediate result being the drastic redeployment of American military assets in preparation for imminent attack. With only an estimate for when the attacks might take place, all efforts were made to communicate the urgency of the Blues' message to the Russians and the Chinese, though Westerson had no idea how effective those efforts had been. She could only hope that they had taken advantage of the opportunity fate had given them and acted accordingly.

Her check of the area completed, Westerson allowed herself a brief moment of rest, removing her helmet and wiping the sweat from her forehead. Summers in Washington were notorious for being hot, and this one was proving to be no exception. She gave thanks that sunset was approaching, as it would bring with it some relief from the brutal temperatures she and the others were enduring.

As she swallowed a mouthful of warm water from the canteen she pulled from her equipment belt, her thoughts turned to Jerry. She had not spoken to her boyfriend in days, but she was sure he was okay. Jerry had informed her of his plans to collect his mother and drive her to his hunting cabin north of Omaha, Nebraska, with the hope of avoiding the growing mess that was the alien civil war. He had been upset with her upon hearing of her intention to remain in Washington and aid the war effort in any manner she could, and that was before she had made the decision to request assignment to the front lines. Westerson had no doubt that he would be furious with her when she told him.

If you get to tell him, that is.

Would she see Jerry again? If not, would he live to see a

world of peace or one torn apart by war? And what if he did not live past the next few days? What if she somehow managed to survive all of this while he did not?

God, no. Anything but that.

"You have to wonder what good all this is gonna do," she heard a quiet voice say from somewhere ahead of her. "If the reports are right, those Gray rifles can shred us to pieces, and they have antiaircraft guns that can pick incoming cruise missiles out of the air like they were standing still."

Another voice replied, "Yeah, and what if they have stuff that's even worse? You remember that movie where the aliens hit all the cities at once and torched them all in like five minutes? How the hell are we supposed to fight that?"

Westerson recalled that movie as well, particularly one scene where the Capitol had been obliterated under the force of a massive energy weapon. She could not suppress the momentary shudder that gripped her as the image played out in her mind. Though the Grays had not as yet displayed technology approaching that scale, what they had shown so far was indeed more powerful than anything in any human arsenal.

If they get past the tanks, what kind of chance are a bunch of grunts going to have?

The Marines who had been talking stopped at her approach, the expressions on their faces letting her know that they had not expected to be overheard by anyone in authority. "Easy, guys," she said. "We're pretty well protected here, and we brought enough firepower to ruin anybody's day. Besides, we've got the edge. They don't know we're here waiting for them, remember?" Her words elicited nods and expressions of relief on the faces of the two young men. Westerson knew that the effect might only be temporary, but it was better than nothing.

I just hope I'm not lying to them, she thought as she continued her tour of the trench.

Given what she knew about the weapons used by the Blue ground forces, though, Westerson wished for some of that firepower now. Unfortunately that was not about to happen, as those Blue soldiers who remained on Earth were still scattered across the world, fighting for their very lives as Gray forces continued to emerge through portals and engage them.

"Listen," someone said from behind her and she turned to see one of the Marines to whom she had been talking. The younger man and others were looking over the parapet of the trench, their attention gripped by something to the east. Putting her helmet back on, Westerson stepped up onto the small ledge that had been fashioned from rows of sandbags and allowed her to peer over the lip of the trench.

Jesus, there it is, right where the Blues said it would be.

Beyond the tanks that sat between the trenches and the far end of the Mall, between the buildings that housed the National Gallery of Art and her favorite of the Smithsonian archives, the Air and Space Museum, she could see the portal forming before her very eyes. It was small at first, merely a ball of disruption that obscured her view of the Capitol Building, but it was growing. She could see a mass of frenzied colors, their vibrant hues intensifying with each passing second. The portal continued to increase in size, quickly moving past the dimensions Westerson and the other Marines had been told to expect. She felt something wash over her skin, an almost electrical sensation that made the hairs on the back of her neck stand up. Was it caused by the portal and the energy it had to be expending in order to connect the two worlds?

"Here they come!" someone shouted even as she caught sight of movement from within the portal. At first there was only the suggestion of something approaching, a darkening of the wash of colors that grew larger. Then a shape formed, assuming mass and detail as it shook itself free of the conduit.

Flat and narrow, the alien craft resembled a black horseshoe, not much larger than a Cobra attack helicopter and possessing comparable maneuverability. No sooner did it clear the portal than it climbed for altitude, moving up and to its left before coming to a stop and hovering over the Mall. More of the craft were exiting the passageway now, one after another, each moving away from the portal to allow the next one to emerge.

They kept coming even as the first shot was fired.

Not from the alien ships, but from one of the tanks. The echo of that first salvo as well as its effects were still rolling across the flat plain of the Mall when more shots rang out, with tank after tank firing its main gun at the new targets. The Gray ships were firing, too, the whines of their weapons ear-piercing even from this distance as Westerson saw energy erupt from several of the U-shaped ships' forward prongs. No longer hovering, the alien craft were now spreading out into some type of combat formation, closing the distance between them and the tanks.

"Are the tanks even hitting anything?" a voice called out over the rising din. Westerson had no answer and there was no time to find one, for now there was more activity at the portal. Ground vehicles were beginning to emerge, along with soldiers on foot, a lot of them. Disgorging from the portal in columns of two, they were spreading out and away from the conduit as fast as they appeared. Dozens of them were pouring forth. More, Westerson knew, than anyone had yet seen.

"God help us," she whispered as she brought her rifle to her shoulder.

43

Waiting in line with his fellow soldiers for his turn to enter the portal, *Kret* Aloquon was still nervous. Squad by squad, he and his comrades were being hustled toward the odd doorway, beyond which lay a battle unlike anything Aloquon had seen in his short though active career as a foot soldier in the Chodrecai army. Scientists as well as soldiers who had already made the trip had briefed him and the others on what they could expect, that passage through the conduit was both quick and painless, though that did little to assuage the anxiety he felt at the idea of stepping through a gateway that would transport him to another planet.

In many respects it was not unlike other skirmishes in which he had fought, where he had been required to step onto a battlefield through the doorway of a transport vehicle. There were few things more dangerous than the precious few moments needed to unload a platoon of soldiers into such a situation, when susceptibility to incoming enemy fire was extremely high. One of Aloquon's greatest fears as a soldier was that he might be wounded or killed before even getting the chance to fire his own weapon, and it was that same sense of vulnerability that he was feeling now.

"This is unreal," he said, more to himself than anyone else.

Still, his fellow soldier and friend, Niytrin, overheard the quiet comment and turned to look at him. "I still have trouble believing it. Can it really be true?"

Naturally Aloquon had doubted the original assertion during the premission briefing, but the statements of fellow soldiers who had already been to the "other side" helped to quell those reservations, if only slightly. Besides, he reminded himself, would the Leadership expend such a tremendous amount of time and resources chasing a falsehood? He thought not.

"I've heard that these humans are better in combat than we've been told," Niytrin said, careful to keep his voice low to avoid being heard by any of the platoon leaders tasked with keeping the lines of soldiers moving forward. The *zolitums* were yelling orders at the top of their lungs with a tenor and ferocity that Aloquon had not heard since the days of his indoctrination training.

Shrugging, he replied, "They will have to be, if they are to have any chance of success against what we are sending to face them." One had only to look around the immense underground cavern and see the bustling activity taking place to know how serious the Leadership was just now. Beyond the columns of soldiers waiting to step through the portal, equipment hummed and vehicles moved into position for transferal. Some assault vehicles had already disappeared into the gateway, apparently already engaging the enemy on the other side. They were softening the lines of resistance and clearing paths for the infantry to move in and establish a foothold.

Aloquon was almost at the portal now, the group in

front of him preparing to go through. There was now a very real tingling sensation playing across his exposed skin, the raw power of this staggering technology already reaching out to envelop him. The storm of swirling colors generated by the conduit was almost blinding at this proximity.

What would they find on the other side? The reports of battles fought on the new world had led Aloquon and his companions to believe that the humans' fighting capabilities were limited, at least in some respects.

Some of the soldiers who had returned from Earth, including a few battle-tested veterans, had told a different story.

Whereas the humans seemed to lag behind both the Chodrecai and Plysserians with regards to weapons and technology, they compensated for that disparity with their determination not to give up a fight easily. With the Plysserians aiding them, any mismatch working in the Chodrecai's favor would be tempered even more. This did not surprise Aloquon, as he expected no less from anyone faced with the prospect of defending their home against an enemy force. He could respect their resolve.

Not that it would make much difference, of course. With the overwhelming forces being pitted against them now, the humans stood no realistic chance of winning the coming battle. If this campaign had unfolded as the Leadership had foreseen it, the crippling blow to the humans' world would be the largest step taken toward their ultimate defeat.

"It is time," Niytrin said as they stepped up to the point designated by their platoon leader. This was it. In a moment they would enter the gateway and leave this planet, perhaps never to return. The *zolitum* was already barking out his final list of instructions, and then came the command Aloquon was both anticipating and dreading.

"Go!"

Aloquon stepped forward and a number of things happened at once.

The sounds of activity echoing throughout the cavern abruptly stopped, drowned out by the energy of the portal. His skin itched beneath his body armor, and what felt like a gentle breeze passed across his face. Though he could see nothing but the dazzling array of colors generated by the conduit, he felt no sense of vertigo or imbalance. There was no sense of falling or of being pulled or pushed in any direction. Movement through the portal was as easy as traversing a passageway into a room of his own home.

As he always did in the last few moments of peace granted to him before he went into battle, Aloquon thought of his wife, Kerrod. They had been married but a few cycles when he had been called to service, and many more cycles had passed since he had last seen her. He had not even been able to communicate with her for some time, so she had no idea where he was or how he was doing. Was she well? Would he see her again?

Then there was no more time for such thoughts, because as quickly as the sensations of the portal had begun, they ended. Kaleidoscopic colors faded away and the odd vacuum that shrouded all sounds around him vanished. The cavern was gone now, too, gone and replaced with the chaos of war.

And another *zolitum* screaming at him.

"That way!" he yelled, pointing one arm in the direction of a group of Marauder assault vehicles that had been assembled in a row next to each other, forming a barricade against an onslaught of incoming fire. "Keep down and wait for orders to move out!"

Reacting as his infantry instructors had instilled into him time and again, Aloquon dashed away from the portal opening and to where the rest of his platoon were assembling. Explosions thundered all around them, chewing up the ground in all directions. The night sky was broken by the illumination caused by the blasts and numerous fires burning all across the broken terrain in which he now found himself, casting light on the bodies of dozens of fellow Chodrecai soldiers and the wreckage of downed assault vehicles. In the distance, he could see large bulky vehicles with what appeared to be large cannons, each of them belching fire.

What? How?

His mind screamed the questions, but he could not seek answers now. Aloquon could hear other soldiers yelling over the sounds of equipment moving into position. Interlacing all of it were the whining reports of uncounted pulse rifles.

"What's happening?" he called out to a soldier, one he did not recognize, crouching down behind the line of vehicles, waiting as he now was for further instructions.

The soldier shook his head. "The humans were waiting for us! As soon as the first of us came through the portal they opened fire!"

Aloquon's mind reeled with the revelation. How had the humans anticipated the attack? This three-pronged assault was supposed to have been classified under the most stringent security. No one outside a small cadre of people had even known of the objectives for more than a few moments before the plan had been put into motion. The soldiers selected for the mission had not even been briefed about their targets until the last possible moment. Even the scientists had been sworn to secrecy, ordered not to reveal the coordinates they had plotted for the three Earth cities until the command to begin the assault had actually been given.

Something or someone had obviously been compromised, yet the Leadership was apparently not calling off the attacks. They could not of course, not with so much at stake and with so many forces already committed to the enormous offensive. Looking over his shoulder, Aloquon saw that more Chodrecai soldiers and equipment were coming through the portal, dispersing into a semicircular pattern that was being pushed outward as more forces arrived from *Jontashreena*. Despite having walked into what amounted to a massive ambush, the Chodrecai had managed to establish a firm position on this side of the portal and were beginning to fight back against the humans.

Aloquon looked about frantically but could not find Niytrin, having become separated from him in the harried moments that followed their arrival through the portal. Where was he? Aloquon did not want to consider the possibility that his friend might be one of the several bodies lying on the ground all around him.

Sitting idle with his fellow soldiers and waiting for further instructions, Aloquon noticed for the first time just how cold it was here. Unlike the temperate climate he had left behind on *Jontashreena*, there was a distinct chill in the air here. He could already feel the cold seeping through his protective garments. The longer they remained here the more adverse the effects of this environment would be.

"Move out!" a voice shouted above the din of combat, shattering his reverie. Aloquon looked up to see another *zolitum* directing him and the soldiers in his group to follow him. The time to press forward had come, and his group would be part of that push. Had a weakness in the humans' defenses been found, allowing the Chodrecai to advance on the city as they had been ordered to do? It did not matter, of course. He was a soldier, sworn to follow the orders of his leaders, even if he did not always know the reasons behind those orders.

Checking to see that the power level on his pulse rifle had been set to maximum as he had been instructed to do, Aloquon rose to his feet and began to run at a crouch, following on the heels of the soldier in front of him. He emerged from behind the line of assault vehicles and saw that another group of Marauders was advancing slowly, providing a moving barricade that would offer some protection from the weapons the humans were firing at them. More of his fellow soldiers were already pushing forward, turning the momentum of the battle back at the humans.

In the distance he could see the elegant city selected for this aspect of the massive assault, the metropolis the humans called "*Moss-koe*." The city had an obvious artistic aspect to its design, with several of the larger buildings capped by a variety of huge rounded domes and ornamental spires that reflected the harsh light of conflict waging beyond the city's borders.

So this is Earth, Aloquon mused as he ran toward the battle.

44

We who are about to die salute you.

Simon DiCarlo could not get the words out of his mind, remembering them as he did from the gladiator movies he had occasionally watched over the years. The images had started playing in his imagination from the first moment he had laid eyes on the immense outdoor arena, the bowels of which he and his companions now hid within.

"My father used to tell me stories of the games they held here," Kel said in a quiet voice from where he stood to DiCarlo's right. "His father would bring him to the city from their home in the mountains for the games. It was a tradition each season for the different provinces to put forth their best athletes in the spirit of honorable competition. According to my father it was a festive time to be in the city."

Smiling at the images his friend's words evoked, DiCarlo replied, "Sort of like our Olympic games. The athletes in those events compete for pride, either individually or as part of a team. They don't play for money or fame, at least not the majority of them."

"I would have liked to have seen the games for myself,"

Kel said, "but such pursuits were abandoned when the War came." Shaking his head, he added, "I wonder if our leaders envisioned how much of our culture would be lost when they decided to declare war on the Chodrecai." He indicated their surroundings with a wave of one massive hand. "It is a shame that what was once a symbol of peace and prosperity has been turned into just another battle-field."

Essentially a huge oblong bowl erected in the center of this once prominent Blue city, the stadium was a formidable construct of stone and metal, though like the surrounding buildings it, too, had fallen to neglect from years of disuse. To DiCarlo it was perhaps three times larger than the football stadium in Kansas City, with a comparable array of columns and struts fitted together to support the arena's shape. The support structure contained a maze of tunnels which allowed the passage of workers, spectators, and event participants to and from any of the dozens of chambers housed inside the stadium.

It also provided a wide selection of places in which to hide. Cubbyholes, air ducts, crawl spaces that allowed access to wiring and plumbing, all of these and more offered opportunities for concealment within the stadium's labyrinthine underground. DiCarlo and Russell, along with a small contingent of Javoquek's soldiers, had secreted themselves within a maintenance tunnel, behind the wall of one of the stadium's main thoroughfares. Grilles set into the walls at regular intervals provided ventilation to the infiltrators as well as a means of observing the goings-on throughout the arena.

DiCarlo grimaced yet again at the constricting straps of the Plysserian body armor he wore as he shifted his position in yet another attempt to get comfortable. "I don't think I'll ever quite get used to wearing this stuff," he said.

Standing next to him, Russell nodded. "I know what you mean. Weird, considering that it's lighter than Kevlar. You'd think we'd be grateful." More important than its weight, the protective garments were far more resistant to the pulse rifles used by both alien armies. Though they might not be the most comfortable thing to wear, DiCarlo could get used to them if it meant not falling before the horrific effects of the alien weapons.

DiCarlo sighed. "I'm dying for a cigar." He did not want to smoke it, of course, not now. But he would have welcomed the taste of the sweet tobacco within its brandy-soaked wrapper. It was with regret that he had smoked the last of the cigars from his rucksack two days previously.

"Are you saying you did not appreciate the *tempra* Javoquek offered you?" Kel asked, more than a hint of teasing in his voice.

Grimacing at the memory, DiCarlo replied, "Pass." Javoquek had introduced him to the hand-rolled concoction made from the dried leaves of an odd-colored bush growing in great abundance around the caves of his small army's hidden base. The result, when smoked, was a noxious dark brown smoke that had made DiCarlo turn green and so consumed Javoquek with laughter that the Blue had fallen off his stool.

He exhaled an exasperated sigh as he looked down the darkened tunnel, not seeing what he wanted to see. "Where the hell is Javoquek, anyway? Shouldn't he have been back by now?"

"Knowing Javoquek," Kel replied, "he is giving everything a final inspection. He is quite thorough and does not leave anything to chance, especially now when so much is at stake."

DiCarlo nodded in understanding. "I can appreciate that, but he's cutting it a little close, don't you think? How much time do we have before your air assault group arrives?"

"If they're holding to schedule," Russell said, "they should be here in about twenty minutes. That's when the fun should really start."

"Fine by me," DiCarlo said as he examined their surroundings for perhaps the six hundredth time. "Anything to get out of here." Though he would not go so far as to call himself claustrophobic, he had never been fond of closed in spaces. Not because of some irrational fear, but simply because he preferred having room to move about, especially in a potential combat situation. The dimly illuminated maintenance tunnel was narrow, no more than two meters across, and not even that wide in some areas where wiring or piping extended from the wall into the corridor itself. It was a tight fit for the Blue soldiers with their bulkier physiques and equipment. Passage through the tunnel had to be undertaken with care, both because of the possibility of snagging a protrusion as well as the noise such contact would make. In a confined space such as this, sounds could be amplified and perhaps heard by one of the many enemy soldiers prowling the inside of the stadium.

That would not do, particularly now.

After learning of the planned simultaneous assaults on Washington, Beijing, and Moscow, a bold counteroffensive had been put into action. Dr. Yagen had used the encrypted communications network, established by belea-

guered Blue forces scattered across *Jontashreena* in recent
years, to make contact with Plysserian scientists working at
other portal locations around the world. After much
covert investigation, it had been determined which conduits would be used to launch the attacks and that
Chodrecai forces were in the midst of marshalling their
resources for the coming offensive.

This stadium, it had been learned, was the staging area
for the hundreds of ground forces assigned to the attack on
Washington. It had taken Javoquek's unit nearly two days of
overland travel to get here, every mile of which had been
through enemy territory with discovery possible at any moment, and presenting only the first of many difficulties the
Blues could expect while carrying out their mission.

Javoquek had hoped to do more here than simply stop
the Grays from moving through the conduit. His plan
called for the elimination of as many enemy combatants
and their equipment as possible in addition to retaking the
portal, but he had designed the operation so that, if executed properly, he and his troops would come away with a
bevy of much-needed weapons, equipment, and other es-
sentials. With Blue forces scattered across the world, obtaining food, ammunition, and medical supplies—to
name the more important items—had become a challenge all its own. Successful engagements against Gray
units were as much about obtaining these items as they
were about advancing military objectives. Such elements
introduced into the already chaotic mix of combat could
be hazardous, DiCarlo knew. A hungry soldier was oftentimes a distracted one, though he had also seen that discomfort and the rewards to be had by besting an enemy in
battle used as powerful motivators.

With the idea of dealing the Grays a huge defeat and the additional lure of the bounty awaiting them spurring them on, Javoquek and his unit, along with DiCarlo and Russell, had come here. Navigating the vast network of sewage conduits and maintenance passageways beneath the city's streets, they had worked their way into the bowels of the stadium. It had taken days of covert movement to deploy their forces into their planned positions without attracting any attention. Similar stealth had been required as the team set about planting explosives in strategic locations throughout the complex.

"I'm still surprised we didn't run into more Grays than we did," Russell said. "Considering the operation they're mounting here, you'd think they'd have tighter security."

Kel replied. "Not necessarily. This city is deep inside Chodrecai territory, and has been for some time. They have no reason to suspect an attack here." Frowning, he added, "It saddens me to think about how vibrant this place must have been before the War. We tried to retake it several times, but were eventually forced to concede it because of the enormous losses we sustained in each failed attempt."

Once more DiCarlo felt sympathy for his friend. What must it have been like to live in a world and know nothing but war? Even his own experience, participating in far more conflicts than he cared to remember, paled in comparison to the life Kel had endured. A life without peace, without getting a chance to enjoy that which he was supposed to be fighting for? The very idea was demoralizing.

A sound from the corridor beyond the wall of the maintenance tunnel caught DiCarlo's attention. Footsteps? Russell's hand on his arm, squeezing his bicep, was enough to confirm that he was not imagining it. He exchanged looks first with her and then Kel, whose troubled expression mirrored his own.

The footfalls were coming closer. Judging by their unhurried pace and the level of noise they were making, whoever was approaching did not appear concerned with keeping their presence hidden.

Squatting down, DiCarlo peered through the small ventilation grille set into the wall. A few seconds passed with the footsteps growing louder before he saw a figure walk past, a Gray soldier. Two more of the aliens were with him, each of them moving in a casual manner down the corridor. DiCarlo did not move for several more seconds as the footsteps receded before standing back up.

"Grays," he whispered. "And they're heading in Javoquek's direction." The unit leader was still conducting his final placement of explosives set deeper in the stadium's underground.

Russell said, "If they find him, or any of the explosives, this whole thing will be shot."

"We cannot warn him," Kel said. "Any attempt at communications would almost certainly be detected. The risk is too great."

"It won't make any difference if they catch Javoquek or find the stuff we planted," DiCarlo countered. If the Grays were alerted before the strike team arrived, the element of surprise would be lost, and their entire assault plan would be shot to hell. There was too much at stake, both here and on Earth, to allow that to happen. Not now, when they were so close.

It meant having to leave the relative safety of the maintenance tunnels, something DiCarlo had hoped to avoid lest any of the Blue assault force tip their hand too early. Of course, he reminded himself as he and Russell and Kel moved out into the corridor, none of that would matter if the Grays found Javoquek or, worse yet, the explosives that had taken so much time and risk to plant. The question now was whether or not the enemy soldiers could be dispatched without attracting any more attention.

Using hand signals, DiCarlo directed Russell and Kel to split up and hug the walls of the corridor, hoping that the dim illumination would conceal them as they moved. Knowing that it would only draw attention if used, he had slung his pulse rifle across his shoulders, securing it tightly so that it would not shift and make noise. Though both he and Russell had become proficient in the use of the weapons there was no way they could use them now. No, he had decided even as he drew the combat knife from its sheath and held its blade alongside his right leg, this would require an act of stealth.

How long had it been since he had killed anyone with a knife? Could he still do it? As personal combat instructors had taught him years ago, it was an altogether different method of dispatching an opponent than using a firearm, and not just in the obvious manner. It required a harsh brutality that could not be softened by killing from a distance. That point had been hammered home for him almost thirty years ago and during his first week in a combat zone when his platoon's firebase was overrun and he found himself occupying his fighting hole with a Vietnamese soldier. The other man was his own age, maybe even younger, and to this day DiCarlo's dreams were occasionally haunted by the look in the boy's eyes as the blade sank home.

Would he hesitate rather than act without thinking, in order to attack purely from instinct and with the aid of training he had mastered long ago? He was many years removed from the frightened young man in a hole in Vietnam and faced with killing or being killed. Truth be told, he was also no longer the hardened combat veteran he had been even ten years ago. The events of the past months had brought some of those skills and memories back with full force, but would that be enough here and now when he would have to face an enemy up close once again?

And what about Russell? How would she react when the time came? He had seen the look of uncertainty and fear in her eyes as his plan became apparent to her, though she had insisted on coming with him and Kel. The Blue had given her one of his own large blades and instructed her on the best way to employ it, but would she be able to do so at the crucial moment?

There was no use debating the issue, he knew, even with himself. There was also no time.

As they drew closer to the trio of Grays, continuing to hug the walls as they moved, DiCarlo could see that all three of the soldiers carried their own weapons slung across their backs just as he did. They were talking among themselves and he even heard one of the aliens laugh.

Not looking for trouble here, he mused. *Maybe we'll get lucky.*

They managed to get within twenty meters before their luck ran out.

At first the Marine thought the Gray had failed to see them pressed against the walls of the corridor as it turned in their direction, but that hope faded when the soldier's head snapped back and its dark eyes locked with his own. DiCarlo saw the look of total surprise on the alien's face as it realized what it was looking at.

"Shit."

The Gray said something to its two companions that DiCarlo could not hear, but the effects were easy enough to discern as all three aliens turned to face back up the corridor, each reaching for their weapons. He did not even try to run. What was the point? At this distance, there was no way the Grays could miss. Time seemed to slow down and the only thing he could hear was the pounding of his own heartbeat as first one rifle muzzle then a second swung in his direction.

Something screamed past his ear and he felt the rush of displaced air on his skin as DiCarlo saw one of the Grays punched in the chest by the force of a pulse rifle and dropped where it stood. He only had a moment to see Kel moving forward from his left, his weapon held to his shoulder.

Having obviously decided that taking out the Grays quietly was no longer an option, the Blue soldier had seized what little surprise and initiative remained and plunged ahead. He was already firing a second time and the round struck another of the Grays in the leg, spinning the alien around until it fell to the floor. DiCarlo only had an instant to duck as the third soldier dodged to its left to avoid incoming fire, raising its own weapon in the process and firing. The shot went wild, causing Kel to drop to the floor to evade it as the pulse slammed into the wall where he had been standing. Regaining its own balance, the Gray brought its rifle up and DiCarlo saw its massive muzzle once more.

Then the alien's face disappeared in the rush of a final whine of energy, its body teetering for a few seconds before toppling over and collapsing in a lifeless heap.

DiCarlo blew out the breath he did not realize he had been holding. Turning to his left he saw Russell stepping forward, the muzzle of her rifle trained on the unmoving bodies of the fallen Grays.

"You okay?" she asked as she joined Kel in verifying that the enemy soldiers were in fact dead. She kicked one of the Grays with her boot but the alien did not move.

Rising to his feet, DiCarlo returned his knife to its sheath. Had there been time, he might even feel actual relief at not having to use it. "I'm getting too old for this fucking nonsense." He nodded in the direction of the Grays as he pulled his own rifle from his back. "You've been practicing, I see."

"Not much else to do around here," Russell said as she turned away from the dead enemy soldiers. "Somebody had to hear this mess. They'll be coming to check it out."

"It was unavoidable," Kel replied, "for they would surely have killed us given the opportunity."

"We have to get out of here," DiCarlo said, his eyes already searching the corridor ahead of them for anyone who might have heard the scuffle.

Then the near silence was shattered by a blaring alarm echoing through the underground passageway. Unlike the other alert signals they had heard since working their way into the stadium's bowels, it was the one they had all been told to listen for and hope they did not hear.

"Jig's up," DiCarlo said. "They're onto us."

Watching as soldiers and equipment continued to disappear through the portal, Dr. Hjaire once again felt pangs of disgust and guilt in the pit of his stomach.

He looked through the observation window of the control room and into the massive underground cavern that housed the portal generator. Chosen for its size and security and located deep inside Chodrecai territory, the cavern provided an ideal staging area for the assets being transported to Earth. Beyond the confines of the room, the immense chamber teemed with the activity of hundreds of Chodrecai troops and matériel. All awaited their turn to pass into the conduit for transport so that they could join in the battle now underway in the human city of *Moss-koe*.

Similar operations were taking place in two other top-secret locations elsewhere around the world, sending assault forces to the humans' planet to attack their other two large centers of authority, *Bee-jing*, and *Wosh-ing-tun*. These three locations, selected by the Leadership as the prime targets in which to launch offensives, had been determined after numerous interrogation sessions with captured humans. Capture these three cities, they reasoned, and conquering the rest of the planet was a virtual certainty.

And none of it would be possible were it not for the well-intentioned yet ultimately misguided efforts of Hjaire and other scientists. *We are to blame for this.*

He had heard some of the Chodrecai talking in recent days as the time for the offensive drew closer. They believed that the humans deserved their fate as punishment for allying themselves with the Plysserians. Most seemed unable to grasp the idea that the humans had as much right to defend their civilization as the Chodrecai had done long ago when the War had begun. Only a few viewed the humans as pawns, unwittingly drawn into the conflict by the Plysserians.

How could he or anyone else have foreseen that all this would happen? The portals, as radical a notion as he had ever entertained in his life, had been intended as a means to finally end the War. No one had ever considered that the gateways could be used as a bridge between dimensions to another world, a world with a thriving civilization that knew nothing of the conflict which had raged between the Plysserians and the Chodrecai since Hjaire's own childhood.

Regardless of what anyone had thought might happen, there was no escaping what had become of the technology he and his companions had labored to create. Instead of contributing to the very survival of their people, Hjaire and the others had given their enemies the means to defeat the Plysserians once and for all, to say nothing of offering up the entire human race for the taking.

Except that the assault was not going as planned.

It took all of the self-control that Hjaire possessed to

keep the smile from his face as situation reports from Earth began to arrive. Carried by haggard couriers who looked as though they may have only just escaped the battlefield with their lives, the news was not good.

"Our forces on the other side are encountering heavy resistance, sir," a lower-ranking officer said to *Nomirtra* Ktrol, the officer in charge of the Chodrecai forces here. "A large contingent of humans and Plysserians was waiting as our soldiers emerged from the portal. The fighting began almost instantly, and unit leaders on the ground have had to scramble to maneuver their forces to defensible positions. They are requesting withdrawal instructions." Hjaire could hear the nervousness in the subordinate's voice as he made his report, and for a moment felt empathy for the soldier.

Such sympathy was fleeting. The Chodrecai was still the enemy, after all.

"There will be no retreat," Ktrol countered. "Not until the Leadership orders it, and they have no intention of doing so. This is our best chance to bring the humans to their knees. We will not get a better opportunity."

Pacing the narrow confines of the control room, the *nomirtra* muttered a particularly vile oath. "They knew we were coming somehow." For a moment, Hjaire was worried that Ktrol might begin to suspect him or the other scientists of somehow getting word out, either to Plysserian forces on this planet or to the humans on Earth, about the coming attack. That he might find proof to support this suspicion did not worry Hjaire, for there was none, though lacking such evidence would not change the fact that if Ktrol were to accuse the scientists of collusion, he would be correct.

From the moment he had received the covert and encrypted communiqué, written in the hand of his longtime friend and fellow scientist Dr. Yagen and delivered via one of the few Chodrecai soldiers who had proven sympathetic to their cause, Hjaire's hopes had begun to soar. Finally, an opportunity had presented itself not only to assist his people's efforts but also to lend aid to the humans who had become unwilling participants in the War.

It had not been easy to determine the locations where forces would be arrayed for the massive offensive on the three prime Earth targets that Yagen had identified, as the battle plan had been classified at the highest levels of the Chodrecai Leadership. Any chance at a counteroffensive would have been lost if Hjaire or anyone else trying to obtain the information had been discovered.

That diligence and stealth had been rewarded, most notably by the reaction Ktrol was having to the latest reports from the battlefield.

"We have to keep pushing forward," the *nomirtra* said. "Our soldiers must be able to move faster through the portal." Turning to face Hjaire, he leveled an ominous gaze at the scientist. "Its size must be increased."

Hjaire had been prepared for this, though. "We can divert the necessary power, *Nomirtra*, but it will take time to determine how widening the portal will affect the stability of the conduit itself." He pointed to one of the computer displays dominating the control room's front wall. "We are having a difficult time as it is. This larger portal is more demanding in its power requirements, and we do not have the proper equipment at the endpoint. It requires constant monitoring and adjustments to maintain the conduit's integrity, more so than we originally anticipated."

"Your problems do not concern me, scientist," Ktrol said, making no effort to hide the menace in his voice. "If we are forced to abandon this offensive because of your inability to provide what we need, then your usefulness to me has ended."

In all the time he had been a prisoner of the Chodrecai, Hjaire had never heard Ktrol lose his composure in any fashion. That he was able to maintain his bearing under almost any circumstances was at times both admirable and frightening, as one could never know what the *nomirtra* might be thinking beneath the stolid military facade. The stresses of the current situation had to be wearing on him, and Hjaire did not doubt for a moment that Ktrol would carry out his threat.

With a sigh of resignation, he directed his attention back to the array of computer monitors. "It will take time to derive the proper calculations," he said over his shoulder. "You will need to clear the area around the portal."

"Time is a luxury you do not possess," Ktrol said before turning to the Chodrecai soldier who still stood at rigid attention and ordering him to carry out Hjaire's instructions.

And it was during that critical moment when the *nomirtra*'s attention was drawn away that Hjaire acted.

Normally the various series of instructions used to moderate the portal generator's operation were long and complex, mostly because of the process used to determine an endpoint for a conduit. This was true even before it had been discovered that the gateways were connecting *Jontashreena* with an entirely new world in a dimension separate from their own. Faced with that staggering revelation, Hjaire and other scientists quickly realized that their job had become much harder. The rotation speeds of both planets coupled with the velocity of each body traveling through space in its own respective dimension had to be factored into the computations if safe passages for their people were to be created and maintained.

For what Hjaire planned now, far fewer keystrokes were permissible, lest he be interrupted by Ktrol or a curious guard. The fingers of his left hand moved over the computer console almost with a will of their own, working at a frantic pace to enter the command string that he had labored for several cycles to create.

The effects were immediate. The portal simply tore itself apart.

It did not fade away in the manner Hjaire had seen countless times when the conduit was deactivated. He could only stand in muted shock as it instead exploded from the center outward, energy pouring forth in a torrential rush. The floor, the walls, even his teeth vibrated under the force of the concussion. Soldiers and workers caught in proximity to the portal were helpless, thrashing about uncontrollably as the sudden onslaught overwhelmed their nervous systems. Nearby vehicles and equipment were affected, too, their power sources crushed by the abrupt liberation of the energy the portal generator had commanded.

"Shut it down!" he heard Ktrol scream over the chaos unfolding in the cavern, but there was nothing Hjaire could do. Feedback from the portal generator had already worked its way back toward the control room as the first of the computer consoles disintegrated with the others following suit heartbeats later. Hjaire threw himself away from the blast but he could not move fast enough as he felt sudden pain in his back and legs. Heat tore through his body at dozens of points simultaneously as he was peppered with debris and he fell to the floor in a heap.

His vision blurring as the pain began to register, he was only just able to turn his head toward the door to see Ktrol also lying on the floor, his chest and face a bloodied mess of skin, bone, and shrapnel. The *nomirtra* was not moving, whether dead or merely unconscious Hjaire could not tell. It seemed ironic somehow to the scientist that Ktrol should die in such an ignominious manner, given the grandiose plans he had entertained for his own advancement as the War shifted its focus to the conquest of the humans. It had been Ktrol, after all, who had first voiced the idea to the Leadership that Earth could be a valuable resource to help replenish their own ravaged planet, so long as the humans could be dealt with.

Not today, I think.

Outside the control room, confusion continued to reign with those who had not succumbed to the portal's destruction. Though he found nothing humorous in what was happening, Hjaire still mustered a smile through his own mounting agony as he heard the cries of pain and others calling for help. He knew those pleas would not last long.

They were replaced by more explosions, these so thunderous that they shook the very walls of the cavern. True to their word, the unit of Plysserian resistance fighters who had assisted in the delivery of Dr. Yagen's encrypted message had been ready to act, waiting just as they said they would for Hjaire to disable the portal. In his mind's eye Hjaire could see the detonation of explosives planted with the aid of supportive Chodrecai, sealing the tunnel that led to the surface and cutting off the only means of escape from the underground chamber.

The screams he heard now were born of terror as those who had survived the portal's destruction, almost two thirds of the force assembled for the attack on Earth, fell victim to tons of falling rock and dirt as the ceiling began to collapse. Even the most generous estimates hoped for by the Plysserians' brutal yet simple plan had called for half of the force to be caught in the attack.

Then the lights were gone and darkness enveloped everything, and Hjaire heard the air circulation system die.

Generators are gone.

He tried but was unable to move because of his injuries, not that it mattered, of course. Where would he go? Escape routes had been cut off and he was trapped and alone in the darkness, helpless to do nothing but listen to the screams of others in the cavern as they futilely begged for help that he knew would never come. The loss of life here would be enormous, and similar carnage was probable at the other two staging sites elsewhere on *Jontashreena* should the assaults on those targets be as successful.

Rock was hammering against the control room's roof now, reverberating through the structure. Though he could not see it in the darkness, Hjaire could hear the ceiling already straining under the weight of rapidly accumulating debris. It would not be long now, a few moments at best.

He was comfortable with sacrificing his own life, considering it small penance for what he and his fellow scientists had inflicted on Earth with their creation. It was the wholesale slaughter of so many soldiers, enemy though they may be, that did not set well with him. Would what he had done here today have any lasting effect, either on the War or those who remained to fight it? Hjaire hoped that, if nothing else, the humans would be given a much-needed reprieve. If the War continued for any length of time, they would need every advantage and means of assistance available to them.

The sound of tearing metal pierced the darkness above him, and Hjaire heard the rumble of shifting rock. Able to do nothing but brace himself for what he knew was coming, he offered one final plea to the people of Earth.

"Forgive us."

Forgive me.

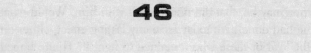

46

Another explosion shook the ground beneath his feet as Aloquon sought cover among the rubble of what might have once been a small building. He hunkered down behind the remnants of a wall as dirt and other bits of debris rained down on him and the small cadre of soldiers in his group.

All around him the sounds of fighting continued. He could hear aircraft in the skies above the battlefield, Chodrecai *Grista* assault craft as well as the slower and bulkier flying vehicles employed by the humans. Even with their lesser technology, the humans were still mounting a formidable defense. Though their aircraft lacked the speed and mobility possessed by the *Gristas*, the human pilots were proving to be exceptional marksmen as they engaged targets both on the ground and in the air with remarkable precision.

The humans were enjoying measured success on the ground, as well. Aloquon had observed the lumbering tracked vehicles with their large cannons firing with uncanny efficiency on Chodrecai ground positions, though the faster and more maneuverable assault vehicles Chodrecai drivers commanded were tempering that effectiveness. Even with their larger numbers, the humans stood no real chance of success on that front.

"Do you hear that?" a voice asked from somewhere to Aloquon's right. Turning to look in the speaker's direction Aloquon saw a fellow soldier crouching for protection behind another pile of wreckage. "Those sound like Plysserian pulse rifles."

Straining to hear above the high-pitched whines of Chodrecai armaments and the distinct reports of the humans' projectile weapons, Aloquon could indeed discern the familiar sounds of armaments used by the Plysserians.

"That would explain a great many things," Aloquon said as he shifted to a more comfortable position and scanned the broken terrain ahead of him for signs of the enemy. In the distance, illuminated by the glare of explosions and fire, he could see fleeting figures running across the battlefield, dodging to and from places of concealment as each side worked to outmaneuver the other.

"They must have helped the humans to prepare for our assault," he said as he finished his survey, satisfied that there seemed to be no immediate threat. "I wonder if our enemies are here, or did they simply supply the humans with weapons?" No matter what approach they had taken, there seemed to be no denying that the Plysserians' assistance had been of great help to the humans, particularly at the beginning of the assault.

However, while the battle had at first seemed one-sided against the Chodrecai, that appeared to be changing now.

With an adequate defensive perimeter now established around the portal, larger mechanized assets were arriving at a steady pace to aid in the fight. There had been no time to establish permanent weapons emplacement to protect the transferal of troops and matériel, so it had fallen to the foot soldiers to cover the situation as best they could. Aloquon and the uncounted soldiers forming this battle group had been pushing outward at a steady pace since their arrival. Skirmishes of varying size and intensity were raging throughout the city as Chodrecai ground forces continued to engage human defenders.

"I cannot believe this cold," the other soldier said. "They did not send advance scouts to survey this area before launching the assault, did they?"

Aloquon could not refute the question. He, too, was feeling the effects of the bitter cold, more so than at any other time he could remember. It was yet one more factor into a fight that was already more grueling than any other campaign in which he had participated. Without heavier clothing to shield them from the weather, the effectiveness of the Chodrecai forces was almost certain to diminish the longer the battle continued.

For the first time since he had been ordered into the fighting, Aloquon turned to look back the way they had come and his heart sank as he realized how little forward progress they had made. The portal and the troops and equipment arrayed around it were still visible amid the smoke, dust, fire, and debris littering the pummeled landscape of the battlefield.

He was still looking at the portal as one of the larger vehicles, a more formidable companion to the *Gristas*, began to emerge from the conduit. At first it was a faint outline that rapidly took on shape and substance as it materialized before his eyes, the dull finish of its armor plating appearing to absorb the light around it rather than reflecting it. Aloquon could see the weapons ports on the front of the vehicle already beginning to cycle back and forth in search of targets even as the hulking machine continued through the transferal process.

Then the darkness was pushed away as the portal and everything around it was enveloped in a tremendous flash of intense light that seemed to explode outward for but an instant before collapsing in on itself amid a torrential rush of air and energy. A heartbeat later the conduit was gone as though it had never existed.

"No!" Aloquon shouted as he beheld the expanding cloud of smoke that was all that remained of the portal. He continued to stare as the storm of smoke and dust generated by the conduit's abrupt collapse washed over the scattered bodies of anyone unfortunate enough to have been in proximity to the overwhelming blast. Farther away from where the portal had been, other Chodrecai stumbled about or writhed and twisted on the ground, they, too, being victims of whatever had happened to the gateway.

The effects of the portal's disappearance were beginning to register across the combat zone. Aloquon heard shouts of triumph and elation coming from all around him, and he recognized the snippets of language as belonging to the humans. Had they somehow orchestrated this as yet another facet of their unlikely defense? How was that possible? What power did the humans possess that allowed them to deal such a savage blow?

As quickly as the lull had fallen over the battlefield, the sounds of fighting were already beginning to reassert themselves.

"Here they come!" someone shouted, Aloquon did not know who. He looked in the direction they had been heading moments ago and saw movement among the rubble and the fires that continued to burn, both ground soldiers and mechanized weaponry. Chodrecai soldiers near his own position were beginning to fire at the approaching enemy, and it took Aloquon an extra moment to realize that they seemed to be aiming in multiple directions. Looking over his shoulder he saw fellow soldiers firing at something in the direction of where the portal had once been. Why? How could the humans have gotten behind them so quickly?

Of course. The revelation came with little effort and Aloquon's stomach fluttered in sudden stark realization. The humans had not needed to work to maneuver into their current positions. They were already there.

"Look out!"

The warning came from his left and Aloquon turned in time to see a line of humans rushing in his direction. Some of his comrades had already begun to fire at the enemy soldiers and he raised his pulse rifle to join in the fighting. The feel of the weapon recoiling into his shoulder was comforting as he watched some of the humans fall in the face of the onslaught while others scrambled for cover. Others were coming up behind the first group, though, rushing to fill the gaps that had been opened in the initial line. Still others were behind that second wave, all of them running and waving weapons as they charged.

"They've surrounded us!" the soldier next to him shouted over the wail of weapons fire. "What are we supposed to do now?"

"Keep fighting," Aloquon replied, taking aim at the line of advancing enemy soldiers. Countless energy charges tore the air apart all around him as the rest of the battle group engaged their attackers.

Even as he continued to fire his weapon, Aloquon pictured the battle scene in his mind. The humans had organized their defenses in a mammoth circular formation with their firepower concentrated inward and with the portal at the center. Impossible as it seemed to him, the humans had not only gained advance knowledge of the pending assault, but had also known precisely where the portal would be. It was a classic ambush on a massive scale. What had begun as an immense defensive effort had now turned into a multipronged counterattack, with the Chodrecai forces at the center of the envelopment.

A figure moved to his right and Aloquon fired at it, the energy charge from his rifle shredding the approaching human. The remains of the soldier were still falling to the ground as two more stepped up to take his place, so close now that he could see the hatred and fear in their pale faces. More than that, he could sense a new quality in these creatures that had not been present at the outset of the battle. They fought with a new fire in their bellies, a fire fueled by the need to protect their homes from invaders and the knowledge that they had somehow gained the upper hand.

Something was clambering over the dirt near his position and Aloquon turned to see the first wave of humans scaling the remnants of the wall he and his companions were using as cover. Jumping headlong into the fray, they screamed and yelled as they fired their crude weapons at anything that moved. Aloquon pulled back from his place on the wall, twisting around in a desperate attempt to shoot at the humans who were now piling over the rubble in droves to engage the enemy face-to-face. Their tactics, though primitive and limited, were more than compensated for with their sheer courage in the face of battle. It was ferocity unlike anything Aloquon had encountered even in the most heated of skirmishes in which he had fought.

He sensed movement to his right and then a human was lunging at him, its own smaller features screwed up in fury as it unleashed a shrieking cry. Then he saw nothing but the yawning maw of the human's weapon as it aimed directly at his face.

We have underestimated our enemy, was all Aloquon had time to think before everything disappeared in a flash of light and a clap of thunder.

47

They only just made it to the safety of the maintenance tunnel before the battle plan went completely to hell.

Anyone in the Blue assault group had been authorized to order the explosives detonated ahead of schedule should Gray forces discover any signs of the invaders' presence, thereby setting the rest of the offensive into motion. Doing so meant risking the loss of the portal and any matériel the Blues hoped to capture, but Javoquek had been explicit in his orders during their premission briefing that one way or another, the Chodrecai would lose this conduit to Earth today.

Therefore, DiCarlo had no way of knowing who might have given the order as, somewhere close by in the stadium, the first of the explosives detonated.

"Here we go," Russell said, and DiCarlo felt the vibration in the soles of his feet and the walls around them shook from the force of the blast. The echo rushed up the narrow passageway from the direction of the stadium's center to meet them. He could see it in his mind, the first of the tunnels leading from the massive playing field collapsing in the explosion, not only cutting off its potential avenue of escape but also trapping hundreds of Gray soldiers under tons of debris. It was a ghastly action to take, DiCarlo knew, but unavoidable given the disparity of numbers between the enemy forces and their own comparably meager contingent.

And it was only the beginning, with the tactic being repeated in the other three tunnels where Gray troops were staging on their way to the playing field and the portal. With luck, a sizable portion of the enemy forces would be taken out of the equation in the first moments of the assault without a shot being fired.

"The strike force will be here in moments," Kel said. "We have to move." DiCarlo and Russell followed after the Blue alien soldier, running almost at a sprint to keep up with the alien's longer strides.

How many Grays would be waiting for them? There was no way many of them could have passed through the portal before the alarm had sounded, DiCarlo decided, which meant that a sizable force still remained on the playing field. With luck they would be disorganized and perhaps even panicked somewhat as the attack unfolded around them.

Attacking the stadium had presented a distinct challenge, one DiCarlo had come to appreciate while sitting in on the meetings Javoquek had conducted and listening to the suggestions bandied about for the best way to conduct the assault. Though air assault units could be used to bomb the target from the air, ground forces were needed to secure the interior of the stadium along with the portal and other matériel they were after.

Sneaking enough Blue forces into the stadium using the same means as the advance teams that had planted the explosives was not practical, as maintaining stealth with so many bodies would have been impossible. Likewise, they could not employ a frontal assault from the ground, converging on the exterior of the structure from several directions, either. Such a maneuver would have given the tactical advantage to the Grays, easily able to fire on troops in the open from well-defended positions inside the arena.

Javoquek had therefore put into play the only option remaining to them, with ground forces being delivered to the stadium's upper sections via airborne troop transports. The soldiers would have to fight their way down to the lower levels, but if the initial strike had worked as planned then the number of enemy troops they would have to face would be considerably reduced. They would also be aided by other air assets providing cover fire during those critical moments as the first soldiers were inserted.

But would all of that be enough?

Guess there's only one way to find out.

It took them several minutes to negotiate the tunnel and make their way onto the arena floor, and in that short amount of time DiCarlo could see that the scene inside the stadium was well on its way toward deteriorating into total chaos.

His heart soared as he saw dozens of Plysserian arrow-shaped aircraft flying about overhead. The now familiar *Lisum* assault ships were weaving an intricate web high above the playing field and the rows of benches forming the stadium's audience seating. Their pilots were laying down an oppressive blanket of weapons fire, tracking and shooting anything that moved.

The air was filled with the sounds of the ships' pulse cannons and the smaller rifles of soldiers on both sides of the battle. Fires burned, smoke and dust polluted the air and bodies were scrambling in all directions. It had been a long time since DiCarlo had witnessed a battle scene of such intensity. Even the firefights back at Camp Growding when all of this insanity had begun had not approached this level of mayhem.

Mayhem's good, he reminded himself, *as long as you're the one dishing it out.*

"Look," Russell called out above the din and both he and Kel looked to where she was pointing. Under cover of the protective fire the *Lisums* were providing he could see larger troop transport craft, each carrying a dozen Blue soldiers, taking turns flying in to one of the open observation decks on the stadium's upper level just long enough to drop their passengers. The soldiers had been well-trained themselves, wasting no time clearing the platform as their ship pulled away. They moved quickly to join their comrades and help push outward from the observation deck and down into the stands, making room for the next batch of new arrivals. It was a textbook example of infiltration into a hot landing zone, the likes of which DiCarlo had not seen in thirty years. Where the hell had these guys been, in 'Nam?

Pulling Russell by the arm, DiCarlo sprinted toward the stands. He did not have to look back to know that Kel was bringing up their rear, searching for threats as they moved and with his weapon ready to fire. Only when he was able to crouch down behind a waist-high, intricately carved stone wall separating the viewing area from the field did DiCarlo even think about breathing easier. There was no sense standing in the open and waiting to be picked off like a target in a shooting arcade, after all.

What he could not see was any sign of the rest of the advance party. Spread throughout the stadium, they had moved in teams of three and four to plant the explosives that had launched the offensive. The original plan had been for the teams to get out of the stadium the way they had come before the actual attack began. With escape avenues cut off by the explosions that had killed or trapped hundreds of Grays and sealed any survivors inside the arena, DiCarlo and the others would have to resort to their backup plan of moving into the arena itself and calling for an extraction by one of the troop transports.

Though some Grays were moving toward the stands in feeble attempts to defend against the attack, most of the enemy soldiers who had survived the initial bombings were bunching up in large groups near the center of the field where the portal was positioned. More bodies than DiCarlo could count littered the playing field, and he saw a handful of Grays, officers presumably, shouting and waving their arms frantically as they tried to speed up the process of sending troops through the conduit. Others were moving away from the portal, spreading out to form a circle around the group.

"They're establishing a perimeter," Russell said.

DiCarlo nodded. "Probably hoping to buy enough time to get the rest of the troops through the portal." How many of the Grays had already made the transit to Earth? What kind of reception was waiting for them? There was no way to know if the warning about the massive Gray offensive had gotten through in time for a counterattack to be put into play in Washington, Moscow, and Beijing. Would they be able to repel the three-pronged assault?

He could not concern himself with that now, though.

A group of five Grays had noticed their arrival and were turning in their direction. Kel wasted no time raising his own rifle and firing at the onrushing enemy soldiers, with Russell quickly following suit.

"On the left!" DiCarlo shouted as one of the Grays managed to bring their own weapon up, but Russell was faster and the soldier fell in a wash of energy. His companion dodged the Gray's falling body and leapt for the wall, so close that DiCarlo could hear the alien's breathing. The Marine swung his rifle around and fired, aiming purely by instinct. The energy pulse punched the soldier in the chest and sent him flying backward to the field below.

As quickly as the small skirmish had started it was over.

"Time to call for a ride, Kel," he shouted. "We're sitting ducks out here."

Out on the field the perimeter had taken on definite shape, with the Grays beginning to return fire into the stands. DiCarlo watched as Blues scrambled for cover, some of them not moving fast enough as they were caught in the blistering volleys of weapons fire.

Behind the defensive line, Grays were disappearing into the portal in groups of ten to twelve and DiCarlo gritted his teeth in frustration. So far, few of the enemy's assault vehicles or other larger equipment had been able to move toward the conduit, as they had been among the first targets selected by the *Lisums* when the attack had begun. Still, though, too damned many of the troops were getting **through**!

Static crackled from the earpiece of his communications headset and DiCarlo grabbed for the unit. Bringing the headset to his ear, he heard the stressed voice of Javoquek calling out orders in his native language. Though he was not wearing his translator headband, DiCarlo had picked up enough of the Plysserian language to get the gist of what Javoquek was saying.

"I think he sees the defensive line, too," Russell said, listening to the exchange on her own comm.

Kel nodded. "Correct. He is calling for the *Lisums* to concentrate their fire on the field and abandon their cover fire missions."

It was as good a strategy as any, DiCarlo knew. Though there was no way for him to count, he figured that enough time had passed since the beginning of the attack that there had to be sufficient Blue soldiers on the ground now to hold their own without needing protection from the air.

Hopefully, at least.

A thunderous explosion shook everything around them. DiCarlo saw fire to his right and turned to see what had once been one of the troop transports consumed within an expanding ball of writhing flame. He could only stand transfixed as the transport plunged to its death, dropping in a spectacular arc to the floor of the stadium. Soldiers on the ground saw it, too, and raced away from the incoming missile but there was nowhere for them to go.

When the craft plowed into the ground it exploded again, casting flaming debris in all directions and catching anyone in the open in a storm of fire.

What the hell had brought the ship down?

DiCarlo looked around the field and saw that a few of the Grays' own assault vehicles had been brought to bear. Others were breaking from the columns of troops and equipment waiting for their turn to enter the portal and moving toward the now firmly established defensive perimeter. They were already targeting other Blue attack craft and the Blue pilots were responding in kind, their evasive maneuvers becoming more elaborate as they continued their mission. Several of the pilots did not react fast enough and they paid the price, their *Lisums* getting hammered by concentrated weapons fire.

The Blue ground troops working their way down from the upper levels were not faring much better, either. At first able to push forward from the landing zone with relative ease, many of them were pinned down now, forced to find whatever concealment presented itself. Those who failed to find cover were caught in the onslaught of enemy fire.

"Damn it," DiCarlo hissed. "They're getting their feet back under them." He could feel the tide of the battle beginning to turn away from the Blues. Another few minutes at this rate and any superiority they had managed to forge here would be lost.

Then he heard Russell cry out in alarm and he jerked his head up to see something moving in his direction. Several somethings, in fact.

It took him less than a second to pull the rifle into his shoulder and press the firing stud. He was rewarded with the weapon's satisfying hum and kick as the weapon spat its energy and struck the first Gray in the chest. The soldier went down but DiCarlo was already sighting in on the next one. To his right he heard the whine of Russell's rifle as well as Kel's, each of them going after members of the group bearing down on them.

"Watch out!" Russell shouted just as a round hit the wall to DiCarlo's left and then something punched him in the rib cage as stone shrapnel peppered his body. Heat and pain ripped into his leg and arm along with the left side of his face and neck. He tried to keep his rifle on the target he had selected but he was off balance, the muzzle of the weapon pointing toward the dirt even as he fell over. The armor saved his back as he slammed into the stone bench behind him, but the impact was still enough to drive the air from his lungs.

His arm, face, and neck throbbed where he had been struck, and his leg felt as though it had gone completely numb. DiCarlo tried to move it but failed. Then it no longer mattered as a shadow loomed in his vision. Instinct told him the Gray could only be a few meters away.

Energy screamed past his face and DiCarlo realized that Kel had fired directly over him, his shot taking the rushing soldier in the midsection and dropping him to the ground.

"Simon!" he heard Russell shout as she scrambled to help him. "Are you all right?"

Swiping his face with his right hand, DiCarlo looked at his fingers and saw that they were covered in blood. Not too much, though. He had been fortunate not to get any debris in his eyes, or that the shrapnel flung at him had not been bigger.

Yeah. Lucky lucky me.

"Help's on the way," Russell said as she gripped his hand in her own. "Kel says we're getting out of here."

Even though the pain was beginning to take hold and he could feel the initial stages of shock reaching out for him, DiCarlo forced himself to focus on the situation at hand. "Javoquek is ordering an evacuation?" he asked through clenched teeth.

"Yes," Kel replied as he moved closer, shaking his head.

"He feels that we have lost the initiative and that we need to pull back before we suffer too many losses."

DiCarlo felt his heart sink as he digested the news. In Javoquek's plan evacuation meant only one thing.

He was vaguely aware of Russell leaning closer to examine his wounds, but he did not acknowledge her ministrations. Instead he looked out onto the field, beyond the Gray defensive line and to the swirling circle of mad color that was the portal. It appeared that once again a way back home was being taken from him and Russell. DiCarlo had known before the mission began that losing the conduit was a very real possibility, but that did not make it any easier to accept now. Even were he not injured there was no way that he and Russell could cross the open ground between their present position and the portal. It, and its path back to Earth, was beyond their reach.

Besides, there were more immediate concerns, such as how he, Russell, and Kel might survive the next few minutes.

The drone of the cargo transport's engine would normally be soothing to the ears of young Seyal, but instead it only added to his growing sense of agitation.

"I hate the waiting," he said to no one, as he was alone in the cramped confines of the transport's cockpit. He had known to expect this type of lull, and the very real possibility that he may not even be needed in the coming attack on the arena. That did not sit well with Seyal, who had wanted to be part of the actual assault, ferrying his fellow soldiers to the battlefield as he had done so for most of his adult life. Despite his youth, he had garnered a reputation as a pilot of consummate skill and daring, flying more troops into combat zones than he could easily remember.

Besides, this was more than just a battle. It could very well be a historic turning point in the War, not only for the Plysserians but also for the humans who had come to their aid on Earth. From everything the intelligence reports had said, the Chodrecai were channeling massive resources into this three-front assault on key Earth targets. Though Seyal held no illusions that the War would be decided by what happened today, he was certain that the outcome of this battle would likely dictate the course of

the War for cycles to come, both here and on the humans'
planet.

And after that?

Seyal had met and talked with the two humans who
had traveled to *Jontashreena* through another portal and
had come to the conclusion that Earth was a place he
would very much like to visit one day. Assuming the
Plysserians won the War, would such a visit even be possible? A question that had been plaguing him, one he had
not had the courage to ask DiCarlo and Russell, was
whether or not the humans of Earth would embrace the
Plysserians as friends rather than simply allies born of necessity once the War was over? Surely there would be re-
sentment among many of the humans, if indeed there was
not already. How would they react when it became common knowledge that the Plysserians were ultimately to
blame for the strife imposed on their planet in the first
place?

There was nothing Seyal could do about that now, of
course.

A beep from the console before him jolted him from
his reverie and Seyal realized it was an incoming communication. Tapping a control to complete the connection,
he spoke into the microphone attached to his headset.

"This is Seyal."

A burst of static filled the receiver built into the headset
and Seyal winced at its volume. The signal was heavily
disrupted, as if the transmitter were located near a powerful energy source. It cleared somewhat, long enough for a
harried voice to break through. *"Seyal, this is Javoquek.
Things are going badly for us, I'm afraid, and I've ordered
our troops to retreat. Start your run."*

It was the order Seyal had been both anticipating and dreading. While Javoquek's command meant that he was finally going to participate in the battle as he had been trained to do, it also drove home the fact that the assault itself was not going well for their side and that extreme action was now required.

"Acknowledged," he said. "I'm adjusting my course now, and will wait for the all clear signal."

Javoquek's response was quick and firm. *"Negative, Seyal. We cannot wait for that! The Chodrecai are rallying against us. You are our last option. Launch your attack now."*

It would take Seyal only moments to get to the stadium at the speed he was traveling. How many of his comrades would still be in the danger area when he arrived? Javoquek was essentially ordering him to attack his fellow Plysserians, and the very idea horrified Seyal. Considering the ordnance he carried aboard the transport, there was no way anyone still on the arena's playing field, or even in the stadium for that matter, would survive his attack run.

Javoquek knew all of this, of course, and that only served to tell Seyal just how desperate the situation was becoming.

Feeling the initial symptoms of shock washing over him, DiCarlo was only vaguely aware of his surroundings. He heard the disheveled chorus of battle around him, including rifle fire as Kel occasionally shot at an enemy soldier that came too close to the trio. There were other sounds, too, including the whine of attack craft engines and orders shouted in languages he still did not understand, his confusion compounded by the loss of his translator band during the previous skirmish.

What he did understand was Russell's labored breathing as he leaned against her. Unable to walk on his own, she had taken up the task of guiding him through the stadium's viewing stands, leaving Kel free to cover their retreat. DiCarlo tried to help, searching for potential threats that Russell might not see, but it was difficult to keep his attention focused.

A sharp stabbing pain beneath his body armor told him that he had at least one broken rib, probably two. Blood flowed from numerous wounds, including one on his forehead that had caked his left eye shut. His left arm and leg were all but useless and he had been forced to discard his pulse rifle in favor of his Beretta pistol, though he was having trouble even holding onto it. The sidearm would be ineffective against a Gray's thick skin and muscle tissue except at extreme close range, but it was better than nothing.

Assuming I can even fire the damned thing.

Where was their extraction point? DiCarlo had lost track of how far they had traveled, but he had no difficulty discerning how slowly they were moving. He could sense Russell starting to tire under the strain of supporting his weight. How much longer would she be able to keep this up?

"You can move faster without me," he said, biting off each word through clenched teeth.

"Don't even think about it," Russell countered between sharp intakes of breath. "We're not supposed to leave anybody behind, right?"

There was more to it, of course, given their romantic involvement during the past weeks, and DiCarlo could not help the pang of affection that warmed his heart at the sound of her words. It had been far too long since the attention of another had enticed him so, but he could not allow that to cloud his judgment, or Russell's. While she was correct to evoke the long-standing tradition of not leaving comrades on the battlefield, she was still his subordinate and he could not allow her to sacrifice or endanger herself on his behalf.

"If you don't leave me, neither of us will get out."

Russell turned her head until her eyes locked with his. "Either we both go or we both stay, and I don't want to stay here. So shut up and keep walking."

An explosion rocked the ground and Russell stumbled, falling to one knee and causing DiCarlo to drop to the ground in a disjointed heap. He grunted as pain lanced through his injured ribs, his breath coming in ragged gasps as he fought to keep from losing consciousness. "Belinda?" he called out weakly, unable to see her from where he had fallen.

"I'm here," she replied and then he felt her hand on his arm. Gritting his teeth he allowed her to help him back to his feet as another explosion jolted them. He saw Kel looking back the way they had come, his weapon in his shoulder and firing. Russell directed DiCarlo to start walking again, continuing to hug the wall that separated the viewing stands from the floor of the arena and keeping the field on their right as they moved.

Most of the stadium was shrouded in dust and smoke, so much so that DiCarlo could not see much past the center of the field. The bodies of Gray and Blue soldiers littered the area, as well as the still burning wreckage of equipment destroyed by the aerial assault fighters. There was still plenty of movement though, with hundreds of soldiers still waging the battle throughout the arena. Di-Carlo heard the savage grunts of soldiers engaged in hand-to-hand combat, having either lost or discarded their weapons in favor of their own brute strength. Bones snapped and blood flowed as the fighting deteriorated to its most basic, primeval form.

"It's getting pretty bad out here," DiCarlo said, forcing the words past gritted teeth. "How much longer?"

Kel made a sweep of the immediate area before responding. "Any time now. We must keep going."

A shriek of power echoed overhead and DiCarlo looked up to see a pair of *Lisum* attack craft diving in toward the center of the field, their weapons flaring as they locked onto a group of Gray soldiers huddled near one of their own assault vehicles. One of the Grays had activated the vehicle's pulse cannon but could not bring the weapon around fast enough before the *Lisums* were on him. The vehicle and the Grays disappeared in a flash of light and energy even as the attack craft pulled up and flew back into the sky, already coming around for another run.

"There!" Russell yelled pointing to a Blue transport that was dropping sharply down into the stadium, plummeting as if in free fall to the arena floor. Even as it continued its rapid descent DiCarlo could see its side doors opening, a Blue soldier visible in the doorway facing toward them.

"It is time," Kel said. "That is our evacuation transport." He handed his rifle to Russell, who took the weapon before climbing over the wall to the field below. In the flurry of motion that followed DiCarlo felt himself lifted with ease by the Blue soldier. Then Kel leaped the wall as easily as he or Russell might step over a footstool, the alien landing on the field with the grace of a cat before taking off at a run across the now broken and battle-scarred terrain.

DiCarlo heard a low rumbling from somewhere above them, increasing in volume with each passing second. Cradled as he was in Kel's massive tattooed arms, it was easy for him to look up and see the source of the growing whine of power.

"Holy shit," he breathed. "Kel, look!"

"I know what it is," the soldier replied as he continued to run toward the transport. "Javoquek has ordered the use of our final weapon."

The shock of the simple statement broke through DiCarlo's pain. "We still have people on the ground!" He and Russell and Kel were still fifty meters away from their transport. Russell was sprinting for all she was worth, barely able to keep pace with Kel who had even slowed his stride for her benefit.

DiCarlo could not take his eyes off the lone craft coming toward them even as it jostled in his vision as a result of Kel's galloping strides. It was growing larger, accelerating as it fell from the sky like a meteor. Laden with explosives and hundreds of gallons of a flammable substance that DiCarlo had likened to napalm when he had first heard about it in Javoquek's briefing, the "final weapon" would indeed be the last strike of this offensive.

And it was coming.

49

Even as the ground rushed up at him through the transport's canopy, Seyal remained in position. With heavy barrages of enemy fire still tearing through the surrounding sky, it was still possible that he might have to take some final evasive maneuvers to ensure that the craft was not destroyed before it reached its target.

His eyes flitted to the bank of displays just below the windshield, the one that showed him the status of the Plysserian evacuation. Updated by each of the transport pilots extracting troops from the arena, it told him how the retreat was progressing. According to situation reports he was receiving, there were still a good number of their troops on the ground, though not nearly as many as when Javoquek had given Seyal the order to begin his final approach. Less than half of the transports that had been used to bring the ground forces to the assault remained, the others having been shot down by Chodrecai troops as the enemy had begun to turn the battle around.

The reports of the surviving craft, with their cold, stark numbers, told him one thing. There would still be Plysserian troops on the ground when he arrived. For the briefest of moments, Seyal considered reducing his speed or even aborting the approach and swinging around for another attempt, thereby buying his comrades additional time to escape.

No sooner did the thought materialize than he discarded it. Javoquek's battle strategy had been devised with timing being crucial to the successful implementation of its various stages. Though the attack had already suffered setbacks and the Plysserian resistance leader had unleashed his planned backup measures to maximum effect, it had obviously not been enough. The final contingency had been called into play.

And Seyal was the soldier with whom that duty had been entrusted. If the portal could not be captured, then it had to be destroyed no matter the cost. The loss of Plysserian lives, even those lost as a direct result of Seyal's own actions, would still be far less than the damaging blow the Chodrecai would suffer today.

Before the attack had even started, Seyal had acknowledged that he may have to remain at the transport's controls all the way to the ground. The idea of dying had, when he was younger, terrified him, but as the War had continued to rage he had gradually come to accept it not only as a possibility but even as an eventuality. Many of his friends had already died in previous battles, some of them willfully sacrificing themselves in order to save the lives of comrades or even innocent noncombatants.

The faces of those friends played across his memory as Seyal arrived at one final decision. He could not bring himself to eject from the transport and drop to safety, not with so many of his brothers and sisters in arms about to sacrifice their lives for the greater necessity of the mission. The choice came with little effort, most likely because at some level, Seyal had made it long ago. While dying in war was itself not a good or even noble act, doing so in defense of something worth fighting for, be it an individual or an ideal, was a notion from which a soldier could draw the strength and courage needed to succeed on the battlefield.

It was that small measure of comfort, along with the knowledge that his comrades would understand the necessity for his next action, that Seyal altered the transport's course one last time and entered the command for the craft to accelerate.

Their evacuation transport had begun its liftoff even as Kel and Russell closed the final distance, jumping aboard as the craft's landing pads left the ground. Kel barely managed to set DiCarlo into a seat as the ship banked upward at a severe angle and accelerated into the sky. DiCarlo could still see the stone and metal of the arena rising up around the transport, and he caught only a glimpse of the larger cargo transport screaming past the ship's open doorway on its collision course with the stadium floor.

"Hold on!" Kel called out as the transport lurched to the left, its nose pointing even higher as the craft gained altitude.

The explosion was audible even over the ship's howling engine. When the shockwave came, DiCarlo reached for the safety bar above his head despite the pain his movements inflicted on his already mistreated body. Everyone else in the cabin held on as the ship bucked and convulsed violently around them, with the pilot fighting to keep the transport airborne.

DiCarlo had seen the damage caused by fuel-air explosives in other wars, but they were nothing compared to the effects of the bomb-laden cargo ship as it detonated near the center of the stadium's massive playing field. His faced pressed to the window port next to his seat, he saw the monstrous fireball erupt from the point of impact, cascading outward in all directions to engulf the arena's interior. With each passing second the radius expanded to envelop more of the field and the surrounding structure, the force of the blast more than enough to envelope the entire stadium along with anyone who might still be trapped inside.

As the pilot regained control of the craft, Russell left her seat and crossed to where DiCarlo was seated. "Are you all right?" she asked as she set about the task of helping him out of his restrictive body armor. Despite her attempts to be gentle DiCarlo still felt a sharp jab of pain as she assisted him in removing the garment.

"He requires medical attention," Kel said as he moved closer. "They will be waiting for us when we land." DiCarlo was too tired and too far along the path to shock to even argue the merits of what a doctor from this planet might be able to do for him. He could only hope that the concepts of mending broken bones and suturing wounds were universal.

Casting another look through the window, DiCarlo could no longer see the burning husk of what had once been the proud stadium. "How do you suppose we did?"

Kel shook his head. "I would imagine that it will be some time before an accurate casualty report is collected. The Chodrecai will likely have suffered significant losses, to be sure, not only in personnel and equipment but the destruction of the portal as well." He paused before adding, "I am sure we lost significant numbers of our own soldiers, as well."

The thought was a sobering one for DiCarlo. Had all of it been enough? He could only guess at the ultimate effects of their attack. Had their actions been sufficient to allow any defenses that might have been marshaled to protect Washington, D.C., to succeed as well? How long would it be before he knew the answer to that question? Never?

"I wonder how the other attacks went," Russell said as she helped DiCarlo into a more comfortable position. "If they failed, then everything we did here might be for nothing."

The idea that it might all have been in vain galled DiCarlo, even the part of him that had long ago grown accustomed to the savage realities of war. Russell was right, of course. Just as the Grays had been counting on a successful three-pronged attack on Earth targets to squelch any prospect of prolonged human resistance, the Blues' had relied just as heavily on their tri-fold counteroffensive to keep the enemy forces at bay. It had been a bold plan, fraught with risk, with the stakes equally high for both victory and defeat.

"Our actions here today might not have any noticeable effects for some time," Kel said. "Such is the reality to which we grew accustomed long ago. It may very well be many of your years before tangible consequences become apparent." He smiled grimly. "I would not worry too much, my friends. There will be much to do in the interim, for all of us. The War is far from over, after all."

Settling into his seat and allowing Russell to dress his wounds, DiCarlo could only agree with his friend.

Though the War had already lasted for years on Kel's own planet, how much resilience had Earth breathed into it? Everyone on his planet was involved now, for the long haul. How many more battles could they mount before their resources, already meager when compared to the technology of the aliens, failed them?

And what of Russell and himself? Would they ever see their home again, or was it better that they resign themselves to the idea that the rest of their lives would be spent here?

The questions remained unanswered, for the moment at least, as exhaustion and the stress of his injuries finally overtook him and Simon DiCarlo drifted into unconsciousness.

Eye
of the Storm

50

"General Thompson, your presence is requested in the Situation Room. General Thompson to the Situation Room, please."

The urgency in the voice on the intercom, something Bruce Thompson had not heard in quite some time, pulled him from the quagmire of reports on his desk and propelled him from his office to the Op04-E control center. Had the Grays finally seen fit to show themselves after lying dormant for more than a month?

Though the massive three-front campaign had technically been a defeat for the Grays, the humans and the Blues who had assisted them in repelling the invaders had paid a dear price indeed. The three targets of the Gray assault had suffered to varying degrees, although none of the besieged cities had fallen into enemy hands.

Moscow had suffered huge losses in troops and matériel as well as enormous damage to many of the city's historic buildings and other landmarks. Despite this, the Russian army had held their ground and finally succeeded in surrounding and capturing those Gray forces cut off when the portal that had brought them from their own planet disappeared.

A similar outcome had happened in Beijing. Though Chinese military forces there had suffered much in the way of damage and loss of life, they had managed to overwhelm the alien contingent through sheer force of numbers. The portal there had vanished as well, leaving in its wake the first clue that some type of coordinated effort had been launched on the aliens' home planet to assist Earth against the Gray attack.

The theory gained strength in Washington, D.C., as the portal there also collapsed, allowing forces arrayed to defend the capital to fight almost to a stalemate. Though the Grays themselves had ultimately been repelled, numerous milestones of American history had either suffered significant damage or had been lost forever. Only the bottom third of the Washington Monument still stood, the remainder of the immense marble and granite obelisk having tumbled to the ground. Several of the Smithsonian Museums had been consumed by fire and the Capitol Building had suffered partial collapse. Civilian casualties were few, thanks to the evacuation efforts that had preceded the battle.

Even after the portal on the Mall had disappeared, the fighting continued for days afterward as Gray forces trapped here broke through the lines and scattered into the city. Losses were heavy on both sides, and the battle lines had blurred in the war-torn streets as each side danced around each other in search of any kind of advantage.

As the days passed, reinforcements continued to be brought into the city and numbers worked against the Grays. Many of the aliens were captured or killed as the fighting waned, while it had been reported that a few had escaped, disappearing into the countryside of Virginia or

Maryland. While the battle itself could be called a victory for Earth, it would take months to assess the costs to this, the focal point of American history and political power. Still, preventing the loss of the nation's capital could only serve as a much-needed shot in the arm for the country's morale, if not that of the entire world.

Scientists and other specialists had long since begun drooling over the remnants of alien weaponry and equipment and the bodies of Blue and Gray soldiers salvaged from the numerous battlefields around the world. How advanced was the aliens' technology? How did their physiology protect them from germs and diseases they were sure to encounter on Earth? These and uncounted other questions required answering, and the wealth of recovered specimens and information would be enough to keep researchers busy seeking those answers for years to come.

Loath as he was to admit it, Thompson had been sensing an unwelcome calm already beginning to take hold in the aftermath of the battle several weeks ago. The Grays had not seen fit to show themselves in the days following those attacks, and there was already speculation in some quarters that they would never return. Though the military was continuing mop-up actions across the city and indeed the entire country, others were talking about how to move on with their lives and put the traumatic events of the past months behind them. While scientists and other specialists studied the remnants of alien technology salvaged from the numerous battlefields around the world hoping to either duplicate the weaponry or develop effective defenses, there were those who sought to proclaim the entire affair a government-sponsored conspiracy, a hoax designed to secure larger defense budgets.

All of it made Thompson's head spin, his stomach ache, and his heart yearn for retirement.

Entering the Situation Room, his eyes darted to the Map Wall in search of whatever development had prompted his summons. The array of screens showed the same things they had been displaying for weeks, each tuned to a different channel with news anchors giving their take on the events of the past month. As they invariably did with any news event, they had run out of anything new to report and the anchors had long since begun to rehash everything all over again.

Thank God for mute.

"What's going on?" he called out, his deep baritone voice echoing in the cavernous room.

"Bruce, you're not going to believe this," General Thomas Brooks called from the room's lower level where he stood next to Lance Corporal Gardner and Max. The three appeared to be poring over something that Brooks held in his hand before the general started up the stairs toward Thompson with Max and Gardner following close behind.

"A squad of Army Rangers was on patrol near Arlington when they came across three Grays. They surrendered to the Rangers, didn't even put up a fight. When they were questioned by interpreters they said that they were looking to be captured, claiming to be part of a resistance movement that's gaining steam on the aliens' home planet. According to them, we're gaining some friends among the Grays." Handing over the items he held in his right hand, Brooks added, "The leader was carrying these, with instructions to deliver them to someone in authority here."

Thompson did not recognize the black rectangle that

his friend proffered, though he was surprised when it felt heavier than it looked. The several sheets of paper, white with blue lines and looking as though they had been torn from a notebook, were familiar enough. "What is all this?"

"The notes are from two Marines, Sergeant Major Simon DiCarlo and Sergeant Belinda Russell."

Recognition flashed in Thompson's mind at the mention of the two names. Looking to Gardner he said, "From your unit, right?"

Gardner nodded excitedly. "Yes, sir. We thought they were killed during the firefight in Missouri, but it looks like we were wrong."

"They've been fighting with the Blues on the other side, Bruce," Brooks said. "The notes are Russell's, detailing everything that's happened to them since they crossed over." Tapping the black wafer in Thompson's hand he added, "That's a data cartridge used by Blue computer systems. Among other things, it contains a complete record of their battle plan against the portals used during the attacks on Washington, China, and Russia. DiCarlo and Russell were part of the team that disabled the portal linking up with Washington."

Thompson's mouth fell open at the revelation. It had been suspected from the very beginning that Blue forces on the other side of the conduits had aided in the timely collapse of the portals during the massive Gray offensive. But to have that theory confirmed, and to find out that two of their own Marines had played a part in that action?

It seemed that the news anchors were finally going to have something new to yammer about.

"It gets better," Brooks said. "There appears to be a growing number of Gray dissenters that have been working to disrupt further efforts to attack Earth." He indicated the cartridge again. "That thing holds information and maps for portal locations all over their planet, whether they're controlled by Blues or Grays. There's also information about new portals that are either planned or already under construction. Many of those locations are near Gray military installations, most likely to facilitate movement of troops and materiel through to here."

"Jesus," Thompson breathed. He now had proof that the mammoth stroke of good luck visited on Earth had been no accident, as well as the much-needed wake-up call that he had been waiting for that the War was indeed far from over. "And you say the Grays are starting to feel sympathy toward us?"

"According to the Chodrecai we questioned," Max said, "it is a small movement of support, but it is gaining momentum every day. It is hoped that if your people can be made to understand how you were drawn into our War, you might see fit to extend the same hand of friendship to them as you did to my people. They realize that it is a difficult proposition, given the extent of harm that has befallen your world."

Thompson sighed. "That's an understatement, all right. Most of the planet won't know about or understand the reasons why you went to war in the first place, much less why we became involved. Many of the people who've survived to this point won't care about becoming friends with those who attacked them. One thing you have to learn about humans, Max, is that we can be pretty self-absorbed until you piss us off. Then we tend to carry a grudge."

Though Thompson expected the Blue soldier to be

confused with what he had said, Max instead nodded thoughtfully. "I have seen some of what you describe already, General, during the time I and my companions have been living among you. This grudge you speak of has affected us, as well, and I cannot say that it is undeserved. After all, we are the ones responsible for bringing this conflict to you. There will be those who seek retribution for what we have done. It will make adapting to life on your world difficult, but we will manage. We will have to, as there is every possibility that this is our home now, as well."

"You helped us," Gardner countered, "you and your friends. Now it'll be our turn to help you."

"He's right," Thompson added. "Many of us know what you've done for us, and I for one won't be forgetting it anytime soon. We'll protect you just as we would protect our own people. Besides, we need you. We've got a long way to go before all of this is over, Max. People want to believe that we've got the Grays on the run, but I think you and I both know differently." He held up the data cartridge for emphasis. "We might have bloodied their noses, but they'll be back. This proves it."

Perhaps it would take weeks or even months before the Grays were ready to launch another offensive, but Thompson knew it would come.

Would Earth be ready?

The first of *Jontashreena*'s three moons was just becoming visible above the mountain-laden horizon when DiCarlo heard footsteps behind him. He did not have to turn around to know that it was Russell, her footfalls much lighter than even the most graceful of their Plysserian friends. Her steps were confident as she navigated the narrow trail up to the hill's small plateau with practiced ease.

"Figured I'd find you up here," she said as she drew closer. DiCarlo smiled at the lack of deductive reasoning that it had taken Russell to find him. The small open area on top of one hill that formed the cover for their underground hideaway had become a favored location for both humans. It was a place where they could go and, for a short time at least, almost forget that they were marooned on an alien world. While the terrain here was somewhat similar to Earth in daylight hours, it was at night when the stars came out that the resemblance took on a more convincing air.

Russell sat down next to DiCarlo, resting her back as he did against the smooth flank of the large boulder he had chosen for his vantage point. With a casual familiarity, she nestled in close to him as his arm draped around her shoulders, each seeking the warmth of the other's body as protection against the mild evening chill. He winced slightly at the contact, his ribs still tender from the injuries he had suffered weeks before.

At first DiCarlo, and then Russell, had been worried that getting medical treatment for his wounds would prove difficult if not impossible, trapped as they were with no way to reach a human doctor. Despite this, the knowledge Plysserian scientists and doctors had acquired from their study of humans even in the weeks before the aliens' existence had been discovered on Earth had proven most helpful to Javoquek's field medics as they treated the injured Marine. That, along with DiCarlo's own first-aid expertise, hard won in more than one combat zone, had been enough to get him started on the road to healing.

"Still no news, I take it," he said as she settled herself, and felt her head shake in response. It was a two-pointed inquiry, one they both had made several times in recent days. No word had yet reached them about the final outcome of the battles on Earth. They had no way of knowing how beneficial the actions of the Blue forces here had been. The lack of useful information was frustrating for DiCarlo, though not unexpected. Confusion and lack of information were tenets of war as much as violence and death, after all.

"Nothing, but that shouldn't be surprising. Javoquek told us to expect that we might not hear anything for weeks, if ever. As far as we know, the Gray operatives who were given our information made it through the portal to China before it was blown. After that, it's all a big guess."

DiCarlo frowned, though he knew Russell could not see it. "That, or they played us and we dropped a shitload of intel right into their lap." At first, he had been against the idea of trusting anyone from the Gray side, especially when it involved trusting any soldier in their Army. He had a particular aversion to advertising the fact that he and Russell were here. Surely, someone on this planet would see the value of two humans now that the War had evolved to include Earth. In the battles that were sure to come, his and Russell's knowledge would be as valuable here as that which Max and other Blues were likely providing to their friends on Earth. That usefulness extended to the needs of an enemy, as well.

Kel and Javoquek had convinced him of the legitimacy of the Chodrecai resistance movement, however, as well as the merits of attempting to communicate with the authorities on their home planet. Perhaps if someone knew they were here and just how far the scope of the War had changed, with Blue forces and resistance cells fighting the Grays from this side of the conduits, they would see the virtue of orchestrating a coordinated campaign.

"Kel vouched for the Grays," Russell said, "but the question is whether or not they can get the information to someone who will believe it and use it. If there's a new push on Earth and they're not ready . . ." She let the sentence trail off, unwilling to give voice to thoughts that disturbed her as well as DiCarlo himself.

Though he knew the Grays were still feeling the repercussions of the Blue counteroffensives, their leaders surely realized that they were now fighting a two-front war and were making appropriate plans. With any luck, Earth government and military leaders had come to the same conclusion and were already preparing their answer to the lingering yet still-potent Gray threat.

DiCarlo was certain that the Grays were regrouping

even as he and Russell relaxed beneath the dim illumination of the *Jontashreenan* moon. There was too much at stake for them not to be planning action. The environmental situation here was still deteriorating, accelerated by the effects of unremitting conflict, and Earth represented a salvation for this planet's war-weary population.

Earth. Even after all the time that had passed since their arrival here, DiCarlo still wrestled with the notion of identifying his home as a planet, rather than a city or a state or even a country as he had done for so many years while on duty in foreign lands.

"Simon," Russell said after several quiet moments, "do you think we'll ever get home?"

DiCarlo shrugged. "With every portal within our traveling range under Gray control? It won't be easy, and I can't see asking Kel and the others to take on the risk of trying to get us to one." It was the first time since they had prepared the packet for authorities on Earth that either of them had actually voiced the question of getting back. Though he had been reluctant to admit it to Russell, DiCarlo had more than once considered the notion that returning to Earth would prove to be difficult, if not impossible.

Further, he also knew that he and Russell represented a vital link between the Blues and Earth, a bridge to unite both their peoples against their common enemy. It had taken him several days of reflection to arrive at his decision, but he had concluded that until the fighting had ended, one way or another, the two Marines were more valuable here than on their own planet.

For better or worse, *Jontashreena* was their home now, perhaps forever. Pulling Russell closer to him and feeling her arms encircle his waist, DiCarlo gave silent thanks once more that fate had seen fit to bring them together. He took comfort from the knowledge that no matter what uncertainty they would surely face here in the days ahead, at least they would face it together.

"Maybe not today," he said as the first hint of *Jontashreena*'s second moon began to crest the peaks of the far off mountains. "And probably not tomorrow, but one day, we'll get back."

One day, after the War was over.

Afterword

"Camp Growding" is a fictional Missouri National Guard installation based on far more than a loose sense on Camp Crowder located in Neosho, Missouri. The actual base is rather small and in addition to the National Guard and U.S. Marine Corps Reserve presence there, it is also home to a junior college and a number of civilian industries based in Neosho.

While I thought that this part of southwestern Missouri would be an ideal setting for the beginnings of *The Last World War*, I also believed that the real Camp Crowder would not lend itself to various elements of the story, especially early on. With that in mind I made the decision to create "Camp Growding" and model it in part on the real base, taking liberties as needed to suit the requirements of the story. This in no way is intended to slight the military personnel serving at Camp Crowder or the citizens of Neosho, who are some of the friendliest people it has ever been my pleasure to encounter.

Acknowledgments

Many thanks to John Ordover, my editor at Pocket Books. After coming to me one day with an interesting notion and then letting me run with it, he coached and encouraged me as I developed the initial kernel into the full-blown story you've just read. In addition, he promised that the tomato juice he spilled all over the manuscript came only after he'd finished reading it. Honest.

And to Kevin Dilmore, friend and frequent writing partner, who let me bounce ideas off him over countless chicken fingers and French fries. We still found time to write other stuff along the way, but he helped me to stay focused on this project more so than he knows, even when he was sneaking fries from my plate. Thanks, Bubba!

Last but certainly not least, to Michi. Wife, best friend, soul mate, it would take another book just to begin the process of explaining how I feel about this woman. She also knows how terrible I am at expressing myself this way. Lucky for me, that old writer's rule of showing rather than telling works for other things, too.

About the Author

Dayton Ward served for eleven years in the U.S. Marine Corps before discovering the private sector and the piles of cash to be made there as a software engineer. He got his start in professional writing by placing stories in each of Pocket Books' first three *Star Trek: Strange New Worlds* anthologies. He is the author of the *Star Trek* novel *In the Name of Honor* and with coauthor Kevin Dilmore he has written several tales in Pocket's *Star Trek: S.C.E.* series.

Though he currently lives in Kansas City with his wife, Michi, he is a Florida native and still maintains a torrid long-distance romance with his beloved Tampa Bay Buccaneers.

Readers interested in contacting Dayton or learning more about his writing, or who simply need proof that their website is cooler and better looking, are encouraged to venture to his Internet cobweb collection at www. daytonward.com.